Light and Shadow

Light and Shadow
Candida Baker

First published in 2025 by Popcorn Press, an imprint of Fair Play Publishing
PO Box 4101, Balgowlah Heights, NSW 2093, Australia
www.popcornpress.com.au

ISBN: 978-1-923236-35-6
ISBN: 978-1- 923236-36-3 (ePub)
© Candida Baker 2025

Cover design by Mathilde Noblet
Typesetting by Ana D. Nedeljković

A catalogue record for this
book is available from the
National Library of Australia

All inquiries should be made to the Publisher via sales@fairplaypublishing.com.au

Light and Shadow

*The story of Eadweard Muybridge, Flora Shallcross Stone
and Harry Larkyns – as told by their granddaughter,
Rosa Maria de Martinez*

By Candida Baker

For Greg

CONTENTS

Prologue

Dearest Beth,

The truth is, there is no truth.

For example:

My grandfather was a murderer. He shot my grandmother's lover dead. The name he became known by was not the name with which he was born. He was not a purveyor of truth. His photographic images, and his life, were doctored in order to be presented to the world as he imagined they *should* be. My grandfather, or so I believe, was the photographer Eadweard Muybridge, born Edward James Muggeridge.

Or:

My grandfather was murdered. He was, according to most sources, a scoundrel, a conman, an ex-soldier, a theatre critic, a quintessential black sheep. He had a thousand unfulfilled ambitions, none of which ever came to anything. But Harry Larkyns, my grandfather (or so I sometimes believe) had one true talent, and that was to love women; to bring hitherto bored and lonely women alive and to make their senses sing with passion. The love of his life was my grandmother Flora Shallcross Stone Muybridge, who was married to the photographer Eadweard Muybridge. When Eadweard (my possible grandfather) discovered that his wife had been having an affair, he sought out his wife's lover, my (possible) grandfather, and shot him dead.

You see, already we have two different stories, and for me, even after a lifetime of searching I cannot tell you which one is the 'truth'.

Who was my grandfather? The murderer, or the murdered? One of the greatest photographers the world has ever seen, or a conman? The facts of both their lives, as I have written them, are irrefutable, and facts are the skeleton of this journey around my life – whatever slippery flesh may cover its bones.

I can tell you for instance, that my father was definitely one Florado Muybridge, even though I never met him and never knew him, but when my mother died, I found my birth certificate… and I saw his name there, plain as day.

But even this 'fact', this 'plain as day' is misleading, because when I say, 'my mother', until the day I found my birth certificate, I had grown up believing, with all my heart, that my mother was my sister; and my grandmother, my mother; and my grandfather, my father.

And perhaps now, I must give you, my friend, something to hold onto, give you something which will not shift underneath you as the sands of time have shifted under me, giving and taking away in equal measure, until… well… until whatever comes next.

Although you understand some of these things, sweet Beth, allow me the license to tell a story, a chronology of sorts, even though, you, of course, know these 'facts' about me. Let me state them for the record.

My name is Rosa Maria de Martinez. I live in the High Country of Victoria, not far from the mountain town of Mt Beauty. The year is 2014, and I am 80 years old. I was born on April 10, 1934, in my family's hometown of Santa Rosalia, in Baja, California Sur. I was born 20 years almost to the day after Eadweard Muybridge, (the man who may or may not have been my grandfather) died. He was born under the sign of the Ram and died under the sign of the Ram. I too, am an Aries, and so was Florado Helios Muybridge, the father I never met. A piece of the jigsaw puzzle, or simply a coincidence?

I am writing this book, if indeed that is what it becomes, because my whole life has been a search to find out who I am, and where I belong; and now as I near the end of my life I wish to write it down. I want to bring alive these shadowy figures of my past. I feel them beckoning me these days and sometimes, most often at the dawn or dusk of the day, the thin veil between this life and the next seems to be as light as gauze, almost transparent, as if I might simply slip over there while I am searching for my 'family', and quietly find myself on my journey of no return.

But I am not quite ready for a one-way ticket Beth. I want to create my own story, because, try as I might, I have not been able to recreate the story of those who came before me to the point where I can 'know' what happened.

So now I will feel my way into this skein of wool, begin the careful knitting, try not to slip a stitch, call forth the ghosts, and make them real.

Chapter 1

Deceit

Oh, how my bones creak when I get up in the morning these days, Beth. I love living alone, and I intend to die alone, although the Department has other ideas, and, although I don't tell you this, they constantly send out young people to check on me. Often though, they drive past, scared, I suppose, by the *Beware of the Dog* sign. I see them stop outside my gate. I see my place through *their* eyes: the tumbledown shed, the two old horses in the front paddock, the old stone house, the dog. It's not a way of life they feel comfortable with, for sure. I wonder what sort of report they file to their bosses when they have not even met me.

But I seem to have been put into the too-hard basket these days. Weeks, sometimes months go past, without a nosey-parker coming to check up on me, and I go along, happily enough. Once or twice a week you, my darling Beth, take me into town to do my grocery shopping, or to the doctors, or the feed shed. You and Will keep an eye out for me, which is all I need, even though you are reluctant to believe it. I do appreciate Will chopping my firewood, and mending the odd fence, and I hope that the plentiful amounts of chili sauce and chili oil I send your way are enough recompense, Beth.

As I've grown older, and passed the age beyond which my grandparents, my mother and my father lived, I think more about Eadweard - although even he died six years before the age I am now. Every decision I've ever made in my life, from the age I became imbued with doubt about my heritage, has held an echo of the actions of my family, or, I should say, my possible family. Eadweard, for instance, was 64 when he retired to England permanently, and although I was much younger than that when I chose to leave Mexico and America behind me to come to Australia, there are similarities even in those journeys we both decided to undertake in the latter years of our lives.

I've often wondered what must it have been like for this grand adventurer, this inventor, this wild man – this *murderer* – to put his larger-than-life aside, and slip into the quiet greenery of his home country?

It was after my mother died, and I found the tell-all birth certificate that I began to create stories in my head about my family, or those I thought had been my family, who became suddenly strangers to me the morning I discovered that the funeral I had attended the day before for the woman I believed was my older sister was the woman who had given birth to me.

I saw my sister's name, *Maria Elena de Martinez*, and I saw another name, *Florado Helios Muybridge,* and I swear to you, on all their graves, I had *no* idea who this person was. I had never heard his name pass my parents or my sister's lips. (And for now I shall continue to call them my parents and my sister because, as I am sure you can imagine, it took me many years before I was able to contemplate that those who had loved me so closely had fooled me so duplicitously. The only way to hold on to their love, until I came to accept the truth, was to continue to love them, as I always had.)

As I say, I had never heard of Florado Helios Muybridge, and if the surname Muybridge rang any kind of tiny bell, it was not an immediate recognition. I did not move in artistic circles. although it could be said that the trajectory of my life has always displayed a certain flair for the dramatic, but if anyone had said the name, 'Eadweard Muybridge', there would have been no obvious sign of recognition.

Of course, that is all different now.

Now I am, as they say in Australia, the full bottle on Eadweard Muybridge. I am also as full a bottle as it's possible to be on Harry Larkyns and Flora Shallcross Stone Muybridge, and on my father, Florado Helios Muybridge when so little has been recorded about them, and so much about the man who may or may not have been my grandfather. I am even the full bottle on some of the people less central to my story, the Governor of California, Leland Stanford, for example, who became a millionaire largely by stretching out railways like a giant spider's web across America's vast interior. He was often referred to as a 'robber baron', and it seems to me, after much consideration, that this is *exactly* what he was. And yet, without Stanford, the story of my (possible) grandfather Eadweard, would not be nearly so rich, *nearly* so exciting, because it was Leland Stanford who asked Eadweard Muybridge to conduct an experiment with a racehorse to see if at any point, all four hooves were in the air. In his backing of Eadweard, Stanford set him on a lifelong journey of photographic discovery.

As I say, as I began this journey of exploration, I created stories, and as the stories became more complicated, any idea of finding absolute answers became as difficult as holding a handful of mist, and yet, at the same time, gradually those stories became my lifeline.

I am going to start towards the end of this story.

Why? Because when Eadweard Muybridge returned to England at the age of 64, he had 10 years left to live, and I so truly feel I, too, am in the last few years of my life now. In fact, dearest Beth, I have my suspicions that it may be much less. Eadweard, of all the characters that create this story, is the one who must take centre stage, the possible tie between us growing stronger as I age. Forgive this fictional deceit; I will begin with what I imagine, how he must, or *may* have felt in the last few years of his life.

So, let it begin.

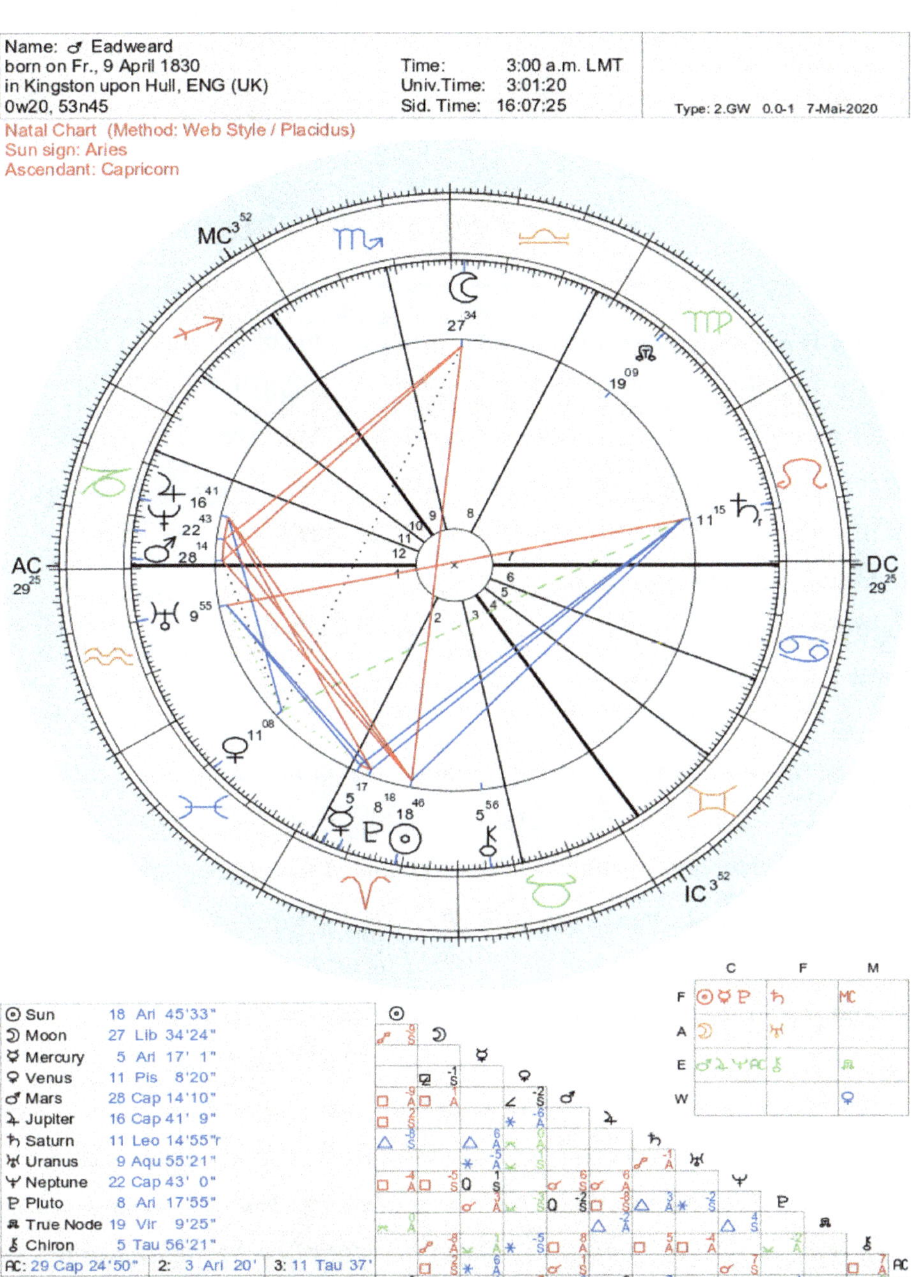

Eadweard's natal chart

Notes: What happens if I give Eadweard the time of 3.00am as his birth, which is one of the most usual times of day/night for babies to make their way into the world? Mars, Jupiter and Neptune all in Capricorn; ascendant Capricorn. Ambition, dogged persistence, an understanding of the dark side, a seemingly very solid, very patriarchal male. A tendency towards depression, perhaps?

Saturn in Leo – is that what gave him Helios? Not an easy placement, the Lord of Time in the sign of the Sun, but one to overcome obstacles, to become very successful in later life.

Sun, Mercury and Pluto all in Aries; the mover and shaker, the go-out-and-get-it person. But Venus in Pisces: Here the rivers flow, deep emotional attachment, but with an element of fantasy.

Uranus in Aquarius: the inventor, the person before his time, the out-there thinker. The man who would think nothing of photographing naked men, horses, animals and bodies, over and over again.

Moon in Libra: the man searching for an elusive truth? Moon in the sign of balance? Perhaps not so much, but yet again, maybe the search for balance, the tendency to not cope well when life is unbalanced?

Virgo in the North Node, Chiron in Taurus. Wounds, and healing. Healing via nature, primarily. Virgo bringing him up against a desire for perfection. Perfect for a bookseller, perfect for a photographer. Perfect, perhaps, for a murderer.

Yes, I think this will do very nicely.

Chapter 2

Conjecture

Early morning sunlight dances on the walls. He feels tired this morning. It is an effort to walk around and shut the light out. It occurs to him he has been doing exactly that for most of his life, shutting the light out, or letting it in, controlling it in some way to meet a desired end. His hand shakes slightly as he adjusts the wooden shutters. As a ray of sunshine lights his hand, he sees with a shock how old it is, how covered in age spots, how wrinkled.

He stands there for a moment, turning his hand this way, then that. He is suddenly reminded of an old woman he met in the jungle in Guatemala, and how her hands seemed like a crab, but she still would have been decades younger than he is now, he thinks. He is too old to be doing this, his hands will keep shaking; he wouldn't be doing this, if it wasn't for that blessed girl, he thinks to himself. He'd put it all away, hadn't he? But where had it all gone? How had it all been so quick? It was there, and now it was almost *not* there. He is almost *not* here, and he isn't ready for it. He isn't ready for the absence of him, even if he will not know about it when it comes. A thought stabs him: perhaps those other two had not been ready either. He quickly turns it away, sidesteps it neatly. Not his fault. *A man has to do something, defend his rights, defend his territory.* He looks at his watch. She will be here soon. A bonnie lass, smiling and rosy-cheeked, waiting for her chance to be made immortal, to have her chance to live forever. She is still young enough not to know that it can be disturbing too, this permanent image of the self, caught in youth. She thinks it is exciting, exciting enough to batter down his resistance. He feels a small stab of pain in his arm. It has happened a few times recently. 'I'll sit down,' he says out loud, his voice echoing in the quiet room. He nods to himself. *That's what he will do, sit down and wait for her.* But sitting, as usual, disturbs him. It has always been too static for him. It allows shadows to settle in his brain. A disinclination to be still is part of the disadvantage, as he understands it, of being born under the sign of the Ram. He remembers one of Flora's friends many years ago coming for one of Flora's occult nights and offering him an astrological reading. He wasn't in favour of those nights, he found the idea abhorrent that something other than his nature was responsible for his destiny; but he agreed, simply to keep Flora happy. The result, brought to him a few weeks later, was, he had to admit, a bit disturbing. He wishes he could remember the woman's name. *What was it? Lavinia!* Lavinia Pettigrew. An odd name, odd enough for him to wonder if it was real or made-up, or perhaps adjusted, as his had been, to suit her character and occupation. She wanted to show him his chart alone and Flora was crestfallen. 'Can't I come too?' she said, her face downturned like a small child. But Lavinia shook her head, speaking to his wife as you would to a child: *No, not this time.*

So Eadweard had found himself in their drawing room having planets, and houses and effects of this square and that trine, and this conjunction pointed out to him, while his reason seemed to split in two; one piece of him watching her from a distance and with a large degree of scepticism, and the other amazed at the accuracy of her descriptions. *How much had Flora told her?*

'Impatience is natural to you, Sir,' Lavinia had said, poring closely over his chart. 'This is quite right for a man under the sign of Aries, but there seems to be a period here where something happened, some accident perhaps?' She'd looked to him for acknowledgement, and he'd grudgingly given it, with the slightest nod. *Flora must have told her,* he'd reasoned. An accident. Yes, my head split apart on the rocks, my very life ebbing from my veins, the spirit inside me taking leave of me and walking around without so much as by your leave, the sheer force of my will to bring myself back within me again.

The agonizing, excruciating ongoing everlasting pain. 'You have not been quite the same since?' He'd nodded again, almost imperceptibly. A painful admission.

Then she began to talk fast, almost as if she was in a hurry to get this over with... words rattling at him like gunfire.

'Mars... tendency to explode, be careful, trying to get you to understand gentleness, understanding... ignore this, something dangerous...' her head bobbing up and down as she spoke. 'Sir, I can see from your chart you are a hard worker, determined in spirit. Your photography! Your ideas, some of them will live on even beyond you. You travel, and you will keep on travelling. You have a huge knowledge of the world, Mr. Muybridge, but...' she'd shaken her head, 'I don't know. There is something in here. I cannot quite make sense of it. I feel as if there may come a time where you may do something you come to regret... be kind to yourself, Mr. Muybridge and to your wife.' 'Of course.' He'd been impatient then. 'Enough, Mrs. Pettigrew. You have given me too much of your time.'

If this, he remembers thinking, was a plot by Flora to have even *more* attention from him, it was not the right way to go about it. Over the years he has often wondered to himself how much 'that woman' as he thought of her, saw. She could not, could she, have seen the exact circumstance? Surely not? If she had, she must have warned him further, or warned Flora. He sometimes thinks she would have done better to have read his wife's chart, to have mentioned to her that fidelity was an attribute required in a wife. 'If that woman could see something, she should have told me. I was not to blame. They acquitted me. They acquitted me!' he says out loud, looking around the room as if to unseen witnesses of his innocence.

Again, the stab in the arm, and there is the other thing too, the thing he has been to the doctor about, and for which there is no cure. It is a race apparently, between his heart and the cancer lying in the depths of his manhood. One of them will carry him off, and sooner rather than later. He breathes sharply.

Enough thinking of this. It does no good to dwell.

It never has.

* * * * *

It does no good to dwell. I, Rosa Maria de Martinez (Muybridge/ Larkyns) can write that sentence, believe its essence and at the same time wonder at it, since dwelling is what I have done ever since that fateful morning when I discovered I was not who I thought I was.

I ask myself: How is it that Eadweard Muybridge did not dwell? How is that someone, who on his own admission, murdered a man, and who also killed his wife by neglect, abandoning the child who (arguably if not his), was his responsibility, learned not to dwell? But it is certainly a fact that Eadweard's career did not appear to suffer one jot from his 'disgrace'. And how is it that a disgraced male will quickly find a way to rise again? Think of any number of politicians, bankers and athletes to name just a few; whereas a disgraced woman, however talented, however small her crime, will often disappear from all view, buried, I believe, under the sheer weight of her own shame.

I know the shame that took my grandmother, Flora Shallcross Stone Muybridge to the grave; I know the shame my mother/sister must have felt at carrying me at the tender age of 16. I have come to understand the crippling effects of shame in my own life. Shame is a visceral, red-hot, molten fire. Shame is black, and cold as death. Shame is unforgiving. Shame stalks you, and once it has you in its icy grip, it never lets you go.

I have done a few things, only a few, that I am ashamed of in my life, and when I remember them, I can hardly breathe for the terror that rises up in me, for the feeling that I will still be 'caught' and condemned. Am I right in thinking that women feel shame far deeper, far longer, than men? Outwardly men, it seems to me, bounce back from job failures, from relationship breakdowns, even from criminal behaviour, in a manner that women *never* can. The Boys' Club will support a man through shame, whereas women, so supportive in so many ways, find shame so disturbing they will walk away from those who are shame-filled, leaving them alone on the sinking wreck of their lives.

A psychiatric nurse once told me that 'exclusion is the first form of female bullying'. My heart pinged in recognition at her words. I'd never thought about it, but it's true. Little girls with their gangs at school. You're in, but then you're not; you're included, you're excluded. Exclusion, for a herd animal, can mean death. Exclusion is to be avoided at all costs. For women, exclusion means no access to the loving support of their kind. It means living with a sense of always being an outsider, of never truly being invited in. It has taken me a lifetime to understand that there is a way to belong, and that is to belong to *yourself* so fully that you never, ever exclude yourself from your own heart, from your own ability to love, to recover, to forgive yourself.

When I look out of the window in my sitting room, where I sit to write or work; when I take a break as I have just done now, Beth, and stretch and creak and walk around, make a cup of tea, and sit once more at my desk, the landscape I look out on is so alien to the one I grew up in, I might as well be on another planet. This, perhaps, is not the time to wax lyrical to you about the wonder of the place in which we live, the soft olive-grey palette of the gum-covered hills, the delicate mountain wild-flowers, the towering hills that surround me, the land to which I now belong. This is more that I wonder how Eadweard, this man who left England as a teenager, who lived in New York and San Francisco, who travelled – oh how he travelled – throughout the US, through South America, to wilderness areas where a white man had scarcely been seen, could bring himself to retire to the sedate, tidy town of his childhood.

I went there. To Kingston-upon-Thames, during one of the periods of time when I had convinced myself beyond a shadow of a doubt that Eadweard was my grandfather. By then I was a woman of some independent means. Hard won those means, and the decision made one evening. Just like that. Before I met you Beth, and the only time I ever went to Europe. (This, of course is a typical Aries trait: Act first, think later.)

Who am I?

The fact is that no matter how I join these dots, I will never truly know. It will be impossible for me to do more than guess whether it is Eadweard the Murderer's blood that runs in my veins, or Harry the Murdered. I can only conjecture, and yet it is in that conjecture, in the lies of my childhood, in the duplicity of my ancestry, wherein lies my story. And I suppose, sweet Beth, if you are to follow my story, and the stories of those that are within this book, having given you the old Eadweard, perhaps we should start at the very beginning, so to speak, and I should give you the young Eadweard, born long before Flora, long before Harry.

Because there is no doubt that Eadweard, my maybe grandfather, is the start of this story.

Chapter 3

Childhood

Sometimes it is all Edward can do to stay still in his room studying when the sounds of the town can be heard so closely around him.

He can hear, for instance, the sound of the barges on the canal, and the crunch of boots on gravel, as the barge owners come to buy coal from the side door. He can hear, and smell, the grain being sifted, bagged and carried into carts; and, then, of course, there's Mr. Brown whose regular announcements of news Edward listens for attentively, not because, at the age of 10, he is particularly interested in what Mr. Brown has to say, but more because this means that, his duties over, Mr. Brown will be once more in his studio, a place where Edward is always welcome.

ʹEdward.ʹ

His mother's voice pierces the fog of Latin verbs in which he is immersed.

He turns to see his mother standing at the doorway, tall and calm as usual, surveying her son's bedroom with a mixture of amusement and concern.

ʹYes Mama?ʹ

ʹMy dear, what is all *this?*ʹ

Edward jumps up, his books forgotten. ʹI'm making a pulley system Mama, look, I'm trying to invent something so that you could have this all around the house, and say if you needed something taken from one place to the other, you would simply put it on the pulleys and it would arrive at the other end.ʹ

Susannah Muggeridge smiles. 'You remind me of your grandfather,' she says.

'Yes.' Edward looks at her expectantly. 'Tell me again about the pigeons.'

'Edward. I'm busy. I came to ask you to go to the store to collect...'

'Just for a minute?'

Susannah pauses, irresolute. 'Alright,' she says, walking across to his desk and sitting down. 'Come and sit beside me.' She pats the empty chair beside her.

'When your father was a child,' she begins, and Edward can already begin to feel the flow of words through his veins, as sweet as warm milk and honey, comforting and familiar... 'When he was a child, his father, your grandfather, owned many barges and horses, and employed many men for his business. He would often drive his carriage to London to buy his wheat or coal, and he always took with him one of his carrier pigeons, and always carried with him a quill, so that when he bought a cargo, he could write on a tiny piece of paper the number of barges he needed. He would put the paper in the quill, tie it under the wing of the pigeon and set it free.' She smiles down at her son's face. 'The pigeon would fly home, here to Kingston, and your grandfather's foreman would know exactly how many barges to send down to London.'

'He was clever.' Edward says of the man he was named after. 'But Mama, now there is the telegraph and the railway, isn't there?'

'Yes.' Susan stands up, and smoothes down her dress.

'And they were invented?'

'Yes, of course.'

'Someone thought of them.' Edward looks up at his mother, 'that's what I want to do, think of things.'

'Yes, well, you can start by "thinking of things" while you go to the store for me.'

'Yes.'

As he busies himself with his boots, his mother picks her way carefully through the intricate pulley system and back to the door, stopping by his desk with its open boxes of butterflies. 'Your collection is growing, Edward. It is impressive.'

Edward joins his mother. He points to his latest find, a glowing russet butterfly, outlined with black, and with a silvery underside. 'Mr. Collins says this is a Large Copper Butterfly, and I am lucky to have found this around here since it comes from the Fens.'

They stand for a moment in companionable silence, while Susan runs her eye over the tiny bodies, carefully arranged by size and colour, some of them still held in place with their pins while they dry.

'Poor little creatures,' she says.

'They don't feel anything, Mama, you know that. I put them in the jar, they go to sleep, and that is that.'

'I know,' she sighs. 'But all the same.'

'It's because they move so freely,' Edward says. 'And then they don't. That is what upsets you, isn't it, Mama?'

'Yes.' She looks at her son curiously. 'It doesn't bother you, Ted?'

He shrugs. 'No. I like watching the movement of their wings in the jar. It intrigues me.'

Susan ruffles her son's hair. 'Well,' she says. 'There'll be no tea if we don't hurry up.'

* * * * *

Have I got this right Beth? Is it at all how it was? Who am I to try to breathe life into Eadweard Muybridge?

But I *do* have the right. I remind myself again and again. I have the right because there is every chance I am his granddaughter. There is every chance that my desire to be surrounded by wilderness, my fascination in the natural world, my independence, that all this comes from Eadweard. For those of you who know his work, you might say – and his love of horses – because of course, it is his photography of horses that in the end made him most famous, and yet I would not say that. After all my years of research, I am not sure that Eadweard Muybridge did in fact 'love' horses. I think he admired them and saw them as an ultimate expression of the movement he was so keen to explore and understand, but 'love'? No. I think that belongs to the other potential grandfather; I think that comes directly from Harry Larkyns.

Why do I make this assumption that Harry Larkyns loved horses? And is it too soon to hint at Harry's wounds: his birth in India, his abandonment in England by his parents when he was only three, the murder of his parents, sisters and brother at Cawnpore in India? Oh Harry, poor Harry. My heart bleeds for him. But he became a dashing figure, a success, of sorts, and a soldier and horseman of note. And he loved, that was for sure. He lived and loved with an air of reckless abandonment, until he was gunned down on October 17, 1874, his essence bleeding away from him that fateful night in Calistoga, California.

Dear Harry, he turns up in San Francisco for the first time, like a bad penny, early in 1873, which gives him exactly six months to establish himself as a drama critic, meet and fall in love with Flora before she falls pregnant with Florado, rip-off a travelling companion of his money, be arrested for financial irregularities, have a Frenchman swear to his gallantry and good character, and begin the unraveling of his life, towards that inevitable night in Calistoga where he will be called to the door while he is in the middle of a game of cards.

In exactly that same year, charted almost daily, there is Eadweard having his most successful year to date. This is the year in which his first photographs of the racehorse Occident are announced; the year in which he photographs the Modoc Indian war; in June a *Catalogue of Photographic Views* is published; in late July those landscapes win a medal at the Vienna Exposition. His young and most beloved wife, Flora tells him she is pregnant. How can he not be feeling on top of the world?

So how can I say, with this little evidence, that it's Harry who loved horses, when it is Eadweard whose photographic reputation will be shot from the successful to the spectacular because of his photographs of a racehorse? Because what I feel, what I intuit in my bones is this: that despite everything he did, and everything he achieved, my possible grandfather Eadweard Muybridge remained, at some level, an outsider, the ultimate observer, whereas my possible grandfather Harry, in spite of his failures, was an engager. Harry loved life too much.

* * * * *

But I am supposed to be writing about Eadweard's childhood, and of course I find I have wandered again.

I am *so* excited. Where have these words been sitting in me all this time? Why have they not made their presence felt before now? Why did I never think of writing my story like this? As a story for you dear Beth? (And do you mind, by the way, if I write it as if we were more like strangers to each other than we are, so that I can say everything, even those things you know so well about me, the confidences and intimacies shared? I think you won't mind. Perhaps in a way it will be a new story for you as well, to see my life in a different light.)

I think all this outpouring began because of the experience I've been having with you-know-who over the past few years, which has tipped me over into an anxiety that has almost crippled me, that almost, at this very end of my life, caused me to leave my home. Almost, but not quite.

I said that people from the department come out to check on me, and that is true. But Beth, there is one car I have come to dread the sight of: that gun-metal Toyota Landcruiser, with all the bells and whistles, a snorkel and a massive bull-bar and not one, but *two* radio antennae, not like my old thing with 400,000 on the clock. No, this one is exactly the kind a real-estate agent/developer would drive in this type of country. Exactly the kind of thing a Mr. James Jarvis, *wanting to buy my property to incorporate into all the other properties he has bought around here so that he can create a residential resort*, would drive. I hesitate to say a bully's car for a bully, because personally I love Toyota Landcruisers, so unfortunately, I cannot really throw that accusation in the ring. If I was younger I would buy the recently released limited Kakadu GXL, with its power adjustable front seats, front and rear air conditioning, 17-inch wheels, a tilt-telescope steering column and a cool box between the front seats.

Fifteen years ago when I sold the horse truck I'd started my small trucking business with when I first moved, before I created the 'Sofia' range of oils you know and love so much and used the truck for moving oils, I bought myself a then-two-year-old automatic turbo diesel and a trailer designed specifically to carry the oils. I have to admit a cruiser not the most sensible vehicle 10 years later for an 80-year-old to own, perhaps even not the most sensible sized vehicle for a 65-year-old to buy, but at that age I still thought I was invincible. Plus, it towed, and still would now, the horse-float I bought for myself as well as the trailer.

Mr. James Jarvis owns his Cruiser and I own mine, and I hope that is where the similarity ends. Because he is the most conniving, bullying, manipulative piece of work I've ever met in my life, and I've met a few.

It started innocently enough. It was about four years ago, at the end of the first decade of the 2000s when the full force of Australian chauvinism was showing itself through a ripple effect of optimism, buoyant real estate prices and a feeling that anything was possible passed, like a joyous Mexican wave, through the villages and towns. Well, certainly that is how it felt up here, didn't it Beth? It would be two years earlier that our first out-of-town resort had opened, up the road from me, and let me say from the outset that I was impressed, and remain so, at the environmental care taken, but the ripple effect from it was that every man and his dog wanted to create 'resorts', and James Jarvis was, and is, at the head of that charge.

I don't think I told you about his first visit, I think I kept that to myself. He came to visit me one morning, with an apparatchik at his side. It was a fine spring morning, cold but not freezing, and I was outside with my horses, brushing off their winter coats. He drove up my driveway and pulled up, stepping out of the car in his R. M. Williams attire.

'Mrs Martinez?' James Jarvis says, walking towards me.

I look at him. 'I am Rosa Maria de Martinez,' I say, and pause, waiting for him to announce why he's visiting.

The long and the short, (and he got to the short pretty quickly let me tell you), imagining I suppose that I would be an easy touch, that I would roll over and show him my soft underbelly as soon as the figure '$500,000' was out there on the table.

'A great idea,' he says. 'Fantastic for the area,' he says. 'Another resort,' he says. 'We would help re-house you,' he says. '$500,000,' he says, 'for your 150 acres. Good money,' he says.

'No thank you,' I say.

He looks quite affronted, as does his apparatchik, who mimics every gesture, as if to affirm that his greatest desire is to grow up and be exactly like this Mr. James Jarvis.

'Of course,' he says. 'You will need time to think about it, not a decision to be taken lightly... I understand.'

I lay my hand lightly on Freya's golden wither.

'I don't need time to think about it Mr. Jarvis,' I say. 'I have lived on this property for decades now, and I intend to die here. Both these horses were born on this property and have lived their entire lives here. I am not now, nor at any time in the future, selling this property.'

A scowl crosses his face. The scowl of the alpha male suddenly experiencing resistance where he expected none.

'Well,' he says. 'Perhaps we can revisit our proposal.'

'You can revisit it all you like, Mr. Jarvis,' I say. 'It won't make any difference.'

And it didn't. But what it started was five years of underhand bullying. And if he thinks I don't know why the Department have suddenly started taking an interest in me, where there was been none, he is a bigger fool than I take him for, Beth. But in a way I suppose I should thank Mr. Jarvis, because it was his constant bullying that spiraled me into an anxiety and depression from which I truly felt there was no return. It was not until the day I realised that no matter if he torched my place, with me in it, I still would not leave, that I also realised he had given me a gift. The most precious gift of knowing finally where I belong. It was the sudden stab of insight, that this place was 'home' no matter what, and that you my Beth, and your family are my family, that allowed me to begin this odyssey around the material I have spent decades collecting.

And I've found the more I work on it, the less anxious I become, which, if he knew about, I have no doubt would upset Mr. Jarvis immensely.

* * * * *

One of the many problems with getting older is the level of concentration I can give at any one time to anything. I get out of bed in the morning with a firm idea of what I am going to do, and by the time I put the kettle on, something else has grabbed my attention. And so it is with this book, or perhaps 'book' is too grand a word for what I am attempting, perhaps 'manuscript' or even just 'journal' is better.

Because although I was fully convinced that I was going to keep on writing about Mr. James Jarvis, for the moment I've become bored of him, although it's the fact that I called him an alpha male (which he most undoubtedly is) that's prompted my next twist. To my surprise, it is Flora that has suddenly come calling. She seems to feel quite strongly, and I'm in agreement with her, that she should make her presence felt early on in this story. And there is absolutely no doubt at all that it is men, alpha or not, that caused the disastrous trajectory of her short life to unfold as it did.

Some years ago, when I first began to truly explore Flora's story, I was intrigued and disturbed by how little psychological delving had been done into her character. It was almost as if history, (written mostly by men, of course), wanted to bury her, to make her simply a footnote to a great man's career. And yet the fact is that Eadweard Muybridge loved her so much that he killed for her. The facts also are that Flora's life was short, and often, sad. I know she was born in 1851, but I cannot find the exact date. She was only 20 when she married a man twice her age, 21 when she became a mother, 24 when she died. She was eight years younger than her handsome, feckless lover, himself only 28 when they met. (Harry, astrologically right at the beginning of his first Saturn return was already a marked man. He would not make the final traverse across the divide between youth, and middle-age, and Flora would not even reach the milestone of the Saturn return.)

What I imagine, or what I have decided on her behalf, if you will give me another dip into my interest in astrology, is that she was a Leo, that she as well as Eadweard, was a fire sign. As a Leo, the need to be loved and admired lay deep in her psyche, and not just to be loved and admired every now and then as with most mortals, but *all* the time. For my poor darling grandmother (and at least I know for certain, that she was my grandmother, since Florado was her son), things went wrong from the early age of 10, when her doting parents died, leaving her an orphan, unwanted by any other member of her family. Perhaps I will give you a sketch of Flora, a précis if you will, of her life from her early happy childhood to the fateful day when she was working in the Nahl art and photographic gallery at 121, Montgomery Street, San Francisco, and a certain tall, bearded man with ice-blue eyes walked in.

* * * * *

Sometimes, when she doubts whether she will ever marry again, or if her life will work out as she had always imagined, with a loving husband and children all around her, Flora looks in the mirror. 'I'm pretty,' she whispers to herself, and sometimes she touches the side of her cheek in the softest of caresses. 'I'm pretty.'

She was only eight years old the first time anybody had called her pretty. Her parents were still alive, and they all lived, as at the time only children can imagine, happily ever after in their house in Alabama. It was a small house for the district, not a large fancy plantation house, but nice enough, white-washed and respectable.

One day some new friends her father had met through work came over for a social visit. They had four children, and before too long they were told to 'run along and play together'. And so, they had, shyly at first until one of them, the older girl, suggested they play hide-and-go-seek, and they did, running here and there in the garden. At one point Flora, who of course knew her garden well, hid in the garden shed, right at the back and was surprised when the boy, about her age, was already there.

'Shhhh,' he said. 'Don't say anything.'

She smiled at him, and even now she can remember what an adventure she thought it was, hiding together while the other children ran around looking for them in the garden. Somehow she was unsurprised when she felt his hand reach out for her, but when he pulled her in towards him, and put his lips on hers, she gasped.

'Shhh,' he said again, and put his finger on her lips, oh so gently.

'You're pretty,' he said gently, and then he kissed her again, and this time – she couldn't seem to help herself – she melted in towards him, taken aback by the strange tingling sensation she could feel running through her body, while outside they could hear the children laughing and searching for them.

The boy's older sister was the first one to spot the shed. 'I bet they're in here,' she shouted, and quick as a flash Flora and the boy separated, so that when his sister burst in, Flora was standing at the back of the shed, and the boy (she never can remember his name, she thinks of him only as 'The Boy'), was sitting on an old tin box of her father's. Afterwards the boy didn't even look at her, and even then she thought that was odd. She remembers wanting him to look at her, wanting him to acknowledge that something had happened, but he behaved as if she was just one of the crowd, and soon enough they all left, with cheerful goodbyes, and shouts of *we'll see you soon* and they were off, gone to a life Flora couldn't imagine even though she often thought of The Boy, particularly in the years to come, as the war came, claiming first her father, and then later her mother, who came down with a fever after nursing the wounded. This is how she learned to think of it when people asked where her mother was. 'She came down with a fever after nursing the wounded,' she would tell them, repeating the words she'd heard her grandmother and her aunt use. That way she managed to give the impression that her mother had died without actually saying that she had. It stopped, too the icy clutch of loss grabbing at her throat and heart.

Getting ready for work, this day, Flora thinks, as she does everyday, about her life as 'Before' and 'After'. 'Before' is the misty landscape of her childhood, when she had parents, a home and a garden, and a shed in which to be kissed. 'After' is everything since; the war, her parents' death, her grandparents' inability to look after her, her sense of not being wanted, of being shoved here and there until a friend of her aunt's, Captain W. D. Shallcross, had, in his words 'taken pity on her', and been appointed her foster father, paying for her education on top of his care for her. She was told by her grandmother and aunt 'you'd better be grateful' on an almost daily basis when she protested that she did not want to go and live with a stranger. Her grandmother would have none of it. 'You'll go and be thankful missy,' she told Flora. 'All he wants is some young company in the house from time to time, and someone to help out a bit in the house.'

* * * * *

It can overtake her anywhere, the feeling of powerlessness. Sometimes all she has to do is see a tall man walking towards her and panic fills her. She can feel her heart pounding, her mouth goes dry, everything in her becomes taut, anxious. Her body is waiting for the next move, for the pinning-up against the wall, the hand thrust between her legs. And as the man, innocent enough, of course, goes past, the panic gradually, oh so gradually, subsides, and she sinks back into herself, becomes, well, just Flora walking down the street, as she is now, on her way to work.

There was a difference though, Flora knows, between Captain Shallcross and the man she ran away from him to marry, Lucius Stone. At least with Shallcross she learned she could control the 'incidents', as she thought of them. Not at first, of course, not until she realised that they had a pattern to them. Once a week, that's what she worked out, after he'd had a few too many whiskeys. After dinner, the dinner she ate with this strange man who had somehow become the only family she had in the world: 'Let me see how you've grown, Lilly,' he'd say to her. And even know she wonders, *why Lilly?* What was wrong with *her* name? What was wrong with Flora?

The servants would retire for the night, and she and the captain would sit in the sitting room, him in his armchair, her perched on the sofa, wondering if tonight was the night, before she learned to judge from the whiskeys, before she saw the pattern.

The first time, she screamed, of course she screamed, she screamed, and she bled, but no-one came to rescue her, and to shut her up he put his hand across her mouth so she could hardly breathe. The first time he didn't even bother with the niceties of at least allowing her to retire first, to go to her bedroom as if she was a normal 14-year-old girl; he simply told her to come and stand in front of him, and when she did as she was told, he picked up his cane, and ran it up inside her leg, so that she instinctively gasped and drew back.

'Stand still,' he rasped at her, and his voice was stern, so stern that she stood still, while he lifted her skirts and feasted his eyes on her legs. 'Well, Lilly,' he said, 'you are growing up.' He stood up and grabbed her hand. 'Let's see you with your dress off.'

'No, please...' Flora tried to back away, but he was strong, far too strong, and as soon as she resisted he put his hand against her throat. 'Don't struggle,' he whispered in her ear, as his other hand began its urgent explorations. Flora began to cry, but it made no difference. He forced her down on the floor, tearing at her clothes, and his, and that's when the pain came – a pain so extreme she'd never felt anything like it before, searing and hot, and as she lay there, pinned underneath him – she knew for certain what she had tried to pretend to herself wasn't true. Her mother and father were dead, they were never coming back for her, she would never see them again, and it seemed to her that she may as well have died herself. As he lifted himself off her, she lay there and experienced a sense of hopelessness so crushing she thought she might as well be dead.

'Go and clean yourself up.' His voice was low, and when she didn't move, he said it again, more urgently: 'Go and clean yourself up.' He walked across to the drinks table and poured himself another whisky, and stood there, his back towards her.

This is what Flora learned. If she read the signs well enough, then she could be in charge of the situation. If, at dinner, there was a certain reckless abandon to the number of glasses of wine he drank, a narrowing of his eyes when he looked at her, then she knew what would come next. She knew she would be sent to bed, that he would arrive not long after, that he would turn off the light and climb into her bed, and that it would be over soon, that the moment would come when he would make a strange grunting noise and withdraw himself, covering her in some wet liquid. On those nights she began to act more coyly, to lead him on just a little, to suggest that she might be available. Anything, she learned, so that he would get it over and done with and life could go back to normal. Until the next time.

At school, which the captain paid for, Flora learned to put aside the night-time memories. At school, she was not Lilly, an orphan with a foster father who was no father, she was Flora, who was pretty enough to be popular.

One day the captain sent her down to the local saddlery to get some reins mended for his bridle.

'Tell Stone I need them by the weekend,' he said to her. 'And don't dawdle.'

Flora didn't need to be told twice to leave the house. It was a rare pleasure for her to get away on her own, and she almost ran out of the garden and down the road towards the saddlery. It was a spring day, and somehow, some tiny spark of optimism pierced her at the very sight of the blue, blue sky and the sweet scent of flowers and blossoms hanging in the air. When she got to the shop, she bustled in, so that Lucius Stone, looking up from his counter was almost taken aback by the breath of fresh air she brought in with her.

'Good morning,' Flora said cheerfully. 'The Cap... I mean, Father, sent me down to get these reins mended. He says he will need them by the weekend – is that possible?' She smiled at him, little knowing that it served to only further the effect that something impossibly fresh and vibrant had just walked into his shop.

'Of course,' he said. 'We can do that, can't we mother?' He turned towards the backroom where his mother sat at the sewing machine, and she nodded at him. 'If it's just reins, it shouldn't be a problem,' she said.

Flora's heart lurched at the sight of what she'd just seen. Just a normal interchange between a mother and son, albeit that the son was old, at least to her, at least, she reckoned, twice her age, with hair already turning a little grey at the temples, but somehow it touched her to the quick, the idea of the pair of them working together, talking together, and yet again the loss of her mother wreaked painful havoc in her heart, so that she had to lower her eyes for fear Lucius Stone would see the tears in them. But he noticed, of course he noticed, how could he not, when the pretty thing in front of him almost visibly wilted.

'Are you feeling alright?' he asked her. 'Would you like to sit down?'

And somehow Flora felt that yes, all she wanted to do was to sit down in this shop full of the smell of leather and horses and stay while the man and his mother worked and talked together. So she sat in the customer's chair in the corner while Lucius Stone brought her a glass of water which she took gratefully; and when he offered to walk her home if she was feeling faint, she looked up at him, and what she saw was a man who wanted to protect her, a man who might look after her, and without even realising what she was doing, she pressed herself just slightly closer to him than was really necessary, as they made their up the street, closer to her 'home'.

* * * * *

It didn't take long, she thinks as she brushes her long hair, ready to twist it up in the bun on top of her head. The very next day Lucius Stone delivered a note to the house asking if she would like to 'take a walk in the gardens' with him. Not something that the captain would have allowed, Flora knew, but as luck would have it he had been suddenly called away on business for a couple of weeks, and had left her, during school holidays, to her own devices, so that Flora seized her chance to escape the house, to escape her thoughts, to escape, for a moment, her life. In two short weeks 'Lilly' would fall into a flirtation with the absolute intent of leaving the captain's house forever.

Even now Flora is surprised at how clever she was, how easily deception came to her. Trained to observe the slightest sign of interest in her by the captain, she used those senses to oh so easily deceive the household, to step out while the captain was away, on little errands, which, she told the housekeeper, he had given her instructions for. To order a new dress, to take one of his suits to be repaired, to have some shoes re-soled, all the while running into Lucius's arms at the first opportunity. The meetings made all the more delicious because he had to break away from the shop, and from his mother, to be with her.

Even though there's been a lot of water under the bridge since the day Flora eloped, since she leapt, (she now knows), from the frying pan into the fire, she still likes to imagine to herself how angry the captain must have been when he came home to an empty house. She is still surprised at how cunning she had been. It takes her aback, sometimes, how she and Lucius had conspired so carefully, so that he had gone to the expense of hiring a carriage, and had waited around the corner from the house, while she casually wandered into the garden with her sketching things, and, if anybody had cared to notice, which they did not, a small bag which contained just enough things with which she could start her new married life. She had sat in the garden, quietly drawing, waiting for the carriage to arrive and when it had stopped, she waited just a few more minutes, before looking around to make sure nobody was watching her, yawned, stretched, picked up her bag and walked out, and into the arms of her waiting lover, so that by nightfall, she was Mrs. Lucius Stone.

She couldn't know exactly how the captain must have ranted and raged, but she liked to think of it, and to feel that for a moment she had wreaked just a small amount of revenge on him.

But of course, it hadn't taken her long to discover that her 'escape' was the reverse of that. She ran from one jailor to another, even though their first night together in a small hotel held for both of them, she thought, the promise of true love. He'd held her so close, so tenderly, so gently, that Flora's disturbed heart had shifted on its axis, had opened then and there to new possibilities, before, that is, they got back to the saddlery the next morning and Lucius's mother discovered what her son had done.

'You idiot,' she'd screamed at Lucius, hitting him around the head so that he shrank away from her like a small child. 'You've brought disgrace on us. How could you do this to me? She doesn't even bring any dowry with her.' And Flora watched in disbelief as her husband of one day began to sniffle and cry. 'I suppose at least she can work,' Flora's mother-in-law said. 'Less for me to do.'

And that is how Flora became, as she thinks of it, an unpaid slave, and worse, an object not just of scorn and derision, but something to be punished when anything went wrong, and treated with downright contempt the rest of the time. She'd lasted a month before she realised she had to make a plan, before she started to steal tiny amounts of money, so that by her 18th birthday she had just enough to run away, this time pleading such fainting illness that even Mrs Stone had agreed she should be left in bed, in the tiny rooms behind the saddlery where they lived. The minute Flora was sure that they were in the shop, and she could hear their now hateful voices raised in conversation with a customer, she slipped out of bed, grabbed her bag, running through the back door as fast as she could. She did not stop until she reached the carriage depot, where, panting and out of breath, she almost threw the money at the man in the ticket office.

'I need a ticket,' she'd said.

He'd scarcely looked up. 'To where?'

For a moment Flora was startled. She hadn't even thought about to 'where', all she'd thought of was to get away. She glanced wildly around and saw there a group of people gathered together near a sign that said 'San Francisco'.

'San Francisco,' she'd said, pausing just for a moment. 'Yes, San Francisco.'

He passed her the ticket. 'You'd better get over there quick,' he said. 'It's leaving in 10 minutes.'

On the stagecoach Flora kept herself to herself, sitting quietly in the corner. She did not want to attract any attention, nothing that might be reported back to put Lucius Stone on her trail. She simply sat, her arms folded in her lap, as quiet as a mouse, and perhaps it was that very quality of stillness, she sometimes wondered, that caused Charles Nahl to speak to her, and to ask her where she was going.

'To San Francisco,' she said.

The painter, as he turned out to be, smiled at her. 'It's a big city,' he said. 'Where in San Francisco?'

She shrugged. 'I'm not sure yet. I have friends there.'

But there was something in the way she spoke that made him doubt it. As a father, he felt concern for her. As he looked down at her, he couldn't help noticing that she suddenly and quickly shielded her left-hand, but not before he'd caught a glimpse of gold.

'You know,' he said, conversationally, in an easy quiet tone, 'my brother Arthur and I have a gallery in Montgomery Street. We're artists, but we also run a business re-touching photographs. If you find yourself in need of work, we may have something for you.'

Flora inclined her head.

'Thank you,' she said. 'That is kind of you.'

* * * * *

Flora looks at herself in the mirror and pinches her cheeks to bring a bit of colour to them. With her hair swept up, and her neat dress, she looks every bit the professional she has become, somewhat to her surprise (and truth be known to Charles and Arthur Nahl's as well). There is a little spring in her step as she leaves the room she rents in the boarding house not too far from Montgomery Street and close enough for her to walk to work.

'I'm pretty,' she whispers to herself. 'I'm pretty.'

She dawdles a bit on the way. The weather is fine, she's stopped looking over her shoulder every time she hears a man's voice. She has a few pennies in her purse, and more hidden away at home. She knows she wants more. She wishes beyond anything for a house, a home, a proper husband, but for now her life is enough.

And so it is, with these things on her mind, that when she arrives at the gallery, she finds both her bosses, the 'Mister Nahls' as she thinks of them, talking to a tall man with a bushy beard and looking with him at something – his work, Flora presumes, as she enters the gallery to the peal of the little bell.

'Good morning, Miss Stone,' says Charles Nahl, polite as always. 'May I introduce you to Mr. Muybridge? He has come to show us some of his recent prints, and I must say, they are very fine indeed.' The somewhat curious-looking man in front of her looks at her with disinterest. His sharp blue eyes, *startlingly* blue, she thinks, run over her in what seems to be so much disdain so that she imperceptibly shrinks back.

'How do you do Miss Stone?' says Eadweard Muybridge. 'I'm pleased to make your acquaintance.'

'Miss Stone will work on your photographs, Mr Muybridge,' Charles Nahl continues. 'She's very good. She has the touch, you know…'

And this man, the photographer, looks at her once more. 'Does she?' he says, and as he smiles at her his whole face suddenly lights up. 'Well, that is very good to hear. I expect that we will work well together.'

Flora is embarrassed by the attention. The man in front of her seems suddenly to be drinking her in, and he too seems affected by it, because he sways a little and puts his hand on his head.

'Mubridge, are you feeling alright?' Charles Nahl looks at the man with concern.

'Yes,' the man replies. 'An old injury, that's all.'

But still, as Flora takes her leave and walks past the two men towards the back room where her work is laid out for her for the day, she knows without a doubt that he is watching her.

Jane Thomas, her working companion and friend, smiles at her.

'Good morning, Miss Stone,' she says formally.

'Good morning, Miss Thomas,' Flora replies.

Flora, Flora, Flora. Poor pretty Flora. She is almost galloping towards her untimely end, and she has *no idea*.

At this time, indeed, it is quite the reverse, she is proud, and why should she not be, of what she has achieved since she arrived in San Francisco. She has a job, a place to live, friends; she has a life, and I imagine that she would be grateful to herself, and for her own will to live for bringing her to this point.

She has no idea that she is walking around with a gaping wound in her soul, that she has what any modern therapist would call 'abandonment issues'

That's what the therapist I saw called it anyway. When the anxiety and depression I suffered during the constant phone calls, demands, letters and veiled threats from James Jarvis led me to a place where suicide became a viable option, I finally allowed you and Will to persuade me to see someone, but not without a fight, if you recall Beth. I didn't want to open any of my Pandora's boxes.

'I know you mean well,' I remember telling you both, 'but I can't see this working.'

It was you Beth, of course, that pushed my buttons. 'If you won't do it for us,' you said to me. 'Do it for your horses. I'm watching you get more and more isolated. Your horses need you. They love you. At least tell me you'll talk to your doctor.'

I shrugged but to be honest, I was touched by your ongoing concern. Some tiny bit of it pierced the almost constant feeling of detachment from my own body, from my own life. Alright,' I said. 'I'll see the doctor, although I'm not promising anything.'

So I went to see my doctor, who was a bit surprised to see me since, despite my age, I very rarely have to see a doctor. I've stayed (and often I think perhaps this is a Muybridge gene) strong and healthy, at least in my body, right up until now.

When I tell my doctor about my anxiety, she asks me some questions. Am I not getting pleasure from things I usually enjoy? I think of how strange I found it when my roses had bloomed recently, and I'd seemed to see them from a long way away. Tick. Do you feel hungry, or perhaps not hungry, more than usual? I think of my strange new habit of often not eating for an entire day. Tick. Have your sleeping habits changed? I think of how suddenly I'm catnapping, how tired I am all the time. Tick. Are you experiencing an ongoing stressful situation? James Jarvis. Tick. And it went on; *tick, tick, tick.*

After a while of this, Jan, my doctor, looks at me with concern. 'Rosa,' she tells me. 'You're most definitely suffering from anxiety and depression.'

I have to say that in some strange way I was relieved to have it named. I actually laugh. 'I thought it was old age,' I say. 'I thought perhaps this is what happened when you're in your 70s.'

It's her turn to laugh. 'Well,' she says, 'growing older is not exactly easy, but no, anxiety and depression are *not normal* – at any age. I think we should put you on some mild antidepressants, and perhaps you'd like to see someone? A psychologist or a counselor perhaps?'

I tell her: 'Yes to the psychologist. No to the pills. Tell me what else I can do. I don't want the pills.'

* * * * *

'I think,' the psychologist, Louise, says to me, Beth, 'we should look at the broader picture here. I think this goes way beyond the current situation. From what you're telling me of your childhood, it wouldn't be surprising if you were suffering from some extreme abandonment issues.'

No kidding.

The truth is that although on the surface, perhaps deeper than the surface, I had a happy childhood, even though Santa Rosalia was not an easy place in which to live. A small hint: when copper was found, the lodes to be developed confirmed their grandiose and wrenching names of Providence, Purgatory, Solitude and Hell. My parent/ grandparents had come to the town when the French company El Boleo opened the copper mines, building houses, and commissioning beautiful and gracious buildings, envisaging, I suppose a town of boulevards, a town of wealth and prosperity. But anywhere where people strive to be rich, the poor will suffer. Of course, as a child I had no idea how lucky I was to live in this somewhat desolately beautiful place as one of those families not dependent on the rise and fall of the mining industry, and the conniving bastardry of the owners who did everything they could not to pay a living wage.

My parent/grandparents had not always lived in Santa Rosalia, they came from Guerrero Negro to the north, where my father worked in the salt mine, and my mother worked on embroidery and sewing commissions. (Will you forgive me if I refer to them as my parents Beth? Even so many decades after their deaths, after my discovery that my life had been based on a lie, I do still think of them as my parents. And they were the ones that parented me.) My father was hard-working. He quickly rose to become a foreman, and was then offered a position as manager of a provisions store in the town. This was a lucky thing indeed, and there they would have stayed, was it not for the fact that they had sent their 16-year-old daughter to a ranch in Texas, through contacts of the store's owner, so that she could learn the business of housekeeping, and in due course she became pregnant to a 59-year-old man, Florado Helios Muybridge.

She was, of course, packed off back home, and this is when they concocted the idea of passing off the unborn child as theirs. (Of course, their version to me was always simple: they moved, shortly before I was born, to Santa Rosalia because my father was offered a job. End of story.) In the mess of real life however, what I have since pieced together is that they must have moved when my sister/mother was around five months pregnant with me. How did they manage the change-over period? Did they spend a long time on the road? Did they, the most likely scenario, decide to dress both mother and daughter in similar clothes to disguise bulk? Did my mother/grandmother wear a cushion to disguise the child in her belly? How I would love to ask these questions!

What lies and tangled webs they must have spun. And what about the fact that my father was 59, an oldish man, if not an old one, and my sister/mother so young, so very, very young? My heart bleeds for them both. Were they both so lonely, so alone that they reached out for each other across the great divide of their ages? Or did he do the unthinkable and take advantage of this young, young girl? Some part of me wishes and hopes, of course, that it was consensual, that it was a moment for both of them. I hope that I was conceived in a moment of love given and received, no matter the age difference, not in a moment snatched from a young, innocent girl. Can I hang on to that, at least for now Beth? I can imagine you telling me that was not likely, that he took advantage of her, that my own father preyed on a young girl. You wouldn't hold back, would you Beth?

But I will, if you'll forgive me, hang on to the idea that it was loneliness that created this unlikely coupling, that it was a sudden reaching out across a chasm of difference and age, and the result was this hybrid, this strange creature, of me.

But to move on for the moment, let's take it as a given that if anybody ever guessed, nobody ever said anything, not, at least to my knowledge, and when my mother/grandmother was apparently delivered of a healthy baby girl, life went on, and my father/grandfather's lucky trajectory remained exactly the same. He worked initially in the desperate conditions of the copper mine but his talent for organization was soon spotted, he was made a foreman and then an office administrator, and later, once more, the manager of a store.

It was almost a karmic replay of his initial career. Of course, my father/grandfather was a Virgo, and so a sense of order was utterly essential to him. Not for him the messy desk I have before me now, not for him my tendency towards what I like to think of as organic chaos. Was Eadweard messy? Hard to imagine. Was the charming feckless Harry messy? Much easier to imagine. But I've always been tidy with my horses. Go into my barn, even today when all I have is my two golden oldies, and you will find everything in order. Even though I haven't ridden for some years, you know Beth, when you sometimes bring the children over for a ride on Thor and Freya, you will not find cleaner or more gleaming tack than mine. Everything in my stable and yards is shipshape, albeit it a little frayed around the edges, but the fact is that the house and I are gradually falling into a quiet state of disrepair together. And that saddens me, since it was me, so many moons ago now, that brought the house *out* of a state of disrepair, and in a sense whilst I was doing it, myself as well.

But to get back to my childhood, to focus for a moment. We lived not far from one of Santa Rosalia's main landmarks – the beautiful little church of Santa Barbara which came to Santa Rosalia, from, of all places, Brussels. What happened was that towards the turn of the century a group of local women asked the wife of the Director of the mining company to ask him if the company would build a Catholic church. He agreed, but he was leaving for Europe for a while, so the matter was postponed. But while he was in Brussels, he chanced upon a church designed by Gustave Eiffel, made entirely of metal because it had been constructed for a commission in Africa where white ants devour wood. For some reason it had not made it to its designated destination, and the minute Monsieur LaForgue saw it, he bought it and shipped it to Santa Rosalia, where I am sure it still stands to this day, the gleaming white metal as pristine as the day it was made.

It was a shining example of the strange multiculturalism of Santa Rosalia. Its first priest was an Italian, Father Juan Rossi, and so an Italian priest and a Belgian church met in a remote Mexican mining town run by a French company. Add to this mix the Chinese workers the French imported to work in the mines, the French themselves, and the Mexican population, and you can imagine this was a town in which a family with a secret could start over; or at least could disguise the secret, and protect it from white ants.

So, this was my childhood, a nurtured and secure one in a town where typhus, and many other diseases, were rife, and funerals commonplace, and yet we escaped. We brought with us my parents' cleanliness and hardworking ethos, and we were, without a doubt, lucky.

And another, less obvious piece of luck for me… the multicultural nature of the town meant that I did not grow up with a Mexican chip on my shoulder, I learned a smattering of different languages, the sting of the loss of Texas was not raked over in our family as it was in others, and my father's job was safe. In fact, we were lucky in many ways, my father had always suffered from a slight limp, with one leg just very slightly longer than the other. It was enough for him not to go to war, Beth, when I was eight years old and Mexico and Brazil became the two Latin countries to sign up as Allies. Nine thousand of us died defending the sane world against Hitler and the Nazis, but my father was exempted.

Was Eadweard lucky? Luckier than Flora that is for sure. Luckier than Harry, perhaps, although Harry threw away his luck, and Eadweard created his. The difference perhaps that pure crystal-clear ambition can make to a person.

This is how I see it. If I put myself as a circle in the middle of a large piece of paper then I can see how each other person, represented by a circle, has touched my life. In my case my need for attention is explained astrologically by my moon in Leo, an aspect of course, I have lent to my grandmother, although for her it is her Sun sign, and therefore with some different effects. I imagine that Eadweard had Leo active in his chart, perhaps in several places. Let's look at just one fact: you don't go round giving yourself the pseudonym ´Helios´ if you're not, shall we say, at the very least confident in your abilities. And Helios, of course, as the personification of the Sun in Greek mythology would be another representation of Leo, the personification of the Sun in astrology.

It isn't hard to imagine that the young Eadweard, still Edward then, with all the fire in his belly, was never going to be happy running a grain merchant's company for his mother; that, like many other young men, he would be drawn towards the New World, a world of exciting possibilities, and we know he had no intention of coming back. And this much I know, mothers weep when their children leave.

My sister/mother and my mother/grandmother wept when I left for America. I remember it still, to this day. I was 20 years old, and I had been working at the store my father/grandfather managed for three years, since I had left school. I was ready for bigger things, and they came towards me, without much effort on my part. The thing was, I was not stupid, and I had a flair for organization (and how I wish I still had it now). The owner of the store, Jacques du Plaix, was an entrepreneurial type, he held no racist attitudes towards Mexicans, or towards anybody, he simply wanted to sell things that people wanted to buy, and over the three years I worked in the store he had become impressed with my book-keeping abilities, and my somehow innate desire to windowdress the store, so to speak. Now, I wonder if those qualities came from Eadweard? After all you had to be organised to be a photographer. It wasn't just 'Smile please!' in those days. My desire to endlessly arrange and rearrange the goods in the shop could easily be linked to a photographer's desire to frame a photograph in the most pleasing way possible. And let me say this is not to detract from my mother's and grandparents input into my character, there is much of them in me, and the person I thought was my sweet sister, who was in fact my sweet mother is, without a doubt, responsible for any softness that lies within the kernel of protective layers I have carefully built up around myself.

What happened was that Jacques du Plaix saw an opportunity to open his 'Mexican' store in Santa Ana, California, and he offered me a job there as the store's bookkeeper.

'You weel halso serve the customerrrs,' he told me, in Spanish, of course, but with his strange rolling French accent. 'Hand, Rosa, you weel make the store 'jolie' huh?'

For me it was a chance to get away – and often I've wondered if my father/grandfather had a hand in it. It sets up another duality for me, did he help along my leaving the family because he was not my father and therefore did not want me around? Or did he simply know there were more chances across the border, and did he want to help me expand my horizons? For obvious reasons I tend to favour the latter suggestion, although in the 'tristesse' of the early morning hours, when all is questioned and nothing answered, I do not know.

But with Eadweard, well, that is easy. He was dying to get away, and there was nothing to be done about it, despite his mother's sadness. And shall we imagine her then, her gracious calm fractured by the news that her son, Edward Muggeridge, is leaving Kingston-upon-Thames, for New York, in all its 'new' glory?

* * * * *

'No.' His mother's voice is tight with anguish. 'Edward, please. No.'

'Mother.' His heart constricts. He has dreaded this conversation for so long. 'I must.'

'Edward. Why? How would I manage without you? First your father, and then your older brother. How will I cope with losing you as well?'

'But mother,' he says gently. 'I am not dying.'

'No, but *America* Edward. You may as well be dead. When would I ever see you again? I cannot lose another. It's too much.'

He steps towards her as if to hold her, to comfort her, but she retreats from him, shaking her head.

'You would see me mother. It's not so hard these days that journey. I have to go, you must know that… how can I stay,' he glances around their living room, spreads wide his arms, 'here?'

'But what will you do Edward? You are supposed to work here, to take over the business in due course. You know that. This is where your duty lies, to us, to your future family.'

For a minute Edward wavers. His mother is so solid in front of him, her gracious form as usual so calm and steady. He glances around the room he's known since childhood, the delicate oval-backed armchairs with their carved legs and lion claws, that scared him so when he was little. Sometimes in the night he'd lain in his bed unable to sleep, afraid that the chairs would come alive, transform into child-eating lions, ready to stalk through the house in search of prey. And when sleep did come the fear had become a nightmare. He can recall it even now, the lions in his dreams chasing him, their hot breath steaming behind him, until he would wake screaming in terror, and in only a minute his mother would be there to settle him, to stroke his forehead and leave a night candle on. It occurs to him that she, even more than his father, had been the central pillar of the family around whom everything revolved. Now, everything in the room is just so. The fire laid for later in the evening, the polished piano, his mother's ornaments. This room, he came to know as a child, was his mother's sanctuary. As he drinks it all in, he realises that this room is *all* his mother, a place where her quiet grace can have free rein, away from her husband and four sons. He wishes for a moment that his parents had had a daughter, that then perhaps his mother would not feel his leave-taking so keenly.

'What will you do, Edward, where will you go? What on earth is it that you can do there, that you cannot do here?'

'I thought I might go to New York.' He says this casually and can hardly believe himself the words coming right out of him like that, as if he had been saying he might go to Oxford. 'I had an idea I might sell some old books there.'

'But why *America?* Even London, or Europe... you could do the same thing there surely? Is it really necessary?'

Edward wants to be honest, he wants to be able to say to her, to even shout at her: *The men of the family die here. I might die here*, but instead he finds himself shrugging. 'I just feel I need to travel,' he says. 'I want to see the world, mother, that's the truth.'

His mother breathes in the deepest breath he's ever heard, and as she exhales, her body droops with sadness. 'I suppose the boy who wanted to invent things when he was little is hardly going to be satisfied by Kingston,' she says. 'Well, you had better tell me all your plans so we can organise your leaving.'

She raises her shoulders just a little and looks him in the eye. 'I hope you will be happy, Edward.'

'I hope I will be successful, mother,' he says, with a smile. 'Then happiness will follow.'

* * * * *

Only a few weeks later, on the eve of his departure, he goes to say goodbye to his grandmother.

'Well, I wish you luck Ted,' she says. She pushes a pile of sovereigns towards him. 'Take these, dear, you may be glad to have them.'

'No thank you Grandma,' he says, gently pushing them back towards the old lady. 'I have no need of them. I am going to make a name for myself in the world, and if I fail, you will not hear of me again.'

His grandmother tries not to smile at the earnest young man in front of her. 'Well, Ted,' she says, 'that seems a bit extreme to me. You would always have a home to come back to. Family is family after all.'

He inclines his head. 'Thank you,' he says. 'I don't know when I'll be back. I will visit, but it could be some time.'

'Yes.' She knows what they are saying to each other. This will be the last occasion they will see each other in this lifetime. 'I understand Ted. Travel safely and have a long and happy life.'

'I will try.'

As he leaves the room, his excitement scarcely contained at the idea that he will be off and away now in only a few hours, his grandmother allows the tears to fall, knowing full well that it is not just for the loss of her grandson that she cries, but also for the losses of a long lifetime.

'Well,' she says. 'I hope he comes back one day, safe and sound, and

I leave it to your care God. I truly do.'

* * * * *

'I have no need of them. I am going to make a name for myself in the world, and if I fail, you will not hear of me again.'

It will be hard for you sometimes Beth, to know where I've let my imagination flow, and what is truthfully Eadweard. Well, that last statement is exactly Eadweard, (or Edward as he still was then). Recorded in family history, passed down through essays and articles and books. The kind of statement a biographer can sink their teeth into. There's a wonderful young man's pomposity to it, isn't there? *If I fail, you will not hear of me again.* What did he imagine he might do if he failed? Disappear entirely off the map of the world? What did he imagine 'making a name' for himself meant? But you've got to give him this – he did not take his grandmother's money. (Harry would have, Harry wouldn't have hesitated for a second. Harry would have asked his grandmother for more money. Harry, I'm pretty sure, would have stolen his grandmother's money.) Eadweard made a name for himself, becoming one of the first travelers to straddle worlds, the New and the Old, moving so smoothly between the two I imagine him almost as a kind of chameleon; here in New York, there in the South American jungle, now sitting on Yosemite's highest point, then back in the patchwork quilt green of England.

Ahhh, my hands have had enough tonight, my imagination too. Bella is restive at my feet. I will raise myself now, and she and I will brave the chilly night air, and once more, as I do every night, I will stand and listen for the night-time noises that reassure me all is well; the sound of the horses grazing, the occasional mournful calling of the mopoke, sometimes a sighting of a deer, or the wombat as he shuffles on his way.

Time, my friend, to put abandonment issues and gaping wounds to one side, time, in fact, to go to bed, and go to sleep.

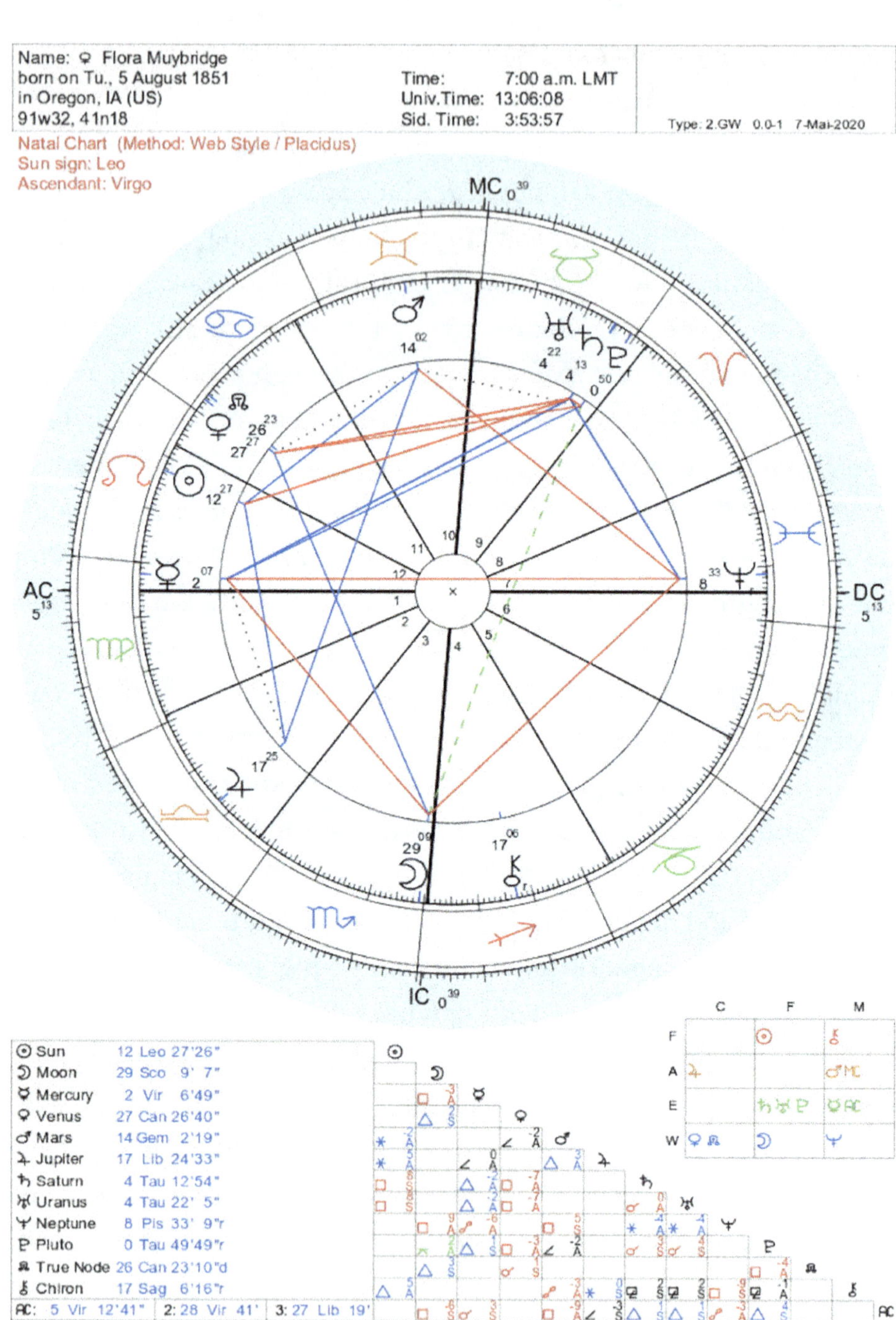

Flora's natal chart

Notes:

Sun in Leo, moon in Scorpio. Powerful, is what you would think straight away, with a lot of physical and psychic energy. A very engaging, but somewhat self-centred personality here, but also one, if these two strong forces are not fully acknowledged, with emotional incongruence. The deep passionate feelings pushed underground, surfacing not always appropriately, a marked sexuality, and the lure of the Scorpio moon with the ability to push towards ignoring others.

Ascendant in Virgo. Interesting. Perfect for work as a photographic re-toucher, or in retail. Someone who can pay attention to detail, but still again, the potential for selfishness, and yet also very sympathetic to those she loves. A tendency to believe she's always right.

Neptune opposite Virgo. This placement can result in an intense fear of being alone. Someone who needs love so much they can't see how much their friends and family do love them.

Chiron in Sagittarius. Fear of a loss of freedom (so searching for freedom where it may not exist), and yet paradoxically Venus in Cancer, so a safe home very important (and hard to give up).

Mars in Gemini, easily bored, needing almost constant stimulation.

Pluto in Taurus, should make for a practical, steady individual, but the effect of Pluto can be rebellious to the point of indulging in compulsive behaviour.

Hmmm. It fits.

Chapter 4

Leaving

Today, I am excited. To begin with there is just the tiniest hint of spring in the freezing mountain air and I do believe the snow has gone. I feel the cold these days I have to admit, and there have been nights when I have shivered myself to sleep no matter how warm my clothes, the house, or my bedding. It seems as if the cold enters my bones and refuses to leave, as if it is the first call of death, that chill.

(I can tell you something about being a woman, Beth – when the menopause hit me with its raging flushes, much worse was what I came to think of as the 'frozens', when a sudden river of ice would flood my body. Nobody tells you about those, so be warned my dearest friend, although of course, you're still young, you'll forget.)

Thor and Freya feel the cold too, as you know, and where once only one sturdy rug would do in the worst of the winter, they now have two through the coldest months, a woollen and a padded winter rug. But this morning my joints are moving, the sky is blue, and later on, Beth, you and Will are coming over and we are all going for a day trip into Mt Beauty for its annual fete day.

What I would like you to understand Beth, is that there is a trajectory, that there is juicy stuff coming. Sometimes my head feels as if it might explode with all the images that are tumbling out of me. Of course there's Eadweard: the tragic stagecoach accident, his scalp opened to his brain, Eadweard perched on the highest point of Yosemite, Eadweard carefully inventing the series of tiny wires that will trip the camera into taking the pictures that will prove, once and for all, that at one *certain* point in time racehorses have all four hooves off the ground. And, of course, Eadweard falling head-over-heels in love with Flora, desperate for her, desperate for the family he believes will be his bedrock.

Then there's Harry and Flora lying together as clear as day, and I can see the sex between them, how he runs his tongue up her spine, and into the warm, moist darkness of her. I see how she finally learns what love is, or perhaps I should say, she learns what *obsession* is, tumbling into a sea of passion, until even Eadweard, away on his work too often, gets wind of it, forbids her to see him, but it's too late, much too late for that. I see my father, the little Florado, his name made up to contain both Flora and Eadweard (and even, perhaps the 'o' as a touch of Helios?), and that is a dark place to visit. The baby, left with his nanny so his mother can continue her affair, his father locked up in jail for months on a murder charge, while his mother's mental state unravels; the toddler now, left in the charge of a stranger, never to see his mother again, then snatched away from that home by his father and taken to an orphanage, where he will stay for 10 years, until his 'father' will come and take him to the ranch in Texas where he will stay for the rest of his life.

And then of course, there's me too. There are so many stories to tell you, so many twists and turns. And the main question you might ask me Beth: Why did you come to Australia? And the answer would of course be – love – love brought me to Australia, and then love left, and what I found to my surprise was that the main relationship in my life was not with a person, but with a *landscape,* and with my horses. I have found in those two things, a space of unconditional love. Although loving those things, loving all of you, brought me to the last love of my life, and I miss him more than I can say.

But before I found the love we search for in another I was taught the lesson to find it right here, in my garden, in this valley, in these mountains. And quickly now, as you all arrive to take me into town, the very idea of love prompts me to imagine how my (possible) grandfather, Eadweard Muybridge, met and fell in love with my (certain) grandmother, Flora Muybridge. It quickens my pulse to think of it. But I am trying, a bit late in life, to learn restraint. I am thinking, yes, but at the very least there needs to be some chronology. As I head into my 80th year, time seems no longer relevant, it jumps around all over the place, (not helped, it has to be said, by my ability to sleep for 10 or 20 minutes at any time of the night or day) but that does not mean some sense of chronology is not relevant for others.

Before we explore that fateful day, let us instead go to the next chapter in Edward's life, and to mine as well, so you can see how this patchwork quilt of love, and life and dare I say it, death, is coming together. Each tiny square a little story, abutting another tiny square. Will I finish it? Is that my job? Or will there be one last small empty corner space left to fill in?

Back in time, on the first of his hundreds of journeys, the young Eadweard Muybridge, (Edward Muggeridge, still,) is leaving England for America, leaving the gentle green hills and sweet-flowing river of Kingston-upon-Thames for the Wild West.

* * * * *

It feels strangely familiar to him, traveling, Edward thinks, watching all the activity on the dock, although the furthest he's ever been from home is a visit to London, and now here he is, waiting to board this massive steamer. He has already memorized her statistics, this *Sarah Sands*, which will take him from Liverpool to New York. He'd reassured his mother on all the safety points.

'She weighs 1,299 tons, she's 215 feet long, and she's a steamer and a clipper,' he'd told her with no small sense of satisfaction once he'd paid for his fare from the sale of his butterfly collection, which had left him with money to spare, to his relief. 'She's got a funnel, four masts, an iron hull and a maximum speed of nine knots – *and* mother,' he'd told her. 'She was built only five years ago.'

He has all his worldly belongings packed into one large trunk, and at his mother's suggestion, some illustrated bird books. 'You never know, Edward, you may be able to sell them there... they may want English books,' she'd said to him, and he had thought it was a good idea.

As he watches the steerage passengers board the ship, he feels a deep sense of relief that at least he could afford a second-class cabin. He already feels different. For the first time the thought occurs to him, that he is not of the masses, and just at that moment he hears a mother call her son: 'Edward!' Her sharp voice rings out: 'Stay with me.' Edward looks at the young woman, haggard and drawn already, a baby on her hip, the young son, the Edward she's called, hanging back, scared no doubt by the moving carpet of people being swallowed by the dark cavernous hole of the opening to the ship. Edward contemplates a strange notion that has come to him, out of nowhere. He does not want to be associated with other Edwards, with steerage passengers, with (and he looks behind him, back towards the entrance to the port), a place such as Kingston-on-Thames.

What if, he wonders, he changes his name. What if he conjures up a past Edward. Hanging over the ship's railing, gazing into the murky depths of the churning water, his mind wanders, glances into the past, pulls out an idea: The Anglo-Saxon version of Edward - Eadweard. He almost punches the air. *Yes! Eadweard,* he thinks. *Ead – meaning wealth and luck – weard, guardian and protector. Eadweard will do very nicely.*

Eadweard, for so he thinks of himself from this very moment on, is intrigued by the life on board ship; this moving microcosm of a universe in which, he notes, behaviours that would not be tolerated on land, seem to be almost, well, de rigeur. *Granted,* he thinks one morning, watching yet another flirtation unfold between a young married woman and one of the sailors, *granted, I don't yet know a lot about the world.* His cabin mate, older than him, a red-faced Yorkshireman, who is travelling to New York for his sister's wedding, seems to relish the idea that life is freer on-board ship, exhorting Eadweard to join him at the bar, or at the inevitable card games, or in pursuing a few of the older, single women, despite himself being married.

'While the cat's away,' he says to Eadweard, splashing himself with cheap cologne, 'although, strictly speaking my wife's not away. I am!' and he laughs uproariously at his own joke. 'You mun come with me young 'un,' he says. 'Have a bit of a laugh.'

But in the main Eadweard is happy in his own company and happy learning about his soon-to-be new home, although he does admit to himself sometimes that it would be nice if he was brave enough to speak to some of the young women he's noticed casting glances his way. He's a little disturbed by the stirring inside his trousers that arises sometimes when he catches a glimpse of curls and a flash of cheekbone under a bonnet. He wonders, when he sees the young married couples on board, at their happiness. He can't help thinking about what he witnesses, the gentle touch of a hand dropped on a shoulder, the secret smiles. He would like to *know* he thinks. (How surprised, how disbelieving would he be if someone was to tell him: the woman you will fall madly in love with is only just now about to be born. A 20-year age difference. Surely only marriages for royal families, for allegiances to be forged, territories gained, would create such an unholy alliance.)

His chance to 'know' arrives somewhat unexpectedly when the ship breaks some of its valve gearing five days into the voyage, returning to

Cork for a few days for repairs. Impatient to get to America, Eadweard finds this detour irksome, although at the same time he is impressed by Cork, the beauty of its architecture, the massive harbour his ship has limped back into. Encouraged to get onto terra firma by his always jovial cabin companion, Eadweard finds the Irish a merry mob despite the terrible repercussions of the ongoing potato famine, and with a few days in port, it's not long before he finds himself in a pub drinking perhaps a little too much than is wise, and sorry to say, within a few hours, he's on his stomach vomiting into the channel between the jetty and the ship, divested of both his virginity and the one pound note he had in his trouser pocket, 'both,' the barmaid who had spotted a young man on the loose, told her sister later, 'as easy as the other to take, although to be sure the pound'll last longer than his love-making.'

It was not, Eadweard reflected sourly the next morning when his unsteady legs and aching head allowed him to climb back onboard ship, the romance he'd built up for himself, but he was eternally grateful he had not taken more of his money on shore with him. It taught him a lesson early in life: to guard his money, and his dignity. He saw the winsome cheekbones in a somewhat different light after that, and was able to feel not even a twinge of envy when his rotund cabin companion set off on his daily excursions, 'for a bit o' fun lad.'

Can I leave him here then for a while? Arrived safely in New York, with his New Name? Although I will admit that for the sake of brevity I have shortened the many versions of his surname he played with. But let's imagine him, this somewhat odd young man, and his early years in his new country. Do we hear of love affairs and marriages, something we might expect of a 21-year-old male trying to make something of himself? No, we do not. In fact, we know almost nothing of his time in New York, although we know he found work as an agent with the London Printing and Publishing Company.

He is lost in New York, my (possible) grandfather, subsumed by the city. He seems somehow already though to have had discovered the art of survival, it seems as if his preoccupation with the worlds of art, science and nature were already unfolding. Why wouldn't a young man of relatively good name and with a keen interest in those subjects, be able to buy and sell books? No reason at all it seems, because we hear that his bookselling went well, well enough to start a bookstore, and in due course for first his younger brother George to join him, and four years later when George dies of tuberculosis, Thomas joins him.

And then what we know is that like so many hundreds of thousands of other new Americans, he decided to 'go West', and that the curious trajectory of his life began to unfold as he makes the decision in 1855, to go to San Francisco, where so much of his future will be played out, where there is so much destiny written in the stars.

Drawn to a city on water, little knowing that this girl-child, this Flora, now only four-years-old, will be the only love of his life. They will marry, and she will become his 'wife', and for all those who come after, not much rhyme nor reason to that. But then there is often not much rhyme nor reason in the decisions of the heart is there?

Marriage. That word. It had to creep in somehow, didn't it? Loaded as it is; happy, sad, dysfunctional, steady, solid, abusive, short, long, never married, spinster, bachelor, divorced, widow, widower. An entire family of words around the idea of coupling. And then there is another family of words isn't there? Words like desire – a word as light as a spider's web, sitting lightly in the mouth, as light and as fickle as the emotion itself. Then there's passion, heavier than desire, reminiscent of a bitter-sweet fruit, it tastes somehow of addiction, potent, bitter-sweet, utterly consuming. And other words too. Bliss, fidelity, infidelity, betrayal, heartbreak, loss, devastation, and more, and more, and more… a waterfall of words cascading toward us, taking us deep into the territory where Eadweard and Flora and Harry lived, where my mother and father met, where I too have dwelt.

I 'coupled'. At least I thought I did. Love is what brought me from California to Sydney, and then fleeing from it took me from Sydney to the Victorian High Country, and then there was one, last desperate journey from a place I can still hardly mention, to here, to home. And perhaps soon there will be this story for you, how a Mexican girl, to all intents and purposes, became an American woman, became politicized, educated, radicalized. How she fell in love and followed her heart, and how her heart was broken and trampled upon, and how, fleeing from the wreckage, she found herself in a landscape where the tiniest of wood orchids can take her breath away, where the warm crushed-apple breath of her horses can melt her into the golden light of infinity, where she now exists, caught in a melting moment, the twilight of her life, opening her heart to those that have dwelled within, that have come before, those that are no more.

I too was drawn to a city on water; I went for love, and love chewed me up, spat me out, and found me instead a landscape, horses and friends. At the time it felt as though my life was over, as if I would never put together the shattered shards of my soul.

To become your true self, do you need to be shattered somehow, Beth? I often wonder about karma, and about the effect of a birth chart on someone's destiny. Take yours, for instance, all that Earth in you – Taurus, and Virgo and Capricorn. You're a nurturer, builder, and sustainer and above all, beyond anything else, the glue that holds your family together. I know when you chose Will against your family's wishes, went against their politics, their mainstream ambitions for you, you fell apart, didn't you? You've told me so, and I believe you. You had to lose one family to create your own, and despite bridges being crossed, connections remade, I know there will always be the shadow of the separation in there.

Eadweard was shattered before he became a photographer. In his case almost literally– his head smashed open, to be never quite the same again. He 'saw' the world differently after his accident. His accident gave us a photographer who seemed to inhabit a world of movement, whilst photography was still a static, representational view of the world, my (probable) grandfather's head saw it as a whirling source of energy.

And how that happened was, he fell out of a stagecoach and on to a rock. Imagine it Beth: something comes along and sideswipes you so completely that it changes your life forever more. I've thought about it often, that defining moment, the stagecoach out of control. Could it have been like this? Does *this* – what I write – allow you to see it, to feel it, to understand the beginning of the road that took a relatively normal man, a bookseller, and turned him into one of the most extraordinary photographers of the 19th century?

Indulge me, Beth. Imagine it.

* * * * *

In the hospital Eadweard gingerly lifts his hand towards his head. He could not have imagined such a headache in his wildest dreams. His worst hangovers are as nothing compared to this.

The nurse, noticing his distress, comes towards him.

'Sir? Are you in pain?'

A grimace forms on his face. 'I believe in as much pain as Saint Catherine must have been on the spiked wheel,' he says.

Seeing the blank expression on her face, he is prompted to explain. 'You have seen the fireworks?'

'Of course, Sir.' She nods, smiling.

'Well,' he says, 'next time you see those pretty sparks remember this – the Catherine wheels are named after the martyred Saint Catherine, who was tortured on the wheel for her Christianity, but when the wheel miraculously fell apart, she was beheaded.' He watches with a perverse satisfaction the falling of the pretty face in front of him.

'I should sit you up for the doctor,' she says, and he imagines she is slightly rougher with his bruised body than before.

Eadweard does not feel normal. This much he knows. He cannot put his finger on it, but it is as if somehow one side of his brain cannot, will not, talk to the other. His senses are somehow more, and somehow less acute than ever. He cannot smell or taste anything. It is a strange sensation being in a hospital, unable to smell the smells he knows exist there: the disinfectant, the food, the indefinable hospital smell. He cannot even taste food. It is almost unbearable. And yet his brain is exploding with a weight of shifting colours and sounds, sensations so filled with clarity they are almost overwhelming. Then too, over-riding everything is a slight smell of burning, so real that at first he had demanded of the nurses and doctors if there was a fire nearby.

He wants to ask his brain *what is it?* He wants his brain to give a logical answer, but there is none. His brain is a jumble of memories, feelings and sensations, as if his normal control levers are all being erratically flicked by some unseen and malevolent mechanic.

Waiting for the doctor, Eadweard once more runs through the sequence of events.

Nothing unusual in the planned trip. Life was going as planned, the bookshop going from strength to strength, despite George's death. Eadweard pauses for a moment, waiting for the stab of sadness to come when he thinks of his brother, but instead he sees images – George laughing, George sick, George's coffin. Exploding images, to the point where he has to hold both sides of his bandaged head.

He moves on in his own story, trying to follow a logical line. Nothing unusual, a stagecoach trip from San Francisco to New York, in order to go to Europe and purchase more books, advertising for commissions for works of art, books and engravings.

Why, he wondered, had he decided to take the coach instead of sailing to New York, as he'd originally intended? But he knew the answer. It was cheaper, and he'd never done it. Cheap and adventurous, a perfect combination. Although he had not considered that he would be in such close proximity to people with the capacity to bore him to tears. There had been one man… what was his name? Mr… Mr. Mackey! That was it. He had gone on and on about his failed business ventures, until it was on the tip of Muybridge's tongue to point out that it was no *wonder* he failed at everything if he insisted on travelling around the countryside talking about it.

But nevertheless, the landscape, the sound of the horses' hooves, the clear brisk air, it was all enough to make a man's heart feel happy to be alive, to feel that almost anything was possible. It was indeed, an almost perfect combination and would have remained so too, if the accident had not occurred, if the carriage brakes had not failed on one of the steepest hills in Texas.

He can still hear the screaming.

'We're going to die!' The stout woman opposite him had grabbed at her husband, 'We're going to die!'

It was almost surreal, the speed at which they were going; the terrified horses with nothing to hold them back, careening down the hill out of control, everything outside a blur. He knew this – he had never known such speed.

The thing in Eadweard's mind: *Get out of here.* Finding his penknife in his bag, throwing himself against the force of gravity towards the back of the carriage, desperately cutting, slashing at the canvas. *Get out of here.* The sheer force of his wrist plunging down through the canvas enough to send shockwaves up his arm, and then, just as he began to edge his way through the opening – *blank*. Absolute nothingness.

'For nine days!' the surgeon who had treated him said, almost proudly, as if he himself had organised this extraordinary event, that his patient should be knocked unconscious when the driver aimed the out-of-control carriage at a tree, and that he should wake up in a hospital bed 180 miles from the accident.

'You're a lucky man, Muybridge,' the doctor had told him. 'One of the passengers died.'

'What was his name?' Muybridge asked, knowing even before the doctor replied what the answer would be.

'I think it was a Mr. McKay,' the doctor replied, somberly.

'Mackey.' Eadweard's penchant for exactitude presented itself. 'Mr. Mackey.' He felt a sudden stab of pain that Mr. Mackey, boring as he was, no longer encumbered the Earth.

'Exactly! Well done, Sir. You are coming along well.'

'That,' said Muybridge, somewhat sourly, as the doctor continued to present himself as a single, then a double vision in front of him, 'is entirely a matter of opinion.'

Chapter 5

Difference

Something different about Eadweard. He wasn't a strange-looking man for his time; his bushy beard and hair were merely indicative of his status as an elder member of an artistic patriarchy, but he had an intensity about him – his startling blue eyes for one thing. And as a child I looked a little odd, a little different to those around me. I had blonder hair, whiter skin and blue eyes. Reports in books and newspapers say that in his later years my father, Florado, looked almost exactly like Eadweard (another plus in the column for Eadweard as my grandfather perhaps). You would think perhaps that this difference might have alerted me as I grew older to the idea that perhaps there were some genetic differences between myself and my 'parents', but blue or green-eyed Mexicans are not as rare as the Hollywood movies would have us believe. My father/grandfather, who truly believed that education was the way to a better future for all Mexicans, told me stories as I grew up, paving, if I'm unkind, the way to a lack of curiosity on my part to my difference; teaching me, if I am kind, more than I ever learned in school about the true nature of being Mexican.

'Mexican, mi hija,' he told me once, when we were working together in the shop and a particularly rowdy bunch of pushing, shoving teenagers had just left, 'Mexican is an ethnicity, not a nationality. Mexicans forget this. We are just another mixed race.'

I did not exactly understand what he meant by that statement at the time, but I think what he was telling me was: Look, we have Native American Indian blood, we have Spanish, we have Andalusian, Catalan — we even had an Austrian Emperor for a while there – Maximilian I of Mexico, no less, who came charging into Mexico in cahoots with Napoleon and a plan to conquer Mexico. He ruled for three years, before America, which had been a bit distracted by its own civil war to take much notice, began to aid the Mexicans, and finally Maximilian the First, the one and only Emperor we ever had, was executed in 1867. Take all of this toing and froing of Europeans, take the odd Austrian dalliance with a local, take the French control of the mines in Mexico, and it's easy to explain why I might have blonder hair, blue eyes, and, if not white skin, a more olive version of my parent/grandparent's darker skin. Also, I grew up loved, most truly and sincerely loved, and because I was loved I was secure, and because I was secure I didn't even question my place in the family, or how I fitted in with those around me. I could not even begin to imagine that they were playing out a betrayal on me every single day of my life. And after half a lifetime of thinking about this, the only conclusion I can come to is that for them it simply became real.

My mother was 16 when I was born, old enough and yet far too young to be a mother; the lie to hide her disgrace, to keep me safe within the family gave me everything an *ilégitima bastarda* would not have had. It also kept my mother safe; no scandal attached to this Catholic family, but I am sure, the Secret of Me is why she never married. A situation which troubled me as her much-younger sister, but which, as her daughter, of course I understand.

Bubbling up under all this is a little volcano of fire and ice, the shadowy figures of Eadweard and Flora, of Flora and Harry, of my mother and father, and all that is – let's not beat about the bush – sex. The messy lava of love and sex, that both created me, and ends with me.

There were boys, of course, I wasn't immune to a girl-child's fantasy that the older boy next door would love me, and there were some teenage fumblings, but it seemed, although I couldn't of course have defined it then, as if there was something about me that did not attract boys in the same way that my friends, whose deepest yearning desire was to fall in love, get married and have a family, managed to get boys they liked to look at them.

Perhaps the boys sensed my difference, perhaps like animals, they smelled I was not quite of the 'herd', and despite the occasional kiss and wandering hands, it seems, looking back as if, on both sides, theirs and mine, there was some essential key element missing in the equation of 'boy meets girl'. At least, that was the case until I moved to Santa Ana, and there, away from home and friends and family, I fell in love for the first time.

I can remember it to this day, as clearly as I can now see the golden yellow blooms of wattle outside my window. It happened, of course, while I was working in the shop. It could not really have happened anywhere else, since at the time my life consisted of the small apartment I could only just afford to rent (with a little extra thrown in by my parent/grandparents to make life just a tiny bit easier for me), and the bicycle I rode to work and back each day. Jacques du Plaix had chosen well for the site of his second shop. Santa Ana had boomed during the war, with its aviation company and army air base and although *Chicanos* weren't regarded highly, they weren't as reviled as they were in many other places, and there was at least an acknowledgement that we too had done our bit in the war. And things were changing. That same year, 1947, the Mendez family won the right for their children to be educated at the white school in Westminster in the case *Méndez v Westminster*, and like a pebble in a pond, the ripples of change were set in motion.

I can't say that I felt the ripples of change in my life immediately on the morning I met one Miguel Francisco Ramirez, but ripples came, soon enough.

I was stock-taking at the time, and José, the manager, was supposed to be serving in the shop, except that he wasn't, because the shop was quiet, and he was in the back office, so when this voice said: 'Excuse me, I'm looking for chayote, do you have some?' I gave only the slightest glance towards the corner.

'The manager will be with you shortly,' I said, concentrating on my pad of numbers.

'But you could look for me,' he said. 'Couldn't you?'

I lifted my eyes. 'I could, but I'm stocktaking. I'll get José for you.'

'I'm in a hurry!' He sounded just a bit annoyed. 'It wouldn't take long to look, surely?'

Just for the tiniest of moments, we glared at each other, and then just before I could say anything, José returned.

'Can I help you?' he asked, and the man turned to José.

'Please,' he said. 'I would like some chayote, and I can't see any in the store. Do you have any?'

And I tuned out, back into the world of numbers, while unbeknownst to me Miguel Francisco Ramirez had decided that I, 23-year-old Rosa Maria de Martinez, was intriguing enough that he would visit the store, not just once, not just twice, but three, four, or *more* times in the next week or so, until finally José said to me one afternoon:

'This man, he is almost our best customer, but I think he visits not just for what we sell eh?' He winked at me, and I felt myself blush from the top of my head to the tips of my toes. A slow-burn if ever there was one, because I had been conveniently pretending that I hadn't really begun to wait until 4.00 pm when Miguel would come by on his suddenly oh-so-regular-as-clockwork visit. I had conveniently been pretending that I hadn't noticed him noticing me, and that I hadn't, not for a second, seen into this man's laughing eyes and wondered what it might be like if he kissed me.

And later, just only a few weeks later, I knew full well how sweet those kisses could be, as he whispered to me, 'my stubborn Rosa,' and retraced with his tongue the journey of that blush.

Miguel. He always thought it was funny that our relationship started with a stand-off, but in a way the seeds of the end were there in that beginning, because finally our stand-offs became our normal default while we tried to balance what we *wanted* from each other with what we were prepared to *offer*.

He was not, as it turned out, (although of course I imagined he was at the time) the great love that would come and shake me to my core, but he was the man who woke me up. And although in only a few years, we would end it by mutual agreement, or disagreement, the beginning of the radicalization was set in place by Miguel, and I was lucky that this true man was my first love.

What is intriguing about my (probable) grandfather, if we follow his chronology, at least as it suits this vague wandering through my life and memories, is why there was no woman, before the woman/girl half his age who claimed his heart?

Was it perhaps, that the stagecoach accident, and his ongoing neurological problems stopped him dead in the young testosterone-filled prime of his life from even considering romance, so hell-bent was he on controlling the strange repercussions to his brain?

History tells us that when he recovered from the accident, at least enough to travel, he made his way back to the UK again, and that his mother, visiting him in London, took matters into her own hands.

Chapter 6

The Aftermath

It is a week since Eadweard has arrived at his uncle's house in London, and Susan Muybridge is worried about her son.

Now, for instance, here he is in the drawing room, and still she can see the pain cross his face. When it does, it's as if a shadow falls across him.

'Edward.' (She still calls him Edward, and even if there is no difference in the pronounciation of Eadweard and Edward, in her mind he will always be Edward. I'm sure that is exactly how a mother would respond, isn't it Beth?)

Eadweard looks up at his mother standing near the window.

'Mother?'

'I think you should see a doctor. I'm worried about you.'

Eadweard tries to dismiss her concern.

'You worry too much.'

'Allow me this,' she says. 'I lost your father, and your brothers, and I almost lost you.'

Eadweard grimaces as he tries to focus on her face.

'I will think about it.'

She nods. She knows her brother is acquainted with someone who is acquainted with the Queen's neurologist. She can wait.

In London Eadweard is out of sorts. He realises he has become a somewhat different person. Not quite an Englishman. He is used to more light, more sun, more openness. He is not used to seeing England with the inevitable bursts of Catherine Wheels inside his head, with the double-vision, blinding lights, and energy emanating from all things.

His uncle's house is in Kennington, a long way from all that is fashionable and busy, but that suits Eadweard, who still tires easily. The headaches and the double vision can return any moment, and on top of that, he's bored. Arranging the purchase of books to take back to America is too simple, and also he is not ready to travel back there yet.

One morning, he wakes early, while it is still dark, far too early for the household to be awake. Getting dressed, he sees his boots are not yet back outside his door, and so he goes quietly down to the kitchen in search of them.

They are easy to spot – all the household shoes lined up, clean and ready to be delivered to their owner. In fact, the internal mechanisms of the household are all on display, thinks Eadweard, as he sits and ties his laces. It is warm in the kitchen, the coal stove heaped up last thing makes sure of that, and from his vantage point Eadweard can see through to the laundry where the washing is hanging. So much washing, he thinks, for one house – his clothes, his mother's, his uncle's, his uncle's wife and his children.

What if there was a way to wash clothes all at once? A machine to help make the daily running of a household easier, he thinks to himself.

'Now that would be a thing to invent,' he says out loud, his mind turning over all the possibilities.

When he returns from his walk, his spirits lifted, his mother sees the time is right.

'I've made you an appointment Edward,' she tells him, 'to see the Queen's neurologist. He is interested in your case.'

'Well,' says her son, obsessed as he is at the moment with the mechanics of this machine that can wash clothes. 'There would be no harm done in seeing him I suppose.'

Sir William Withey Gull, 1st Baronet of Brook Street, is intrigued by his new patient, this tall, upright man with the piercing blue eyes, and the slightly-less-than-English accent.

'Tell me about life over there,' he says, while he's examining Eadweard. 'I find it hard to imagine.'

And so Eadweard describes New York, how grand and busy it is, how brash in comparison to London, he describes the massive landscapes he has seen, the beauty of San Francisco; and all the time Sir William watches him, watches the way he puts a hand to his head every now and then, asks him occasional questions about his vision, about his mood-swings, about his heightened imagination.

As a first step, Sir William prescribes outdoor activities for this new patient. It's obvious to him that Eadweard is suffering from frontal lobe domage, that part of the brain that controls emotions and behaviours is damaged. *But how much damage? That of course is the question,* he thinks to himself. *How much damage?*

Six years Eadweard stays in England. He sees Sir William regularly. They have a lot to say to each other these two, with Sir William's belief in science, his writing on subjects as diverse as anorexia nervosa – identified and named by him – paraplegia and Bright's Disease. (Jump with me here for a moment into the future Beth. Who could have possibly imagined that in the 1970s a conspiracy theorist would suggest that Sir William Withey Gull not only knew the identity of Jack the Ripper, but despite being at the time of the murders, 71-years-old and not well, *was* Jack the Ripper? Despite any evidence at all, somehow this idea stuck, long after this man, who was a champion of so many causes, had left this Earth, and it proves to me yet again, the slippery nature of the truth, or at least how a truth can be disputed, undermined or twisted by another 'truth'.)

I wonder what Sir William would have made of Eadweard's interest in astrology? Not much, I can't help thinking, and yet it is Sir William, a scientist through and through who actually determines the course of Eadweard's life, with an almost magical suggestion.

'It's the exploding colours I see,' Eadweard explains to him one day. 'It's as if I see the energy *inside* everything since the accident. My eyesight is different these days –sometimes sharper, sometimes more diffuse. Sometimes I feel as if I'm living in a world nobody else can see.'

Sir William has been making notes on his pad, doodling with intent, when the idea occurs to him.

'Have you thought about taking up photography Muybridge?' he says, suddenly, out of the blue. 'I've been thinking you need an interest. I think the art – and the science – of photography could interest you.' (In fact, he knows, this brain in this man needs more than an interest, it needs an obsession, it needs to focus on one thing, and one thing alone.)

Eadweard is intrigued. 'The science and art of photography,' he says. 'That is an interesting way to look at it.'

And so this is what Eadweard does. First he invents a washing machine, then he studies the science of photography, and at the International Exposition in London a few years later he has two inventions, one for a photographic plate process, and one for a washing machine.

And finally, Beth, when Eadweard has mastered the wet-collodion process, when his head is as well as it will ever be, he returns to America – to the land of open skies, to the city of San Francisco, to the water, to the meeting of Flora, and to his destiny.

Chapter 7

The Calls

As for me and my destiny, I had always imagined that it would be in America, and when Miguel and I were in love it really did seem to me that I had already come such a long way from home, living and working in America, that this would be where I would stay. But perhaps in meeting this man who taught me from the start about the inequality of the Mexicans in America, who taught me to think for myself, to question the status quo, to demand more from my life than I had ever imagined I might achieve, it was inevitable that the student would outgrow the teacher and that I would need to leave him.

This is how I became radicalized; this is the trajectory that led me to the great love of my life, that led me in turn to the greater love of my life – Australia. A thousand miles from where I lived in Santa Ana, in Texas, was the town of Westminster. Now, Westminster had become, by the time I was 24, the birthplace of a fight for rights for Mexican Americans, or 'Chicanos', as we were known. You have to understand that in much of postwar California and the Southwest we were still excluded from 'Whites Only' theatres, swimming pools, restaurants, parks and schools. And I say 'we', because at this time I was a Chicano, with no idea that the blood of England's green and pleasant land flowed through me. By the time I arrived in Santa Ana, the upholding of the ruling of *Mendéz v. Westminster* was sending ripples of change throughout the Southwest, and Miguel and I were riding its coat-tails.

In 1944, a Westminster woman, Soledad Vidaurri, took her children, and her brother's children to enrol at the 17th Street School in Westminster. Although they were cousins the children looked quite different, Soledad's had fair complexions and features, and Gonzalo Mendez children were darker. The administrator looked over the children and said the two blonde ones could stay and the others would have to register at the 'Mexican' school. Soledad was furious at the discrimination and went home without registering any of the children in either school.

At that time Mexican schools were typically housed in run-down buildings, they had less experienced teachers than the Anglo schools, they had shabbier books, less expensive equipment; and where geometry and biology and science were taught at the Anglo schools, Mexican schools focused on teaching industrial skills to boys and domestic skills to girls.

One school superintendent in Texas told his fellow educators: 'You have doubtless heard that ignorance is bliss; it seems that it is so when one has to transplant onions… If a man has any sense or education either, he is not going to stick to this kind of work. So, you see it is up to the White population to keep the Mexican on his knees in an onion patch.'

Gonzalo Mendez and his wife Félicitas had both come to the US as children, their parents fleeing political turmoil in Mexico. Gonzalo's family had owned their own ranch, but now they had to work as laborers in the citrus groves, so when Gonzalo married Felicitas, the pair of them set about saving money in order that they could lease their own ranch, and by the time their children were of school age, they were a prosperous couple, employing people on their ranch, and they were proud of their American citizenship. Imagine their distress and shame when they were told that their children are too 'dark' to attend the good school, the 'American' school in their area.

They made a decision to stand up for their rights, for their children's rights. Gonzalo took a year off work and began a campaign, Felicitas minded the ranch and the home; they hired a lawyer, they challenged the segregation and they won, not once, but *twice,* when the school appealed and the original decision was upheld.

And like ripples in a pond, this one result began to affect communities far and near, including Santa Ana. Because although it was Miguel who originally became first intrigued, and then involved, passing out pamphlets and beginning to talk locally about the injustice of segregation, I too began to question my place in society, to wonder if I was meant to be a shopkeeper's assistant all my life, or if I was destined to be a worker, a wife and a mother, or if there was some faint possibility that I might become something else. And what I decided I wanted to do in this postwar America where Mexicans had laid down their lives for the United States, only to come home to a country which still treated them like second-class citizens, was to become a teacher. And so I studied at night school to gain a qualification that would allow me to be a teacher's aide, and from the moment I became a teacher's aide, I knew without a doubt that I wanted to become a teacher, and gradually, step by step, I was led, it seems to me, by something larger than myself, to the University of California, in Berkeley, and towards the man who would sweep me off my feet, promise me the earth, break my heart, and ruin my career, all in a period of a few years.

I still have the catalogue from the University's *Bulletin,* for the Fall and Spring Semesters of 1954–1955. It was 25 cents, and I remember as clearly as if it was yesterday the combination of excitement and overwhelm I felt when it arrived in the post. It was pages and pages – 400 to be exact, a book in itself, all about the University, and as I glanced through it, I couldn't help noticing the deadlines, the Last day for This, the First day for That, all seemingly in a different language, with courses for subjects I'd never even heard about. I remember sitting down in my one and only armchair and wondering what I'd done, and whether I, Rosa Maria, had any right at all to dare to become a teacher, and at my age, as well. After all I would be a good five years older than most of the college students; I would be, I knew in advance, out of place, and it was something that bothered Miguel deeply, despite his radical politics.

'You will not be the same as them,' he said to me, early on in one of our circular discussions. 'You will be different.'

But I already knew that, and I knew it because I already carried difference within me, and this was before, although not long before, my sister/mother, before my mother/grandmother died, before I saw those words, *Florado Muybridge,* on my birth certificate, before my life as I *thought* I knew it crumbled in front of me, as insubstantial as fairy dust.

Miguel. He did not ask me to marry him until the final months, until it was becoming clear to me that I was truly going to to *do* this thing; that I had the qualifications to apply, that I could do this, and I suppose for him this was when he could feel me slipping away from him, from everything he'd imagined we would become. Perhaps, if he'd asked me earlier I might have said 'yes'. In fact there was a time, early on, when I was so in love with him, I was desperate for him to ask me, but he, the radical one, went on about 'freedom' and 'choices', until I fell for it, and I wrapped up and tucked away my desire for a husband, a home, a family. And like a wasted muscle, it shriveled, until there was, in the end, nothing left.

Looking back, I can see that many of these pivotal occurrences occurred during my first Saturn return, this time of shedding or commitment to a path, and in my case both those things happened. (As an example, Eadweard's accident happened when he was 30, when his first Saturn return was still active in his chart. It was not his destiny to be a seller of rare books.) But perhaps, before we look at Martin, and how he burst into my life, there is a trajectory there, a trajectory of loss and grief and confusion, so that one thing led to another in the same way in which a line of dominos will tumble with one tiny flick of the wrist.

The call. The first one. It came from my sister/mother.

It was late at night, and I was asleep. Of course, in those days I did not have my own phone. The house I had my room in had a telephone, and my landlady was not too impressed with her household being disturbed at one in the morning. When I heard the ring, I had no intuition it was for me, not even when my landlady thumped on my door, did a chill run through my veins, I simply got out of bed, put on my dressing gown and slippers, went downstairs and picked up the phone.

'Rosa, my Rosa,' Maria was crying, her voice shaking with effort, so that now, suddenly I felt cold, as cold as ice. 'It's Papá, it's our darling Papá… mi pequeña niña…'

I sank to the floor, there was not even the possibility of staying upright. I put my head on my knees, and I heard the words falling on me from a great height. My father had suffered a massive heart attack, right there at home, he had died just a few hours before. His body, my sister was sobbing, was still warm.

'Come home,' Maria said. 'Mi pequeña niña, come home.'

My little girl. It was not her sister she wanted to come home, it was her daughter, but it would be some years before that thread unraveled, some years before those words came to me in the middle of one of my wakeful nights, and by then she too was long gone.

And so, I went home. The first of the three journeys towards the day when I would stand there in the home I'd grown up in and realise that not only was there nobody left for me, I was not even the person I'd imagined myself to be, and I swear Beth, that I have never felt more alone in my life.

But for this first close experience of death was so visceral it took my breath away, and what I remember most from this distance away, was learning that grief and laughter are so closely related. How could it be? I wondered, after I got home and threw myself into my mother/grandmother's arms, that we could cry so much? And how could it be that just a few minutes later, we could remember something about Papá, and laugh all together, the three of us. His three women. Mexicans, of course, do death well. We wailed and cried, but we also cooked and called in our friends and family. We mourned and celebrated in equal measure, throwing ourselves into the sensory experience, until we were immersed in it, dripping with sorrow and giddy with laughter.

And when it was done, when my Papá was buried and gone, and it was time for me to leave once more, I do think that even though both those women who were so dear to me held on to the secret of my birth, that we were completely united in our love for the man in our lives, for the rock he had been, and that we mourned him well. And somehow, by the time I boarded the bus back home, something else had happened for me: I knew for certain that I was going to go to university, and I knew that even if it meant leaving Miguel and everything I had built around me, I was going, and nothing was going to stop me.

To say I was heartbroken when I left is probably not absolutely accurate. To say I *believed* I was heartbroken would be closer to the truth. Because, although it was my choice, and although it seemed in many ways as if something more powerful than me was guiding me to this choice, it was devastating to leave behind not just Miguel, but Jacques, Jose, the shop, the friends I had made, the life I'd carved out for myself.

Sometimes I wonder, if I had not lost so many people in such a short space of time, would I have fallen in love with Professor Martin Bailey, Lecturer in English? A lover of fine wine, a man with poetry flowing through his veins, a lover of women – in short, charming, seductive and, it has to be said, narcissistic. A man who had bettered himself by leaving behind his somewhat mundane career in England for the promise of 'advancement' in Australia, and had parlayed that into a three-year contract in America. A man who had started out as a little fish in a big pond, and by various means, fair and foul, was on his way to becoming a big fish in a big pond. A man, who, let's face it, bore a remarkable similarity to Harry, my other (probable) grandfather.

It was not what you could call instant attraction. After all, he was my teacher, and newly bruised from the loss of my father, Miguel, and my friends, I was barely keeping my head above water, and as for my heart, it was hidden from sight for the moment. Under lock and key.

The professor, Martin, I suppose I should say, encouraged us to have opinions, but at first, despite my years with Miguel, I was as quiet as a mouse in the classes where young men and women bandied around ideas, batting them like tennis balls, here to there, some landing, some falling shy of the mark. In these active discussions I took no part, not feeling I had much to offer to their constant banter, and quite frankly often bored by the inevitable and compulsory studying of say, Mark Twain. My heart and mind longed for something more, without knowing exactly what it was. It was yearning to find its literary wings, and one day, as it happened, Martin made it quite clear to us, his class, that he too was bored by the books we had to study. Out of the blue, almost, although it is quite likely I was daydreaming at the time, he exhorted us to: 'Think outside the square.'

'Have any of you read *Lady Chatterley's Lover*?' he asked, 'or Flannery O'Connor, or even *Gone with the Wind* with a subversive eye? Are any of you aware of Charles Bukowski? Do you read the Beat poets? If not, why not? Never mind what you're reading for this degree, tell me what you *read* not what you READ.'

I remember the ripple of confusion running through the class, but for me, and perhaps for a few others too, I felt as if my veins had been opened. I understood what he was saying – be made uncomfortable by what you read. The time of the classics is coming to a close. Embrace it.

He paid me no notice at the end of that class, as the students crowded around him, eager for his reading list, and I left as I usually did, alone and silent, but I knew he had given me what I had been seeking – permission to learn. I threw myself into the world of books: I began to look for books about Mexico, books by Mexicans, poetry, books brimming with ideas. I began to think about women, women's rights, racism, sexism and of course, I began, little by little to fall in love with, or at least to project love on to the man who had set my brain on fire.

Perhaps nothing would have happened if it wasn't for Jane Amos suggesting that I join in with a group of students who had decided to go to this event, the 'Six Gallery Poetry Reading' in San Francisco.

I sit here, and I write those words, and I look out at my mountains, at my gum trees, at the bluest of blue Australian skies, and I can scarcely believe that it was me, that I was there that night, the night when some have said Beat poetry was well and truly born.

I didn't want to go, truth be told, I felt out of place. I couldn't embrace the outlandish dress that had begun to emerge on campus as a way of standing out from the crowd. I felt, in every sense of the word, an outsider. We'd gone in two cars, and the other girls seemed so knowing, so sophisticated in comparison to me; they smoked endlessly, and talked of poets and writers and ideas, and all the time I was silent. When we got there, Martin was there, and I remember feeling surprised. I don't know why. After all he was our English teacher, he was interested in modern literature, why would he not be there? He chatted to us for a while before the readings started, and somehow as the other girls moved away – finding friends, mingling in a way that was completely beyond me, I found myself standing next to Martin, and somehow the night got underway and we were still there, next to each other.

I was there the night that Ginsberg read 'Howl'. And on the night that Ginsberg read 'Howl' in public for the first time, Martin, my professor, kissed me. Sometimes I think it was almost by accident, that it just so happened that it was me next to him and not someone else. Is that what fate is then? A simple 'accident'? If another student had been next to him, and he'd kissed her, would he have fallen in love with her? Is fate so random – so *wanton?* When Ginsberg finished reading, the room, which had gradually fallen so silent you could hear a pin drop, erupted into a maelstrom of clapping, and cheers, and whoops, and all of us were intoxicated by what we'd just heard. All of us were filled with a little wine and a lot of excitement, a pulsating, throbbing urgency that here was something new. That *we* were new. And as we stood, and clapped and whooped, Martin grabbed my hand and raised it in the air, and then suddenly pulled me to him, and kissed me. Taken by surprise, I was almost literally thrown off balance, and into the space of him, into a liminal moment where nothing existed beyond 'us', and the kiss, which had begun as this cheerful celebration, went on, the softness of our lips and mouths surprised to find the other, dropping further and further into the moment so that it seemed I was standing in a midnight pool of infinity, suspended in a moment of rapture so complete that I could even feel the edges of my body blur towards him, as if every part of me was dissolving into him.

And then.

Someone jostled us, bumping into Martin, so that he fell into me, and I, in turn, stumbled. Martin held me by the arm and steadied me, and then he smiled. A great big endearing smile.

'Well,' he said. 'Rosa.'

I blushed and then blushed more to find myself blushing. I could feel this deep rosy glow descending or ascending, both at once perhaps, as I smiled back at him. Of course, I was already gone, totally and completely absent without leave from everyday life, a cocoon of wild fantasies swirling around me as if from nowhere, so that it was all I could do to pull myself back from the sudden film of 'us' that was playing itself in my head and into the reality of the noisy, smoky room we were in. He took another step towards me, and perhaps, who knows, he might have kissed me again, except that at that moment Jane burst out of the crowd.

'Oh my God, Rosa! That was unbelievable! Wasn't it? Aren't you glad you came with us?' She didn't even pause or want an answer. 'Come on,' she said, grabbing my arm, 'these guys have asked us back to theirs. There's a whole bunch of us going. Some of the poets too. It'll be cool.'

What could I say? I didn't want to go. It was the last thing I wanted to do after my sudden unfolding. I wanted one of two things: to be with Martin, or to be back in my own room, reliving what had just happened. I did not want to be in some smoky crowded house where a bunch of people would be getting high. I stood there, rooted to the spot.

'I don't know,' I said. 'I'm not sure…'

'Well, *we're* all going.' Jane's voice was just the slightest bit testy. 'So you'll have to come.'

'It's fine Jane.' Martin's voice was reassuring. 'I'll take Rosa home. I'm leaving now anyway. I've got class to teach in the morning.'

'Rosa? Is that okay?' The relief in Jane's voice was so strong, I could almost have laughed.

I nodded. 'Yes.'

'Well…' Jane paused. 'See you tomorrow then. Thanks Martin.'

(And this was something I'd found very confusing at university, that students seemed to know which teachers they could call by their first name. It seemed as if some of them gave a permission slip into the ether; but for me these nuances were unreadable, along with, it would soon transpire, numerous other nuances to do with human behaviour.)

But Martin did not drive me home. He did not drive me home until the next morning, when I just had time to shower and change and head back to college. And by that time our lives, or at least, I had believed it was our lives, had changed forever. The plot would unfold as the plot would unfold. Where were my choices that night? I made a choice to be there, in that place at that time. Did I make a choice to be kissed? I made a choice to keep on kissing, I suppose, feeling this rich melting of me into him.

I made a choice to go back to his place.

There was nothing in his apartment that suggested I was about to have my clothes taken off by a married man. Actually, that's not quite true, there was one photograph: a smiling woman, two small children, by a rock wall with water behind them. As he poured as a drink, he saw me glance at it.

'My sister.' he said. 'She lives in Sydney with her husband and two children.'

I nodded. 'You're lucky to have family.' I was made bold by the night, the kissing, and, I imagine, by the alcohol.

He looked at me curiously. 'But you have family?' he said. 'I always thought Mexicans had big families.' Then he laughed. 'That's a bit of a clichéd thing to say, isn't it?'

'Yes,' I said and I paused. 'It's a long story.'

'Ah,' he said, passing me my drink. 'Perhaps it should…'

I couldn't have agreed more. 'Perhaps it should.'

He lied to me. Just like that. And yet again I found my way into a situation where people were not what they seemed, where relationships were not what I believed. But I also did not tell him the story of 'me' immediately. I did not tell him that twice more the call had come to go 'home' in the space of only a year. My mother/grandmother's heart broken by the loss of her husband, my sister/mother believed. No medical imperative for my grandmother to die, but she did; she faded away, and my sister/mother's heart was also broken, by the loss of these two loving parents who had held her secret for my entire life.

That time, when my mother/grandmother died, it was a strange mourning for me. I think now Beth, that my soul somehow knew it was my grandmother, because as sad as I was, I could not join my darling sister/mother in her deep grief. I thought at the time it was because of my new, big life. I thought I was the most selfish person on the planet not to be able to feel what I ought to feel, what my sister/mother was feeling, as she wailed and keened, and I watched her from somewhere far away. This far away place that became, over the years, the locked and secret planet to which I could move in the blink of an eye.

But then, only a year later, before the start of Martin and I, the next and final call came from our neighbour that my sister had died. I fell, Beth, I fell down, just like people do in the movies. My back slid down the wall, and I crumpled on to the floor into the tiniest version of myself, and a wail rose up from deep within and let itself out into the early morning air, and I held myself, swaying from side to side as our neighbour, Gloria, told me that my sister had not wanted me to know, but that she had been sick, diagnosed with breast cancer, and she had died only a few hours before Gloria called me, with Gloria there with her.

Why did my mother not tell me she was sick? Dear Beth, I've asked myself this question so many times, and there are so many answers. When she was the only one left, why could she not tell me she was my mother? Had she made some pact with her parents, my grandparents that she never would? That third and final journey home, I knew that I would never be going back again. I knew that I could not go back to a country now so filled with loss for me.

How my mind whirled, Beth, during those strange days. I'm not even sure I can give you an accurate account of it all. I locked it all away in my secret vault and threw away the key, you see, and even now, it's hard to write about it.

My darling mother was laid out for burial at home for the vigil, and I had so much to thank Gloria for beccause when I arrived our home was already filled with people who had known her, with food and drink and gifts for me, the one left behind. I walked in on a cloud of grief, being hugged and cried over and fed in equal measure. Knowing what I know now about the Western way of death, I think at least I was lucky that this Mexican way of celebration was there to hold me up through those strange first days.

I sat with my sister's body and felt such an unfathomable loss I thought I would break into pieces, but I ate, and drank, and reminisced with all our neighbours and all our friends; even the children ran in and out, grabbing food on their way to yet another round of games. It was beautiful Beth, in its Mexican way, even more touching because this was the death of a 38-year-old woman, but even so, for Mexicans death is the start of a new journey, and that is what everyone around me was celebrating.

Only Gloria could see the depth of my pain and she was gentle in joining me and holding me in it.

After the burial, and my sister/mother was of course buried with her parents, with our 'parents', came the task of sorting out the house. I had cause to be thankful to my hard-working grandparents, still my parents at that moment in my head, because they fell into the 50%

of Mexicans who owned their home. It was modest by American standards, but it was theirs, and now it was mine to do as I wished with, and what I wanted to do was sell it, leave Mexico and never look back. When I told Gloria the day after the burial that is what I was doing, she broke down. 'But we will miss you all so much,' she told me. 'So many years we've lived next to you.'

So many years, and yet even she never knew, or never guessed, the secret I would find out on the third day of clearing up, when finally I could bear to enter my sister's room, when I found the box with my birth certificate, when I saw my sister's name in the box where my mother's name should be, when I saw the name *Florado Muybridge*. When my life turned upside down in a nano-second, so extreme that for the second time in a week I slumped to the floor, this time in equal parts of astonishment, dismay, and, I have to say, excitement.

Because, Beth, it made sense! Like a dark house suddenly illuminated, corners of my subconscious came forward to greet me. This memory, that memory. My sister was my mother! Of *course* she was my mother, this was why she had loved me so fiercely, why my grandmother stepped in so often, did not allow her to brush my hair, or to dress me, or to cuddle me when I fell over. A wave of memories washed over me, and in each one I saw – of *course* she was my mother.

I did not expect to be angry, Beth. I think I was angrier at her for dying than anything else. But I did become angry. For many years I carried that anger towards all three of them, my grandparents and my mother, that they could have betrayed me like this, that they never saw how cruel it was to keep this from me. I don't think I will ever understand how they kept this pretence up forever. Not once in my lifetime did I have the chance to put my arms around my mamá and call her by that sweet name. *Mamá.* I had reserved that name for my grandmother, and love her as I had, she was not, never had been, that sweet and gentle mamá my sister, I could see, had tried so hard to be.

And so the trajectory of the next part of my life began, as the Mexican part so brutally ended. The house packed, the belongings sold, given away, burned even, the house put on the market, and I returned to my home, to America, to university, with a birth certificate in my purse that would allow me to get a passport, to travel, to lead an exciting life, to not live as my mother and grandparents had – in a small town in Mexico, the shadow of a secret hanging over them all their days. The money from the house would be enough for me to invest a small amount and have some in the bank. This, I already knew, was unheard of freedom for a young Mexican woman. I did not know exactly how I was going to look after my money, but I knew from the years of working with my father, of working for Jacques in the store, that I would guard this gift, and that it would be my chance to always have a small amount of independent means.

My counsellor recently told me that people struggle with two main areas of their lives – relationships and finances. I haven't lived a rich life, and if it hadn't been for a particular circumstance, and the building of my essential oil business, as you will find out about in due course, I could never have found the home I found here.

But could it be possible, Beth, as I move inexorably towards the end, that I have managed to reconcile both these vital forces? That would be something, wouldn't it? Because the fact is that for years, in fact for decades of my life I thought that if I could love someone enough, I would be happy, I would be loveable, that love alone was enough to mend the hole in my soul.

With Martin I was blinded by love. As we became more and more involved, as we found more and more pleasure in each other's bodies, in each other's company, I ignored all warning signs. I think perhaps ignoring the 'signs' was deeply embedded in me by my childhood.

The fact that he flew to Sydney for the holidays, for example, the fact that when his 'sister' and children occasionally flew into to visit him, every single trace of 'me' had to be eradicated. He was persuasive and adamant about the protocol of no-one ever knowing about us because of his position as my professor, but he always said that once I graduated, and enough time had passed, we would announce our love to the world. It was enough for me to gloss over the rest.

(Which, is of course, exactly what my maternal grandmother did with her darling Harry. She glossed over his abominable track record as a liar, cheat and thief. She borrowed money from her husband for her lover, she turned a blind eye to his gambling, to the necessity that he leave town when there were debtors out to, well, kill him in all probability. And, finally, the ultimate betrayal. At his funeral, another woman in hysterical tears, flung herself on to his coffin. Oh, he loved her, for sure he loved her, but Harry was missing a moral compass in every area of his life. He was not going to stop sleeping with other women because he 'loved' Flora.)

We settled into a rhythm, Martin and I, behaving like a married couple outside college, in his apartment. At college we were student and professor, and our socializing was limited to those events where we would both have found ourselves anyway. You might ask how on no-one guessed, but once I had fallen for him, I didn't bother with the slight friendships I had made any longer, they simply fell by the wayside. I was content with Martin's presence, content with his explanations, and when I was not with him, I was busy reading and studying. Two-and-a-half years can pass quickly if you've spun yourself a story that has a happy ending. If you've allowed yourself to fall for a lie, or worse, become part of the fabric of that lie – as Flora did too. You do not enter an affair imagining catastrophe, and yet where there is an affair catastrophe will always be the consequence.

I'll never know what Martin's thought processes were behind his decision to suggest to me that when his contract was up, and he was due to go back to Sydney I might like to go with him. I could comfort myself, as I tried to do for some years, by saying that he truly loved me and he truly believed we would end up together, but actually I think, like many men, he simply wanted to have his cake and eat it too.

There's a moment, when some inner knowing flickered, and then because of my own desires, disappeared.

We were having dinner at his place, discussing the merits of this sudden and exciting scheme. Sydney! I couldn't believe it. I'd never thought to go to Australia, but it seemed like a perfect adventure.

'I'll be able to meet your sister and her children at last,' I said. 'I can't wait to get to know your family.'

And there it was. A frozen moment. Something blank crossed his face. Just for a few seconds. 'Yes,' he said casually, and then he got up, taking his plate into the kitchen.

I was hurt. It had been such a spontaneous thought, and it seemed to have created an atmosphere that simply didn't match the words I'd said. I wondered for a moment, *was it because I was Mexican? Was he, after all, ashamed of me?*

'Don't you want me to meet them?' I asked him.

He turned back towards me. 'No…' he said. 'It's not that at all. It's just… oh well, never mind. I'm sure it will all work out.'

That phrase haunted me for years. *I'm sure it will all work out.*

Little by little, we planned the great move. I did not even demur when he said he wanted to go ahead of me. He had, he said, some business to attend to, and if he went ahead he could find us a flat somewhere and set it up so that when I arrived everything would be ready for us to start our new life. I think I was so busy discarding and packing and planning that it didn't even occur to me that this was an odd thing to do. I was thrilled at the very idea of what seemed like the inevitable progression towards marriage, because, I would reason to myself, if he wanted me to live in Australia with him, surely he wanted us to get married. I was not about to burst my own bubble.

And so, in due course, Martin left to set us up for our new life, and in due course so did I, discarding another skin on this strange journey towards this current, and last, incarnation of 'me' in another place.

Place. Already I had come so far from the land, the town of my birth, but as we flew in over Sydney, my heart was literally in my mouth at the sight of the beauty of the city below. The Opera House was not yet finished but it was already a grand sight. It seemed as if Sydney was determined to make itself as beautiful as it possibly could for me that day. The deep green/blue of the water, the white streams of spray from the boats on the harbour, the clear blue sky, red roofs and greenery everywhere took my breath away. I was overjoyed, overwhelmed at the idea of so much beauty in my life, at the idea that I was about to start a new life with the man I loved in such a wondrous place.

What I did not find out for many years was how much I needed 'place'. Even now I envy those third, fourth, even fifth generation locals, the ones who 'belong'. And now the last laugh of the universe is that here, in this place, which has gradually come to be 'home', to be my 'place', my spirit is slowly leaving, spending as much time floating above this land as on it. Perhaps we could be divided neatly into two sorts of people, the nomads and the gypsies, and those that stay put.

There's no doubt, Beth, that both my grandfathers, as I often think of them, fell into the first category. The world was their oyster. It was there for the shucking, and shuck it they did.

And suddenly there I was, arriving in Sydney, waiting for the grand moment when I would throw myself into my lover's arms.

Chapter 8

Sydney

It was doomed from the start, and I had no idea.

When I finally arrived in Sydney, tired and jet lagged, I scanned the crowd for Martin's face, longing to throw myself into his arms. At first, it didn't dawn on me that someone was holding up a placard with my name on, I simply kept on scanning, and looking for my love. *Where was he? He had to be here, didn't he?*

But as I came out into the crowd waiting at the bottom of the handrail, a man stepped forward. 'Rosa Martinez?' He asked.

I nodded. 'Yes?'

'I'm your driver. I'm here to take you to Rose Bay.'

I glanced around. 'But Martin,' I asked. 'Surely Martin…'

The man simply shrugged. 'I don't know anything, only that I'm to pick you up and take you to Rose Bay.'

My heart flip-flopped against my ribcage. What had gone wrong I wondered, as we drove through the alien city streets, why couldn't Martin be there to meet me? It's what we'd organised via our constant letters to each other, confirmed in a rushed telephone call.

The driver was silent and that suited me. I had no desire to speak with a stranger, to embarrass myself by asking him: *Why is my love not here?* And if he had spoken to me, I might well have cracked.

I gazed out at this new city that was going to be home. It was a strange feeling to have absolutely no idea where I was, but when we got close to Rose Bay, and suddenly the harbour opened up in front of me, I felt as though I was falling into a new world of colour. It was as if a painter had streaked across a canvas a splash of skyblue, a stripe of crimson, the clarity of titanium white, greens of every hue dotted here and there, and all of this sitting on headlands overlooking this vast expanse of blue-green water filled with yachts, and ferries, and *craft* of all kinds. Despite myself, my worry and my fear, I felt my spirits rise. *If this was where we were going to live,* I thought, *what could possibly go wrong?*

The driver stopped outside a block of red-brick flats. 'Number six,' he said, as he hauled my suitcase out of the boot. 'That's your destination.'

My destination. It was a strange way of putting it. 'Thank you,' I said to his already departing back. I never have quite got used to the Australian propensity for either cheerful over-familiarity or what seems to be downright contempt.

I pressed the bell for Number Six, and through the intercom I heard his voice, 'Rosa? Is that you? I'll be right down…' And as soon as I heard his voice my heart took flight.

If I was to tell you of his running footsteps down the stairs, his oversized hugs, his chatter: *I'm so sorry, something came up at the university, I couldn't get away,* the flowers in the flat, the foods I liked in the fridge, the thoughtfulness – everything as if it was, well, shall we say, a home, you might say well, what was wrong with that then?

When we had deep sex, the sex after absence, the merging again, what was wrong with that?

When we ate together afterwards, and laughed, and talked, what was wrong with that?

When I suggested we take a walk, and suddenly he froze, just a little, was there something wrong with that?

And so began a life based on a lie.

I look back at that year now and wonder to myself, how could have I been so gullible, how did I let myself be taken in?

The answer to that of course is that I wanted to be taken in. I did not want to see the obvious truth staring at me straight in the face which was that Martin was leading a double life. It became clear on one crisp autumn day in the Blue Mountains, when, as usual, we had slipped out of town for the day because (as I saw looking back) it was only out of town, that he would dare risk holding my hand in public or giving any public displays of affection.

So there we are, leaving the small junk shop in the main road, laughing about something – what? I don't remember.

A couple are walking towards us, but we're engrossed at that moment, looking in a second-hand shop window, full of things no-one in their right mind would ever want. We don't notice them. As they daw level with us, the woman says, 'Martin! Is that you?' And then, in that way that people do when they are re-stating the obvious: 'Nick... look, it's Martin!'

'I can see that,' Nick, a man around Martin's age, I guess, holds out his hand. 'How are you?'

'I'm good.' Martin shakes Nick's hand vigorously, but says nothing more, everything about him suddenly stiff.

I wait to be introduced, but instead an uncomfortable silence falls over us, as chilly as the autumn wind whistling up the main street of Leura.

'Well...' the woman is hesitant, looking at me curiously. 'How are Sally and the kids?'

'They're good. Yes. Fine,' Martin says.

The woman tales a plunge, and turns directly towards me, and she just leaps straight in, jackboots and all.

'Such great kids,' she says. 'Aren't they?'

'I haven't met them yet,' I answer truthfully. 'Martin's sister seems very busy.'

And there it is. Silence so thick you can cut it with a knife. As if someone's just died. Martin looks at his boots. Nick looks at Martin, I always think looking back, with a slight sense of sympathy, and the woman, well, the light of evangelical truth shines in her eyes.

'Oh,' she says, crisply. 'Sally's not his sister. Sally is Martin's *wife*.'

And I must say Beth, I never knew it was possible to get so many syllables into one short word.

The woman, Justine, I later learned, moves away. 'Come on Nick,' she turns one last time. 'We really must go.'

Nick shrugs his shoulders at the sight of his wife's disappearing back, and follows her.

I don't know what to do. Fury and sorrow course through me, and at the same time I seem stuck there, unable to move.

'Rosa.' Martin touches me on the arm, and I instinctively recoil.

'Rosa. We should move.'

'Move?' I almost spit the word. 'Where? Somewhere where you can hide me and nobody will ever find us? The desert maybe...'

'No,' Martin's voice is calm, reasonable. 'I mean, from here.'

'Oh.'

We move. We move away from the window. We move back to the hotel, we fight, and I cry, and we fight, and we move back to the city, and we fight, and I cry, and in the end, I find I have some small shred of dignity and I tell him to leave.

'But I found this place,' he says, looking for all the world like the toddler I'd realised in an instant he actually was. 'It's my place.'

'You have a "place",' I tell him. 'It's called "home". It's with your wife and children. I have nowhere. Until we work out what to do, I'm staying here.'

As he is about to leave, I demand he give me the key back, and he did.

And that was how it ended. Another betrayer left my life, but despite my war wounds I somehow managed, Beth, to keep hold of what would sustain me.

I was already a survivor, but it took me many years to recognise the strength in me.

Chapter 9

Helios

But my grandmother was not to be a survivor, although of course, she does not know it yet Beth, in the chronology of this writing, if you like. At this moment she cannot possibly imagine the changes that will be wrought in her short life, when on that fateful day the photographer Eadweard Muybridge meets her at the Nahl gallery. And all I can imagine is that he was smitten by love, as strongly and as completely I was with Martin, and that she was smitten by the idea of love, the idea of safety, of marriage and home and children, and a position in the world.

We could imagine it, couldn't we, Beth, that day when Flora arrives at work, a day like any other day, but not like any other day, the day fate steps in and takes a hand in not one, but four destinies, writing a strange course for Flora, for Eadweard, for Harry and for Florado. And further of course, for my darling mother, for me… and how curious that I will be the end of this line. The final fullstop, when it comes to that.

But we are not quite there yet.

Eadweard carefully walks out of the shop into the sunlight. The top of his head is throbbing in a most peculiar way. Sometimes, and he has grown used to this, when he is depressed, he feels as if his brain is constantly undergoing some sort of heavy transformation, so that every thought feels filled with lead, and every movement as if he is swimming through a viscous sea. Sometimes the plates in his head seem even to mimic a tremor in the earth, as if they are being pulled apart. But now, right now, he is experiencing something entirely different. A lightness of being has entered him, a sense of golden wellbeing is coursing through his body, and rather than feeling heavy, his head feels as light as air, almost as if the top of it has exploded and everything lovely he has ever seen or known is both leaving and entering him on a pillar of light.

He holds out a hand and places it against the wall to steady himself, and walks uneasily around the corner, out of sight of the shop, so that he can lean back against the next shop façade and rest a moment.

So this is what they talk about when they talk of 'falling in love', he thinks to himself with amazement, and he realises that all his life he has been waiting for this feeling, waiting and wanting to understand those undercurrents of electrical energy he has seen pass between people, but has never experienced himself. Images of the women he has known flicker through his mind: Sarah, the Irish girl, and the others, which has not excluded the occasional lady of the night. But this!

Flora's face dances before him. She is short, much shorter than him, he thinks, already fascinated by the 'why' of his attraction. And of course, young. Not his usual type, he thinks, no, not at all. Normally it's an older woman of independent means, someone who requires nothing of him emotionally. But Flora, her dark eyes looking up at him, seemed already to be asking him a question. There was a sadness in them Eadweard wanted immediately to erase. What could such a young girl of 19 or 20 know of such sadness, he wonders, and feeling now slightly more secure in himself, as the cascade of energy in his body begins slowly to settle, he starts to make his way up the street, pondering on the proper protocol for asking this Flora Stone out.

But fate and Eadweard are on the same trajectory and when he goes, a few days later to collect the photographs he had sent for retouching Flora is alone in the shop. When she hears the bell she comes out of the backroom where she had been working.

'Good morning, Mr. Muybridge,' she says to him, pleasantly enough, he thinks, his heart somersaulting through his ribcage at the sound of her voice, at the sweet, sweet sight of her. 'I'm afraid Mr. Nahl has gone out to meet with his brother, but your photographs are ready.'

Eadweard gives a tight, nervous cough – his throat, it seems to him, suddenly so restricted it seems almost impossible to speak. 'Thank you,' he manages to say, and then stands there *like an idiot,* he thinks to himself.

'Would you like to see the photographs Mr. Muybridge?' She prompts him gently.

He nods, and coughs again. 'Yes,' he says. 'Thank you.'

'I will get them,' she says, and for a moment that seems like an eternity, disappears from his sight. As she walks back towards him, she smiles at him, and his heart feels again as if it will burst out of his ribcage. All he wants to do is to take her in his arms, and as his head, overwhelmed by the sudden rush, begins its explosion into thousands of shards of light, he has to put his hand out to the bench next to him in order to steady himself.

'Are you all right?' Her voice comes to him from another galaxy, and he grimaces at the effort to calm himself, but he nods, and manages to speak.

'An old head injury,' he says. 'It comes back from time to time.' *What will she think of him,* he thinks, *this strange old man.* But she simply nods.

'I will get you a chair,' she says, calmly, 'and a glass of water. Sit for a moment until you are quite recovered.'

As he sits there, Arthur Nahl arrives back in the shop, all fluster and apology.

'My dear Sir,' he says. 'I am sorry not to have been here. I hope Miss Stone has looked after you?'

Eadweard nods. 'Indeed, she has been most kind. The head – you know – it plays up sometimes. She is fetching me a glass of water.'

Arthur nods. 'I am glad to hear of that, and sorry to hear of the head. But my dear "Helios" if I may call you that, let me just say what a privilege it has been to work with your photographs these past days. Yosemite! The sheer magnificence of it, and you Muybridge! I think even Watkins has not come near the magnitude of your photographs. They are stupendous.'

Eadweard can hardly bear the attention, the words slide off him while he nods and smiles, but all he is waiting for is Miss Stone, Flora, to return with his glass of water. A glass of water for which he has no real need, but he would make himself a dying man if it would bring her back towards him. Every sense is waiting. As he continues the conversation with Arthur Nahl, even the memory of scaling the cliffs at Yosemite is nothing in comparison to this desire to see her, the desire to be seen by her, and as she comes back, carefully holding the glass of water, it's all he can do not to leap up and pound the table and demand what took her so long.

'I hope this will help you feel better Mr. Muybridge,' she says to him as she passes him the water, and he gulps it down as if it is the last drink he will ever drink, a benediction from an angel, and then she bows her head slightly and leaves – leaves! When he stands up he almost slams the glass down on the table, and Arthur laughs at him. 'Steady on, old chap,' he says. 'You'll spill water all over your precious prints if you're not careful.'

'Of course.' Eadweard pulls himself together. He has an image of picking himself up bit by bit, and restacking his body, except that he can never be *quite* the same, he thinks, now that he has been hit by this strange force of nature.

'These are for your subscription series?' Arthur Nahl is bending over the prints, examining them minutely, checking for any unseen blemish or instruction not fulfilled by his retouchers.

Muybridge nods. 'Yes, and possibly for a guidebook to Yosemite.'

'Well, they are magnificent.'

Eadweard inclines his head. 'Thank you Arthur,' he says.

'No need to thank me. I hope our girls have done your work justice. The younger one, Miss Stone, she is relatively new to the work, but she seems to have a natural talent.'

'Yes,' Eadweard keeps his tone measured. 'Indeed, I am very happy with the work.'

'Good. Well it is advantageous for us to have the great photographer "Helios" associated with the gallery, and we are delighted to be of service…' He pauses for a moment. 'You know,' he says, 'my wife and I are holding a small garden party this coming Sunday. It is our son's first birthday and we thought we would celebrate with afternoon tea. I wonder if you would care to join us?'

'Of course.' Eadweard inclines his head. 'I would be honoured.' Dullness seems to be running through his veins. He cannot think for the life of him how he can ask if Flora will be there without it appearing strange, and yet if he were to go and she was not there – what a waste of time that would be.

'Yes.' Arthur taps the table on which the prints are resting. 'Charles and I have had good fortune in our business and our life, and so a small celebration seems in order. There will be a few fellow professionals you'll know Muybridge, I'm sure.'

And with that Eadweard has to be content. He thinks, but he is not sure, that Charles is saying people associated with the gallery will be there; he thinks but he is not sure that will mean Flora will be there;

he thinks but he is not sure that he can wait the full five days until Sunday rolls around.

At night, alone in his apartment Eadweard can think of nothing but Flora. He replays their meeting over and over again in his mind. One moment he wonders what it is he sees in her. *She's a little plump,* he says to himself, *her features are not well defined.* He calls her suitability for him as a partner into doubt. *She's so much younger... I could be her father.* The next second he is imagining the slight disarray of her hair at the nape of her neck, the curve of her cheekbone, the smile when she looked up at him, and he knows he loves her more than he has ever loved anybody. He knows that although he has only spent an hour in her company, he would walk over hot coals for her. He knows he must possess her or die in the attempt, until his brain feels fit to burst with doubt and passion, and he claps his hand to his head.

'You are a bloody fool, Muybridge,' he shouts at himself. 'A bloody fool! Do you hear me?' The only thing that will quiet his brain, he knows, is to think about another obsession, and not one involved with physical desire. Already, he has held himself, rocked himself, imagined himself inside her, but it curbed him for only a few minutes. His mind casts about wildly, images flicker in front of him, and at the forefront is Yosemite. *Yes* he thinks, *come to me.* And there it is, the canyon arrives in all its glory, and he begins to plan. 'The next trip,' he says. 'I will think about the next trip.'

In bed that night when Flora visits him, dancing across his vision, enticing him, beckoning him, he resolutely turns away, imagines instead towering cliffs, the sandy colours shot through with purple haze, the sheer grandeur of the canyon, the waterfalls, the green meadows and the massive sequoias. He sees himself walking through the valley. He runs through the logistics; he will need, he knows, two assistants along with the pack train. Then there is the list: the 'darkroom' tent, the plates, collodion, silver nitrate, chemicals of various sorts and the camera, of course.

Gradually, as he ticks each object off in his mind, his breathing relaxes until at last he sleeps.

At the Nahls, everything is in what you might call an 'organised fluster'. Mrs Nahl is putting finishing touches to the vases of flowers; the weather has held fine, little Samuel's tooth, which had been bothering him, popped through: 'Just like a tiny daffodil,' she had crowed to her husband this morning. 'Or a pearl. A perfect little pearl.' Her son had been magically restored to his normally calm and happy state, something for which Mrs Nahl was extremely grateful given the imminent arrival of 50 people, and even as she decides the moment has come to remove her apron, the girls, Miss Stone and Miss Thomas arrive, having been promised to her by her husband as extra helpers for the day.

'My dears! Perfect timing. How lovely to see you both.' She gives them both a warm smile. 'Thank you for giving up a few hours on your precious Sunday, I do appreciate it.'

'It's a pleasure Mrs Nahl,' Flora says, and Jane nods her head in agreement.

'Well, come with me and I shall show you the plates to take around.' She pauses for a moment, 'and of course,' she adds kindly, 'you are our guests as well, so once you have helped us serve the food, do please feel free to socialise.' (She hopes she has managed this with diplomacy.)

'It's a bit of a bother,' she'd said to her husband when he'd presented her with the idea as a way to solve the extra help needed for the day. 'I mean, Arthur, they are not exactly servants are they? But they are also not our friends, are they?'

Arthur had been amused. 'They're young girls, Lizzie, they'll be happy to earn a little extra for a day off and be able to chat to people as well.'

By the time Eadweard arrives, the garden party is beginning to fill up. He could not bear, he had decided, to arrive early, in case Flora was not there, and then he would have to stay until it was polite to leave, but equally, he could not bear to arrive too late, in case she was there, and he missed the chance to speak with her. As it is, as he arrives, Charles sees him at the gate.

'Muybridge! My dear man, come on in and meet people.' He guides him by the arm to a spot where two men are standing.

'Muybridge,' he says, 'meet my brother-in-law, the estimable Mr. Lowry. He is an accountant, if ever you should need one. Something every family should have, eh Frank?' Nahl laughs, and Muybridge is left in no doubt that this family joke has been told before.

'Delighted to make your acquaintance Sir,' he says, politely.

'And yours, Mr. Muybridge,' says the estimable Mr. Lowry.

'Muybridge is a photographer,' says Arthur. 'The great "Helios", as he is known. We are privileged that he is associated with the gallery…' and with that he moves away, leaving the two men at a loss for words.

'I imagine,' says Mr. Lowry, choosing his words carefully, 'that a great deal of work goes into the making of a "photograph".'

'You imagine correctly,' says Eadweard, feeling for all the world like one of the butterflies he would pin as a boy. They stand in awkward silence for a moment until Eadweard cannot bear it a second longer. 'Excuse me,' he says simply, and moves away, while Mr. Lowry nods at his retreating back. Eadweard moves through the crowd – there are a few people he knows, and they nod and wave as he wades through the sea searching for Flora whe he suddenly hears her laugh. (Later he will ask himself how he even knew it was her laugh, he had never heard her laugh before that moment, and yet his whole body trembled.)

He turns towards the sound and sees that she is offering sandwiches to a group of people near the steps leading up to the house. Abruptly he strides through the crowd, arriving, just as he had hoped, as she begins to walk away with sandwiches. His blood feels thick and thin at the same time, as if it is staggering around his body, and he almost lurches himself in front of her, so that she stops, pulled up short.

'Why,' she says, looking up at the tall man in front of her, 'Mr. Muybridge, it's you.'

'Yes.' He stands now, mute, *like a fool*, he thinks, *say something, anything.*

'The sandwiches look attractive.'

'Yes,' Flora smiles up at him. 'I believe they are very nice – would you like one?' She holds the plate out to him, but he shakes his head, but then, as she smiles again, and goes of course, to walk away, he says, and he cannot believe how raspy his voice sounds: 'Yes, I will, I believe I will,' so that she holds out the plate, and he makes a great welter of choosing one, all the time knowing he must say something, and say it fast, so that suddenly, as he stands there, sandwich in hand, it hits him with a lightning bolt.

'Miss Stone,' he says. 'I just wanted to say I very much appreciated your work on my photographs. You have a deft touch, a deft touch indeed.'

'Well, Mr. Muybridge,' she says, 'It was a pleasure to work with such beautiful material. I particularly love your clouds.'

'I was wondering,' *nothing ventured nothing gained*, he thinks, 'would you consider perhaps meeting me for tea at the Empire State one afternoon?' He sees the frown and the fleeting hesitation cross her face just as the other girl crosses in front of them with a plate of food, and to his surprise her name forges through the mists of his memory. 'With Miss Thomas,' he adds, quickly. 'I would be delighted if both of you would join me for afternoon tea. A small thank-you for the excellence of your work on my Yosemite series.'

And now, she smiles, and the slight tension around her eyes ebbs away. 'Why, Mr. Muybridge,' she says. 'That is very kind of you. I will talk to Jane, and I am sure we would both be pleased to meet with you. Thank you.'

He bows slightly. 'No,' he says. 'Thank you. Shall we say three o' clock in the afternoon next Sunday then?'

Flora nods her agreement. 'I will confirm with you, Mr. Muybridge when I have spoken with Jane, but that arrangement sounds suitable.'

All the time she is speaking, Eadweard is drinking all of her in – the peachiness of her skin, the way the sunlight is falling on her, lighting one side of her face, the thick hair piled high on her head, and still that air of vulnerability she exudes, so he is swept up again with the desire to simply take her in his arms, to protect her forever. He realises with a start that she is talking to him.

'Mr. Muybridge? I must do my duty now and take around the sandwiches. I fear they will dry on the plate if I stand here any longer.'

'Of course, Miss Stone...' he stands aside and watches her as she moves off, circulating with a social grace he has never been able to find, he thinks, but still he finds it in himself to make the effort. He congratulates Mrs Nahl on their son's charms, he speaks with both the Nahls, since Charles is there too, about the studio, about their art; to continue the never-ending discussion on the difference between art and photography, but all the while he is waiting for Flora to return to him with a 'Yes' or a 'No', feeling that his entire happiness depends on the proclamation of one of two tiny words.

Just as he as he is beginning to think that perhaps he has read the situation incorrectly, and that perhaps she will not confirm, or decline, a man comes towards him.

'Mr. Muybridge?' he says, holding out his hand.

Eadweard nods.

'Sir, I'm delighted to make your acquaintance. My name is Lloyd Tevis, and I work with Mr. Leland Stanford as his General Manager on the Pacific Union. We are both long-term admirers of your work. I am sure you know of Mr. Stanford's interest in the railroad and I was wondering whether perhaps we might be able to talk with you about the possibility of photographing some of his work for posterity.'

'Of course,' replies Eadweard, not blind to the business opportunities inherent in such a suggestion. 'I would be delighted to meet with Mr. Stanford, whenever such an opportunity presents itself.'

'Well,' says Mr. Tevis. 'That is excellent news. I will organise a meeting next time Mr. Stanford is in town... so good day to you Sir, for now.'

* * * * *

Was that an abrupt ending?

Well, it had to be. I heard the sound of your truck, Beth, and that was it. I had to go. It's hard to leave what I'm writing while it runs through me like a constant river, or perhaps it's more a massive jigsaw puzzle – these little pieces: this one here, that one there – am I right?

I move them around, placing and replacing, cantilevering until they seem to fit. I still can't see how it will all come together, but something makes me carry on. I suppose I had become accustomed to the idea that after I die, I would leave nothing behind, that my existence would be wiped from the planet, and with it any knowledge that my life had been connected with Flora and Eadweard. It's not as if, in the past at least 50 years, that the art world has not been aware of Eadweard's work. He has been experiencing a revival. Once or twice I've thought of contacting the 'authorities', of producing my birth certificate, of saying I am here too. But then, in the end, I felt that it would not suit me to open myself to others. In this way, I can do it. In this way I can leave a story behind for you all Beth, for my family.

I wonder if you would remember today in the same way as I will? And that is part of the strangeness of memory isn't it? That we all remember differently.

There we are, racketing over the mountains in your old Patrol, and there's been plenty of ribbing over the years between us on the value of a Cruiser versus a Patrol hasn't there, Beth? May and Brock in the middle seat with you, James and Joe in the back; me sitting up like Jackie in the front seat with Will, and soon enough I see your hand resting on Will's shoulder, just for a minute, lightly resting there while we chat about the weather, and I know this is the sweet, silent communication between you both, and that even after 25 years you wear it proudly.

'So,' says May, who has just turned 17 and is all bristly edges, almost literally in her case, since the only way to rebel in a small country town is to stand up somehow, and May has adopted Goth as her look, with purple spiked hair, a nose ring, and those clunky boots. 'Don't expect me to hang around you guys all day.'

I can almost see Will stiffen beside me. He grips the steering wheel tightly, and that's when your hand arrives on his shoulder and rests there, ever so gently.

'Of course not love,' you say to your eldest daughter. 'We'll just catch up with you around the town. No big deal,' you say. And both father and daughter deflate, the last almost reluctantly, I think, and I'm trying not to laugh at this small family drama, while James and Joe punch each other cheerfully enough in the back, and Brock gazes out of the window.

And me? Well, I chatted with Will about the spring lambing season, and you put in with your two cents worth, and part of me is with you both, with the grown-ups you've become; and part of me still remembers your own youthful rebellion. Dear Will, a farmer's son, falling for the hippie girl who came to town on a whim, all flowing dresses, headbands and beads, and their most unlikely coupling. Do you see it as clearly as me, Beth? There you were when I first met you, living in the shack Will built, eking out a living with his handyman work, showing a surprising ability to make chutneys and jams to sell locally, but still, nevertheless, dirt-poor, judged by Will's parents, Will made an outsider in his own community.

But here you are now, solid and substantial as you like. Although I remember the dark times too, you sobbing in my kitchen that you couldn't take the isolation anymore, Will slamming up to my place shouting at you. Even though of course he was really shouting *for* you, for fear that you were leaving, that the love of his life was about to leave his heart in a wasteland of devastation.

But I do believe you've both made it through to the calm waters beyond the rapids. I hope that I've been a refuge for you both, Beth, I really do.

Do you remember the first time I met Will? It was some years after I'd bought my property, and I was down the front on the road boundary re-doing some fencing, when a grotty old ute pulls up on the side of the road, and this wild-headed youth sticks his head out.

'It's not going to work unless you have strainer posts,' he says. 'It'll never stay up.'

I stand back and survey my somewhat crooked handiwork.

'You're the woman from America that brought the place, aren't you?'

'Bought,' I say absent-mindedly.

'What?' he says.

'Never mind,' I say. 'Yes… that's me.'

'I'm Will,' he says. 'Beth, that's my wife, we live down the road, next property but one. I could give you a bit of a hand if you like?'

So next thing you know, there we are working alongside each other as if we've known each other for years, not minutes, and Will gets stuff from his ute from time to time, muttering to himself, and flinging bits of this and that into the air, and then coming back whistling to his work, as if he's got all the time in the world to help a complete stranger.

A few hours later and a couple of glasses of my home-made lemonade and we're done.

'Sweet,' he says, downing the last drops of his second glass. 'Beth'd like that. You could teach her how to make it.'

I've been trying to think how I can repay this startlingly disheveled angel, and there it is.

'Sure,' I say. 'Why don't you bring Beth over for dinner? You can tell me about life in the valley and we can get to know each other.'

He pushes his hat back, sweaty blonde locks sticking to his forehead, and grins.

'You're on,' he says, and we shake hands on the deal, cementing unbeknownst to us, Beth, unbeknownst to you, still at home, not even knowing that Will has been helping a complete stranger, a lifetime friendship in the making.

And that story is more interesting, at least to me, than the story of our day in town, which is everything you and I knew it would be; down-at-heel floats, desultory out-of-tune school orchestras, the smell of fatty foods, and worse, much worse, a certain Mr. James Jarvis strutting about the town as if he owns it, a false smile fixed on his face, until he sees me, and his smile drops and he glares at me, whispering something to Mr. Apparatchik beside him, so that they both laugh, and I see the gesture, the finger pointed at me, but I do not flinch, not this time, not anymore.

The trouble is that in my mind, time is no longer linear. It's been a slow progression, this caving in of the sharp edges, of the absolute finite nature of time as it once existed. Now it jumbles itself, parallel universes present themselves, not always conveniently, as I move backwards and forwards, or more correctly sideways across this material, these stored stories of my ancestry. When I write I get searing flashes of connection. James Jarvis is a bully, Flora was bullied, bullied to death, and I feel it now acutely. I didn't understand, not for the longest time, why I should be so blessed to find another family on the other side of the world, until I saw it was to teach me about true love, of a kind that would not hide the truth, uncomfortable as that might be on occasions. I could not write of Eadweard's old age until my bones creaked with weariness, until my brain began the process of giving in, until I became content to live within several realities at once.

Until, I suppose, I no longer cared, or care what anybody thinks of me.

Twenty-three. That's how old I was when I met Miguel.

Twenty-four. That's how old Flora Shallcross Muybridge (Stone) was when she died: destitute, heart-broken, an orphan with two marriages and an affair behind her, and to my mind, a sufferer, almost without question, from abuse from her guardian. Separated from her two-year-old son, unable to look after him, her last words: 'I'm sorry.'

Ahhh, my heart bleeds at the idea of this young woman dying in such shame and sorrow – there was not even a specifically cited cause of death. She manifested it seems, nervous unidentifiable symptoms after Harry's death, and these seemed to move about her body, creating malaise wherever they landed, and whether they were psychosomatic or not, they were real enough to kill her.

But what of before? What of that brief couple of years where she was Eadweard Muybridge's wife, and so soon after Harry Larkyn's lover, and (at around the same time, and there's the rub) the mother of young Florado. Why did she marry a man twice her age having freed herself from Lucius Stone? She didn't need to – she'd hauled herself up from her difficulties, she had a job, she had a life. She was young, pretty and vibrant, and then Eadweard fell for her, and from the little that is written, it seems she for him as well.

I've left them there, haven't I, the three of them, Eadweard, Flora and Jane Thomas, the agreement set to meet for tea, and perhaps we should join them there because there had to be, I think you would agree, a pivotal meeting, a meeting in which wheels were set in motion, a meeting when Eadweard Muybridge would discover that Flora Shallcross Stone was in a difficult situation, and he was able to offer her help. I think that is where we will go now, to the tearooms. Perhaps it is a beautiful day in San Francisco, a little windy, which is normal, but the sky is as blue as the flash of kingfisher's wing, and for all three of them, even for Jane Thomas, this has been a little moment out, a time to savour and enjoy.

Perhaps, because Eadweard would be so impatient if we spent too much time dallying over the sandwiches, and the service and the small talk; we are entering towards the end, when the conversation is, you could say, getting interesting.

* * * * *

Eadweard looks at his watch, discreetly he hopes. It's not that he is not enjoying this tea-time experience, but he arrived at the tea-rooms with one purpose, and one purpose only, and that was to ask Flora out, to see if she would come with him to the theatre or to a concert, and so far the conversation has been a string of cheerful banalities of the kind he normally abhors, while he has been sitting there in an anxious state of desire.

But just as he's thinking that the opportunity to speak to Flora will never arise, Jane Thomas excuses herself from the table, and suddenly, there it is – he and Flora alone, and when Flora suddenly smiles at him, it's as if a band around his heart cracks, and the sunshine floods in.

'This has been a great treat, thank you Mr. Muybridge.'

'The pleasure is all mine, Miss Stone,' he says, and is surprised to see a sudden shadow cross her face.

'I would that it was "Miss Stone",' she says.

'I beg your pardon?'

She looks him squarely in the eye.

'You should know, Mr. Muybridge, that I am married,' and as Eadweard's heart leaps into a vortex of pain and confusion, she leans forward towards him.

'Let me be clear,' she says. 'I am in the process of getting a divorce from my husband, Lucius Stone, on the grounds of mental cruelty, but it is not easy to find out how to proceed.'

Eadweard does not know what to say. His brain is utterly bamboozled by the images pouring in. His beautiful Flora (because he realises, in his mind, she is already his), married, with another man, how can this be? But then that she should suffer at all, with anybody – how could that be? And again, if it's true that she was – is – married, then what better way for him to help her, than with this problem? Out of the corner of his eye he sees Jane Thomas heading back towards the table, and he has only a minute to stake a claim.

'You're shocked.' Flora says.

'No, no, Miss, I mean, Mrs. Stone,' he says. 'Surprised perhaps, but not shocked. But you know, if you would like some help with these proceedings, should you need to know a good lawyer or have someone to guide you through these legalities I would be more than happy to help.'

There, he thinks, it's out. It might not exactly be taking her to the theatre, but it's out, and just in time.

'Would you? Mr. Muybridge, that is very kind of you! Jane, Mr. Muybridge has said he will help me with my divorce difficulties, which is kind of him, is it not?'

Jane, whom Eadweard would have difficulty recognizing anywhere even after spending an hour in her company, so peripheral is she to his one intent and purpose, puts her hand over Flora's.

'I'm glad,' says Jane. 'Thank you, Mr. Muybridge.'

* * * * *

And that is exactly what happened. Eadweard helped Flora get her divorce from Lucius Stone on the grounds of mental cruelty, and during this process they fell in love, she left the Nahl gallery to work in a haberdashery shop, and on May 20, 1871, they married.

A question would have to be, did she fall in love with him, or only him with her? If we could ask her, what would she say? Would she say that he was charming, helpful and kind, perhpas good-looking as well, tall and upright with blue eyes, and a sharp keen gaze? Would she acknowledge that perhaps what he offered her was what she felt she needed most in her life – the golden quality of safety? He had everything; an increasing amount of income, his comfortable rooms in San Francisco, his reputation, his financial help and support, and, most importantly, his name, to give to her.

And what did she bring him? Her lively young self, full of desire for life, full, after her rocky start in life (whichever way you look at it) of a desire to have fun, with just enough complexity to entice him and intrigue him.

How did they meet each other in the bedroom? Should we go there? It's a private place after all, but in the end, the bedroom will make or break a couple, won't it Beth, and it seems as if in the end the bedroom broke them, and so to wonder what it was like for them, is perhaps not so strange if what I am doing is (and this suddenly strikes me now) looking for love. I am looking for a 'love' connection between all these people, so let us be not embarrassed to spy on them, after their quiet marriage and small reception, because, after all don't forget, Flora is a divorcee, and Eadweard not the type of person to make a great display. Flora, let's say, was content enough to have found her way to safety, and fully understood that as a divorcee discretion was the better part of valour, even though, tragically, it was a lesson she would also soon forget.

The older man and the younger woman is hardly an unknown scenario, but strangely, although we know of Flora's already colourful past, there is nothing about Muybridge, no suggestion of a previous relationship with anybody, anywhere. Hard to imagine though that a good-looking single male, traveling as much as Muybridge did, had not had at least the occasional liaison. But what about Flora? Perhaps, despite the age difference, she has at least as much sexual knowledge as her second husband.

In my chart she has her Venus in Cancer, the home-lover, but oh, the Scorpio moon, the moon of deep compulsion, creating a conjunction that would explain not just her ability to attract men, but her passionate desire to be loved. I could explain it, or I can just say, well, there they are at last, alone in his rooms, everyone gone. There is just them, a newly-married couple, and we could take it from there.

* * * * *

'At last,' the man says, and smiles at his bride.

'Yes,' she says. 'Edward.'

He holds out his arms, and she walks into them, resting her head against his chest. His hand strokes the top of her head, rhythmically, soothingly, and she slides her hand down his back, feeling the male strength of it, allowing her hand to slide across his shoulders, over his hips.

He tilts her face up towards him, and kisses her with deep, warm kisses, and – 'undo my dress,' she says, turning her back towards him, and he unhooks the sweet baby-blue poplin so that it falls at her feet, and there she is, her corset, and petticoats and more hooks, until finally she's free, and turns towards him, her full breasts taking his breath away, and now she touches him, stroking him through his trousers, so that it's all he can do to restrain himself from coming then and there. He tears at his buttons, and she helps him until he too is free of his clothes, and then she drops to her knees and takes him in her mouth. He gasps both with pleasure, and with a sudden unexpected flash of pain that she's done this before, and then she stands, turns and walks to the bed, lying on it, open and waiting for him. He drinks her in, the languid sensual beauty of her, the ripeness of her, and as he mounts her, he cradles her right breast in his hand, his finger and thumb circling the nipple and she begins to give urgent, breathy sounds, soft moans that throw him over the edge so that buried in the deep dark ocean of her he thrusts, feeling the juice of her running over him like a river. And Flora, oh, she is lost in it too, for the first time in her life feeling the full essence of a man who loves her, knowing he's on the brink, and she arches her back slightly, holding herself, everything inside her waiting for him, until yes, here he comes, and as he does, he says her name over and over again, 'Flora, Flora, Flora…' and she feels the deepest part of her open up into a flood of molten lava, and she says the words she has always wanted to say, and to mean: 'I love you.' And then they lie, their breath subsiding, him resting in her, on her, their eyes closed, sunk in their separate/together worlds, until the sounds of life make their presence felt – a shout in the street, the bang of a door. He rolls off her, and she moves herself so she lies on his shoulder, and together they simply drift off, into a sweet sleep.

* * * * *

Oh, I do remember you know Beth. Even though we age, the body, and perhaps more importantly, the mind, never forgets the feeling of desire. Even when the act of love has long since gone, the memory of it all a rivulet rather than a rushing sea, it's there. In the past 10 years, since Pete died, I've thought a lot about love, not just because of my interest (or obsession, some might say) with Eadweard, Flora and Harry, but because as I am gradually moving away from this physical plane of existence I am noticing, more and more, love as an almost tangible energy running between everything natural, everything good. I have begun, I think, through contemplation on the idea of love, to understand the love of mystics and saints for God.

Take, for instance, the dawn chorus. It happens, does it not, every day, the same wondrous occurrence, the sky filled with the sounds of thousands of birds waking up and celebrating the new dawn. They sing, they fly, they literally open their hearts to the universe. The magpies throw back their heads, they carol their liquid song into the early morning air. And yet, it is only in the last year or two that I have really *heard* it. These days it is part of my morning ritual to get up in the pre-dawn dark, make a cup of tea, and wait, suspended almost in the waiting, for the first bird sound. First one, then two, then three – and then, suddenly I can't count anymore, the air is alive with nature's composition, and its beauty leaves me breathless.

If it's warm, I sit on my verandah in rapt contemplation, if not I sit in my chair, and breathe the sounds into my soul. And it's in this space, this unearthly moment between night and day, that I wonder about my crossing. How it will come, and in what manner? Will I hear the dawn chorus on the other side? At the same time, to take this back to 'love', my daily Concert of the Dawn produces in me a feeling of such euphoria that it reminds me, it really does, of the sensation of being in love, and how sweet that was.

Flora was swept off her feet. It just occurs to me that we share this in common – a great love that came to nothing. *Why,* I wonder, *did Flora fall so heavily for Harry so soon after marrying Eadweard?* After all, in so many ways Eadweard gave her what so much of her must have been craving and yet he left her alone almost immediately, pursuing, of course his photography, as he would, as he should, but leaving Flora, unfortunately, to her own devices, and Flora, sympathetic as I am to her plight, might just not have been, as they say in Australia, 'the sharpest pencil in the box'.

Just weeks after they were married, he was off photographing lighthouses on the Pacific Coast for the US Lighthouse Board, a few months later he was in Texas and Arizona, at one point photographing the Pima County Courthouse in Tucson, and the participants in the Camp Grant Massacre trial, and on and on, leaving his young bride too alone, Beth. And just around the corner are two meetings – Eadweard will meet Leland Stanford, and produce 23 negatives of Stanford's mansion, and Stanford will commission him to commence Eadweard's instantaneous photography of horse movement, to prove that at one point when it's galloping all four hooves are in the air.

And Flora, poor Flora, will meet and fall in love with the handsome and feckless Harry.

Chapter 10

The Outing

After we had been 'caught' in the Blue Mountains, or should I rather say that after Martin had been 'caught', because after all, what had I done other than to love a man I thought was available – after that, it was not going to last long.

You could put it down to a mixture of all sorts of things. The confirmation of my internal belief that everybody lies, to Martin's absolute inability to commit to either his wife or his mistress, but perhaps most of all to my piqued Mexican pride. Because despite everything that has happened to them, Mexicans are a proud race, and I am no exception I know. I have cut off my nose to spite my face many times in my life, but in this instance I undertook my own act of murder and I have never forgiven myself, even though I believe it is a woman's choice to do with her body as she will. At the time it felt as if my actions were not just necessary but lifesaving, but I have felt the loss so keenly of the little soul I set adrift, whose presence in my life I said a vehement 'No' to, that not a day goes by when I don't think of her. And for some reason she is always a 'her', Beth, and I wonder to myself who she would have been if I had let her live. Then there was this too, that the 'doctor' Martin found, his last act to be so evidently eager to get rid of this new, sudden, inconvenience encumberance that if I hadn't known before that our relationship was over, I knew then, on the day he said he was 'busy', and couldn't drive me there. And the doctor he found, as I said, was a butcher, and after a series of infections, the scarring was so bad that I was told I would never fall pregnant again, or that if I did I would have a hard time carrying 'it' full-term.

At the time I didn't care. Or I thought I didn't care. It wasn't possible to imagine that I would ever, having now been betrayed not just by my parent/grandparents, but by the man I believed would be my husband and the love of my life, be capable of loving that ferociously again, and to be honest, there is still truth in that. For three or more decades, until the time had passed when I could possibly conceive, I believed I did not want a child. I believed myself when I told myself that Martin's baby was better off not being born, that I was destined to be by myself on this Earth. But let me tell you, I am a Mexican Catholic, and we know all about guilt, and sorrow and regret, and paganism as well, so at the same time that my Anglo-Saxon brain could logically forgive myself, could tell myself it was all for the best, my Mexican Catholic brain never, ever let go of the sorrow, of the sheer animal terror of that day, when I was delivered to a small dark room in Chippendale, when I experienced such pain as I hadn't imagined had existed when the life was sucked from me, and such crushing sorrow afterwards I could not stop crying, until I did, and swore never to cry again.

And I did not, not for several years.

There are reasons, and they will become obvious to you Beth, why I have to speed up my story, and I am hoping that I have intrigued you enough with my journey so far, that you might be asking; but Rosa, how did you get from an apartment in Sydney to the Snowy Mountains? How did that happen? Why the Snowy Mountains? What trajectory could possibly have taken you from there to here? Perhaps you might ask me, when you'd recovered from your abortion, why did you not go home?

And to that I would say, but Beth, that is the nucleus of this story, I had no family, or none that I cared to reconnect with at that time, and I had no home. Home was not Mexico, with its vexed memories of betrayal, happiness, childhood and poverty. Home was definitely not America where I had been a misfit right from the start, and home was certainly not Sydney, where I'd gone in the expectation of living with my lover, (and truth be known, carrying deep within me the dream of a marriage, of children, of a loving and lie-free family). Instead, there was more betrayal.

I sometimes wonder if it was Flora's betrayal that ate so deeply into Eadweard's psyche that he never entered into a relationship with a woman again. If he did, he kept it entirely secret. There are no letters, no photographs, no newspaper cuttings, absolutely nothing to record that he ever let a woman into his life again. But for all that, he was luckier than me at that time in my life. At least he had a final home. When he was called back (perhaps by a similar time bomb to the one that is lying in me) to the land of his birth, he was indeed going back to something familiar, to something known.

I got a taxi 'home' from the clinic alone. Martin's cowardice once Sally knew about me was absolute, his running back to the bosom of his family immediate. He sobbed when he told me he couldn't do it 'anymore', and was hurt when I replied tartly that I didn't know he'd been doing it at all. Mexican fury filled my veins, I swore at him in Spanish, I threw plates, I vented. I also told him that I would be staying in the flat, and he could take his things and go, I told him I would let him know once I knew what I was doing. I told him, and watched him closely for his reaction, that I thought I might be pregnant, and his face went ashen.

'What do you want to do?' he said, and with that one word 'you', all hope flew out of the window.

'I want you to find me somewhere I can go and have it dealt with,' I told him, and he put his head in his hands.

'If that's what you want,' he said, pushing the dagger in just a little further.

'It's what I want,' I said. And swallowed my pride enough to tell him: 'You will support me for as long as I need you to, but I will guarantee you that when I am ready, I will leave, and you will never hear from me again.'

I took a few months to recover. What I remember most. Crying. Crying for my parents/grandparents. Crying for my sister/mother. Crying for every life and person lost to me. Crying with my broken heart, crying for my lost child. We Mexicans never do anything by halves.

Then one day, I woke up, and I was all cried out.

Just like that.

I remember it was a beautiful autumn day in Sydney, and I went for a walk in Rose Bay along the harbour wall. The sun skipped across the water, the wind rippled the silvery blue surface, and I walked myself to the Italian coffee shop nearby where I knew there was life, and warmth, and even a little laughter. I sat there and nursed my coffee, and indulged in a sweet pastry, and for the first time in many months I felt my blood hum in my veins, tickled by the idea of possibility.

But despite this little flow of optimism, tiny sensation of hope there was still the cinder-grey pall of doubt and despair. Because, after all, what *was* I to do? In a country where I knew no-one except a man I never wanted to see again, in a place that would not even recognise my degree, where my workplace experience meant nothing, where I was living off my small nest-egg and another man's guilt. It was not for me. But what was? I swung wildly. I would go and work in some remote outback town; I would find a way to take up my studies again and stay in Sydney; I would go back to America; *I would, I would, I would…*

This is what I learned during this dark time. Projecting into the future when you cannot see one, will actually destroy you. As sure as white ants can hollow out a building, leaving it looking intact, projection will eat into your very core, so that even though you may look the same on the outside, in my case I think, a reasonably attractive woman at that stage, inside you are shrivelled and despairing, a shadow of your former self.

Would you like details Beth? Can you imagine what I looked like back then? Medium height, as you know, not too thick-set, but strong, although with enough curves for men to find me attractive; my permanently slightly tanned skin not dark enough to make me completely 'foreign' but a little exotic. Men noticed me, I knew, when I walked on my now-inceasingly lengthy hikes up and down the hills of Rose Bay. Wavy hair, light-brown – an exact midway colour between an Anglo-Saxon and a Spaniard if you will. Blue eyes flecked with green. A reasonably healthy physique, you would say, if you were judging from the outside Beth. But inside, well, that was a different story. Inside lay pools of poison, lakes of loneliness, deserts of doubt.

But still, I walked, and in my walking every morning I somehow had enough sense in me to become a homing pigeon, and fly myself to the café. My last stop on the way home. The place for my coffee and pastry, where conversations ran on the airways, and people lived their everyday, ordinary lives. They got to know me by name, the Italian couple Giovanni (Gio) and his wife, Maria, who owned the cafe.

'Rosa!' they would say cheerfully. 'Good morning... how are you today?' And even that small interchange was good. It let me know I still existed, that people could still see me. I had not become the ghost I often felt myself to be.

One day I was in the coffee shop, and it was bedlam. It looked as if two of the waitresses hadn't turned up. People were waiting for food, which was sitting on the bar from the kitchen long after the bell had rung to say it was there.

I don't know to this day what compelled me to stand up and help, but I did.

I simply bustled into the service area, collected plates, matched them up with the table numbers and started serving. Gio and Maria were so flustered they couldn't even bring themselves to tell me to stop, and so I cleared tables, took orders, delivered them, cleared up and wiped down the coffee area until finally after an hour or so, the breakfast rush began to subside.

Gio wiped his forehead with a tea-towel.

'My goodness Rosa, you save our lives,' he said, grinning from ear to ear. Maria nodded. 'You are an angel,' she said. 'I will make you a special serving of iced coffee and cake.'

I did try and protest that I really didn't need more coffee, or cake, but she was having none of it, and soon I was sitting down with them, chatting, and my veins, frozen from so long without friendly conversations, began to thaw, so that I began to tell them a little (judiciously I might say) about me.

And that, Beth, is how I came to work at Caffe da Nonna. Giovanni and Maria. Saints. Lifesavers. Lovers of life. Shouters, in the best Italian tradition.

At first it took me aback. My natural Mexican tendency towards fulsome expression, having been dampened down and down and down by the strange twists and turns of my life. It was not a sensation I enjoyed, being overwhelmed by emotion. The first time Giovanni shouted at me: 'Whadda you mean there ees no basil at the markets?' I burst into floods of tears, to his complete surprise. 'But Rosa,' he said enveloping me in a bear-hug, 'Eets not your fault there ees no basil...'

'Well,' I said, 'why are you shouting at me?'

'Because I have no basil,' he said, his shoulders reaching up to his ears, his hands out in wide dismay.

'You must shout back at him,' Maria told me firmly. 'You must shout: "Eets not my fault there ees no basil Gio, so no shouting at me!"' She grinned. 'You could say, you fat old man...'

'Hey, woman...' Giovanni turned towards her, but she is gone, singing about her business, while I dabbed a napkin to my eye and ponder this strange turn of events.

Later, back in the flat that evening with a glass of wine, I tried to remember what it was to be what you might call 'emotionally expressive'. I realised, that other than my furious rant at Martin, I had spent so many years denying grief, denying anger, that I had also, of course, denied joy and happiness and peace. I had mistaken, and I'm sure I was not the first woman to do so, lust for love, and it had cost me dearly.

The loss of everything, family, country, my baby. It was too much for one soul. I froze myself, and the process of unthawing was uncomfortable to the extreme, but gradually working with Maria and Gio – the café named for Gio's mother, who still came in, a small Italian woman dressed in black, with hardly a word of English, the Grande Dame of the café, and of the family – some warmth crept back into my broken being. Their eight-year-old daughter, Noni (named after her Nonna), would come into the café on her way home from school, tucking into an afternoon treat with such delight it always made me smile.

Noni was never short of friends; who wouldn't want to be friends with someone whose grandparents owned a café. But sometimes it was hard to be there, sometimes it felt as if the fate that had brought me there was also taunting me with everything I did not have, would never have. It took me many years, decades in fact, to understand that 'fate' was telling me that families exist everywhere, in every form, that the purpose of the heart is to belong, and in the belonging the family is created. At the time I could only see what I did *not* have, not what I *had*, but it was a step on my healing journey and there were many moments of pure joy and laughter.

In due course, I kept my side of the bargain, I left Martin's flat and rented a one-bedroom unit for myself between Rose Bay and Bondi, close to the café. I could easily walk to work, to the beach, to the harbour and around the edge of the Golf Course. I could, on a fine Sydney day, absorb myself in the insanely colourful, chaotic beauty of this water city. As if I was putting together the shattered pieces of a mosaic, I felt that even if the little cracked tiles of me would never make a perfect whole, then at least, the glue was beginning to hold.

I began to enjoy my new life. Gio and Maria discovered that I had an eye for display, and a head for numbers. I became an integral part of the team, and they loved me. They were even able to take a few family holidays and leave me in charge, and I relished the responsibility, but still I knew this was not a forever answer to my life, I knew that at some level my heart was still questing. I was like the German Shorthaired Pointer dog I'd befriended on my walks, who would occasionally stop in her running, one paw up, her nose thrust forward, a quizzical expression on her face as if to say, *where next, what's that, shall we GO?*

What I found, as I moved forward into this life was that at the same time I was fitting in, making the occasional friend, resting my soul and spirit and body, was that I was not quite 'of' the life I was living. And that the stronger I got, the stronger that feeling became, so that all the swims in the cold Bondi water, all the long, long walks, all the laughter and conversations and kindness began to seem a long way away from me, as if someone else was living my life. Was this still a manifestation of depression? Probably, and yet without it, I imagine I would not have had the courage, when the time came, to move.

But first there was my first Australian Christmas to come to terms with. Of course, Maria and Giovanni asked me if I would like to spend

Christmas Day with them, and I was grateful, even though I did wonder how I might cope surrounded by an extended Italian family in a small space. I was beginning to find the grey and humid heat so oppressive, that on my walks, even early in the morning, it was hard to breathe. Everything seemed out of kilter. Why, I wondered, did Australia sport reindeers and snow-scenes and play 'Jingle Bells; why was every shop decorated in an homage to a Northern Hemisphere Christmas, while we all boiled in the sultry weather, and people everywhere it seemed were planning meals that included hot turkey, hot ham, and hot Christmas pudding? It was mystifying to me. I felt as if I'd fallen down an Alice-in-Wonderland rabbit hole, where nothing made sense.

Surely in 190 years or thereabouts of inhabitation the population could have adjusted Christmas to the climate, instead of apparently doing their best to do the opposite?

As the celebrations got closer, I was in for a surprise though, when I asked Maria what time I should go to their house, she looked at me in consternation.

'Oh no, no, no,' she said. 'We do not 'ave our Chreestmas in the 'ouse. We go to Nielsen Park, we 'ave a BEEG picnic, everybody, they come, and stay there till ees not so hot anymore. You will come with us because there are not many buses Chreestmas Day.'

My heart leapt. The rabbit hole receded. A picnic! By the harbour, in a spot I'd already visited a few times, where I could swim. This, I thought, was more like it, and more like the festivities I'd known in Mexico as a child, because even though Christmases then were modest in comparison to the massively commercial event it is today, we Mexicans have always known how to party. The Christmases of my childhood weren't crammed into a mere three days, they went for almost a month, from mid-December to early January, and were swiftly followed by Candlemas in February. Despite my shock at the unrelenting heat of an Australian summer, of course, it was only since my American Christmases, always spent alone, and there is nothing more alone than being alone at Christmas, that I had experienced a cool Christmas. Mexico was balmy at Christmas time, and the revelers made the most of it.

I think what I remember more than anything else was the explosion of poinsettias – *flores de nochebuena* – Flowers of the Good Night, most literally. The flowers with which we celebrate our Christmas Eve, our nochebuena, their rich vermillion celebrated in crazy profusion, colour pouring from every tiny adobe; and of course, the nacimiento, the Nativity scene, played out in every village square and town centre, with houses laying out their own personal interpretations of Joseph and Mary, the manger, the animals, the Three Kings and the shepherds.

But here's a funny thing. When I saw the Nativity Scene in the David Jones shop windows in the city, Baby Jesus was already in it, long before Christmas. In Mexico Baby Jesus isn 't added to the scene until December 24th. I almost laughed at loud at the idea that the country of my birth, so colourful, so, I don't know, *random* in so many ways, should take this one point of logic and stick with it. *How could Baby Jesus be in the nativity scene when he hasn't even been born yet?*

Our *nochebuena*, December 24, was the night-of-nights, with feasts and celebrations leading, of course to mass, to religious fervour, penance and renewal. I'll never know if it was because of only half my DNA being Mexican, or some psychic sense of betrayal, of always being the outsider, but Christmas was always a difficult time for me. I watched the colourful joy, I participated in the family life, or, perhaps I should say, in our family lies, and I wanted to enjoy it, to throw myself my into it, to abandon myself to what I believed was my heritage, but it was often too much for me. I would retreat to my room to read, throwing myself into a fictional world when the real world felt unreal.

How do you reconcile the blood that runs in your veins if it comes from two diametrically opposing forces? How do you reconcile the dark wine blood of Mexico, the weight within it of the invader and the invaded, of the pagan and the papist, the knowledge of the other world, of ritual, of magic… of mayhem, mixed with the blood of the Anglo-Saxon with its need for order, its embarrassment at the very idea of (obvious) excess, its logic and its rules?

I think it was that Christmas Day that I glimpsed for the first time ever that perhaps here in Australia I could walk the path of both ways, and so indulge me a moment Beth, while I take you there, back in time to that day at Neilsen Park, back in time to the overflowing car, packed with food, Gio and Maria in the front, me hugging various tins and baskets and containers in the back with Nonna, making our not entirely safe way along Rose Bay Road, turn left at Kincoppal, see the harbour open up in front of you, breathe the salty air down into your lungs, inhale, try and stay calm, while Gio looks for a parking space, and Maria bosses him around, so that he holds up his hands in despair: 'You wanna park the car woman, you park the car – you don't even 'ave your license…'

'I can drive better than you with NO license, old man…' Maria says defiantly.

For a minute I think we're going to park just there, almost in the middle of the road, but the Catholic God is out and about today, and an early morning swimmer is leaving, right by where it seems as if we are patiently waiting.

'See?' says Maria, 'because I tell you what to do we have the perfect parking.'

Gio decides discretion is the better part of valour, and there we are at last, and I'm almost tumbling out of the car in my excitement. We're early enough to get the spot they want, down under the trees at the back of the changeroom, and I'm a bit surprised by the fact that they don't actually want to *see* the water, but no, Maria tells me, this is the spot because later games will come out, the children will play soccer, there will be bocce, she tells me, and shows me the box, with the beautiful balls, each with their individual marking.

'You will see,' she says, 'we need a lot of room!'

And then, suddenly, as if out of nowhere, it seems as if half the Italian population of North Bondi is gathering, there is a tsunami of Italians (to mix up my cultures), flooding down the hill, carrying eskys, tables and chairs, with rugs, and containers of food, and children, and even dogs, a kind of instant al-fresco village, right there, under the gumtrees, while over the hill the call of the glistening water is too much for me, I'm compelled to go for a swim.

I stand at the water's edge and relish the idea of the shark net. I'm terrified of sharks, and I'm not the strongest swimmer. I never really learned how to swim properly, and I have no idea what to do with my breathing. I watch the swimmers, some of them so lazily graceful it takes my breath away as they plough up and down the length of the swimming area. But no matter my style, I must get cool, and so I dip myself into the cool green/blue water, gasp at the sudden chill. It seems, as it always does, to be some form of extreme baptism, where just for an instant everything is washed away, and for a moment I am remade, all sins wiped out.

Looking back, I should say that I never imagined in my wildest dreams that it would be that day that would somehow ignite my fire for life again, or set me on a path towards my destiny. Even though that destiny was still yet unknown, not even a glimpse of it showing, with its twists and turns, its intent it would sometimes seem, to break me, and the corresponding angels sent, it would also seem, when I could take no more. But all that was yet to unfold, as I walked back from my swim, as happy in that moment as it was possible for me to be.

Oh, I had moments that day, that large gathering of family, all that delicious food, I found myself once or twice back in the land of my childhood, back in Mexico on feast days, back with my parent/ grandparents and my sister/mother. I had to pull myself out by sheer force from tumbling into the pit of memory and loss. I tried hard to keep a grip on myself, as I was drawn into the family, introduced to this person and that. Sometimes they would all speak in Italian, and similar as it is to Spanish, I could not understand it all, and it would seem as if I was not even in Australia, but instantly transported to Europe.

But then.

He arrives late. This last cousin. His car broke down, he explains, he had to wait for the NRMA. Christmas Day. He shrugs his shoulders and opens his hands.

'Never mind,' says Maria, giving him a kiss on the cheek. 'You are here now. Eat. Drink. We are all here!'

She sees me sitting on the edge of one of the concrete tables under a shady tree, where I am nursing yet another plate of food, pushed at me by an overly zealous Nonna.

'Rosa!' she says, 'Rosa, meet Antonio, he ees the very last one, I promise.'

I think to myself that then they have saved the best until last, because Antonio, well, he is sweet to look at, let me say. Olive skinned, green-eyes, chocolate-brown hair, and tall. I am used to Gio and Maria and their brood, all small and feisty, but somehow this Anotnio has a few extra inches.

'Hello Rosa,' he says. 'It's nice to meet you. I'm Tony.'

'Pfff,' says Maria. 'Tony. Antonio is such a nice name... you young ones always making things more Australian. '

Tony, let's call him what I would always call him, laughs.

'You never let it go, do you Aunty? Well, Antonio for you, then.'

He doesn't have an Italian nuance in his voice, but still his accent is softer than most Australian voices, richer somehow. Enough to stop me in my tracks, really.

Shall I spare you the journey to his bedroom, Beth, in his house at Cremorne with views of the harbour? Or tell you just a little bit? Feed you a tiny morsel, just to intrigue you, not to overwhelm you. The way he follows me to the water's edge when I go for my next swim, laughs at my swimming, and I am not the least bit offended. Or how he glances in my direction from time to time while the younger tribe clamber over him, beg him to play soccer, or bocce, and he lifts his eyes to mine with a smile in them so deep I want to run into his arms then and there. And somehow, we organise the inevitable. When the time comes to pack up, he oh so subtly intervenes when Gio and Maria are packing the car, says: 'A few of us might stay behind and enjoy the sunset, I'll take Rosa home if you like,' and Maria, all flustered, says, 'Well, Rosa, if you're sure?' Because she's tired now, it's been a long day, she's not her usual Italian momma-self; her hypervigilance is down, for once she hasn't noticed the signs, for which we will have cause to be grateful.

What is wrong with me? I wonder, as we speed in his car towards his place. Is it something to do with the Christmas food, the Christmas wine, the goodwill towards all men. Because I am certainly feeling goodwill towards this man. He has a tape deck in his car and he is playing Neil Young's *Harvest Moon.* We're quite happy listening to the music, we don't seem to feel the need to talk much. I am curiously at peace with what we are about to do. My Catholic guilt is absent without leave, my body is tingling with anticipation, I feel as if I am Sleeping Beauty, woken from a deep, celibate sleep, and yet, somehow what I already know is that this thing that is happening, is a healing, not a future.

And as we fall inside his front door, he kisses me, and his kisses are sweet indeed, nectar for my mouth. Our tongues touch, withdraw, he pushes me up against the wall, and his hands explore me, and I reach for him too, but then he says, 'Not here,' takes my hand leads me to his bedroom, and sets himself to the task of undressing me – not, on this hot summer's day, that there's much to undress. I remember my summer frock even now, a swirling pattern of rich deep blues and greens in light cotton, with buttons down the front to the waist.

'Lucky for me,' Tony says, undoing one then the other, until my bra is revealed, and then he cups his hand over my breast.

'Beautiful,' he whispers. 'Beautiful Rosa.'

Oh, it was a good coupling. That is all I will say. It was good, no, great sex, and both our spirits rejoiced in it. And now, when the men are gone, and there are no more couplings to be had, I still remember Tony with such deep affection, and what I did not know that evening, as we lay around together, was that I would have cause to be extremely grateful to him not once, but three times in the deep unfolded future of my life. I think if I had the 'sight' I have now, I could perhaps have said there was something about us – an ongoing story perhaps, that allowed both of us that greatest and rarest present of all in a relationship, the gift of no pressure.

I feel sure that sometimes people come mysteriously into our lives, and it is their pleasure to serve us, to give us a hand, and we do not have to feel guilty about it, as we so often do, because in the great infinite wisdom of the universe, this is how it is, sometimes we help, and sometimes we are helped, and how blessed are we that these unforeseen, sometimes most unlikely angels arrive in our lives?

Because as Christmas Day turned into Boxing Day, and I slept the deepest sleep of my life, on the drive home to my small flat in Rose Bay, when he said his easy goodbye to me, dropping a goodbye kiss on my head, and telling me that he would call me soon, I was sure he would, but I also knew that I would not be waiting, as I had with Martin for his call, and I was sure that for him, it was the same. He would not pursue me, or lie to me, or cheat on me, but I understood, and was content already about this unstated fact, that both of us would move on.

When I went back to work the day after Boxing Day though, and the café was so quiet, Maria looked at me suspiciously.

'You seem different,' she said. 'What ees it?'

I shrugged. 'I don't know,' I laughed. 'Just a lovely Christmas with all of you, I suppose.'

'Hmmm,' she said, her eyes following me as I concentrated on putting out the salts and peppers. 'You are laughing too, well, that ees something good.'

Something good. It was.

We saw each other once a week or so, sometimes less. I found things out. He was 35, his parents had been wise. They were early migrants, between the wars – they'd sensed trouble coming and got out. They'd done their time in a 'refo' camp, and done it tough, Tony's father's qualifications as a chemist not at all recognised in Australia. First they'd worked as cleaners, then started their own small cleaning business, always with an eye to owning land, to growing grapes. In the end, by a stroke of luck, (if luck is a thing, which I'm not entirely sure about), they'd bought a small, deceased estate, a rundown vineyard in the Riverina, producing the Botrytised Semillon for which the region, he told me over dinner one night, was already well-known and for which it was rapidly becoming famous.

'I have no idea what that means,' I say.

'Aha,' he says, 'well, you'll find out at the end of our meal.'

He tells me about dessert wines, about the fungus that attacks the grape and how it metabolises some of the acids within the grapes, creating an extremely high sugar content.

'Botrytis is in most vineyards,' he says, 'and it can wipe out an entire vineyard if it's not controlled, but in the right environment, it produces a truly beautiful dessert wine.'

And it was extraordinary, this deep yellow-gold liquid, slightly viscous in texture, sweet but not cloying.

'I can't believe I'm drinking something created by fungus,' I say. 'Nature is truly wonderful.'

Over the next few months, I learn his life's trajectory. Leaving school to live with relatives in Melbourne to study business at university; stints in Italy working with relatives on other vineyards, back home to Australia, to a job in Sydney working for an export company.

'It's all carefully planned,' he tells me. 'One day I'll go back to the Riverina, marry a nice Italian girl, and run the vineyard, bringing it a new lease of life as my parents get older and want to do less. At least, that's the theory, and at the moment that's what I'm sticking with.'

Was there the slightest shadow of a warning there? Or was it even a blunt STOP sign? A warning to not fall in love.

I didn't take it so at the time, but looking back it probably was. But for me it remained this singular relationship. I loved spending time with him, in bed or out, I was happy to see him, but I did not mourn or pine when I did not see him.

I told him 'stuff' about me, but I chose carefully. I did not tell him about my sister/mother my mother/grandmother my father/grandfather, or about Eadweard or Henry or Flora. I guarded those things deep within my heart. I was not, anyway at that time, actively searching information on my troubled ancestry. That was to come later. Sydney seemed to have infected me with its streak of hedonism. I felt lighter there than I had ever felt before, or in some ways would ever feel again, even though – or perhaps because – I knew I would not stay there forever.

I did tell him about Martin, about what I believed was a relationship not an affair, about the flat, and about the abortion.

'My poor Rosa,' he said at the time, and held me close. 'My poor, poor Rosa. So hard for a Catholic girl, that must have been so hard.' I understood with a deeper level of clarity, the path for his life – there could never be marriage with a woman with my kind of past.

But I was trying to turn my kind of past into my kind of future, and as the summer days began to wane into a softer autumn, and the heat gave way to the occasional cool night, I could feel a strange internal longing to be on the move, I didn't know where to, or even really why, but somehow I knew that my time in Sydney was coming to an end.

I even spoke to Gio and Maria about it, to warn them I might be moving on, but they were determined I would be staying.

'Rosa!' said Maria, as we sat for a post-closure cup of tea, or shots of espressos in their cases. I always wondered how they could drink that strong, bitter, small coffee and still sleep at night.

'You cannot leeve, where will you go? What will you do?'

She reached out over the table and touched my hand.

'Gio, tell this girl, she belongs here.'

Gio looked at me very seriously, his eyes raised under his bushy brows. 'You belong here, Rosa. We weell look after you. You know that.'

I remember I smiled at them both. 'You're probably right,' I said. And I dropped it, at least with them.

But the seed was planted. I scoured the employment pages of the *Sydney Morning Herald.* I imagined just heading off on a bus, or train, stopping at a country town, and somehow, magically, finding work and settling in.

Tony was supportive, but not at all in favour of my plans. 'You'd hate Australian country towns Rosa, there's nothing going on in them,' he told me once when we were having breakfast together on a lazy Sunday morning. 'You need something more exciting, more vibrant.'

'Well, what exactly?' I asked. A little impatiently, I have to say. The itching was getting worse as the weather grew cooler, and almost every day this strange tug towards an unknown destiny grasped me around my heart. It was not that I had fallen out of love with Sydney, not that I didn't still marvel at the beauty of the harbour, the kindness of the strangers who had nurtured me, the miracle of Tony's arrival in my life, all these things had served to help fill the deep and empty void lurking within me. Sydney had helped fill, but not cured, the desperate desire to know where I belonged, and at that time the equally desperate desire to know to whom I belonged. Yes, I knew I could have stayed in Sydney and built a life; but an adventurer's spirit ran in my blood for sure, whether it was Harry's wanderlust or Eadweard's ambitious work, or Flora's desire to get away, the result was the same. I could not stay in the first place I had landed in. Whether I might come back, like a homing pigeon, would be another matter.

One evening when I'm home in my apartment alone, just watching television I seem to recall, the phone ring, and it's Tony.

'Rosa,' he says. 'Rosa, Rosa, Rosa...'

I'm worried from the tone of his voice that something terrible has happened, immediately catastrophizing – Gia, Maria?

'What?' I ask. 'What's happened?'

He laughs. 'Nothing. But I've solved your problem.'

'Which one in particular?' I say, thinking of all the things we'd talked about.

'The immediate one. The one about where to go next. Even though it means you'll leave me, so I wondered if perhaps I should even tell you, but I decided that wouldn't be fair.'

My hackles rise a little. 'I don't need you to solve my problem,' I say tersely.

'Oh, but you do,' he tells me confidently. 'Wait until you know what it is.'

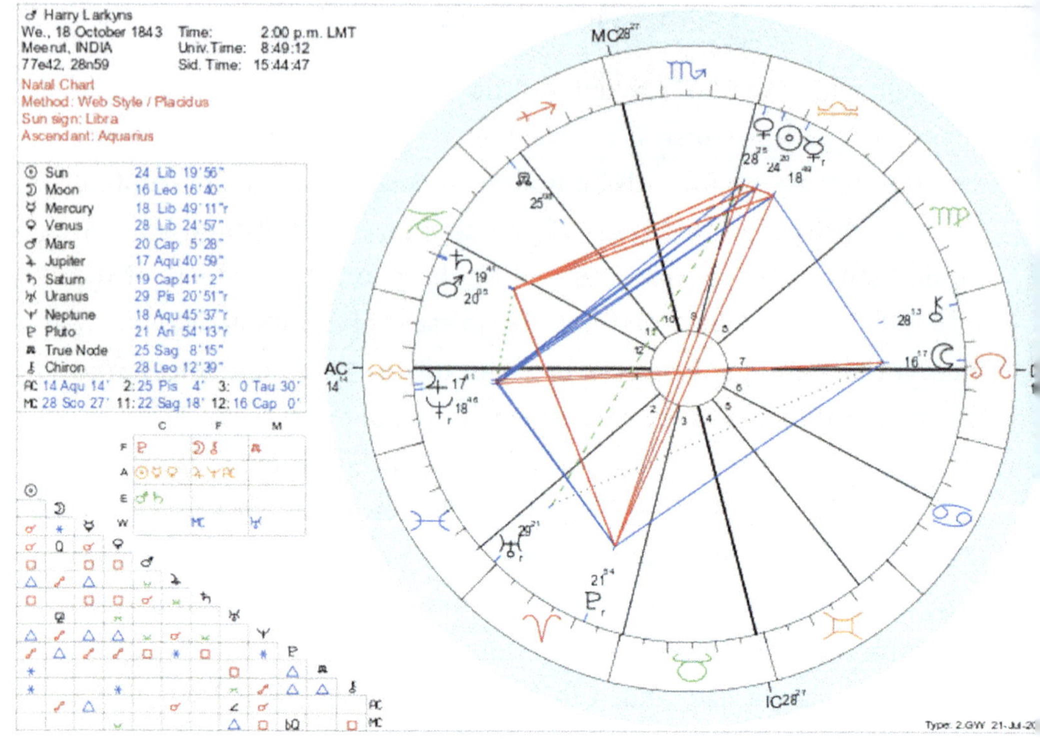

Harry's natal chart

Harry Larkyns

Born on 18th October 1843, died on 17th October 1874. 31 years old. A neat Libran balance there – killed the day before his birthday.

Sun in Libra, moon in Leo, he saw himself perhaps as a heroic person. A huge sense of freedom and adventure with a cheerful nature (he needed that!), but also a lot of pride. Aquarius rising; that would have given him a natural tendency to be sympathetic towards others, but to be unpredictable in love affairs.

Jupiter conjunct Ascendant. Someone who will always do things to excess with a kind of wistful hope that the ambitions will work out.

Sun in the eighth house. Now that's interesting, denoting as it does an indication that near middle age Harry would experience a crisis, which, if traversed successfully, might have taken him to a prolonged and happy life.

Poor Harry. He missed that tide in the affairs of men.

Chapter 11

The Meeting

Confidence. It's a male attribute in the main, isn't it? Confident males, and I don't mean bullies, have a certain air about them. Eadweard was confident in his professional abilities. Harry, well, he was confident in his ability to hustle. But I've met men like Harry, and of course what lies beneath is the opposite of confidence, what they are hiding is a deep insecurity about their own worth. They create the opposite impression as they flit from here to there, trying for all their worth to bring their lives into a cohesive whole and at the same time practicing sabotage, wreaking havoc wherever they go.

Here's a hypothetical question, one that can never be answered.

If Flora hadn't fallen for Harry, would she have fallen for someone else? Was it the sheer force of Harry's easy-going, handsome, wayward charm that seduced her? Would she have grown-up into someone who was quiet and content, would she have become a mother again, been the companion and lover Eadweard so ardently expected and wanted her to be?

Do you want to know how they meet, Beth? They meet at the theatre; one of the main forms of entertainment in San Francisco at that time, and not a form of entertainment (which came out in the trial) of which Eadweard was particularly fond. His young and pretty wife goes to the theatre with friends; his young and pretty wife goes out a lot, without him.

* * * * *

Flora laughs these days, laughs on a whim, at anything and everything.

It seems to her as if she has been sleepwalking the rest of her life; waiting for this moment to wake up, waiting to feel this tingling throughout her body, the way the nerve ends in her fingertips dance with pleasure, the way her stomach contracts at the thought of *him*.

She thinks about him every minute, every second of every day. Even when she is asleep his presence invades her dreams, so that when she wakes she has to gather herself back into her body, into her bed, into the space next to the man beside her, the man who is her husband.

It's easy to divert herself from any task. All she has to do is remember how they met.

She'd gone to see *'Don Giovanni'* with her friend, Emily, and her husband. Two married women, one husband. Where was hers? That she can't remember. Yosemite perhaps, somewhere anyway, photographing anything and everything.

'I never see you anymore,' she'd said to him one day, when he was packing for yet another expedition.

His answer? 'Well come with me then Flora!' He'd turned to her. 'That's it. Come with me!'

And this was interesting she thinks now, because it was before Harry, and yet she had almost recoiled from the suggestion, with no idea why. She did not want to be in close proximity to her husband for days on end, and she couldn't even explain why.

She made vague excuses, *not enough notice, work to do at the studio, she was going to the opera*. He didn't seem to mind too much.

'Ah well,' he'd said. 'If you are busy…'

Later she thought, yes, busy waiting for *that* moment. It seemed as if every molecule in her body knew there was a meeting out there for her and it was her destiny to be there.

They meet during the interval. Emily's husband goes to get drinks from the bar and returns with a stranger in tow.

'Flora my dear, let me introduce you to a friend of ours… Mrs Muybridge, Major Harry Larkyns. Major Larkyns is reviewing 'Don Giovanni' tonight ladies, for *The Examiner.*' And Mr. Peter Barlow, a man of integrity and honour, the husband of her best friend, makes the introduction with a flourish.

And Harry? Oh Harry. His eyes, they sparkle and dance at the sight of her. He sees her immediately, sees *more* than her. Drops into fantasy. Medieval, he thinks, yes, a blue dress with gold thread, she sits by a river waiting for someone… for a knight at arms, for him.

'Delighted to make your acquaintance Mrs. Muybridge,' he says. Turns to Emily. 'Dear Mrs. Barlow, you look lovely tonight.' Bends low over her hand and kisses it, so Emily laughs and pulls her hand away. But his eyes, Flora sees, are not looking at Emily, they are looking directly at her. It is not Emily's hand he is kissing. It is hers.

He makes her wait three whole days, before he makes contact. Oh, he has danced this dance before; and of course, being Harry, there's some money he needs to 'borrow' from a friend, there's a review he needs to write, there's a card game to go to, but he knows she is waiting for him, he can feel it in his bones.

As for Flora, she goes to work, no longer to the gallery, no, she's moved to a haberdasher's closer to home. It suits her better. There is more contact with people, and a little more money. She tries to focus on anything but the idea of Harry, but at night it is his laughing brown eyes she sees, and it is the idea of him, as she lies in her bed alone, that allows her hand to stray around the soft curves of her breasts, and down further, to the warm, moist folds between her legs, and the gasping, flooding warmth that subsumes her is not for her absent husband, but for a lover who has not yet arrived in her bed, at home, although he will, soon enough.

In India, he tells her, they have their own breed of horse.

'We chaps didn't think much of them at first. Indian horses, how could they amount to anything? And they're funny looking things, Flora. They have these ears that bend in and almost touch. They don't look quite right at first. They have these long thin necks and straight faces, and they often slope forward, and they have an extra gait, a sort of ambling trot. But they're amazing horses. Brave and fast and true. Hmmm...' he buries his face in her hair. 'Something for Eadweard to photograph there.'

She looks at him and smiles.

'Shhh,' she says. 'Don't mention him in here.'

His hands slide up her body, begin their soft caress of all her rises and falls, his fingers squeezing on her nipples, his mouth following his hands, while her sighs turn into tiny, hushed noises of pleasure. She fascinates him, the way she gives herself to love. He's never met a woman whose appetite for physical pleasure matches his own. It's a shame she's married, he thinks, because this time he might even have considered asking her himself. He sometimes wonders if it's about time he settled down.

What Harry has learned in his life is pretty simple. If you think up a good enough story, generally people will believe you; if you move on often enough then people can't catch up with you; and lastly and most importantly, women just want to be loved.

He has seen this with great clarity, ever since the mother of one of his school friends had reached for him one day, sensing something about him, looking for some comfort she obviously did not receive from her husband, he supposed. Comfort Harry was only too happy to offer.

That was of course, how it had started with Flora. They had met at the opera, and he could tell immediately that she was intrigued.

It was such an easy recipe. An older husband away a lot, a bored beautiful young woman at home on her own too often.

It would have seemed almost criminal *not* to fall in love with her.

Harry knows this – if he looks at a woman in a certain way, if he slides his eyes up and down her body, if he presses her lips to her hand for just a second longer than he should, and smiles up at her at the same time, she will almost always melt for him, and if she doesn't, well, there is no point to pursue her because there are so many out there who are happy to heed his rutting call.

Over the years he has perfected the technique to a needlepoint sharpness, knowing within a second whether a woman will give in. He has it down to such perfection that it is almost second nature. He can even think of other things; what wine he might drink with dinner, for instance, or where his next dollar will come from, while he is setting the trap for his prey.

But Flora is beautiful enough to actively engage all his senses, and to his astonishment, still does.

'When next my love?' he says, caressing the nape of her neck.

'I shall send a note with Susan.' Her eyes are soft. 'I miss you.'

'I miss you too.'

He hears himself, and yet he's still not sure. Does he love her? He thinks perhaps that in this lifetime this is as close as he will get to knowing love. Uninvited, as usual, the memory comes in. He's six, and he's just been told to say goodbye to his sister, because, he's been told by his aunt, he is lucky to be going to boarding school. He goes, instinctively to hug her, and his uncle stops him.

'Shake hands with your sister, Harry, that is what young men do.'

And he does, he shakes hands with his sister, and walks out of her life, as surely as his parents walked out of his, three years earlier. He shivers.

'Show me your scar,' he says. 'I want to see where I cut you.'

She turns onto her stomach, her legs stretched out behind her, and he runs his hand down a tiny ridge behind her thigh.

'If you're going to cut me, do it where *he* will never see it,' she'd told him, brave as any soldier he's ever met, not a word while he used his knife to slice gently the soft flesh he had caressed only moments before, sucking the blood into his mouth.

'We're one, now,' he'd said.

'Forever?'

'Of course, forever.'

* * * * *

Did you know Beth, that abandonment can cause paralyzing feelings of panic? I mean, I suppose that would be obvious, but what I learnt from my therapy sessions was this: those feelings leave a deep tracing on the nervous system. They run like an underground river through the deep arterial system of our bodies, carrying molecules of loss and danger, and adrenalin. Those of us with this faulty wiring are prone, of course, to either running away in an attempt to avoid the feeling (which is useless since it travels with us), or, until we break the pattern somehow, condemned to replay it, over and over again.

And in this triangle of Eadweard, Flora and Harry, only Eadweard, no matter what the odd workings of his mind, was not carrying abandonment with him in his circuitry. Poor Flora, of course was, but what you don't know yet Beth, is Harry's story and if I give it to you here, in its most encapsulated form, you will, I'm sure cry with me for this baby, this boy, this child, this young man who bled to death the day before his 31st birthday.

Harry was born on October 18, 1843, in Meerut, in the East India Company's Bengal Presidency. His mother, Emma, was Scottish, his father George, a fairly undistinguished officer in a regiment of the Bengal Horse Artillery. When he was born, his older sister Conny, was a year older than her baby brother.

Harry was six months old when the family returned to England, to live in Argyllshire, and those two-and-a-half years, during which time his younger sister Alice was born, were his only and brief taste of family life. When Alice was one, and Harry was three, his parents returned to India with Alice, leaving Harry and Conny behind in the care of various relatives, while Alice was sent back to England when she was six to be educated.

He never saw his parents, or the subsequent children born to his parents in India again. They were brutally murdered in the Cawnpore massacre of June 1857, and by the time of the massacre Harry had already spent years being shuffled from boarding school to boarding school, including one in Belgium.

Not only that, but despite being absent from his life, his mother seemed to have decided that Harry needed disciplining from afar, and despite sending mainly kind and loving letters to the daughters she left behind, little Harry was singled out for hell and damnation zealotry. 'Insubordination is the root from which every sin springs,' she wrote to him. 'The eye that mocketh at his Father and despiseth to obey his mother the ravens of the valley shall pick it out and eagles eat the same.'

Even, Beth, when his mother knows that the case is hopeless and that she, her husband and the three children they have had in India are going to die, she writes one last letter to her children in England, telling Harry: '...if you could see the position that your brother and sisters are in at this moment you would weep over ever having pleased your own desires seek your God & serve Him & please him & always hate whatever is sinful'.

Always hate whatever is sinful.

How, in any world, was Harry, who turned into a handsome young man and in due course was awarded cadetship in the Bengal Infantry, himself leaving England for the country where his family had been murdered, ever going to have peace and tranquility flowing in his veins?

When he met Flora, orphaned, abandoned and abused as a child, and by then a lonely, pretty young wife, their circuitry recognised each other immediately. They were inexorably drawn to each other by need and desire, their gaping wounds looking for salvation. And in they fell to the molten lava of love, burning those around them, setting the stage for the scorched landscape to come.

* * * * *

There is so much written about Eadweard, so much evidence of his existence on the planet, and yet, at the same time, he is a difficult man to get to know. He does not give up his emotional secrets easily – if at all. But with my poor grandmother, the reverse is true; so very little is known about her, and yet somehow each of the tiny droplets of 'self' she left behind allows me to feel her in my bones.

For instance, Flora had two miscarriages before she managed to give birth to my father. Now that is a bald statement, is it not? Flora Muybridge had, according to their housekeeper, Susan Smith, two stillbirths before she successfully delivered a boy at four in the afternoon on April 17, 1874. (And here's a small curiosity, because what that date tells us is that Florado, like Eadweard, was an Aries.) Harry was already in Flora's life by the time she fell pregnant with Florado, but she had actually met him, and they had become lovers, two years before, only a year after she had married Eadweard. You can see the 'What if', in there, Beth can't you? The two miscarriages, and the pregnancy all took place during the time Harry and Flora were lovers.

At the trial Eadweard told the court that he had first met Harry in the early part of 1873 (presumably after March though, which Harry spent in jail after he'd managed to embezzle $3,000 from a young heir to a fortune, Arthur Neil). It was Flora who introduced her lover to her husband. It was her lover who then, quite frequently, asked her husband for advice on artistic matters, because as well as being the drama critic for the *Post,* Harry was also its Arts writer. It was Harry who helped Eadweard write advertisements for the paper for his photography business, while at the same time, and let's not beat about the bush here, he was fucking Eadweard's wife.

The truth is nobody will ever know if Florado was Eadweard's or Harry's son. But abandonment was waiting for little Florado, as sure as night follows day, wasn't it? His mother dead by the time he was two, left in an orphanage when he was three, taken to a ranch in Texas when he was 10, and never saw his (supposed) father again. That was a heavy load to tote, for sure. My heart bleeds for the father I never knew, and for me, to be honest, and the legacy of loss I was gifted.

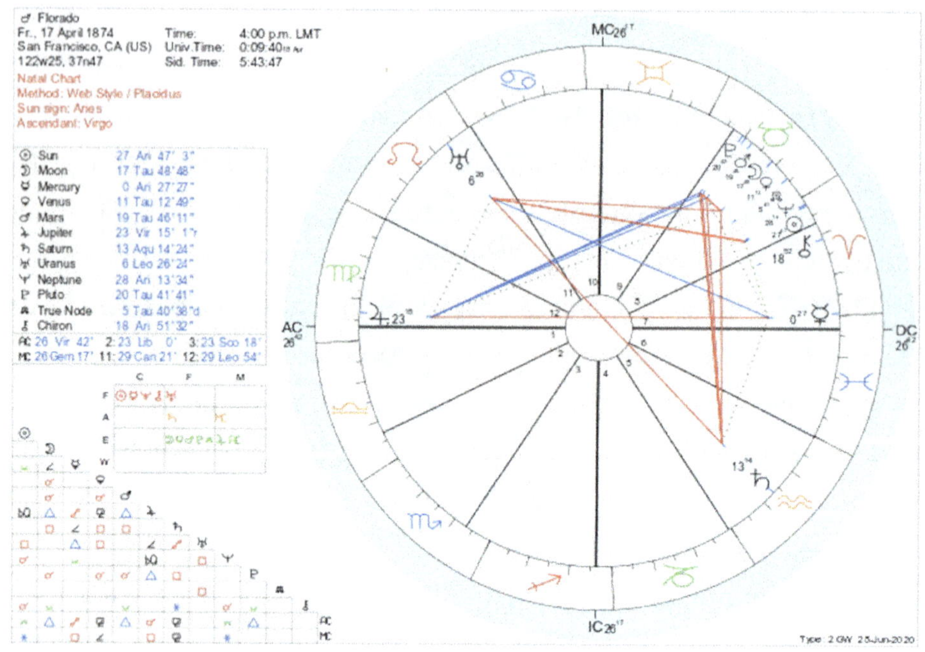

Florado's natal chart

Notes: Five planets in Taurus! The reason why he was happy to stay at the ranch in Texas for most of his life perhaps? Almost as if he needed this amount of grounding to cope with the early distress in his life.

Natural tendency to be quiet and practical, and ascendant in Virgo also allowing for a personality drawn towards advising and counseling others. Was this how he met my mother, was he kind to her? The chart of a gentle man, for sure.

The Wounded Healer Chiron in Aries (his sign, his father's sign), the personal injuries, psychological and physical (the orphanage perhaps), difficulty of expressing the true self. Definitely the sense of a destiny at work here, but so very different to the parent(s) in his life. Even his north node in Taurus — making his way towards more safety, more security.

Was he happy? Perhaps so much earth kept him settled to be happy enough.

Chapter 12

The Snowy Mountains

Tony drove me down to Thredbo, to the Silver Brumby Lodge, where I would be working through the snow season, and maybe further on if everything worked out. He knew the owners, and it was true, he had managed to find the 'thing'.

The very idea of going to the mountains excited me. For the few weeks between leaving Sydney and getting on the road, Sydney suddenly felt constricting.

I had no idea what to expect. I hadn't even really understood that there was a snow season in Australia. My image of Australia was only what I'd learned from Martin, or gleaned for myself, and I was definitely still suffering under the delusion that it was basically a land of desert with a few big cities clumped around the edges. I had put aside my love of books, my interest in the world, in everything other than learning to survive in this strange new land. I was trying to seize happiness from its beauty, to forget aside my ancestry, my heartache for my missing family, for the foetus torn from me, for also, I think a yearning for the days at university, when a world of opportunity seemed to open up before me. I had been left stranded by myself on a giant desert island, and it was all I could do to get through a day, until I had found that I was still alive, and that optimism still flowed through my veins.

We took the coast road. 'Longer,' Tony told me, 'but more beautiful.' We stayed the night in Bega, and when we checked in, it was as a married couple, Mr and Mrs Russo. The middle-aged woman running the reception desk glanced off-handedly at my hand, but if it was to catch me out, it didn't work. When my mother/grandmother had died, I had kept her wedding ring. I wore it on a chain around my neck, but if I felt anxious, I would put it on. It was a way to feel close to my lost family I suppose, but it had its uses, and I had slipped it on my finger as we left Sydney, my belongings all piled up in the back of Tony's Peugot.

He'd taken me to say goodbye to everybody at the café.

'But they'll know then,' I protested. 'They'll know we've been seeing each other, and I've kept it secret.'

He laughed, as Australians say, like a drain. 'Of course they know,' he said. 'You think they're blind?'

And certainly neither Gio nor Maria blinked an eye when I turned up in Tony's car, having told them only vaguely that I was getting a lift to the Snowy with a friend.

'You weel come back and visit us Rosa, for sure,' Maria said.

Gio nodded. 'Yes, and when you don't like thees cold place, you weel be back!'

We hugged and hugged, and I thought of the goodbye as I lay in the bed with Tony in this country town Travelodge. Another goodbye to him, coming up, not one I was looking forward to, another cutting loose. After we'd made love, gently, quickly, as if getting the last lovemaking out of the way was a good idea, so we could concentrate on the journey – both of staying true to the purity of our commitment, to have no commitment, I lay awake for a long time after he'd fallen asleep, my mind filled with the images of the green-hills sloping to the surf we'd passed that day, the crisp autumn air of Sydney already giving way to cold, a cold I'd never experienced, and I was glad of the thick knitted jumper that Nonna had made for me, and the gloves that little Noni had given me.

But then, the next morning, how can I tell you what happened to my heart as we drove inland now towards our destination? As we rose and rose into the eucalypt-covered hills, every tree seemed to be calling me: *Come closer, come closer, fear not, you're on your way home.*

But even adventurers have to fill their cars, and so we stopped for petrol somewhere. I forget now where it was.

I stepped out of the car to breathe in the crisp, cold, not quite yet snowy air.

'It's beautiful,' I said.

'Too right,' the attendant nodded. 'God's own country around here.'

The first, but not the last time I would hear that phrase. *Godzone,* I thought, that's what it sounded like. *God's Own Country, in the Godzone.*

As we drove on, I wondered about Eadweard. What had he felt the first time he saw Yosemite? Oh yes, I knew there was no comparison, me in my comfortable car with my driving companion, my friendly chauffeur, and an easy four-hour trip to our destination, and Eadweard with a team of pack mules, and helpers on hand, carrying with him his portable dark-room tent for his cumbersome wet-plate collodion process, gone from San Francisco for months in a valley still wild enough for the images he brought out to confirm him as a leading photographer of the day.

Nothing so wild, nor so grand for me, and yet the closer we got to our destination, I could feel some strange beating of my heart, as if it was trying to push out of its earthly confines to see a grander vision of the world.

I tried to explain to Tony. But he laughed.

'It's the altitude,' he said, patting me on the knee. 'That's all.'

But that feeling has never left me, is with me even still, when I am in these mountains, and why Australian mountains should call to a half-Mexican-half-American woman with English blood in her veins, I will never know. I've often wondered if this is evidence of Harry's DNA? There were rumours he came to Australia after his time in India, before his fateful decision to go to San Francisco, to reinvent himself as a theatre critic. And I've experienced that too, the reinvention of 'me' from this, to that, to this, but Eadweard, despite his many talents, stayed true to his strongest lathe – his photography, the legacy he would leave the world.

And what do I leave? This manuscript, for what it's worth, Beth, my land, a few people whose lives I've touched, some wisdom passed on perhaps, some love given, my little business. It used to feel not enough but more recently an acceptance has crept into my bones, almost against my own will, that perhaps, because it 'was', it is enough.

But on that day, when we were soon to arrive at the Silver Brumby Club, when I would meet the next couple who would have such a profound effect on me, when I would, any minute now, say goodbye to Tony, not knowing if I would see him again, certainly not knowing that he would come to my aid again, all of this was unknown.

It happened so quickly. One minute we'd stopped for Tony to put the snow chains on, the next we were driving up and up and up and I was gasping at the white snowy beauty unfolding as soft as as a sea of endless feather pillows around us, and there we were being welcomed by my new bosses, Peter and Sally Hughes. There were hellos and a cup of tea, and suddenly, almost before I could register it, Tony was gone, back on the road, and I was being shown my room, plain and simple, a single bed, a wardrobe and a chest of drawers, a rug, and a few pictures on the wall, and that was it.

I stood for a moment by the window looking out at the white surrounds, and I felt a stab of gratitude for the blue, green, red and white of Sydney, its cheerful hedonism, the café and the smell of espresso coffee, for the love of Gio and Maria and their family, and an aching pain that Tony was not there. And yet, even in those first hours, underneath the loss, underneath the unfamiliarity, there was a fluttering excitement trembling through my body. I was away from the city, I was in the mountains, I was somewhere I wanted to be, somewhere most importantly, that I had made a conscious choice about, and in many ways the decisions I'd made in my life had always seemed in some ways inevitable, but this one was mine, and mine alone.

Eadweard, of course, made decisions alone. He had become used to making decisions about his life since the time he left England as a young man. As he became surer and surer of himself as a photographer, as he gathered success to himself, as his wife and her lover involved themselves in deeper and deeper emotional turmoil, Eadweard's photography gathered momentum, much as the trains of his major mentor had sliced across the American landscape, Eadweard was on a trajectory towards fame, and nothng was going to stop him.

* * *

It was, Eadweard knew, an important moment. Sitting with the Stanfords in their San Francisco hotel suite, he listens to Mr. and Mrs. Leland Stanford with the utmost attention. Photographing houses, he thinks, is not usually in his repertoire, but for one of the richest men in America, well, he would do it.

Jane Stanford's voice breaks in on his reverie, as she offeres him some more tea.

'So that is settled then? You will photograph our house for us, Sir?'

'I would be delighted, Mrs. Stanford. Delighted.'

The Stanfords rise as one from the sofa.

'We were most impressed with your Yosemite photographs, Mr. Muybridge, most impressed.' Jane Stanford smooths down the folds of her dress. 'We have, as you may know, had occasion to travel frequently, but rarely have I seen photographs which for me give full realization to the beauty of the country in which we live, Mr. Muybridge.'

Mubridge smiles. 'I thank you, Mrs. Stanford. Your praise is generous. I will be delighted to photograph such a stylish home.'

Jane Stanford inclines her head. Eadweard is struck by her quiet elegance, and by her husband's attention to his wife's words.

'So that is organised then. You will come and photograph the house, while you are in Sacramento.' Mrs Stanford rests her arm lightly on her husband's.

'Indeed. It will be my pleasure.'

Her husband holds out his hand.

'It's been our pleasure, Sir. I do believe you and I may have something further to talk about. To my mind, something rather more exciting than houses, Mr. Muybridge, although, curiously, both beginning with the letter 'H'. But we shall wait and discuss it in due course.'

Eadweard nods.

'Of course.'

Stanford pauses for a moment, unsure how to say what he wants to say next, and decided it can wait. He will explain later to the photographer that he wants none of this 'Helios' pseudonym. What he wants is the photographer Eadweard Muybridge. And what Leland Stanford wants, Leland Stanford generally gets.

On their way home, Stanford gazes out of the window of the carriage, lulled as usual by the sound of the trotting hooves. He thinks immediately of Charley, of course. Little Charley, now the magnificent Occident. What a horse! He can feel his heart rate rise again. How many times had the horse re-paid that initial $4000 investment? Too many to count! Stanford smiles to himself, knowing what he's going to ask Muybridge – he's going to ask him if he can do the impossible, if he, of all the photographers in the world has the technical expertise to capture a horse's movement instantaneously.

'You're smiling my dear?' His wife turns to him. 'A penny for your thoughts.'

He smiles back. 'Horses, of course, Mrs. Stanford.'

She shakes her head. 'I swear I do not know what to do with you my love! I wish you would remember what the Doctor said.'

He smiles again. 'I do remember my dear.'

Of course, he remembers his doctor's post-railroad advice. 'You need an outdoor activity, Mr. Stanford,' he'd been told. 'Something to take your mind off politics, something to connect you with the outdoor world. This nervous exhaustion of yours will pass in time, but I believe you should take a vacation from your normal activities. Are there any hobbies you like to pursue?'

He'd had to think. Not much had come to mind. 'I like the occasional bet on a horse,' he'd replied, thinking that it wasn't much in terms of an 'outdoor' pursuit.

But his doctor had been enthusiastic. 'Horses!' he'd said. 'Just the ticket. Lots of fresh air, another interest.' But he had reckoned without the character of his patient, as he has since pointed out to Stanford on his not infrequent visits for a check-up. 'I meant,' he'd said on one of those visits, with a pursed mouth, 'for it to be a hobby, not an obsession.'

Me too, Stanford wanted to say, and would have, but he felt it might lead to more conversation on this matter of horses. Stanford had no desire to discuss his latest ambitions, which included not only the desire to revamp the entire traditional training system to emphasize speed over endurance, but also this new project – to prove that at one point in a galloping horse's gait, all four hooves are in the air at once.

As his darling wife Jane pointed out one evening to him, not unkindly: 'Dearest, you have swapped your obsession with locomotives for an obsession with equine locomotion.'

He remembers his laughing response. 'You are right my dear, as usual. I wanted to run the fastest trains, and now I want to train the fastest horses.'

And what he knew immediately as soon as the sentence had left his mouth, was that he needed land. Land to have the space to breed the horses he wanted to breed, land to have the space to train the horses he wanted to train; land to create the best facility in the world, where he would employ people with the greatest understanding of horses in the world.

From the hotel step, waiting for his horsecar, Eadweard watch the couple enter their carriage. There was something about them, he thinks to himself. Even beyond the fact that Stanford had the bearing of an ex-Governor of the state, it was more than that, there is a quiet certainty about the couple together he finds himself envying.

He had believed, when he first met Flora, that she was the most exquisite, most beautiful woman he had ever met.

And of course, he was not the only one. Rulofsen's portraits of her had captured her beauty on camera for the world to see. Now that was an unbearable jealousy, that the gallery he'd moved to, and where Flora had also gained work retouching, should have taken the photographs of his beloved *he* might have taken.

The way she worked on the re-touching – expertly, gently. She cared for images is what he knew, or thought he knew, the moment he met her.

He had waited 40 years to be fully in love and he embraced the condition, plunging himself into the fever, into the pleasure and pain. He could not live without her, he told himself in the beginning. She was as necessary as air to him.

Even so, though, there were times when he wondered. He could not help but find it just a little shocking how much Flora seemed to enjoy the act of intercourse. He had to remember – she was a married woman when she met him. Young and beautiful and a woman with a level of experience that made him, he had to admit, anxious. He was retrospectively jealous of her husband; that anybody should have opened up this flower other than him, was such a painful thought he could hardly bear it.

And that was it, he thought now, turning away from the window. It was how she opened for him, soft and warm and inviting, the small smile on her lips, sometimes even touching herself, inviting him to look, serenely content in her beauty. She showed him a thing or two, and he was not fool enough to turn it down, but it bothered him. That was the truth, even though it was her very sensuality that had drawn him to her, like a moth to a candle.

Chapter 13

Mountain Life

Horses. They became Leland Stanford's obsession; they became an obsession for Eadweard. Little did I know, when I went to work in the mountains, that horses were waiting for me.

I'm here to tell you Beth, that working through a snow season isn't all beer and skittles. A lot of the work was cleaning and housekeeping. In a small lodge like the Silver Brumby, and with the different skill sets I'd acquired, I made myself useful; I could clean and housekeep with the best, but I could also serve in the bar, and, most importantly, help with the accounts. My deep desire to belong in these mountains gave me an extra impetus, and while I mightn't have been as young or pretty as some of the girls that had come to work, to save their dollars (because there wasn't much to spend their money on) or to learn to ski, I could put in the hours that I hoped would mean Peter and Sally would keep me on at the end of the season, so that I could see the mountains as the snow melted. I wanted to experience *every* season there.

Strangely though, I didn't have much interest in skiing.

I spoke to Tony a few times on my days off, especially in my first few months.

When he asked me if I was enjoying skiing, I told him. 'I don't know, it's so, well, rushed. I mean, you're standing there, you take off, and in a minute or two, it's over, and if you want to do it again, you have to get back in the chairlift and get to the top again.'

His laugh was so loud I almost dropped the phone. 'But the rush is exactly what people love,' he said.

'I don't think the rush is my thing really,' I told him. What I didn't tell him was that I thought I'd found my thing, or at least my mountains in winter thing – cross-country skiing.

Tomas, the Swiss ski instructor at the lodge who was over in Australia for the season, suggested it to me, when I showed my disinterest in normal skiing.

'Why don't you like skiing?' he asked me one evening when a group of us were all sitting around the fire having a late-night drink, while those who'd had a day off told tales of their escapades on the ski slopes.

'I don't know,' I told him. 'It just seems like you don't really have time to enjoy the scenery.'

'But that's the point,' said one of the other girls, Lulu, I think her name was. 'You're not really there to enjoy the scenery, you're there to go fast.'

I shrugged. 'Not *my* point,' I said.

Tomas leaned forward. 'You know in Switzerland that many people do cross-country skiing. "Langlauf", we call it or in German, "skilanglauf". In some small places people travel between villages on their skiis. I think you would like this.' He nodded his head with precise Swiss certainty. 'I am sure you would.'

Which is how I found myself learning to cross-country ski, first with Tomas, and once I had mastered the sheer joy of the technique, being allowed out, when I had spare time, with small groups who, like me, preferred the sensation of travelling to the sensation of rushing. I think learning to master, and love, cross-country skiing gave me a deep insight into my own personality. I began to understand that I need space, and time to 'process', as they say these days.

As we began to come through the worst of the winter, the snow still thick on the ground, and not yet melting, but with the storms that could come in from anywhere at anytime having lessened, I was allowed, if I didn't go too far to ski-walk (as I thought of it) by myself, as long as I said which direction I was going in and I wasn't gone for more than two hours. They were sensible restrictions. If the weather changed and I was out there on my own it could easily be a disaster, and so I was sensible, in the main. It was on one of these small excursions out by myself that I saw my first brumbies.

I remember that I was on a relatively flat stretch, not that far from the club, when I suddenly got this curious feeling that someone was watching me. I looked up, and this 'someone' was a beautiful buckskin horse – although I did not know the name of the colour then, I only saw he was a deep creamy beige with a black mane, silhouetted in the treeline above me, standing in the snow.

I stopped dead in my tracks, and gazed at him, drinking him in. I knew nothing about horses, but I could see how powerful he looked, his mane so long in contrast to the only horses I'd ever seen, man-owned and tamed. I say 'he', although I couldn't have known from that distance if it was a stallion or a mare, but in my instant fantasy he was a stallion. He was certainly, I was soon to discover, the sentinel, and therefore most likely the stallion.

He could see me watching him – I could see him watching me. From a distance of 100 metres or so, his eyes were fixed on me. Was I a danger, his every molecule seemed to be asking, or was I not worth bothering about? I stood there gazing at him, his muscular beauty, the sheer sculpted beauty of him, and time seemed to stand still. I drank in the clear blue sky, the gracious snow gums in the tree line above me, the white snow and the caramel-coloured horse, for what seemed almost to be an eternity.

Then suddenly a crow sounded an alarm, 'caw-caw-caw', and I don't know who jumped higher, me or the horse. He wheeled around, and just like that he was gone, and as he turned, he whinnied, and suddenly there was the sound of other horses, and a quick flash of their colours, grey, black and this distinctive caramel, and they were gone, leaving me breathless.

I felt like a child. I wanted to call out: *Come back, come back and play!* I wanted to have a tantrum, stamp my foot and say, *I want to see those horses again,* but most of all I think what happened to me that day was that out of the blue I yearned to *be* a wild horse. I wanted to be part of that herd, to have that freedom, that grace. All this of course long before I knew how they were rounded up every year, or the terrible long years facing the horses as animals not native to Australia when it seemed almost as if they must be punished for the presence on this land.

All this, and more, was to come, but for that moment it tapped into the dichotomy that perhaps has haunted me forever: to be free, but to belong.

I turned around after that, ski-walking back to the house with my heart singing. I was still unclear about my future, but I knew one thing with certainty, that one way or another *there would be a horse* in it.

* * * * *

Sometimes, Beth, when I think of that unresolveable tension between freedom and belonging, I think of you. I've watched you grow from a fierce young woman, into a compassionate, patient mother, always there for your children, and for your Will. I've loved watching you two grow into each other, two trees side by side, your branches touching and mingling closer and closer to one another, protecting each other from the storms of life, so that even when all is not good between you, your internal compass has remained the same – that you are here to take care of yourself, your husband and your family. You've taught me the love of belonging, and in the teachng, I've unwound the wound of my beginning, that my sister/mother could not show me the love a mother has for a chid, and my mother/grandmother could not show me the genuine love a grandmother has for her grandchild; my father/grandfather could never quite be my father, never quite be my grandfather. With my real father, well that is a little different, it's hard to miss what you've never known.

When I think of his story, I feel a deep compassion for him. I wish I'd known him, of course, I miss the idea of 'father', but the loss of him – perhaps because it was undiscovered until I was an adult – has never been as extreme a pain as that of finding out those I loved were not who I thought they were.

I have this memory. I'm about three-years-old. I've been playing outside, and I fall over and scrape my knee. I run inside, crying, and my 'sister' is by the stove. She turns towards me and opens her arms, and I'm running instinctively to her. I want to bury myself in her skirt. Suddenly, my 'mother' is there, she walks between us, stopping me in my tracks.

'Don't cry Rosa,' she says. 'It's not that bad. Sit here and I'll clean it.'

My 'sister' turns away, back to the saucepan on the stove, and glancing at her back I see waves of grey sorrow rising from her, and I'm sad too, but I don't know why.

My 'mother' cleans and bandages my knee. 'There,' she says. 'All better now.'

I nod.

All better now.

I stayed on after the snow season. The younger staff mostly left with the melting snow, back off to cities, or off for more traveling. We'd all grown fond of each other, this eclectic group of people brought together by their desire to experience the magic of the mountains in the winter, but now the beaches and the coast called to most of them.

By now, I'd become useful, once more showing my talent with figures, and so I had in essence two jobs; doing the books, and housekeeping in the lodge. I was paid for both roles, and so my money, with really nothing to spend it on, combined with my savings, was mounting up.

As spring began to reveal itself, I decided it was time to buy a car, so that I could explore the mountains on my day off (always, in the back of my mind with the intention of being able to drive into walks where I might chance across that brumby, or any brumby herds I could find, once more). Of all the doubts about my future, two things were sure. I loved the mountains, and I wanted to know more about horses. I also already knew the car I wanted. A Toyota Landcruiser short-wheel base J40, two-door, hard-roof. It was a mountain man car, and I wanted to be a mountain woman.

They were the vehicle of choice for people working in the mountains, solid and reliable, not the most comfortable, with a tendency to pitch a bit over bumps because of the short wheel-base, but I had my heart set on one, and it wasn't long before Bill, the mechanic in town, rang me to tell me that one of the park rangers was selling his personal cruiser because he was being supplied with one.

'It's in good condition, Rosa,' he said. '$2,500, 10 years old, goes well. She's got some miles on her, but she'll last forever.'

I laughed. 'I'm not sure I'll last that long Bill, but she sounds good.'

'She's a great unit,' he said. 'You can't go wrong. Drop into town and come and give her a test drive.'

So that was how I came to love the Cruisers. The country world seemed to be made up then of people who were Land Rovers or Cruisers, and I was the latter. I loved her from the beginning. I've always had Land Cruisers, and it seems as if I will have one until the day I die.

'What are you going to do with it?' Wendy teased me one night over dinner. 'Travel around Australia on your own?'

I shrugged. 'I don't know,' I said. 'I might.'

She looked shocked. 'Rosa!' she said, 'that wouldn't be safe...'

Would it have been, or wouldn't it have been? I'll never know now, but it might have been a great deal safer than the decision I made when I left the mountains.

I passed a whole summer at the Lodge, and it was a happy time. The snow gave way to the glorious spring wildflowers, and the warmer days but still freezing nights suited me. Tony, still waiting for the 'wife' he could take home, visited a few times, and they were carefree weekends. He'd bring packages from Gio and Maria, who seemed to think that nobody ate in the Snowy Mountains. Boxes packed with tasty salamis, in-season fruit – that was hard to come by – fresh crusty bread, and we'd head off in Dawn, as I'd decided to call my 4WD, going deep into the National Park to hike, and to search for my elusive brumby, armed with the binoculars I'd bought for the task.

Unwittingly, through my quiet stalkings of these majestic wild horses, I was learning about horse 'families' in a natural, if unusual way.

One day, while we were hiking near the top of one of the plateaus, we chanced across a herd of about eight horses, mares with foals at foot, some yearlings, a big grey stallion, and other mares. I think they knew we were there, but we were far enough away, to not be a bother to them, so we waited a while, watching them.

I told Tony some of what I'd noticed. That the stallion was not the only hyper-vigilant member of the mob, there'd be two or three mares as well, usually his favourites, who kept the herd in line.

'Watch a while,' I whispered. 'I'll bet one of those mares will push another horse away from its grass, or tick off one of the babies.' Sure enough, it didn't take long, and one almost jet-black mare began to show signs of being the Head Teacher.

Tony laughed, and immediately the little mob froze, heads up, before the stallion indicated he was comfortable enough to graze, and the others followed suit.

That night, after we'd made love, and boy, how my body craved that after however many months had passed since his last visit, he said to me: 'You know, I like this new Rosa.'

'What do you mean?' I said, sleepily.

'You seem, I don't know, surer of yourself, stronger – kinder even. You're a good woman Rosa, and don't you forget it.'

And that's exactly what I did. Just a few months later, I went out and forgot it. Looking back, trying to make sense of what came next – and I have raked through that ash for decades, let me tell you – I wonder now about that over-used word: karma.

Why did I throw away this new, strong, more contented Rosa? Was it inevitable that the scarred landscape of my psyche would do this to me? That simply to be contented was not something I could do at that time? Was it, as fanciful as it might seem, some deep ancestral connection to my grandmother, to Flora?

In the end, curiously, it was Easter in the mountains that pushed me out of my comfort zone.

Whenever anybody asks me about Mexico – or Mehico, as people like to say, with a sly little grin, as if the cliché in the old movies of 'Mehicans' as slightly inferior could just be true, where my mind goes to immediately is the rituals of the complex country I was born in, and to which half of my lineage belongs.

In Mexico we celebrate Easter not just for a few days, not even just for a week, but for *two whole* weeks; for Semanta Santa, Holy Week which begins on Palm Sunday and ends on Easter Saturday; and Pascua, which starts on Easter Sunday and ends the following Saturday. Schools and businesses close down, families take holidays, and we celebrate the last days of Christ during Holy Week with elaborate devotional ceremonies and rituals. Of course, leading up to Easter is Lent, and our Carnival, as well as the day before Good Friday, is dedicated to the Virgen de los Dolores, the Virgin of Sorrows, where we focus on the pain and sacrifice of Mary knowing that Jesus had to die to save mankind.

But it doesn't end there, that's too simple for us. The Spanish brought with them their warfaring, torturous ways, and in defeat we embraced the Catholic Church with a fervour hardly seen elsewhere. Penitentes prove their faith by whipping themselves or carrying religious objects on their backs; the actor playing Jesus in the reenactments wears a real crown of thorns and carries a massive cross for miles to the scene of 'His' crucifixion. Actors prepare for this part for months beforehand.

Then there are the Judases. We got that idea from the Spanish Inquisition, when we started making dolls dressed like Spanish inquisitors and burning them as a protest against Spain burning people for heresy. This burning fever has stayed with us, and for centuries now we have created giant papier mache Judases which are hung up and blown-up with fireworks, paper limbs scattered through the street, picked up by children as souvenirs.

Easter as religious ritual; Easter as political commentary; Easter as the story of Christ; Easter as a time, curiously, of street-food, to cater for the millions out and about taking part or watching all the ceremonies; Easter as living art, the millions of candles and palm fronds, for instance; Easter as theatre, in which we cheerfully mangle our Passion Plays to include Aztec drums and flutes.

In Guerrero a large wooden statue of Christ travels on a donkey led by children on bicycles and a group of young children dressed as angels.

You get the drift.

And yet, Mexico has never taken to the idea of bunny rabbits and chocolate Easter eggs as a religious concept.

So there it was, this simple thing that marked my 10-month anniversary in the mountains, when I discovered that really, nothing much happened at Easter.

A lot of families would come to stay, it was explained to me, there would be an Easter egg hunt for the children. If anyone wanted to go to Church no doubt there would be a service in Jindabyne, and there would be Easter Sunday breakfast with hot cross buns, but that was really it.

Now, it's not that it wasn't all lovely. It was. It's not that I was bored with the scenery or even the place itself. I wasn't. But there was just this pinprick of dissatisfaction. I realised that the longer I stayed at the Lodge, and the closer we came to another winter season, the less I was exploring this country I felt so strangely drawn towards adopting as my own.

It was time, I decided, to move on.

Chapter 14

Choices

Moving on. I had a choice. I could have stayed, and perhaps given what was coming next, I should have stayed, but the choice to leave was mine alone.

It was Eadweard who made the choice for Flora, to move her on, or at least to move her away from San Francisco, away from Harry Larkyns, for a while. Six-foot-tall Harry Larkyns, who spoke numerous languages, boxed like Jem Mace, could shoot more bottle necks at 20 paces than any man had a right to, who could ride horses like an angel, and took Eadweard's wife riding too. He could charm the devil, could Harry Larkyns. He even, as I've said, charmed his lover's husband for a while, helping him design advertisements for the *San Francisco Chronicle,* all the time organizing assignments via little Florado's nurse, Susan Smith.

Do you know Beth, there is a psychological school of thought that says that when we are living with a secret that is too hard to bear, we will find ways to let it be known?

Husbands or wives or partners will leave evidence – not consciously of course – but subconsciously wanting the very thing they are trying to hide, usually an affair of course, to come to light.

* * * * *

'You know Mrs Muybridge, your riding's getting better and better,' says Harry, helping his lover down from her horse.

'Is it?' she says. 'Well, I have a good teacher, Major Larkyns.'

She presses closer into him, whispering to him, placing the next domino in line.

'Come to my rooms,' she says. 'He's away until tomorrow.'

'Are you sure?'

She nods. 'I'm sure.'

'Give me a few hours.'

If he had not taken that few hours, then perhaps he would have been gone from Mr. and Mrs. Eadweard Muybridge's rooms, Beth, by the time Eadweard came home a day early from his photographic assignment. Perhaps history would have unfolded differently, although I don't think so.

Maybe, on that day when Eadeaward gets home early, to find his wife and her lover embracing in the front room, maybe, as he chooses to walk the last mile, while his assistant unloads his 'Flying Studio' from their latest adventure, maybe he is already precoccupied with what he will find at home. Because Beth, what I imagine is that after two miscarriages, a baby and an ongoing affair, perhaps Eadweard wants to move Flora out of San Francisco for the most personal of reasons; perhaps Flora is not so interested in her wifely duty anymore, shall we say?

She blames it on having a baby.

'I'm so tired,' she says to her husband. 'I'm sorry. Maybe tomorrow?'

But walking home now, thinking of all these 'tired' nights, Eadweard knows this is a lie. There will be another excuse tomorrow, and the next tomorrow and the next. He knows too, that this is not just to do with having a baby, as it was not just to do with being pregnant. His wife has withdrawn from him, and in the deepest part of him, he senses the terrible truth – that she loves another man, and when she lies next to him, feigning sleep, as silent and as still as she can be, he knows this too, she is awake, as he is, but she will soon fall asleep, and he will not.

He remembers a night shortly before he left for Yosemite, when she came home late from the theatre. They went to bed, and she turned away from him, and within minutes, it seemed, his wife was snoring, her gently guttural sounds escaping into the cool fall air. Once he would have huddled closer to her, spooned around her for comfort until the speed of his brain was quieted by her presence. But there was no such comfort to be had there these days. His whole body felt as if it was being attacked by pins and needles, his temple near his old injury throbbed. Carefully he slipped back the covers, his feet searching for his slippers on the cold floor, he picked up his clothes from the nearby chair, and slipped out of the room.

Despite all this, as he nears his home, he can't help walking a little faster, he is eager to see her, he can't wait, in fact, hoping against hope that she will be there waiting for him.

But it was not to be, was it Beth? Instead he came home and found her in an 'embrace' as the history books tell us, with Harry Larkyns. Eadweard orders Harry to leave, he rants and rails at Flora, and then he makes the decision, he will send her away to her aunt in Oregon with Florado, and that will be an end to this business.

In the morning, Flora is distraught. 'But Eadweard,' she says, 'I don't want to go away. I am happy here in San Francisco.'

He notices that she does not say, 'with you', just that she's 'happy'.

He shrugs. 'My mind is made up Flora. I am going to be away for some months with this latest job, and I believe it will be good for you – good for us – if you are not here going, shall, we say, to the theatre a good deal and perhaps, how can I put it, not quite fulfilling your family duties.'

She begins to cry, snuffling like a small animal in distress. 'Eadweard,' she says, raising a tear-stained face to his. 'Please?'

'It is all arranged, my dear. You leave later this morning, so we shall breakfast and Mrs. Smith will help you pack your things. Let's have no more discussion about it. I shall allow you $50 per month for your expenses, so I expect you'll be comfortable.'

He turns away from her to leave the room, and wishes, how he wishes, that her sadness at leaving is for him.

This will put a stop to it, he thinks. *Once and for all.*

What is that expression Beth? Absence makes the heart grow fonder. Perhaps if Eadweard had been a different sort of man, he might have understood what a pointless exercise separating Flora and Harry was. Florado's nanny, Susan Smith, continued to act as their intermediary, with her house the mail address for the lovesick letters between the pair. Graphic letters, by all accounts, from Harry.

But here's a thing to throw in the mix, just when we might be feeling a bit of compassion for Flora, married to a man more than twice her age, separated from the love of her life, when we know there's worse to come, there's another version of events, suggested by Harry's letters, suggested by Flora's own timetable. It's likely Beth, that she went to Oregon entirely of her own volition. She caught the Portland Steamer to Oregon at exactly the same time as a troupe of wandering minstrels, Maguire's California Minstrels, whom she'd met through Harry at the theatre. According to Harry's tortured letter to Susan Smith, she did not even take a change of clothes with her, and worst of all, for him, she made no contact with him.

Mrs. Smith, he writes, our lovesick Harry, *I assure you I am sick with anxiety and doubt, the whole thing is so incomprehensible and I am so helpless. I fear my business will not let me go to Portland and I see no other way of hearing of her.*

– If an angel had come and told me she was false to me, I would not have believed it.

– I cannot attend to my work, I cannot sleep, and the longer matters stay like this the more I suffer, besides even if she does write me now, I

shall not know what to believe. I cannot help thinking of that speech of hers to you the day before she left, when she begged you not to think of ill of her, whatever you might hear, it almost looks as if she had already settled some plan in her head head that she you would disapprove of.

And yet Mrs. Smith after all that has come and gone, <u>could</u> she be so utterly untrue to me, so horribly false?

Poor Harry. He even went as far as to write a 'personal' ad in the Portland Papers: 'Flora and Georgie, if you have a heart you will write to H. Have you forgotten that April night when we were both so pale.'

Georgie. His name for Florado Helios Muybridge. George was the name of Harry's murdered father and Georgie the name of his brother, also murdered in that terrible massacre. No doubt, then that he believed the child to be his. No wonder he was so heartbroken at the idea that she had betrayed him. And what, Beth, of the April night? That's what tugs at my imagination. Why were they both so pale? It was both Eadweard's and Florado's birthdays in April. Was it to do with one of those? Was it perhaps even to do with the birth? I wish I could ask my grandmother these questions, I wish she could fill in the blanks for me.

But Flora was incensed by Harry's suggestions of infidelity, and said so, not just in a letter to Susan Smith's, but also to Harry himself. Nevertheless, though, even though she found The Dalles dull and gloomy, she stayed there, not even bothering to return to San Francisco when her husband finally returned from his trip, photographing the coast for the Pacific Mail Steamship Company. When Eadweard had packed Flora off to Oregon, little Florado was only a few weeks old; five months later he didn't, as far as we know, even attempt a reunion with his wife.

Isn't it terrible Beth, that even though it was Harry who disturbed the marriage, we like Harry more than we like Eadweard? It's Harry we want to hold and comfort, it's Harry we want to see reunited with his beloved. Is it because we know his time is coming soon? That like his father and his brother before him, he too will be killed; murdered because of his love for another man's wife? For his Flora?

And you might ask me Beth, but how does it happen, with Flora away in Oregon, with Harry working in the mines, with him being away in Calistoga, with Eadweard back in San Francisco, working on the photographs of his last massive project. How on earth, with all this separation could the situation become so inflamed?

Well, I can tell you Beth in one word: Money. Filthy lucre.

For a man who was well-off, Eadweard had a bit of a mean streak, it seems, and perhaps understandably with the rift between them growing ever since Florado's birth, was not inclined to pay bills associated with Flora, including to Susan Smith, who in October had still not been paid for attending to Flora during the birth in April and her ongoing care after the birth. When Eadweard returned to San Francisco, Flora wrote to Mrs Smith and begged her not to take the debt further, assuring her that she would look after the situation, but Susan Smith had had enough, and hired the services of a debt collector. Flora wrote again, offering to pay her more than the original amount if she would drop the suit, but Mrs Smith pushed ahead, and was awarded her $100, plus costs, in a Justice's Court.

Oh, what a tangled web we weave, when first we practice to deceive, dear Beth, because during the hearing, Eadweard produced evidence that he had in fact given Flora the money to pay Susan Smith, and suggested that Mrs Smith was involved in a money laundering scheme. Mrs Smith then produced a letter from Flora acknowledging the debt and mentioning Harry. Eadweard became immediately agitated, saying: 'It was strange that his wife should mention Larkyns' name so familiarly'.

What had giddy Flora spent Mrs Smith's money on, Beth? On

dresses, and ribbons and bows with which to adorn her 23-year-old self with, most likely. On frippery to make herself pretty for her lover. Of all the pieces in the puzzle leading to Harry's murder, this one has a pulsating neon light around it, doesn't it? I think at least, that's how Eadweard saw it, with his damaged head. I think that he walked out of that courtroom, his heart beating fast with distress, with images dancing in his brain he could not be rid of, not even that night. I think he spent a sleepless, troubled night haunted by his hatred of Harry, and his despair around Flora, because the very next day, he set off to settle the matter for once and for all. He went off to visit the one person who could give him answers: Susan Smith.

* * * * *

He feels as if he's been awake for ever, as if he has never slept. Lying in the bed that once held such promise for him, he berates himself for being a fool, over and over again.

I cannot endure this a moment longer, he thinks to himself, *I must know.* Who could help him? Who would know, beyond any doubt Flora's comings and goings? Her daily affairs? Her *affairs?*

And clear as day comes the answer: Susan Smith.

Of course! Muybridge almost hits his own head with his hand. Why didn't he think of it before? In his experience it is always the staff who know everything. Who better to tell him of his wife's comings and goings than her nurse? Every inch of him wants to go there now, to find out *now.* He imagines the scenario – him slamming down his fist, insisting, Mrs. Smith resisting at first then suddenly capitulating, giving him the name, the reason for his unhappiness.

As the night passes, slowly, oh so slowly, Eadweard roams his rooms as if he is a stranger. What does he really know of it, he wonders, this place where he spends so little time, and where Flora spends so much. By the time the first rays of light begin to pierce the sky, he is beside himself with sorrow and anger, and he can contain himself no longer.

He sets off, braced against the cold, for Mrs. Smith's house. He will have answers, he thinks, no matter what they are.

At first, she does not answer the door.

'Mrs. Smith,' he calls. 'It is I, Mr. Muybridge. Please let me in.'

She he arrives – scurrying, surprised to see him. She has her money now, surely, she thinks, time to let it go.

'Is something wrong, Sir?' she asks, 'with your wife? Or with the baby?'

'No, no,' he says. 'At least I don't think so… but Mrs. Smith, I must talk to you.'

'Of course,' she says. 'Come in.'

In the living room he paces, trying to find the words – *how do you ask*, he thinks, *has my wife been unfaithful? Will Flora's own nurse answer him with the truth? Or will he be fooled again?*

Mrs. Smith knows what he will ask her. How could she not when she has witnessed the comings and goings these last several years, she thinks to herself, when it was even Major Harry who brought Flora back to the house when her labour had started. But she stays silent. *Let him begin it,* she thinks, *not me.*

And at this moment she notices, just as he does, the photograph of Florado, a present from Flora for her, the nurse.

Eadweard reaches out for it, almost in slow motion it seems to her later, as if he knew what must follow.

'Who is this?' Eadweard gazes at the baby. 'Who is this?'

'It is your baby, Sir.'

'But I did not take this photograph! Who took this, and where?'

'Your wife sent it to me from Oregon. It was taken at Rulofson's.' She prays to herself that he should not turn it over, that he will not see the inscription, that he will place it back down on the table.

Eadweard feels hot molten fire running through his veins. Another photographer has taken a photograph of his baby? Why? And why has he not seen this photograph? Instinctively he turns it over, and the words he sees only increase his distress.

'My God!' He shouts the words into the early morning air and his voice slices the silence with its fury. *'Little Harry!* What is this? What is this? You must tell me Mrs. Smith – I order you to tell me.'

How soon he wishes he had not asked. Slumped in an armchair his head in his hands, the nurse's words rain over him relentlessly. At one point he holds his hand up in front of his face, and Susan Smith feels a surge of pity for this cuckolded husband, *but*, she thinks, *that is what you get when you marry someone half your age.* Still she tells him, on and on, the visits, the letters, the familiarity. So that even though she spares him the absolute worst – the undeniable chemistry between the two of them she's witnessed time and time again – he is left in no doubt of two things: that his wife has being having an affair with Harry Larkyns, and that Harry Larkyns is the father of Florado, that most beloved, late-arrived child Eadweard had come to assume, before he met Flora, would never enrich his life.

Finally, he can take no more. He holds up his hand.

'Mrs. Smith,' he says. 'Thank you, you have told me enough.'

'I am sorry, Mr. Muybridge,' Susan Smith replies.

'Yes.' He picks up the photograph. 'I will take this. Thank you.'

Through the curtains the nurse watches him leave her house, watches him stand at the bottom of the steps, watches him as he stands there, gazing into the distance, watches him as finally he walks away.

* * * * *

In the street, Eadweard's head is throbbing. His body has begun to shake. Already he knows what he has to do. He knew even as he was being told the sordid story, even though now, as he makes his way first to the San Francisco Art Association, and then to Rulofson's, he can hear his mother's voice as clear as day inside his head. *No good will come of this Edward,* she tells him, *you never know, do you, when to leave well enough alone? You always have to go too far. Leave it my dear son, mend the bridges, do not blow them up.*

But Eadweard knows he must leave his affairs tidy. He must in fact, leave nothing to chance. He spends the day sorting, tidying, and organizing; unremarkable tasks for a remarkable day, but they quiet his brain, and any way, they must be done, for if the desired outcome is not forthcoming then Eadweard's business matters must be in order.

Finally, it is done, and Eadweard, glancing at the studio clock, sees that the time has come. He must start the next part of the journey.

* * * * *

William Rulofson, strolling back to his studio after lunch, is in a good mood. Business has been brisk recently; San Francisco's urge to build and better itself, has led to him lining his pockets with families and people wanting portraits. And as for his Mary, she has a fine eye for the placement of objects, for retouching, and for the gentle art of persuasion that photography must use to coax the best out of occasionally reluctant subjects.

He is, he knows, a lucky man. He would almost, he thinks as he climbs the stairs towards his studio, be inclined to whistle, if it were seemly. It is then that he notices Eadweard coming down towards him.

'My dear chap,' he calls out, noting the deathly pallor of his colleague's face. 'Are you all right?'

And Eadweard, seeing a friendly face in the midst of the volcano in which he's living, crumples onto the stairs.

'No,' he cries out loud. 'No, I am not "all right".'

Rulofson runs up the stairs as fast as he can to the crumpled figure above him.

'My dear Muybridge,' he coaxes. 'Come up, please, let us get you off the stairs and into the studio.'

Muybridge, like a child, obeys, until he finds himself led by his friend into the lady's dressing room next to the studio. Through the fog in his brain, he notices the accessories, the mirrors and the hanging clothes, everything so soft and feminine, everything reminding him of Flora. Her very presence seems to be here in all these accoutrements, and he reaches out involuntarily for a dark blue dress, burying his face in it.

'If anything should happen to me, Rulofsen, please will you make sure my wife is looked after?'

Rulofsen puts an arm around Eadweard's shoulder. 'My dear man, what could possibly happen to you?'

Eadweard shudders. 'But still,' he insists. 'If it does. Will you promise?'

'Of course. I promise. You have my solemn oath. But what is this about? Why so sad?'

Eadweard shakes his head. 'I am unable to tell you, Rulofsen. It is too painful, too horrific – too shameful to tell.'

Rulofsen gently guides Eadweard to one of the chairs. 'Sit,' he says. 'We have the time. I can listen, and I will not judge.'

'Oh.' Eadweard gives a hollow laugh. 'I think you will, Sir, when you hear the sordid story, when you hear…' and his voice rises higher, 'when you hear how I have been cuckolded and made a fool of by a man I never trusted, and how my life has been ruined and left in tatters. I think you will judge us all in this story as fools. But I will not be made a fool of, that is the truth of it.'

Rulofson nods agreement. 'No, of course not. I would not think it.'

Although of course, he has noticed, how could he not, how much Muybridge indulged his young wife, and he had heard – who had not – that she spent much time indulging herself. He remembers how surprised he had been when Muybridge had fallen for her so hard. Of course, he himself had thought she was beautiful. It wasn't why he'd hired her for the studio, but it had certainly helped.

Except that by the time Eadweard has finished telling him the sordid tale of Harry Larkyns and his wife, and even though Rulofsen would never say the words, he knows what Eadweard himself knows, that Eadweard was indeed, a fool.

'One or other of us must die.' This is Eadweard's final and dramatic proclamation. 'I will find him, and I will kill him, or die in the attempt.'

'Muybridge! My dear man.' Rulofsen moves towards him to comfort him, and puts his hand on his shoulder. 'Nothing is as bad as that. Nothing, surely, is worth taking a life over?'

'Sir.' Muybridge is suddenly stiff, almost formal, as if he has not just loosened his tongue and let all manner of secrets out. 'You have been too kind, but I must go. I have an appointment.'

And despite Rulofsen's entreaties, his attempts to stall, to keep him talking, Eadweard virtually throws himself down the stairs, in his desire to be away from there, to catch the ferry he has planned to catch that will take him one step closer to his destination.

* * * * *

This is all he can think of – that his wife willingly gave herself to another man, that the child, Florado, is not his. Another man penetrated her, another man – *let me name him,* he thinks, *Harry Larkyns* – loved her, explored her contours with his lips, his fingers, with *himself.*

Everything falls into place. How she distanced herself from him, how she was always busy, how, *my God,* he thinks to himself, *how she spent his money on her lover.*

He mutters to himself under his breath, and people, he notices, avoid him. He doesn't care, he has no desire for anyone to speak to him, to try and deter him from his chosen course of action. His fingers clasp tightly around the revolver hidden beneath his coat. The metal is cool and soothing to touch, and he strokes the gun.

He remembers rows about money, always about money. How he would go away on his photography trips and find out that Flora had run up bills all over town. She had even once kept the money he'd given her to give to Mrs. Smith, he recalls, and still he talks to himself under his breath.

I told her to stay away from him, I warned her what he was like, I said, I will not tolerate this – and what did she do? Flaunted me, cuckolded me, made a fool of me. Well, no longer.

He is grateful for the speed of the ferry, even more grateful for the new railroad that will take him from Vallejo to Calistoga in four hours. *Amazing,* he thinks. *Four hours. Who would have thought? Once it would have taken me days.* And he knows that would have been too long, there would have been time for doubt, for those around him to intervene, time enough for Larkyns himself to escape. He is grateful for the modernization of San Francisco, and to the railroad. He thinks, for a moment, of his benefactor, Stanford. What will he make of what he is about to do? Eadweard wonders.

'No matter,' he says out loud. 'Larkyns deserves it.'

By the time he gets to Calistoga it is late, and it is only Eadweard's luck that he personally knows the owner of a small livery stable that sees him setting off with a horse, buggy and driver.

Eadweard tells the man he is out to find Major Harry Larkyns.

'I've heard he's at Pine Flat,' he says, casually. 'I have some news of some importance to deliver.'

The owner, checking buckles and traces, pauses. 'No,' he says. 'He was there, but he's moved on. He's at William Stuart's Yellow Jacket Mine. That's where you'll find him. He's been working as a surveyor this summer and fall.'

'Much obliged,' says Eadweard settling himself into the buggy for the drive.

As they drive into the night, Eadweard feels again the pistol in his hands. He wishes he could check it is in working order without arousing suspicion. He breathes deeply. He could ask, he supposes, a thought crossing his mind. He could simply ask.

'George?' He says to the driver, 'George, isn't it?'

The young man nods. 'Yes, Sir.'

'Is this road safe do you know?'

George nods. 'Safe enough, Sir.'

'So there is no danger of us being stopped by robbers?'

'Aint much chance of that, Sir. I drive this road often, and with so many people out here now, you're quite safe.'

'I see. Thank you.'

In the dark, Eadweard frets. Hard to ask if you can discharge your Smith & Wesson if there is no danger, but still, he thinks, perhaps he can pursue this line without suspicion if he makes himself seem a scared and nervous traveler.

'George?' he says again.

'Sir?'

'I understand what you're saying, but I am wondering, due to the lateness of the hour, and my lack of practice at travelling at this time of night, would it bother the horses – or you– if I fire my gun, just to make sure sure?'

In the dark George grins. *We've got a fraidy-cat here*, he thinks, unaware of his passenger's reputation, unaware of the thousand perilous situations Eadweard has flung himself into without a thought.

'No, Sir,' he says. 'It won't scare the horses.'

Eadweard breathes a sigh of relief, and brings out his precious weapon, aiming out of the window and high into the sky. The sound of the discharge splinters the night for a fraction of a second, and somewhere far off a dog barks, then all is quiet again, apart from the steady sound of the horses' hooves.

'Thank you,' says Eadweard. 'We can be safe now.'

'Yes Sir,' says George diplomatically, although he thinks to himself that even with a revolver he would not set much store in this old man with his long white beard and crazy blue eyes keeping them 'safe'. He chirrups to the horses, and they continue on their way, to their destination, to the house where Harry Larkyns is staying.

* * * * *

When they pull up outside the house, Eadweard feels curiously calm. Knocking on the door, he half expects Larkyns to open it, but it is another man, who invites him in.

'We're playing cribbage,' he says. 'Not exactly poker, I'll admit, but we have the ladies here, and we always welcome a fresh hand.'

'Thank you,' says Eadweard, 'but not this time. I simply have a message to deliver to Harry Larkyns, if he is with you. I won't keep him long.'

The man nods, disappears towards the back of the house. 'Harry,' his voice calls out, 'there's someone here with a message for you.'

Harry comes to the doorway, laughing over his shoulder at the same time, so that Eadweard shudders at the insouciance of him, that he can be so cheerful after what he has done to Eadweard's life.

Harry shades his head with his hand against the dark night sky. He cannot, for the life of him, make out that it is his lover's husband standing outside.

'Who are you?' He asks, curious.

Eadweard takes a deep breath. 'My name is Muybridge and I have a message for you from my wife.' He squeezes the trigger, and the bullet is true, piercing Harry's heart.

Eadweard stands there calmly as Harry claps his hand to his chest. 'My

God – what have you done?' he cries out, even as the pain sears through his body. He runs, *as if that will help,* thinks Eadweard, watching as Harry takes off through the house, and now men are arriving from everywhere, there is pandemonium. A man points his pistol at Eadweard and orders him not to move, although Eadweard is immobile, and simply shrugs at the order. He has no intention of moving. He listens keenly and he can hear through the shouting someone calling: 'It's no good… he's dead.' And Eadweard's heart, his still beating heart, is satisfied.

The men escort Eadweard inside and into the parlour, forcing him into a chair.

'I apologise for the interruption ladies,' he says, for all the world as if he has come in uninvited to a tea party.

* * * * *

If, between his arrival at the house and the death of his enemy, time stood still, if those minutes were a viscous, sticky eternity, then afterwards, it seems as if time is in a jolting, tearing hurry – where everything was calm, now it is distressingly staccato and violent.

Impossible to explain to the three men who seem to think it is necessary to guard him with their lives, that he has no intention of fleeing as they truss up his hands behind his back, and manhandle him back into the wagon, where George is still waiting, standing beside the carriage, his hands trembling on the reins, while he tries to digest what he has just heard and seen.

'What's your name?' the tall, bearded fellow who pulled his pistol out to cover Eadweard, asks the driver.

'George, Sir.'

The man nods. 'George. Well, we're commandeering your wagon here to take this man to Calistoga. We'll bring it back as soon as we're able. In the meantime, you go on into the house and someone will make you something to eat and drink. You look like you could do with it.'

Eadweard looks at the young man he led into this misadventure. 'I apologise, George, for the inconvenience,' he says again, but George cannot meet his eyes. He stares off into the distance, as if he has not even heard the words.

From the steps another man calls to George: 'Come on in, we won't bite.' Reluctantly George leaves his wagon. 'You'll look after the horses Sir, won't you?' he asks the bearded man, who seems to have put himself in charge. 'They'll be tired.'

'We'll look after them.' The bearded man looks at him keenly. 'It's not your fault,' he says, suddenly understanding what's wrong. 'You weren't to know.'

George lowers his head. 'No.'

'I tell you what… we'll take the horses back to the stable for you, and then we'll get you back to Calistoga in the morning – how would that be?'

'Thank you.' George is grateful for this kindness, Eadweard can see, and so is Eadweard on George's behalf.

'Time to go.' and so saying the bearded man leaps up into the driving seat, and they start back down the mountain at a terrifying speed.

The men talk of lynching him. The man sitting next to him, shoves him roughly.

'Hanging's too good for him,' he says. 'We should stop the horses and do it ourselves right here and now. We should avenge poor Harry's death.'

Avenge poor Harry's death?! Eadweard can't believe his ears. He feels like telling them the story, explaining the kind of monster Harry really was, but he senses the futility of it. *Even so,* he thinks, *I would rather face a jury than die right here and now.*

The bearded man, Tom, seems to be the self-appointed leader. 'No need to make things worse,' he says. 'We're taking him to Napa jail. That's what we said, and that's what we're doing.'

Chapter 15

The Riverina

He hits me.

I slump against the wall, holding my hands above my head.

'No,' I sob. 'Liam, please. I'm sorry, I'm sorry…'

He towers above me. There is desperation in this still point of-almost-silent waiting –the only sound, my teary breathing.

Shakes his head.

'Fucking bitch.' He ricochets down the hallway.

I take my chance, run to the spare room. That's a laugh, the spare room. When do we ever have people to stay? I can hear him in the kitchen. I have the time it takes him to get a beer to lock the door, to slam the chest of drawers against the door, and I manage it. I know he'll be too drunk to push it in. He may even forget to stagger back towards me, he may just sit at the table keeping up a monologue of swear words, until he stumbles to the sofa and passes out.

He'll be contrite in the morning I know. He won't remember the worst of it.

'Babe,' he'll say. 'Jeez I've got a head on me. I must have had a few too many. How about some breakfast?'

And me? What am I doing in this room? Waiting for my breathing to return to normal, waiting for panic to subside, waiting to lie down fully clothed on the bed, waiting for sleep to come, to take all of this away, to dream of my mountains, to dream of the brumbies. They come to me in my dreams, I've learned their colours, the duns and greys, the bucksins and bays, the black and white, and – my favourite – the beautiful golden palominos. Every ripple of their manes, and swish of their tails, every moving moment I'd witnessed in those herds, reminding me that freedom does exist.

I can hear you Beth, from here, from the future, asking: 'But Rosa, why didn't you leave? Rosa? What happened?'

I would have to shake my head and say, *I don't know, I don't really know*, even now, what happened. Except that I married this man, this Liam. And that once more I had mistaken lust for love, once more, just as with Martin, I had been conned into believing that someone loved me. It hurt so much that some days I thought I might just die from the hurt.

Some days I thought I really didn't care if he beat me to a physical pulp.

But I am here now, lying on the bed, dreaming of the horses, willing them to gallop through my veins, to take with them this latest memory, erase it from my body and mind, rise up with me, as I do, out of my body for the moment, rise up and out, float out with me through the ceiling, of the bedroom, up through the roof, burst out into the open inky-black night sky, turn now, look down, and you see the tops of the gumtrees surrounding the paddocks; you see, in this good season, green shoots of grass in this small 10-acre property, you see paddocks with water troughs, and in some of the paddocks you see horses. Not the wild horses of my dreams – no – these are a mixed bunch, and I might say to you, read the energy of these horses, these, in the main, are not relaxed horses. These horses are somehow unsure, in unfamiliar terrain.

These horses are waiting – just like me – for the next move.

* * * * *

Liam. He arrived in the packing shed about three months after I'd found a job on a navel orange property and boy, if I'd thought that working in a mountain lodge was hard, now I really knew the meaning of the word 'backbreaking'. At first, just another traveler on the fruit-picking route, I'd slept in the bunkhouse with the other backpackers, but gradually, as Jim and Mary realised I was going to stick around a while, I'd graduated to my own small 'donga', one of a few tiny cabins not far from the house. The first few weeks, learning the art of harvesting the navels – take the whole orange in your hand, twist and place gently in the bag your hand – all I wanted to do was to run back to the Lodge, but something kept me there, some sense that I wanted to master this challenge I seemed to have set myself.

One week, on my day off, I drive into town to ring Tony. He knew I'd left the Lodge, but we weren't in touch regularly. I would send him postcards from time to time, but distance and time had worked naturally to create a space between us.

I ring him at work, and he's pleased to hear from me.

'Rosa!' he says. 'How are you?'

We chat for a while, about this and that, about the weather, the Riverina landscape, Sydney. I ask him how his work was going: 'Fine,' he tells me. 'Busy, but fine.'

There was a pause. What we call in Spanish, a *pausa embarazada*.

'I've got something to tell you,' he says.

And I know, straightaway I know. Every muscle in my body tightens, while I wait in that split second for his news.

'I've met someone,' he says.

'Ahhh,' I say, lightly, much more lightly than I feel. 'I'm glad for you.'

'Thank you.' He pauses again, and it seems to me he's asking permission to tell me about her.

'Who is she?'

He gives a tiny exhalation of relief. I'm not going to be 'difficult'.

Strangely though, perhaps, for all the murkiness I've lived in and with all my life, clarity is a strength. Tony and I had always been clear. We weren't the kind of couple built to last a lifetime, we were friends first and foremost, who had enjoyed each other's company, and each other's bodies, but the parameters were clear, and I wasn't going to sully them now, even though deep inside, a small river of grief at the inevitable loss of what we shared, was tracing its way through my veins.

'I went home for a family gathering,' he tells me. 'She – Sofia – was there with my cousin, Ellie.'

'That's nice.' The platitude hangs in the air.

I suddenly don't want to talk. I don't want to hear that he's fallen in love, that she's the *one*. I'm sad, and a bit jealous, and a lot lonely.

'I have to go,' I tell him. 'There's a line of people waiting for the phone.'

'Oh.' He sounds a little disappointed. 'Well, never mind. I'll come and see you when I'm down that way, I'll take you out for lunch and we can catch up.'

He means it kindly, but we both know it's a lie.

'That would be nice,' I say. 'Anyway, that's great. Good luck Tony.'

And I put the phone down. Just like that. And burst into tears. Just like that. I walk back to my car, and the now all-too-familiar sense of isolation descends on me, a grey mist of rejection, of failure, of being completely and utterly alone.

I suppose, looking back, you could say that I was easy pickings, that Liam didn't exactly have to work too hard to win my bruised heart; it was pretty much out there for the taking, coincidentally, perhaps because it was the same afternoon he came into the shed. I'd once more graduated to helping with the books a few days a week, and even though this day I wasn't working, I needed to be around people, to hear the banter and the rise and fall of voices, at least.

Mary looks surprised to see me. 'What are you doing here?' she says. 'Haven't you got somewhere better to be?'

I laugh. 'Apparently not.'

He turns, the man, at the sound of my laugh.

He's at the other end of the shed talking with Jim.

He's wearing jeans, a shirt and boots. He has a mop of tousled light-brown hair, and the bluest eyes I've ever seen.

'Now that's a lovely laugh,' he says, looking at me, but talking to Jim. 'Who's this you've been hiding from me?'

Jim shifts sideways, the tiniest hint of a shift.

'That's Rosa,' he says, almost blankly.

'Rosa. Well, hi Rosa, I'm Liam. Lovely to meet you from the other side of the shed.'

'Nice to meet you, Liam.' I take a breath and turn away, only to see Mary staring at me.

He didn't ask me out straight away, but he took to dropping into the shed.

He had a small business trucking horses around New South Wales and Victoria, and he doubled up during citrus season, using his truck to deliver oranges, or sometimes even loading the back with horses, and the front with enough boxes to add a little 'cream' as he called it, on the top.

I began to wait for the sound of his voice.

'G'day Mary, Rosa, how've you been? Missed me?'

'Not one bit,' Mary would say, cheerfully, while I put my head down, and pretended he wasn't there. But he knew, oh, he knew, that while he chatted, passing over money, picking up boxes, talking about the weather, crop prices, horse prices, anything and everything that passed for conversation in those parts, he knew that I was glancing at him, drinking in the maleness of him, his laughter, and the twinkle in his eyes.

Mary warns me. She's blunt about it.

'If he asks you out, don't go,' she says, one day, just after he's left the shed.

Of course, I was curious, and after all, wasn't it curiosity that killed the cat?

'Why not?'

She eyes me thoughtfully. 'He's a nice bloke, Rosa, but there's rumours. He hits the bottle, they say, and when he does – well, I don't want to tell tales out of school but there's been a few girls crying after a night out with him.'

'Oh,' I say, and of course it piques my interest even more. *Perhaps,* I think to myself with the insane arrogance of someone about to enter a relationship with an abuser, *perhaps they weren't right for him.*

And for a while, it did seem like that. From our first 'date' – a picnic at the side of a river – he was kind, and funny, and gentle. Hardly anybody's idea of an abuser. We only kissed that day, nothing more, but it was obvious it would be more, and quickly as well, because there was pure fire in the kiss, a recognition that our bodies were made to fit each other.

In the years since, I've often thought about my grandmother. I think this is how it was for her with her lover, with charming, feckless, unfaithful Harry. She could no more have resisted him than she could get out of the way of a tornado. How much of that is pre-destined? How much just simply that I had no boundaries, no sense and a whole heap of loneliness going on?

But in the next few months even Mary changed her tune. Seeing me so happy, seeing Liam so cheerful, she said to me one day: 'Well I wouldn't have credited it if I hadn't seen it, Rosa, but it looks like you've tamed the Wild Boy.'

And I smiled the smile of a cat that had got the cream, the smile of a woman whose body was loved inside and out, and when he asked me, just three months later to marry him it seemed the most natural, the sanest thing to do in all of the world.

I remember that I rang Tony to tell him. He had an odd reaction.

'You're not doing this because I'm getting married?' he asked.

'Of course not. I love him.'

'Good,' he said. 'I just wouldn't want you to do something you might regret.'

After our chat I was outraged. I wondered how he could possibly have the arrogance to assume that *he* was anything to do with my decision. What it made clear to me at the time was that the friendship with Tony, I decided, (with a remarkable amount of childish petulance I can see now from this distance), was over.

Our wedding was beautiful, simple and fun. Jim and Mary had lent us the barn. We made a virtue of the orange boxes, and used them as seats, with piles of them everywhere. We dragged in some old pieces of farm equipment, bought some bales of hay, chucked around some old saddles and bridles, and *hey presto* – we had an American barn party on our hands. We had a barbecue outside, and everybody bought food and wine. This was a concept that astonished me, even after a few years in Australia. The idea that you could get married, and people would bring food and wine to it, well, it didn't seem right to me, but Liam was sure.

'They'd be concerned if we didn't do it, Rosa,' he said. 'They know we're not rolling in it.'

I told him about the day I'd first gone on a picnic in Sydney with Gino and the family, and they'd said everyone was bringing a plate.

'You don't have to if you don't want to Rosa,' Gino said, but I thought to myself that it was a great idea, and so I took along an empty plate, a knife and fork and a glass. It had set the tone for the entire afternoon with everybody taking turns to rib me.

Liam thought it was the funniest thing he'd ever heard. 'I'm marrying a Mexican,' he said, shaking his head. 'How did that happen?'

Well, it happened, and it was a beautiful day. There was absolutely no indication of the chasm that would open up under me in such a little time. Even now I wonder how he did it. How did he disguise his true personality from me so completely for all those months – or was the Liam McDermott I knew for that time, the *real* Liam McDermott? Was the man who made his presence felt only a few weeks later, such a short time later, the interloper, an illusion, even perhaps an evil spirit?

The first time was mild of course, because this is the thing about abusers and their abuse. They know, somewhere in them, that if they came at you with full force straight away, you'd leave. You wouldn't have built up the months of doubts, of insecurities, of desperately wanting to be loved, of fearing what will happen if you do leave.

They're clever, far too clever for that.

Still, with Liam, I'm sure the alcohol played a large part.

Do you hear that? Do you hear that I can still make an excuse for him all these decades later. As if being drunk makes abusing someone less terrible.

It was, of course, what Jim and Mary had warned me about. That he turned, and when he turned, he could be violent. But I hadn't seen it in him. He'd curtailed his drinking during our 'courtship', during the honeymoon period. Maybe, I think, even now, maybe he was truly happy with me during that time, and so he didn't feel the need for it; maybe he was just simply on his best behaviour for a few weeks; but whatever it was, there came a Friday evening when he went down to the pub, and I chose to stay home. He was late back, later than I thought he would be, so I went to bed.

It was in the early hours of the morning that I hear him come back, hear him curse the dogs as he walks past them, and they start to bark.

'You fuckin' mongrels,' he snarls. 'Shut the fuck up.'

But you know, I'm not that surprised at the slurring and the swearing, and the stumbling as he staggers in through the front door. I almost think it's funny. He's had a night out on the town with the boys, and he's drunk, I think. I get out of bed, pull my dressing gown on and go to offer him something – a cup of tea, painkillers, I don't know – something to comfort him.

It's when I see him that I realise how drunk he is. His eyes are red, he's holding himself up on the back of a chair, and he looks, to use a word that's become popular since – feral.

He stares at me for just a second before firing the first shot. 'What the fuck are you looking at?'

'Nothing.' I smile at him, still oblivious, still feeling kind. 'You obviously had a good time. Sit down and I'll get you a cup of tea.'

'What the fuck do you mean, I had a good time?' Before I can even move, he springs away from the chair and pins me against the wall.

'Liam!' I instinctively put my hand up to take his down, but he presses it in further. 'I didn't mean anything. I meant…' I pause. 'I meant it seemed like you'd enjoyed yourself.'

'Of course I fucking enjoyed myself,' he almost spits at me. 'I wasn't here with you pretending to play the happy Mr & Mrs, was I?'

I remember the terror that ran through me as if it was yesterday.

Not Martin I think, *not all over again.* My eyes widen, and that seems to make him even more angry.

'Don't fucking look at me like that,' he says. I lower my eyes and say nothing, silently praying for him to take his hand from my neck. The next few seconds seem like an eternity. We stand in this dark limbo, his breath thick and heavy with alcohol pouring over me, his thumb and forefinger pressing into each side of my neck, my silence as loud as his breathing, until he suddenly flings himself away from me.

'Fuck you,' he says, stumbling down the hall towards the bedroom.

I stand there, silent and terrified. I wait until the bedroom door closes and then I walk as quietly and quickly as I can to the spare room, which isn't really a spare room at all but more a room full of spare junk Liam's accumulated over the years. But it has a sofa, and the spare linen in it, and enough furniture to block the door, and I swear I hardly draw a breath until I'm in that room safely. I lie on the sofa, and draw myself up into a little ball, waiting for any sound that might tell me Liam had got up again, but soon, blessedly soon, I hear the sound of snoring, loud enough to tell me he was out for the count, and I can relax, but while my mind kept telling me that I was safe, or safe enough, my body shivers with fright for what seems like hours, until finally, just as the first bird sounds in the sky, and the palest dawn light shines through the blind, I fall into a deep sleep.

Why didn't I leave that night? Why didn't I just throw my meagre possessions into the cruiser and head off to Mary and Jim's. They would have taken me in, no questions asked.

I think I was ashamed. Ashamed, and of course, surprised. I wanted, I suppose, to believe that this was an anomaly, that it was a mistake and it wouldn't happen again.

Can you read that sentence, Beth, and not feel a chill for the icy blast of despair that was so inevitably about to enter my life?

Can you, even if you, my friend, have never felt the weight of a man's fist into your face, into your back, into your lungs, into your stomach, can you imagine just for a moment what deluded optimism, what fire of love and lust would keep me there? What level of contrition would bring me to open my heart again and again?

And of course, he is contrite.

I wake to the smell of bacon and eggs, coffee and toast wafting into my room, a smell of such normality that for a second, I wonder if I'd dreamt the night before, but my hand moves unhesitatingly to my neck, to the bruising on it where he'd held me so tight, and again a sense of dread washes through me.

What had he done? What had I done? What had we done?

'Come on,' Liam's voice is light and cheerful. 'Time to rise and shine Rosie girl. Coffee's up...'

I wrap the blanket around me, move the chair I'd put under the doorhandle and walk out into the light of day.

'Morning,' he says. 'Jeez I've got a headache on me. I must have put away a few too many last night...'

He turns back to the pans, while I stand there, bemused to the core. Did he really not remember? Was it a one-off, an aberration, should I mention it, or just let it go and hope for the best.

I search for the words. 'Yes,' I say. 'Well, you weren't quite yourself that's for sure.'

He laughs. 'I can only imagine.'

My hand flies up to my neck again.

'Liam?' I *have* to ask, I *have* to know if he remembered anything.

'Yes?'

'You... well... you were very angry last night, you actually scared me. Don't you remember?'

His body goes very still, that's what I recall now. How still he was, his back to me at the stove.

'Did I?' he says. 'Sorry Rosie. It won't happen again.' He turns to me and opens his arms. 'I'd never do anything to hurt you, you know that.'

And so it begins.

Will I spare you the gory details? How far I sank? The make-up I bought to disguise the bruises – the long-sleeved shirts, the glasses. Jim and Mary weren't fooled. Within a few weeks of the cycle starting, they'd heard he was down at the pub every night. One day in the office at the back of the shed, I was standing by the filing cabinet sorting through some papers, and Jim and Mary were talking next to me. Mary suddenly flung her arm up to shoo away a fly, and like a frightened horse, I flinched away, covering my face with my hand. She looked at me intently.

'Are you okay?' she asked me gently.

'Yes.' I lied quickly, easily. 'I'm fine. You just startled me.'

She exchanged a glance with Jim.

I wonder, even now, why didn't I just break down and tell them then and there? But the truth is, I know what it was at the time, it was that dreaded pride of mine; the curse of anyone with Spanish blood. How could I have been so wrong? And of course, they'd warned me, which made it worse. Plus, I'd so quickly fallen into a habit of protection. I tried to work every day that Liam was at home, and to take my days off when he was away trucking horses. But it wasn't much use, because it was not the days that were the problem, other than the result from the abuse the night before. In the day there was remorse, and sorrow and promises not to do it again. It was the night that was a battlefield.

But despite everything, I clung to loving him. I didn't want to lose another man, another life. I was sure I could change him, if only I loved him well enough, and never, in my wildest dreams could I have imagined why he was drinking, and the wild sad story that was about to unfold.

It's blurry now, that time frame. From this great distance I can't quite pin it down, it's more like a memory of emotion than dates and times and places, but what I *do* know is that after some months of the sad and dreadful turn our marriage had taken, our lives were changed irrevocably early one morning with the arrival of the police at our door. It was a morning when Liam was due to pick up horses, and take them north, and even in his addled state he never drank the night before a job, so I was always safe that night, or as safe as I had come to feel I could be in his presence. I remember I'd cooked dinner; he went out to check on the horses, we watched television. Nothing strange, or bizarre or out of the ordinary, nothing to prepare me for the next morning.

I heard them arrive while Liam still slept. I wondered what the noise was, two cars in our driveway. Somebody dropping something off for

Liam, I supposed, waiting for the cars to drive off, but instead there was the sound of doors slamming, and then a loud knock on our door.

Imagine this if you will:

I get out of bed, grab my dressing gown and peer out in the early-morning light to see four policemen at our door.

'Liam!' I turn to him, but he's still snoring loudly. 'There's police here.'

He doesn't even move a muscle, so I shrug. It's probably nothing I think, maybe one of his mates from the pub's got into trouble. I go down the hallway to the front door and open it.

One of the police, a tall man, moves forward.

'Mrs McDermott?'

I nod. 'Yes,' I say. 'That's me.'

'Is your husband Liam McDermott here?'

'Yes,' I say, still not worried, still just curious. 'He's asleep. Can I help you?'

'We have a search warrant with us,' he says, his voice as cold as steel. 'Please get him. We need to search the property, and any vehicles you might have.'

'For what?' I'm outraged. 'Why? What on earth could we possibly have that could interest you? We have horses and fruit here, that's it.'

The four of them exchange glances. I can see the look that passes between them, a look of whether I know something. But I know nothing. Nothing.

'I'll get him,' I say. 'I'm sure he'll be happy to answer your questions.' But just as I turn away, Liam appears behind me.

'Can I help you officer?' he asks, cool as a cucumber.

The tall one passes over the search warrant.

'Liam McDermott,' he says, 'you'll need to stay here with Detective Rowan, while we search your property. We have reason to believe that you have drugs in your possession.'

What does he do, this Liam of mine? This man who has become such a stranger to me in the past few months. The man I've loved so intensely, the man I now feel so unsafe around. I watch him closely. He shrugs.

'Look away,' he says. 'You won't find anything here. Knock yourselves out.'

The tall detective looks at him curiously. Is he disappointed, I wonder, at this cool as a cucumber reply?

'Oh,' he says, 'Mr McDermott, we will, and we'll start with your truck.'

I think I see a ripple of fear, a widening of his eyes, a line around his mouth. Does the detective notice it?

Liam shrugs again. 'Help yourself,' he says.

Three of the policemen stride purposefully back towards one of the vans. They open the back, and two large German Shepherds jump out – sniffer dogs, I'm guessing, and when I glance at Liam this time, I see him wipe his hand across his forehead. I've seen it before, when he's worried about something. I feel a sudden cold stone in the pit of my stomach. I think I might vomit.

I realise I have no idea what you call a policeman.

'Excuse me,' I say as politely as possible to the man who is obviously 'guarding' us. 'Would you mind if I get dressed, and make a cup of coffee? Would that be all right?'

As soon as I've said it, I think I sound absurd. We're apparently in the middle of a drug bust, and I'm asking if I can make coffee, but the policeman, a constable I find out later, looks me up and down, and seems to decide I'm no immediate threat. He shrugs.

'I guess so,' he says. 'We may as well sit inside as stand outside.'

And with that we all three troop in. I lead the way to the kitchen and put the kettle on.

'I'll be back in a moment,' I tell the young man.

Liam looks at me as if I have a secret plan, but I have no secret plan at all. All I have is a desire to have proper clothes on, and a desire to have just a few moments to process this – because along with the stone in my stomach is something else. I won't call it jubilation, because that sounds too harsh, too celebratory, but some tiny piece of me is thinking: *Perhaps this is the end of it. Perhaps I can tell them he hits me. Perhaps I can be safe again.*

By the time I get back to the kitchen, I can see that Liam is visibly tense. He's tapping the table with a couple of fingers, and 'our' guard is sitting quietly at the table.

'Coffee?' I say brightly.

'Thank you. I don't mind if I do. White and two sugars, please Mrs McDermott.'

I almost say, *please don't call me that. You have no idea what that name has become to me,* but I smile. 'Of course,' I say. 'And you, Liam?'

He looks up at me, and I recognise this look. It's the look of fear. I know it because I know what passes through my body when he's about to hit me, and in that instant, I know that he's guilty, and that they are going to find something.

'Coffee,' he says. 'Yeah. Alright. Why not?'

Oh, sweet Jesus, this waiting seems to go on forever. In my head I recite the Lord's Prayer in Spanish:

Padre nuestro, que estás en el cielo. Santificado sea tu nombre. Venga tu reino.

Hágase tu voluntad en la tierra como en el cielo.

Danos hoy nuestro pan de cada día. Perdona nuestras ofensas,

como también nosotros perdonamos a los que nos ofenden.

No nos dejes caer en tentación y líbranos del mal. Amén.

Over and over, Padre nuestro: Our Father... forgive us our sins... I am a child again, at church with my parent/grandparents, my sister/mother, my life is tumbling as I sit there, my hands around my cup of coffee, the policeman silently looking out of the window, Liam tapping the table slightly, just with his index finger – he won't look me in the eye. What has he been doing? *Our Father, who art in heaven...*

And then, suddenly, the sound of dogs barking, silence again, then ripping sounds, and Liam looks at me now, straight in the eyes, and I can see the terror in him, and I know his goose is cooked.

For the first time, it occurs to me, he may have cooked *mine* too, that I am implicated in this thing, and I have absolutely no idea what it is. My blood is doing the strangest things. I am hot, and cold, I feel as if I might faint. I feel jubilant. They will take him away. I won't be hit again. I feel desperation: *my boy*, I think, *my darling boy, what happened, what have you done?* I feel fear. What does this mean? Does it mean prison? Does it mean the annhilation of another life? How can I cope if everything I thought was solid disappears again, and yet, if it takes away this pain, this cycle into which I have become locked, this must be good.

I am innocent, I know that, but already a tiny voice is battering me. I didn't do enough, it tells me, it was my fault; I should have changed him. I didn't love him enough to make it work. On and and on it runs the river of unreason, while we wait in that kitchen, and I stand up and hold on to the back of the chair, to keep myself present, at least physically, in the universe.

Until, and even though by now, I know we're both expecting it, there they are, the other three of them, tall and burly, dressed in their blue, taking up so much space.

The main one, the detective I later learn in charge of this case, steps forward. 'Liam McDermott, you're under arrest on suspicion of possession and dealing of marijuana and cocaine,' he says, his face as blank as a wall, stony-faced, literally. 'You do not have to say anything, but it may harm your defence if you do not mention when questioned on something which you later rely on in court. Anything you do say may be given in evidence. Do you understand?'

Liam nods mutely.

Not enough for the man in blue. 'Do you understand?' he says again, as he nods to one of his men, who steps forward with handcuffs. Handcuffs.

'Yes, officer.' Liam stands up and holds out his hands. He is quiet, biddable, as if every ounce of lifeforce has left his body.

The detective looks at me. 'Mrs McDermott, we would like to take you down to the station for questioning. Would you agree to accompany us?' He's remarkably polite, so polite that of course I don't understand that I could say 'No'. I'm just feeling a huge surge of relief that I'm not being arrested as well.

'Yes,' I say. 'I'll come with you.'

And so we leave, me in one police car with two policemen, Liam in another with the other two.

I had asked if I could feed the dogs and horses before we left, and to my surprise they'd agreed. I felt already as if I was a criminal, as if I must have known something, even though that was not the case. We'd walked across to the dogs' yard, and to the paddocks, where the horses were waiting for their morning hay, oblivious to their sudden change of circumstance. It was lucky we had no overnighters, only Liam's three, I'd never quite taken to them, I wasn't yet a horse woman, but I didn't wish them harm, and I enjoyed looking out of the window watching them graze.

But now, well, what would happen to them? *I'll have to care for them,* I thought, and to my surprise the idea was pleasing. As I collected hay from the barn, and the policemen helped – again to my surprise – I looked sideways at the truck. Where had they found the drugs? They'd closed it up again and it looked as it always did, so where had these illegal substances been hiding. I decided that ignorance was my best defence and pushed the thought aside. With the dogs off their chains and in their day-yard, and breakfast for them done, I smiled brightly at the men in blue.

'I'm finished,' I said, with as much cheer as I could muster.

I need to speed up here. I need, I'm sorry, to shortchange you a little. This morning I was out feeding Thor and Freya and it happened again – that pain, a squeezing pain. I know what it's warning me about, I know what's coming. I don't know when, exactly, but I know it's on its way, darling Beth, and there's nothing any of us can do about it. And even if there was, you need to know, I don't want anything done. I'm spent. I don't want to spend my last months, weeks, days, hours in a hospital being jabbed and treated to no effect other than to delay the inevitable.

I've had a long and interesting life, and in these last few months the often elusive quality of happiness, the state we all so ardently wish for, has come upon me so often and stayed so long, that I begin to understand that my time here is almost done. I've learned, I suppose, that no matter where I came from, no matter what has been done to me by whom, no matter the cruel blows of fate, no matter how alone and cast off I might have felt, I am not defined by any of these things. Tue res mi familia Beth, decreed by the laws of the universe, for reasons neither of us may fully ever understand, and my other 'familia', my horses, well, they run forever in my veins now, and if that was Liam's only gift to me, I have a lot to be grateful for.

Let's wind it up for now. Perhaps, if I feel I have time, I will come back, dot the i's and cross the t's, but to give you closure, to give you chronology, I didn't realise at the time, that when I was answering all the questions the police asked me as truthfully as I could, they threw in a small curve ball, which I didn't see coming, and to be honest, even if I had I don't think it would have changed what I said.

They said to me at one point: 'So last Saturday night, when you and Liam were at home, he didn't receive any phone calls to your knowledge…´

´Not to my knowledge,´ I said, ´because he wasn't at home.´

Am I making this exist in retrospect? I can't be sure that I actually witnessed this tiny flicker pass between the two detectives. I can see it now, but I honestly don't think I saw it then.

It wasn't long after that they let me go, they thanked me for my cooperation, but they would not let me see Liam.

And in quick succession, a précis if you will, of who, what, where, when and why – I had betrayed him. Perhaps he had expected that I would automatically understand he needed an alibi, perhaps he thought I loved him still. And in a way, he would have been right about the 'love', at least at first, because my confusion at my loss of him was so extreme that after the young policeman drove me home, I dragged the doona from the bed, I locked all the doors, I put the chocks of wood inside the windows, I closed the curtains, and I curled up on the floor and cried like a baby, waiting for its mother to come and pick it up, waiting for the comforting sweet sounds of unconditional love to soothe my broken heart and my still-bruised body. Or even perhaps, and much worse, waiting for blows to rain down on me, to tell me that I was still alive, and that Liam was still there.

How long would I have stayed like that if I hadn't heard the dogs bark, a car pull up, the sound of feet on gravel? In my foetal state, I froze, the tears stopping as suddenly as they had started. Instantly I imagined it was the police again, that they'd come for me this time, that Liam had told them a story about me, had dobbed me in for something I hadn't done.

But then the voice came: ´Rosa, are you okay? Rosa! It's Mary – we heard… are you okay.´

Into clouds of relief my spirit fell, the tears falling again, but sweet tears this time, tears of sugar, not salt I swear, as I hauled myself up from the floor, and unlocked the door, and threw myself into this woman's arms.

(It's only now, in this instant, that it occurs to me, how lucky I was that everywhere I went – curiously, until I came here, and became the older woman – there was an older woman there to watch out for me. Did my maternal sister/mother, my mother/grandmother have something to do with this? Did my paternal grandmother, the luckless Flora, know that her die was cast when Eadweard was acquitted, when she became the shamed one, with no-one to turn to, no-one to comfort her? If I had any hand in organizing these women's businesses, in Sydney, in the mountains, here on the flat Riverina, then I should thank myself for some deep foresight, because without Mary there for the next few months I am not sure what would have become of me.)

Police. Court. Law. Murder in one century. Drugs, abuse and a woman who was lucky to escape with her life in the next. What a strange family history. And while we are waiting, Beth, for me to tell you the next piece of the puzzle, the strange and unusual circumstances that allowed me to arrive in this valley, we can't leave Eadweard where he is, can we? Because even though we have passed the mid-point in this strange tale, and passed that most dramatic moment, the shot that ended Harry's life, the consequence of which would be that Flora would soon be dead, we still have Eadweard's trial to come, and you will read how a guilty man became, against all odds, innocent.

* * * * *

Where was Flora the night Eadweard shot her lover? Not, according to history, in San Francisco. Still, in fact, away in Oregon, hiding perhaps from Eadweard, and who knows, from Harry as well?

Patrick Mulligan is not one to mince words.

'I am sorry to have to tell you,' he says, 'that your husband has been arrested on a murder charge, and he is currently being held in Napa jail, pending his trial.'

'I see.' Flora holds on to the side of the table, her knuckles white. 'Do you know who his victim was?' She knows, of *course* she knows, but she must hear it from their lips, she must hear his name spoken.

'Yes ma'am, we do.' Mulligan pauses for a moment. 'It was one Major Harry Larkyns. Was this man known to you?'

Flora's body crumples underneath her, and the sobs – she can hear them herself, as if they are coming from somewhere else, from someone else, and she is powerless to stop them – are answer enough. The detective exchanges glances with his sergeant, indicating clearly enough that the younger man is to stoop and help her up; the detective has no desire to touch a woman who has cuckolded her husband and caused her lover's death. Such a woman is not the sort of person he understands, he thinks.

Florado, confused by the strange sound coming from his mother, crumples up his face and starts to cry as well, and this time Mulligan has no problem with comforting him. He scoops him up in the manner of a seasoned father. 'Shhh, little one,' he says. 'Everything will be all right.'

At the table, Flora slumps forward, crying still but more silently. Mulligan gestures to the kettle. 'Sergeant Waters,' he says. 'We will make Mrs. Muybridge a cup of tea.'

'Thank you.' Flora raises her tear-stained face to him, and he cannot help but be moved by her beauty. He wonders what will become of her.

'What will become of me?' she says, as if she has read his mind. 'What will become of me? Of us?'

As Sergeant Waters places the tea in front of her, Mulligan finds it in his heart to offer her comfort, however false it maybe.

'I am sure you will be looked after, ma'am,' he says.

She nods. 'Yes. Thank you.'

Chapter 16

Napa Jail

They treat him so roughly, throwing him out of the carriage, pushing him in through the door, forcing him into a chair, Eadweard could almost smile with the foolishness of it. He is one, and they are three – he has no weapon, and no intention of hurting anyone. His work is finished.

The sheriff, a slight, nervous man, is at pains to make sure no injustice is being done. While he's completing the paperwork, Eadweard sits quietly on the bench, flanked by two of his bodyguards.

'So you are sure,' the sheriff asks the big, bearded man in front of him who seems to have appointed himself the unofficial sheriff, 'that this man was the man who shot your friend?'

The man nods fiercely. 'It was him and only him, sheriff, ask him yourself, he won't deny it.'

The sheriff turns his head towards Eadweard, who simply inclines his head in agreement.

'You don't deny you shot this man dead?'

'I don't deny it,' says Eadweard, calmly.

The sheriff can't help feeling a slight frisson of pleasure that he has a real murder to deal with – them being in less and less supply in recent years.

'What is your name?' he asks the prisoner.

'Eadweard,' says the man, and spells it: 'E.A.D.W.E.A.R.D Muybridge,' and for good measure and from experience, spells his surname also.

The name means nothing to the sheriff, but one of the self-appointed bodyguards leans forward.

'I know that name now I think of it,' he says, his brow furrows with the effort of recollection. 'Harry mentioned the name…' he exchanges looks with the bearded man. 'You're a photographer, are you not?'

'That is correct,' says Eadweard, politely.

'Well,' says the bearded man, looking down at the sheriff. 'San Francisco photographer shoots dead his wife's lover… you'll be all over the papers in a couple of days.'

Eadweard is surprised to hear this precise rendering down of events, and yet at the same time, he could almost, if it were appropriate, he thinks, congratulate the man for putting it so succinctly.

An hour or so later when everything is complete, and Muybridge is safely locked up in his cell, the sheriff contemplates that statement. He rocks back and forth on his chair for a few moments. Five o'clock in the morning, not too early, surely, he thinks to call the editor of the local paper – before the big wigs move in, he thinks.

* * * * *

Eadweard is not unhappy in the cell. He lies down on the small bed and wraps himself in the blanket, and stares at the ceiling. He has no idea what tomorrow will bring, lawyers, he supposes, journalists certainly. Will it bring Flora? he wonders to himself, although he thinks not. He wonders when Larkyn's funeral will be, and whether Flora will go. His mind allows itself to wander into fantasy – Flora arrives, with Florado in her arms, to reassure him Florado, is in fact, his child, and that she understands why he did what he did, and that she will stand by him. Soon, however, even the force of this misplaced optimism is overcome by exhaustion, and finally, he sleeps.

Chapter 17

Flora

Flora returned to San Francisco after Harry's death. She would have to, wouldn't she, Beth? She would need to be where she'd last seen him, where her home had been for the last few years, where she'd known some happiness and love in her life.

I don't know where she stayed, and that bothers me. I can't think she went to her marital home, but in a way why should she *not* have gone there? She would still have had possessions there, a key to the door; it would still be paid for at this time. Perhaps she is strong enough at this stage to do this, to go back to the rooms where she has loved two men, perhaps she even imagines that although she has lost her lover, and her husband, the fact that her husband is guilty will mean that she might somehow be able to achieve her heart's desire – true independence.

Perhaps, initially, she wasn't going to go to the funeral; perhaps she didn't think she could bear it, but then when the day dawned fine and bright, and she had managed to put aside her early morning tears, she finds herself, almost against her own will, dressing in black. She carefully chooses each item of clothing to disguise, rather than draw attention to herself. She wants no one to recognise her.

'I wish I could take you little man,' she says to Florado, who is playing on the floor, 'but you would give me away, I fear.'

She can feel the familiar sensation of tears rising, unbidden, but she swallows and keeps on. She seems to have cried her whole body out in the past few days, she thinks. Her eyes have sunk, and she has dark lines around them, even her skin feels dehydrated from lack of moisture, from the loss of her tears.

She went to see Mrs. Smith, slipping out of the house late one afternoon when she hoped there was no chance of a photographer or a reporter jumping out at her, as had happened the first few days.

In the same parlour where her husband had found the photograph, she accosts the nurse.

'You told him,' she says. 'Why did you tell him?'

Susan Smith feels a surge of anger at the young woman in front of her, she cannot believe Fora had so misunderstood the possible consequences of her behaviour that even now she is passing the blame.

'He saw the photograph, Flora. He read the inscription.' Flora knows she called her 'Flora' on purpose. There will be no more Mrs. Muybridge for her.

'Where is Hatty? Is she in?' Suddenly Flora hopes to guide the conversation back to safe ground. She does not want to feel the nurse's blanket condemnation of her. But Hatty, well, Hatty has been her friend these past few years, even working at Rolufsen's as Flora had done in her time. They'd taken to each other immediately, and she misses her friend.

'Harriett is out,' says Smith, of her daughter. 'She will not be back until later.' She vouchsafes no further information, but the message is clear – there is to be no more friendship. An icy blast whips around Flora's heart, and a foreboding so deep that it is all she can do to stand up with any degree of dignity to take her leave.

As Flora leaves her former nurse's house, Susan Smith does not even bother to stand up.

'You can see yourself out,' she says, and Flora understands that this is the least of what Mrs Smith wants to say, that in fact she wants to pour insult after insult onto Flora, so that Flora will truly understand what her nurse thinks of her, and that she has, in fact, hated her.

But now, dressed and ready to go to her lover's funeral, Flora gathers up Florado so she can leave him with the neighbours for a few hours and steps out into the bright San Francisco sunshine.

* * * * *

She need not have worried that anyone would recognise her. The funeral is a much larger affair she had imagined it would be. She is dressed in black, with a veil, and nobody pays any attention to her. She is just another mourner in the eclectic crowd gathered to farewell her lover. She recognises some of them: journalists from the newspaper he wrote for, actors and actresses from the shows he reviewed, some of them with her at his side. She can see the coffin from where she is sitting near the back of the church, and it causes her heart to spasm. Some part of her refuses to believe that her Harry is in there, that he will never again walk this earth, put his arms around her, kiss her, whisper sweet blandishments to her. How can it be, she asks herself, that he was alive only a few days ago, and now because of Eadweard, he is not.

And still the tears fall, even when she is not sobbing, they simply fall, as if even her eyes are in mourning.

As the coffin leaves the church, there is a commotion, a woman – Flora recognises her at once as an actress she's seen around the place – breaks free from the pew and throws a huge bouquet of flowers onto the coffin. The actress sobs uncontrollably following close behind the coffin as the coffin bearers leave the church. 'Harry,' this woman wails. 'Harry.'

Flora clasps her hand to heart. She wants to demand of Harry: *What is this? Who is she? Why is she crying? Was there somebody else then, all along? Where you just playing with me?*

It's too much for her, the idea that Harry wasn't faithful to her; the implication that she cannot even treasure her memories of herself as his only love, too hard to bear. She hurries away. She cannot stay to see the coffin being lowered into the ground. She must get back, she thinks, back to her home, to her child, to something that will ground her back into the reality of daily life. *I will divorce Eadweard,* she thinks. *He will have to provide for me and for Florado.*

Just for a moment she allows herself to imagine a brighter future, and it comforts her body and her senses to hold the possibility close to herself that everything might, after all work out for the best. Even without Harry.

Chapter 18

The Trial

In some ways Eadweard finds jail surprisingly comforting. From the moment he was shoved, much more roughly than was necessary, to his way of thinking, into the small cell that he now occupies, it was as if a huge weight had been lifted from him. He felt it the moment he shot Harry Larkyns. Eadweard suddenly knew, with the utmost clarity, what had been wrong with him these last few years, even since before Flora had become pregnant with Florado. He winces now at the memory of the child's name, conjured up by both of them as a loving conjunction of everything he thought was good between them that was, in fact, just a travesty.

What had been wrong with him, the unease he had felt for these past four years was that Flora, his wife – *his wife* – had been sleeping with another man.

Lying on his narrow bed, Eadweard often contemplates this fact, sometimes with a cold fury, sometimes with a deep, dark pain. A dizzying array of emotions, from heartbroken grief to a huge relief that he is as rid of her as he is of *him,* can visit him anytime of the day or night.

On the whole, Eadweard does not mind his incarceration. His needs have always been simple, and once the sheriff determined that his prisoner was, in fact, a gentleman, Eadweard has been allowed to bring in anything he wants to make his life comfortable. His meals come from the nearby hotel, he has clean, wholesome bedding, a writing desk and books. He has lived in conditions with much less than this, and he finds it accords him, when he is not obsessing over what has happened, a certain simple peace to be in this small space.

His friends are impressed, even if they are somewhat disturbed and confused by his detached acceptance of the stark reality that he is a murderer.

Rulofsen, for instance, visiting him in the first week, cannot help but be curious about his friend and colleague's state of mind. When the news had spread like wildfire through the city, he had turned to his wife. 'I saw him,' he'd said, and couldn't quite determine if he enjoyed the vicarious thrill he felt run through his body: 'I saw him just before he caught the ferry to go and shoot that poor man.'

'It is not what we are used to in San Francisco these days,' his wife replied with her customary common sense.

'No,' he said. 'No indeed.'

Of course, there was an unlooked-for consequence of the press coverage and Muybridge's notoriety. The gallery had been flooded with people all week wanting to buy a print. Sitting with him in his cell, having passed over a good supply of books and writing paper, Rulofsen mentions this.

'You're making more money in jail, than you could out of it,' he tells Muybridge.

Eadweard is surprised. 'How?' he asks.

Rulofsen shakes his head. 'Because everybody is talking about you. You are the cause célèbre of the moment. I'd hazard a guess there wouldn't be a dinner party or social gathering where you name doesn't come up.'

'Really?' Eadweard looks up out of the tiny, barred window – his only glimpse of the outside these days. 'What do they say?'

'Well,' Rulofsen pauses, not wanting to condone his colleague's action, but wanting, too, to pass on comfort. 'You would be surprised how many people sympathize with... well, with what you did.'

'Yes.' Eadweard points to his desk. 'Look at these letters. Not a one, not even from women, condemning me.'

They look at each other, the word 'condemn' hanging between them. If he is found guilty of murder in the first degree, Eadweard will be condemned to death. This they both know. Rulofsen's heart is heavy. *How can Muybridge get off,* he wonders to himself. *How can it be possible?* He murdered – he admits it, what, or who, can possibly save him? And yet Eadweard, as if reading his thoughts, stays calm.

'It's not over yet,' he says. 'I have good lawyers.'

'Do you have help?' Rulofsen knows full well that Eadweard, who cares almost nothing for money, (at least when he's the one spending it) a serious character flaw in Rulofsen's opinion, does not have enough to cover massive legal bills.

Eadweard nods. 'I will have enough, thank you. Stanford will help.'

'That's good news.' Rulofsen is relieved. Leland Stanford's bankroll would be almost limitless, and within that will lie his friend's best chance.

'He's sent Pendegast to see me.'

Rulofsen nods his head vigorously. 'With him at the helm you will have a good chance, my friend.'

'He wants me to plead insanity.' Eadweard gazes up and out of his small window. 'But I am not insane.'

Rulofsen, who is not quite so sure, acquiesces nevertheless. 'No,' he says, agreeably, 'but perhaps to be found insane is better than the alternative if you are found guilty – which is death, Eadweard, you must know that.'

There is a long pause, so that Rulofsen begins to wonder if his friend has even heard him. But Eadweard at last turns to him.

'You know,' he says conversationally, 'I righted a wrong. That is all.'

Rulofsen pushes back his hat and scratches his head. 'But that is not how society sees it, Eadweard, you must know that.'

'I've never been much of a one for "society", Rulofsen. Indeed,' he says, his face suddenly lighting up, 'once this is over, I shall go somewhere where "society" can claim no hold over me....' He grasps the sides of his temples with his hands. 'But where?' he asks. 'Where shall I go? Where shall I go? I know... yes... South America. As far away as possible from all of this. Rulofsen, that's it! The steamship company – I talked to them some time ago.'

Eadweard stands up, pacing, his long legs eating up the tiny cell. He runs his hands through his hair. 'Yes!' he says, excitedly, 'that's the idea.'

Rulofsen stays quiet, he doesn't like to say that perhaps the steamship company will not want to sponsor a murderer, or even worse, and what he suspects will be the case, that Muybridge simply cannot escape a guilty verdict, by virtue of the very fact that he is guilty.

* * * * *

Pendegast is at him again the next day.

'My dear Sir,' he says, with just the slightest note of exasperation in his voice. 'It must be insanity. There is no other possibility.'

Eadweard protests again, but with a little less certainty. He is being worn down by the pressure of it all. 'But I am *not* insane.'

Pendegast and his junior exchange glances. Pendegast is no fool, he's done his homework.

'Muybridge,' he says, 'you've told me about your stagecoach accident. I've made further enquiries and let's just say that on occasions your behaviour is known to be, well, erratic. We need something. The judge and the jury need something. We simply cannot go into the courtroom and say to them that you found out your wife was having an affair and so you planned to shoot dead her lover!' He snorts, the sound a mixture of laughter and derision. 'It just won't do. You will be found guilty, and I have no intention of that outcome occurring.'

Pendegast is already planning that this case will be a high point in his career-that the jury will find a man obviously guilty, to be innocent. At night he lies awake planning his speeches; he knows right from the start that he must appeal to the jury, that the bottom line must be *how would they feel if they were cuckolded*, but to satisfy society, there is no choice – Eadweard must be mad.

From deep within himself, Eadweard sighs. He feels a minute unraveling of himself. He is not used to relinquishing control, but relinquish he must, he realises.

Almost as if he is echoing Pendegast's thoughts, he speaks. 'If I must be insane,' he says reluctantly, 'I suppose I must.'

* * * * *

When Eadweard is conducted into the courtroom for the first day of the trial, he almost faints dead away at the sight of the crowds. He pauses infinitesimally, and the sheriff and his deputy, sensing his hesitation, tighten their grip.

He gives them a wry smile. 'Don't worry gentlemen,' he says. 'I'm not going anywhere.'

The 'audience', and this is how he comes to think of them, an audience at one of those benighted plays Flora insisted on going to, gasp as he enters. At first, he bows his head, but then pride gets the better of him, and he raises his eyes, catches sight of people he knows. His friend, James Hutchings, is there with a notepad, and others – reporters and artists from newspapers, even photographers.

As he reaches the desk at the front of the courtroom where he must sit with his lawyers, he says to Pendegast out of the side of his mouth. 'I feel like a monkey in a circus.' He is not used to it. *I am a private man,* he thinks.

Pendegast looks straight ahead. 'Well,' he says quietly. 'If they want a show, we will give them one. And you will be the star, Sir. Never fear in that regard.'

Muybridge glances at the lawyer beside him, his plump, well-fed stomach, the slightly florid countenance, the general air of affability oozing from him, and is not so sure who will be the real star of the trial.

Does it take hours, minutes or seconds for the judge to arrive, for the usher to say: 'All rise...' Eadweard cannot be sure. Time seems to contract and expand as he begins to hear a version of himself described, a version where so much rests on the result of the stagecoach accident and his subsequent injuries, that he begins to feel, that perhaps they are right, perhaps, after all, he *is* mad.

'And Sir,' Pendegast booms at him, glancing at the jury, gauging sympathy levels to the most minute degree. 'You were in fact, in a coma for NINE days with your injuries, were you not?'

Muybridge assents. 'Yes, I was.'

'We have here the neurological reports from your surgeon. He says you suffered thenceforward from double vision, confusion, mood swings and that you were disoriented, is this all true?'

'Yes,' Muybridge agrees to this strangely half-lit character portrait that is apparently him. 'Yes. It is.'

But naturally Pendegast cannot leave it at a murderer's word. No, he has amassed those people who saw his client on an almost daily basis; those people most qualified to testify that this grey-haired, grey-bearded gentleman accused of murder, did not make a pre-meditated plan to take his wife's lover's life, but acted in a moment of complete insanity.

They parade themselves before the packed court, the all-male jury, and in front of Muybridge himself.

He hears that Mrs. Smith recalls that he often could not remember whether he had fed the canaries, and would ask her why she had, when he had already given them hempseed and had forgotten.

'Did this happen often?' asks Pendegast, solicitous, as if forgetting is not something everybody does every day, thinks Eadweard.

'Quite often Sir,' says Mrs. Smith. 'Once, he tapped his head and said – "Ah, dear me, Mrs. Smith, I feel bad here sometimes".'

What Eadweard would like to do is to leap up in his own defence. He would like to grab Mrs. Smith by the shoulders and shake her, and say to her: *You were the messenger, you knew my wife was having an affair, all the times I felt I was going mad, felt there was something going on, not once did you let me know by any hint. Perhaps if you had been honest with me, I would not have felt so bad, so uneasy in my head.* But he sits there, his eyes forward, hands under the desk, apparently quiet, his inner turmoil stilled by the knowledge that he is literally in a fight for his life.

But still, to Pendegast it is obvious that over-feeding canaries is not exactly a sign of madness, and he has more cards up his sleeve. He has Mrs. Smith's daughter, Miss Smith, Flora's friend, who works at the Rulofsen gallery, who testified that her friend's husband was, in her words, *peculiar.*

Pendegast pounced. 'Peculiar, Miss Smith, in what manner?'

'Well, he was easily excited and often nervous, Sir,' she says.

'But a good husband?'

'Oh yes,' she says, 'a good husband. Always kind and indulgent.'

Not the kind of man, Pendegast seemed to be suggesting, who deserved to be cuckolded.

But as for the next witness, his friend, his colleague, his gallery director, Eadweard is astonished to hear how unreliable, how downright *peculiar* he, Eadweard, has apparently been in his dealings with Rulofsen.

'You found him,' suggests Pendegast, 'difficult to deal with did you not Sir?'

Rulofsen nods vigorously. 'He would consistently make agreements with me and then break them, or not remember them the next day.'

'How often would these lapses of memory occur?'

'Oh, over 40 times in the two years we have been working together,' says Rulofsen.

Eadweard raises his eyes towards his friend. *Et tu Brute?* He thinks to himself. Did you find this *mad*?

'Was he particular in his financial dealings?' Pendegast leans towards Rulofsen sympathetically, one sane man to another: 'Was he *reliable?*'

'He was immensely frustrating. He would never make a view for money if he did not see beauty in it, but would drop his tools and pack up at once.' Rulofsen nods to himself, as if *in his opinion this alone must make a man mad,* thinks Eadweard, who himself has felt sorry on occasions for Rulofsen and his mad pursuit of the dollar. 'Also,' adds Rulofsen, after a moment's consideration, 'he will often stay up all night reading – generally some classical work, and once he dropped the matter of a $700 bill rather than pursue it with Mr. Crocker who questioned it.'

Eadweard could almost laugh, if it wasn't his life at stake. *Reading,* he thinks, *well if that's how you judge a man's sanity, then I am mad indeed.* While the court room drones on around him, he suddenly sees Flora dressed to go out to some evening event, while he sat in his favourite chair, a book in hand, Florado asleep in his room.

'So,' his wife had said to him archly, raising an eyebrow, tapping a foot from beneath her dress. 'I cannot persuade you?'

'No,' he'd replied. 'I am happy here, my dear. I shall see you on your return.'

Only now can he see the look of relief that crossed her face. Imagine if he *had* gone, if he had actually seen her speak with her lover. He would have known, and perhaps in that knowing the outcome that had occurred might have been different. *Or,* he thinks bitterly, *it might have been the same. I might simply have shot him dead that night instead.*

As he comes back from his reverie, he realises that Rulofsen has stepped down, only to be replaced by Silas Selleck, who is also denouncing his sanity on the grounds of his lack of business acumen. *I would not buy this if I were the jury,* thinks Eadweard. And indeed, as each person of his acquaintance takes the stand, if Eadweard were to judge himself, he reflects, it would be to say he was, perhaps, eccentric. His mind drifts again, as condemnation whirls about him.

'Before he went to Europe, he was pleasant and agreeable... afterwards he was untidy and his hair turned grey ...'

'Sometimes he would be so lost in vacancy he would not recognise me...'

'No doubt it was madness to sit on the edge of the peak at Yosemite...' *Madness,* thinks Eadweard... *no, no, the purest form of sanity.*

He does know, of course that he was *not* the same after the accident, he knows only too well the headaches, the lapses of focus, a certain obsession that crept into his character coupled with a certain intolerance not there before. That's why he went to England, he thinks, to find a cure, only to find there was no cure other than time, and for him the enhanced ability to take these odd perceptions, hallucinations and ideas and turn them into images. But madness?! Who could have climbed the point and not sat on the rock – that massive jutting piece of granite, 3,000 feet above the valley floor? It would, he thinks, have been madness *not* to climb it.

And so it goes, for three whole days. At night, alone in his cell, Eadweard cries for himself, for everything he has heard, for this poor, cuckolded, damaged, deranged human being that is apparently *him.* When Pendegast visits him on Friday morning, he is in a cheerful mood.

'Fear not,' he says to Eadweard, clasping his arm. 'We are home and hosed. I'll have the jury eating out of my hand by the end of the day, I guarantee it.'

'I hope you are correct Sir, for if they do not "eat out of your hand" as you say...' Eadweard tries to keep his face straight, manly. 'Well then, I will die.'

Pendegast looks at his client in amazement, as if the very thought that Eadweard just might possibly be found guilty has not even crossed his mind. 'Courage, Muybridge!' he says. 'By tonight you will be a free man.'

By the time of his closing speech, Pendegast is in his element. 'I cannot ask you to send this man forth to family and home – he has none. Across the arch of his fireplace where once was written the words *Home – Wife – Child – Content and Peace*, there now appears as a substitute for all, placed there by the destroyer, the single awful word *Desolation*.'

He pauses for dramatic effect – opens his arms – this is where, should he have been so inclined, he might have acknowledged his client's actions, but he knows exactly what to do: he will simply leap that chasm, as surely as Muybridge stood on the precipice at Glacier Rock. Pendegast, will choose to be oblivious to the dangers around him. 'But I do ask you,' he says, his voice soft and persuasive, caressing, almost, 'to send him forth free – let him take up the thread of his broken life and resume that profession upon which his genius has shed so much lustre – the profession which is now his only love. Let him go forth into the green fields, by the bright waters, through the beautiful valleys, (*will they get the religious allusion,*)' he wonders, even as he speaks, 'and up and down the swelling coast, and in the active work of securing shadows of their beauty by the magic of his art, he may gain "surcease of sorrow" and pass on to to his allotted end in comparative peace.'

He gestures his hand towards Eadweard, and then lowering his head slightly towards the jury, he takes his seat again beside his client. Somewhere in the room Eadweard can hear the sound of crying. He feels like crying himself. The enormity of what is to pass soon is beginning to weight on him. Soon he will know whether he will live or die, he thinks, and deep within him a trembling starts. Despite Pendegast's encouraging look, he can't help it, he can feel a sense of impending doom and it is so extreme he can hardly take in the prosecution's words, although he does hear the last resounding sentence: 'You have no right to ignore the law, and you must find the prisoner guilty unless you conclude he is insane.'

And now Eadweard plunges into the longest 12 hours of his life. Pendegast shakes his hand firmly before the sheriff takes him away to his cell while the jury deliberate. 'Don't worry,' he says. 'You will be a free man very soon.' He strides off down the street towards his hotel as if he has not a care in the world. 'I will rest myself,' he says to Eadweard, 'and my junior will sit inside the courthouse.' He taps his somewhat corpulent stomach. 'No point in wasting away. Some food and drink are in order. It's been a long day.'

How lucky he is, thinks Eadweard, he does not have a care in the world, for ultimately in the end, what is it to him if I live or die? And his bill will be paid whatever the outcome, whereas he, back in his cell, is shaking with cold. He wraps himself in his blanket, but it's not enough; nothing will stop the shaking, *nothing* he thinks, short of hearing that he will be allowed to live. He puts his great overcoat on, the one he has taken with him on so many adventures, the one under which he hid the pistol with which he killed Harry. He wonders if he regrets his action and is surprised to find that he doesn't. That, despite everything that has followed, he would do the same thing again – just perhaps in a place where no one could see me, he thinks wryly.

And where is Flora while he is waiting to hear the verdict, he wonders. Is she careless as to his plight? He suspects so, since there has been no communication from her. *Surely you did not expect any,* says a logical voice in his head. *You shot her lover dead. Well, no,* he thinks, *I didn't expect any, but still. It would have been nice to know that she cared whether I lived or died.* And there is still this: he still cannot help the fact that he desires her. He cannot help himself that her shadowy form fills his dreams, that sometimes he wakes like an embarrassed teenager in his cell, empty with unrequited love, love that once had a place to live, and now has nowhere. He almost wishes he could feel the desire for her now, on this night which might be his last on Earth, but it is only in his sleep she comes to him as she once did, willing and open; in his waking hours she is the harlot that cuckolded and destroyed his life.

But the memory of when he first saw her, now that is something to sustain a man, he thinks. He has replayed that film in his head, that series of mental images, over and over again, since the moment itself. It has kept him company on his travels, comforted him during times of distress, infuriated him and finally, saddened him, that such hope, such infinite optimism for the future – the sudden knowing that this was *the* one, the one he had been searching for forever. Again, it plays itself in his mind; how he had gone to Nahl's Gallery to see about some retouching of his some of his San Francisco photographs. He had been introduced to her across a photograph he was poring over with absolute attention.

'This is Flora, Flora Stone,' Nahl had said. 'She will work on your photographs, Muybridge. She's very good. She has the touch, you know...'

And Eadweard looked up, and in that second, his heart, his 40-year-old heart, which had begun to feel as it might never experience the pure passion of love, flipped over.

It was her confidence, he thinks, even then.

'Mr. Muybridge,' she'd said. 'Your photographs give me so much pleasure. It will be an honor to work with you.'

She'd smiled up at him, and he was lost. He'd thought her button nose the most entrancing thing he'd ever seen; she had, (and he winces even now to think of it) even at half his age, that look of knowing, a look that made him want to grasp her then and there, to kiss her with such force that she would forget any kisses that had come before. It seems so long ago, and it seems like yesterday, as if, if he worked hard enough, he could conjure her up here, now, in front of him. If only he could imagine it all away, every bit of it, and particularly *him*.

God damn it, he thinks, *I cannot sleep.*

He forces himself to think about his photography, about Stanford, and their project. He owes Stanford the bankrolling of the court case now as well. He must live to finish this, he thinks. He knows this – there is more, much more to do. He has stopped shivering now. The overcoat has worked the magic the blankets could not do. He is deep in a cocoon of warmth as he imagines a camera to himself... *how do I do it,* he wonders to himself. *How do I stop time, take it apart so I can see the inner workings of movement...*

He feels himself drifting a little and although part of him wants badly to stay awake, to face each minute of this long wait, another wants only oblivion, to be unaware of his uncertain future, to know only when it is finished and done with, what will be his fate.

The next thing he knows the long red fingers of dawn are touching the bars of his window, and the drunk in the cell next to him is shouting that he knows his rights. The sheriff and his deputy are both laughing at him.

'You ain't got no rights,' the deputy, Daniel, says to the drunk. 'Leastways not until you're sober.'

He comes to Eadweard's cell, a mug of coffee in his hand. 'Morning Muybridge,' he says. 'You want some coffee?'

'Thank you.' Eadweard has never quite got used to the American accent and how it drawls out words. Coffee, for example, how does that become *cawwfeee* he thinks. Not even a drink they drink in England. They don't even understand how to make the stuff there. Here it's strong, bitter and useful; there it's weak, grey, tasteless and does nothing.

'You feeling alright?' Daniel has been his jailor these past few months, but he's not against him, Muybridge knows that. He told him one day, *Fellas've got off for worse'n what you done Muybridge, that's for sure.*

Muybridge nods. 'As well as I can be under the circumstances Daniel.'

Dan nods. 'I expect your lawyer'll be here soon.'

'I expect.'

'Well then... I'd better get on. Let me know when you want us to let you out.'

'Thank you.' This kind favour of the last several months, that Muybridge can use the toilet and washroom and that he does not have to do his business like an animal where he sleeps and lives and works, has surely been an acknowledgment that he is still, after all, a gentleman, thinks Muybridge. But will he be a gentleman in a few hours? Or will he be a criminal who has been sentenced to death? And if so, none of these things, coffee, noisy drunks, his ablutions – none of it will matter anymore.

Muybridge thinks back to the Modoc War, to the corpses he had seen on both sides. Is it better, he wonders, to know the time of death, or that it should come quickly, out of the blue? At least though, if he is to hang, the job will be done properly, he assumes. He will not die in agony, shot in the stomach or half-scalped.

After his porridge, and his coffee, and his ablutions, it is still only 7.30 in the morning. He has no idea how long he has to wait to hear if he will live or die. He begins to tidy his papers again. The small writing desk he had brought into the cell, and the bookcase beside his bed now full of books and papers and photographs and ideas. *Ideas,* he thinks, *it is ideas that predict a future. We have ideas because we will be here tomorrow.* But it is not long before he can do nothing, the waiting almost unbearable except that somehow it must be born.

At around 9.00am, William Wirt Pendegast, refreshed by a good night's sleep, and by the look of his stomach, a good dinner and breakfast, calls in to the jail.

'It's looking optimistic my friend,' he says through the bars to Eadweard, who jumps up in an instant.

'Really?'

Pendegast nods. 'I've bribed the boy taking in drinks.'

Even in extremis Eadweard laughs. 'I suppose you have,' he says.

'Indeed,' says Pendegast. 'The most reliable source of information to my mind. He says they were deadlocked for most of the night, with five for conviction and seven for acquittal…'

Eadweard gasps and holds his throat in a sudden gesture of protection.

'But no,' says Pendegast. 'Do not disturb yourself unduly. The tide is turning your way, two more have turned for acquittal. I predict by noon you will be a free man, my friend. A free man. So now you must ready yourself, Muybridge, we must wait out the hours at the Courthouse. I will request that I am allowed to accompany the Sheriffs and yourself across the road.'

While Pendegast is gone, Muybridge fusses with everything on his desk. He can't help touching the books, the papers, the pen and ink. These are his things, his hands have held them, his mind has thought about them, they hold the imprint of him within them, he thinks; they are the closest thing to loved ones that he has at this time, and although he is not much of a one for superstition, he touches each object three times, carefully, with intention. *For luck,* he whispers. His hand brushes over the small stone he brought back from Yosemite after his first visit, and he swiftly picks it up and places it in his pocket. And then, there it is, suddenly, the noise of Daniel and Pendegast, the noise of the cell door opening, the noise of them talking at him, over him, around him, the handcuffs going on, and the walk – the shameful walk – back across to the Courthouse, past the gawping onlookers and into the crowded room, every single person in there waiting to know: will this man who shot dead his wife's lover live or die? By the time he sits down, his handcuffs released as he takes his seat with Pendegast at the small table in front of the Judge's bench, he is trembling all over, his body once more attacked by cold, no fire through his veins, rather an icy Hades, the ferryman already waiting.

Pendegast places his hand over his. 'Now now,' he whispers. 'Do not take on so, Muybridge. This will go your way. You will see.' Eadweard nods, but he is travelling far away even as they wait. Thoughts bounce through his brain like staccato bullet shots. *I have to write a will and to whom will I leave everything? To Florado? No! Not now, he is not my child. No,* he thinks wildly, that is not the answer. His brain begins to explode with the swift tiny lights he has become accustomed to seeing since the accident, so that all he can do is to lean forward and hold his head in his hands, press his hands against his eyes; literally hold himself together.

And then, suddenly, so suddenly that now Eadweard wants time to stop, the waiting a mere nothing in terms of what is to come, the door opens, and the judge is ushered back in. As one the audience and the players rise, the rustle of the clothes, of their chairs, drowning out the usher's superfluous command. The jury file back in, all men, all married.

'Gentleman of the jury, have you reached your verdict?'

The head juror, a quiet, upright man with a serious demeanour, nods. 'We have your Honour.'

'How do you find the prisoner?'

'We find the prisoner, Not Guilty.'

The judge leans forward. 'And on the grounds of insanity?' There is a hopeless optimism in his voice.

'We find the prisoner sane, your Honour.'

Eadweard slumps forward, his head on the desk. He can scarcely believe the words he has just heard and yet it is not the honeyed elixir of hope and freedom running through his veins that he had allowed himself to imagine, instead his entire body begins to quiver with cold, tiny icicles of shock running up and down his spine – little electrical currents which begin to pop in his brain, so that everything is a sea of fizzing confusion. As Pendegast bellows in triumph and pandemonium erupts around the courtroom, Eadweard slumps forward, falling, although he does not want to, how he does not want to, into the deep space of a convulsive fit. It takes over his whole body, and as he jerks on the floor, more pandemonium erupts. Into this noise the judge directs his disappointed words: 'In that case I have no choice but to set the prisoner free.'

Through the distortion of his senses Eadweard hears the words, but all they do is increase the uncontrolled twitching of his limbs. People loosen his collar. He is vaguely aware of Pendegast bending over him.

'We've won, Muybridge, we've won. No need to take on so. Calm down, man, calm down.'

The judge, his authority over-ruled, his legal judgment usurped, finds the scene so distressing he hurries from the courtroom. From the corner of his eye, Eadweard sees him go, but still he is unable to stop this unseemly, *unmanly* twitching, until finally, it does, at last, begin to subside, and Eadweard has no idea if he has been in this altered state for minutes, or hours. As his body slumps into exhaustion, he feels somewhere in him such a monumental unwinding of tensions that it seems he could sleep for days – right here and now on the courtroom floor. But they are all chivvying him along: his legal team, the onlookers that are left, even the courthouse officials, and so he allows himself to be helped to his feet by Pendegast, allows himself to be supported out of the courthouse and into the bright midday sunlight, blinking with surprise as the small crowd outside erupts into applause.

'There,' says Pendegast. 'You see. They are for you, Muybridge. They know you are Not Guilty!'

Not Guilty. The words slide into his veins like honey. Even as they walk through the crowd towards the hotel, the sense of shame and despair of the last three months begins to fall away. *All those men*, he thinks, *found me Not Guilty. They would have done as I would have done.* He walks a little more upright, a little freer, relishing each step across the road.

'Sam is getting your things from the jail,' says Pendegast. 'No need to go back there. We've done everything and we've booked you into a hotel room for the afternoon. Sleep, bathe, recover, and then back to San Francisco by tonight.'

'I cannot begin to thank you,' says Eadweard. 'I am most truly grateful.'

'My dear Sir,' says Pendegast. 'It has been my pleasure.'

Just as they reach the other side of the road, two women – Eadweard has noticed them on the edges of the almost exclusively male crowd – step forward. They both spit at his feet.

'Murderer,' snarls one, and then they both walk on.

'Hey!' shouts Pendegast. 'He was found Not Guilty.'

'Yes,' says one of the women, pausing for a moment. 'By an all-male jury.'

Pendegast shrugs. 'Take no notice Muybridge. This thing will blow over in no time now, you'll see. You did what any right-thinking husband would do. You stood up for your rights.'

Eadweard nods. 'Yes,' he says. 'I know.'

And now, where so recently there was no future that he could contemplate without the spectre of the hangman's noose intruding itself upon his imaginings, now there is, to his surprise, a warm glow in his heart, a feeling of relief and gratitude so overwhelming it has even overtaken his grief and anger.

He is, quite simply, glad to be alive.

He turns and grabs his lawyer's hand. 'You'll come to dinner tonight?' he asks. 'You'll come and join us? Help us celebrate your brilliance and my freedom? As soon as I am able, I shall be off to South America. I have a lot of work to catch up on, but I should be delighted if you would join us. What do you say?'

Pendegast is touched. 'My dear chap,' he says. 'I'd be delighted. Delighted.'

Eadweard nods. 'Well,' he says. 'That's settled then.'

* * * * *

And so, after his prescribed rest, Eadweard travels back to San Francisco, a free man, traveling the same journey he took those months before. A stagecoach to the train, a train to the ferry, the ferry back across the bay. He is in awe of the light, of the air, he can taste the salt on his tongue, his eyes follow every movement; the wake of the water, the seagulls on the wing, everything shifts around him, a phantasmagoria of sight, sound and smell. He touches his own sleeve just to feel the material under his hand, to sense his living arm, to know that every part of him is still alive.

But despite his newborn sense of wonder there is a question-mark in his heart. He wonders how it will be to return to the rooms he and Flora have called home these past few years. He tries to imagine them. He's asked Mrs Smith to send a cleaner through, to clear up any mess, although he knows, of course that Flora and Florado will not be there, and his heart clenches. He cannot bear the thought of ever seeing either of them again and yet he cannot bear the thought of *not* seeing them again. *How,* he thinks, *can I stay in San Francisco when I may bump into them at any moment?* As if a tap of bile has been turned on his throat, his joy at his release suddenly feels like acid in his mouth at the very idea of seeing Flora.

'What can I do?'

'I beg your pardon?' The man next to him, also gazing out over the side of the ferry, looks at him curiously.

'I'm sorry.' Eadweard touches his hat politely. 'I did not mean to speak out loud.'

The man nods, then looks again.

'Do I know you?' He looks closely at Eadweard. 'You look familiar.'

'I don't believe we've met.' And abruptly Eadweard moves away, before the man may realise *why* he seems familiar. *I cannot live like this,* he thinks. *I must get away, and soon.*

When he arrives back at his rooms, Eadweard pauses at the front door. Just for a moment he experiences a fanciful sensation that everything he has just been through has been a dream. That in fact, inside that door, lies the life he left before he shot Harry, that perhaps, he considers for a moment, there is even a life within those rooms without Harry in at all, that Harry, in this life, has never even existed.

Inside these rooms Flora is right now getting Florado's dinner, she is humming to herself (always a sign of her contentment), waiting for him, her husband, to come back from a day at the studio. How would it be, he thinks, if this life, this family life was there, inside the door, just waiting for him.

But of course, it is not so, and as Eadweard takes a breath and steps into the unwelcoming silence of what was his home, he is astounded by how much it hurts to be back in this place. Out of nowhere tears come, falling, it seems, of their own accord, as he walks around the rooms, sees how everything connected to Flora and Florado has gone – as if they have been expunged from the earth, as if they never were. He steps into the bedroom, and his heart hurtles into his throat at the sight of the bed. He goes to the dressing-room to get a clean suit, and turns, automatically to Flora's side of the small room, the side where her dresses would hang, so many of them, he would often grumble to her, *why does one woman need so many dresses?*

And she would laugh, 'Now Eadweard,' she would reply, 'You want me to look nice!'

He cannot sleep in the bedroom. This he knows. Even when he will come back later from the dinner, perhaps a bit the worse for wear, he cannot sleep in the bedroom.

He grabs his suit, and on his way out, the quilt from the bed. He will sleep on the sofa. After his months in jail, the sofa will seem like luxury.

* * * * *

Arriving at the restaurant, freshly bathed and dressed, his beard trimmed, Muybridge, despite his acquittal, is nervous. *What will they think of me,* he wonders, *those who have not seen me since... before.* As he enters the restaurant he is directed towards the private room where they are eating tonight; he can feel his heart beating like a caged bird – *with a cat sitting just below waiting to pounce,* he thinks. For a second it reminds him of Yosemite and the extraordinary vertiginous effect of the cliffs. He remembers how he had wanted to photograph it so that people would understand not just the beauty but the *angles* of the place. Once, out on a tiny rockface, leaning over as far as he could, he had almost slipped. He'd watched the misplaced gravel descending down for what seemed like forever, his heart beating crazily against his chest. How strange, he thinks, that such an effect can be brought on by a high mountain or a roomful of people and feel no different.

But, of course, he should not have worried. As he walks into the room, the first person he sees is Pendegast.

'My dear fellow!' Pendegast moves towards Eadweard, his arms out. 'You already look so rested...'

He turns towards the assembled company. 'Here he is my friends,' he announces dramatically. 'The man of the hour.'

And it seems, as his friends and colleagues crowd around him, slap him on the back, shake his hand and congratulate him, as if this is indeed what he is – a hero, not a criminal. Later on in the evening, when the port is making an appearance, and ties and lips are loosened, Pendegast finds him again.

'One thing I will say,' he says to Eadweard, leaning into him. 'Don't pay her a cent more than you have to. I would not have you pay her at all, by the time she takes you to court, and you're forced to pay her, you'll be long gone, travelling up some remote river in South America, no doubt."

Muybridge shakes his head. 'But that is not my intention,' he says. 'I have said I will support her.'

'Support the woman who was unfaithful to you? And has a child by another man? You were found Not Guilty. What can she try and do? Divorce you? On grounds of what? Cruelty? I hardly think so.'

Eadweard flinches from the words, from the tone, from the suggestion that it is all not *quite* over, and yet at the same time, in some way, he feels a relief; and more, he feels a surge of anger at the very idea that he had been thinking of paying Flora. *What for,* he thinks, *for cuckolding me, for making me rot in prison for all those months?* He nods. 'I hear you Pendegast,' he says.

'Good.' Pendegast nods. 'Well, I see your benefactor looming… good luck Muybridge,' and with that he excuses himself, back to his end of the table, where the men, their ties loosened, the port and cigars on the table, are enjoying themselves mightily.

Leland Stanford, who has been biding his time, extends his hand. 'Muybridge,' he says. 'A good result.'

'Thank you.' Eadweard extends his hand. 'It's good to see you, Stanford.'

'You too. I was beginning to wonder if our project would be stalled forever.'

Eadweard smiles. 'Well,' he says. 'An advantage of being, shall we say, away, was having a lot of time on my hands to think about how to proceed…'

Stanford smiles. 'You interest me, Sir. Very much.' He pulls up a chair. 'Show me…'

Chapter 19

Flora

She wakes early, shivering in the cold, the pain in her spine and her joints that has been haunting her recently, starting again. She rises quietly, quickly, so as not to wake the sleeping child, and moves from the tiny bedroom into the other room, that now houses everything she owns.

The pain claims her attention like a jealous lover, shooting red-hot pokers through her body and gripping her with such force she doubles over. She holds on to a chair, her knuckles white with the effort of staying upright, of not giving in completely. As the spasms subside, she breathes a sigh of relief. *I should go to the doctor,* she thinks, and immediately tears well up. Once it would have been natural to her, but now, as automatic as the sensible thought was, comes the next one, hard on its heels: *I have no money.* The misery of this statement is so complete, she has to sit down. She places her head in her hands, and feels so alone, so bereft, that even the tears will not flow, the sadness is deeper even than tears, as cold, and deep and wide as the bay itself.

How had it come to this? Once, not long ago, only a very few years ago, she had everything a woman could want – a husband, a home, her son, a circle of friends, enough money to live, if not the high life, at least a life without worrying.

Now, she thinks, *I have nothing. No husband, no home, no friends, no money – not even Harry, especially not Harry.* It was still an unbelievable thought. Despite everything that had happened, part of her still expects that her lover will waltz in through the door any day now, and scoop her into his arms, laugh at her with his deep throaty laugh, kiss her with his sweet gentle lips, mumble sweet nothings into her hair until she throws back her head and laughs for the sheer joy of loving him.

But he is not coming. He cannot ever come.

If it wasn't for the few pieces of furniture she has left which she is forced to sell one by one to buy food and pay rent for, she would be no better than the homeless people who live nearby in the small park Flora and Florado scurry past on their excursions out, which are few and far between these days, since Flora finds that any amount of exertion makes her so tired it is not worth the effort.

At the thought of Florado, she feels tongues of fire leaping in her stomach. *I love him*, she thinks, *what will become of him? Even his own father refuses to recognise him.* How can it be that Eadweard cannot see that Florado is his? Why had she ever written those words on the back of the photograph? *Little Harry.* Because the sheer desire she felt for her lover made her wish her child was his, because Harry wanted it as well.

'If Florado were mine,' he would say, 'we would be a family.'

She can see it is getting light outside. Her boy will be waking soon.

She has to try again to reach Eadweard. She has to make him see that it was not all her fault. She was not completely to blame. How could she be? No matter even if the judge and jury had set Eadweard free, exonerated him, left her branded forever a monster, faithless wife, an outcast, there is one tiny part of her that knows: *this was not all my fault.*

She looks towards the desk where the letter she had started the day before sits, and knows she must write again quickly, quickly, before the child wakes, before the day with all its lack of comfort, begins.

May 15ᵗʰ, 1875 San Francisco

Dear Eadweard, I am writing this letter to you, because I am not well. I have not been well for some time now. The events of the last few years have taken their toll. I expect that you will have been disappointed by Judge Wheeler's decision to grant me the sum of $50 per month, as I have not seen this money since his decision and particularly since you remain convinced, no matter what I have said to you, that Florado is not your son.

Perhaps you will continue to travel, as you have already done, thereby making it impossible to retrieve any money from you, or to have correspondence with you.

With no money to my name, ill-health, and with my family turned against me I cannot see that I am much longer for this world, and so Sir, to one whom was once the most beloved person to me I have decided I must write in the hope that when I do leave this Earth, this letter will be found with me, and passed to you so that you will – I pray most ardently – accept Florado as your own, and do what thus far you seem unable or unwilling to do, to forgive the child the sins of the mother.

Of these 'sins' I too feel that I can no longer lose anything, since I truly have nothing left to lose, except the love of my – our – child, and I fear for him when I have gone, I wish to write an explanation. Will you read it? I fear not. If you do read it, will you understand it? I also fear not. But I will at least put down on paper for someone, if not you, at least I hope someone, to see that Flora Muybridge was not quite the sinner she was made out to be and that her actions were a consequence of what, was for her, the most dreadful thing that can befall a married woman, an absence of love and affection from the man she called her husband.

I will never forget the day we met – only five years ago. How entranced I was by you, you seemed so strong and sure of yourself, so in your element as you showed me your prints and explained your work to me. It seemed destined at that point that we should love each other. It seemed you felt it too, you leant against the fireplace and looked at me, and I felt I knew not which way to turn for it seemed as if you could see straight through me.

*You discovered, of course, that I was still married (in name alone) but you seemed at the time to be so understanding of my unhappiness in that union, I could not have foretold for a moment that you too would become for me a source of such unhappiness...*Flora's pen hovers over the paper; she can hear Florado stirring. She feels weak at the thought of the day ahead. She can feel herself getting a temperature. Her head is so heavy on her shoulders, she wonders if she could just place it on the desk in front of her and never move again. The doctor is baffled by her condition, the strange inflammation that has invaded her body, and it seems, increasingly threatens her mind itself. She had sat there in his office, Florado on her knee, and she had seen, oh yes, she had seen the way the doctor had looked her up and down. There was no pity there. He must have known the story, she understood from his glances, from the tight disapproval around his mouth. *I don't have long,* she thinks. She mouths the words quietly, sadly, and bends again to her letter.

And my unhappiness, Eadweard, was simply this, that once we were married you took so little notice of me, I may as well have not existed!

Did it not occur to you that because I loved you, I wanted to become part of your life? It seemed your obsession with your photography, and with your horse project was far more important to you than I could ever be.

I fell in love with Harry because I was lonely, because I wanted to be loved, because my heart was breaking with the sorrow of being married and yet having no husband.

Sometimes it seemed to me as if you fell in love with me because of certain qualities I possessed, and then, once we were married those same qualities became undesirable. I felt judged by you, Eadweard, every minute of every day. I lived in a prison, and you did not even notice it. I could not say things I thought without fear of reprimand, I could not laugh, nor dance or sing, without you frowning, or asking me to be quiet. I could not, Sir, express my physical desire for you, yes, for you, without you indicating to me most clearly that this was not my place.

Eadweard, when you killed Harry for the sin of loving me, you killed not only him, but me as well. I have been told by the Chaplain at the local church, which is the only place where I receive any comfort in these last days, that I should forgive you. I imagine you feel that it is your place to forgive me. I am trying hard to forgive us both, and to remember the love that was there in the beginning, and not this horror I am living in at the end.

I do pray to you Eadweard, that you will find it in your heart to forgive me, and to accept Florado, who has only ever loved you as his father.

Flora

She sighs and puts down the pen. She can hear Florado stirring and summoning up all the energy within her she goes to her child, who soon, too soon, will be deemed an orphan.

Chapter 20

The Jungle

Just to digress for a moment, although in a sense, what I am giving you is several lifetimes of digression I suppose, Beth, it was landscape that brought horses into my life.

Of all the horse sports that exist, the one that brought Eadweard to horses, via Leland Stanford, was racing. At a time when horses were still, despite Stanford's increasing spider-web of railways across America, the backbone of a nation, Eadweard was asked to indulge a rich man's folly, to see if he could create a system of continuous photography of horse movement to prove that at a single moment all four hooves were in the air at the same time, so that just for that split second, less than a second, a horse could be, in fact, I suppose, flying.

Almost a year after he married Flora, in April 1872, Eadweard fulfills his commission to photograph Leland Stanford's mansion, and begins the process that will – despite everything he's achieved so far – shoot both Eadweard, Stanford, and the horse, Occident, to world fame.

Not that Eadweard, ambitious as he was, believed that what Stanford was suggesting was achievable. He didn't. But money talks, so even though Eadweard knew very well the limitations of the cameras of the day at capturing motion, which usually presented itself as a blur, Stanford's offer of $2,000 (around $65,000, Beth, imagine that), was enough to intrigue Eadweard.

And just so you know why it was such a hard task Beth, it was because in those days the shutters were too slow; in the main photographers still used a manual piece of equipment: the lens cap, a piece of board, even their own hat, to cover and uncover the lens, making their own wet collodion solution, poured onto a glass plate, which was then primed in a solution of silver nitrate. This whole process was literally hundreds of times less sight-sensitive than modern cameras, and yet Stanford was asking Eadweard to use equipment that needed a 14-second to one minute exposure on a bright day to capture, for all time, the continuous movement of a horse. In this case, Stanford's beloved trotter Occident (who, by the way, had his own stake, the Occident Stake, named after him at the Sacramento Racetrack).

It was a strange pairing, the wild-looking photographer, with his intense blue eyes, and bushy hair and beard, and the ex-governor, with his limitless bank account and his various mansions; but they were in it for the long haul, at least until they weren't.

Stanford's $2,000 didn't go far as it happened. The project ended up costing him $50,000 – over a million dollars in today's money, Beth, that's pretty pricey, isn't it? All of it simply to satisfy a bet Stanford had with a friend. Plus it took five years to complete, mainly because his photographer of choice killed Harry Larkyns, was charged with murder, jailed and went through a lengthy trial, with his legal team backed by Stanford's deep pockets.

And all of this causes me to think about the idea of shame again, for women and men, and the difference between them, even perhaps of how the public perceive shame and wrongdoing in the sexes.

* * * * *

In Guatemala the rain is like nothing Eadweard has ever experienced.

Sometimes, trekking up a mountain, in search of a village, a view, a *photograph*, he feels for the first time ever as if it is all too much.

The rain is heavy, warm and almost endless.

Lying in his tent at night, the rain mocks his tears, the overflowing grief in his heart, the eternal question: What happened?

Nevertheless.

He will not be taken for a fool. And a fool and his money are soon parted. He'll be damned if he'll pay the money the judge has ordered him to pay. For another man's son!

Sometimes he can't help imagining the conversations he might have had with her if the story had been different. How he would have arrived home, how excited she would have been to see him; how he might still be writing her letters, explaining the sights of this odd country where European sophistication mingles with Native jungle lore, and how the smell of coffee is everywhere, permeating the senses with its bitter sweetness.

Dear Flora,

You should see the coffee plantations here. Anywhere that it is possible, they are planting it to meet the increasing demand of coffee-drinkers around the world. Even in the very sunniest of places, such as San Isidro, they place frames over the plants to protect them from the heat, the native women pick them, and the men spread the berries on platforms to dry in the sun.

Muybridge suspends his imaginary pen and ponders for a moment the fortuitous circumstance of the Pacific Mail Steamship Company sponsoring his journey to Central America and Mexico, so he would not, could not, be tempted to speak with his ex-wife.

He had wanted to capture the beauty of the buildings and landscape in stereoscopic cards from the moment he arrived. How else, he thought, could he show the world the churches and the monuments, the gracious town squares, the jungle and volcanoes?

Not that these are his only work. He is also busy creating a series of prints. He does not know quite how many, but he can see it already. There will be a collective title. Something along the lines of *The Pacific Coast of Central America and Mexico; the Isthmus of Panama; Guatemala; and the Cultivation and Shipment of Coffee.* In the dark he nods to himself. This will do nicely, he thinks.

He is pleased with his work. There is no doubt it eases him. And if at the end of a long day, resting in a lonely bed, his thoughts, despite his best intentions, turn to Flora, to how much he still, even now, desires her, if his hand finds himself erect under the blanket, and begins a caress that will end in a sigh of despair, *Flora...* then who will ever know? No-one, not him, least of all him, will attempt to recall this. And if, after that momentary minute of forgetting, the image of a laughing man, all moustache and blue eyes appears in front of him, well, he is strong enough, surely, to push him away.

As the tropical rain eases, puts itself away for the morning hours, he too folds up his pain. It fits neatly inside one of his many jacket pockets, along with the lemons he sucks on throughout the day, (a habit he had acquired after he once read that Captain Cook had prevented scurvy by providing his sailors with limes) his rolls of film, and, still yes, even now, a photograph of Flora.

Eadweard stays in Guatemala for nine months, alternately drifting in the sea of his imagination and his world of technical expertise: this moment, this exact moment of light and dark to capture the exquisite berry, the winding road, the villagers washing, the waves captured in a moment of motion on the beach, frozen forever.

It begins to suit him. He no longer notices the heat, the humidity. He is casting everything aside.

One day when he is carefully surveying a town square, eyeing its inhabitants with the same impersonal eye he has for their museums or libraries, a young man comes running towards him.

At first, preoccupied with his cameras, Eadweard does not so much register the slight disturbance around him, the ripples and the pointing, until the young man arrives at his side, out of breath and panting.

´Señor Muybridge?´

Eadweard nods.

´Señor Muybridge, I have a telegram from America.´

What he reads is that his by-now ex-wife, Flora Shalcross-Stone-Muybridge has died.

What he doesn't read is that Flora has died of shame.

Her very last words to the people around her, ´I'm sorry.´

She was 24 years old.

Chapter 21

Florado

Eadweard adjusts his tie and smooths his hair.

He is not used to the company of small children, and this one, of all the children in the world, bothers him.

'So Florado,' he says, trying to sound friendly, neutral, 'you will come with me.'

The little boy, his large eyes so reminiscent of his mother's, glances up at his father.

'Yes Sir,' he says, as he has been taught.

The woman smiles. 'He is a good boy Sir. I am glad you are taking him with you. He has been lonely since his mother died.'

She looks at the somewhat imposing figure in front of her. She knows who he is, of course. It's hard to imagine this tall, well-dressed man shooting another man, or causing any kind of scandal. But there is something about the way he carries himself, straight and somehow stern. He is tanned from his visit to the jungle, and his blue eyes have a steely quality about them. He is not a man to get on the wrong side of, she is sure.

Eadweard turns his head and gazes at a painting on the wall.

'I am taking him,' he says, 'in order that I can place him in an orphanage. This child has no parents as far as I am concerned, Madam, and therefore an orphanage is the correct place for him.'

And before she can say anything, before a word can leave her lips, he bends down and extends his hand to Florado.

'Come, Florado,' he says. 'We must go. Thank you for your care of the child, Madam. If there were any costs incurred, please send the bill to my address. Florado, say goodbye.'

'Goodbye,' says the child obediently, walking trustingly out of the door with the man he knows only as his father.

As they stand on the steps of the orphanage waiting for the door to open, the smell of antiseptic seeps out from every crack, from around every window, from under the door.

Florado wrinkles his nose and holds tight to his father's hand.

At least, thinks Eadweard, *it is a clean place.*

The girl that greets them is starched and crisp. She ushers them into the hall, where they wait for the Matron.

She arrives soon enough, bustling skirts and clanging keys.

'Mr. Muybridge,' she says. 'We have been expecting you.' She turns to Florado. 'And you, Florado, isn't it? You are going to come and live with us. I am sure you will enjoy it. There are plenty of children here to play with.'

She turns to Eadweard. 'It would be best for the child if he were to go with Emily so we can discuss arrangements for his care. Are you ready to say goodbye to him now, Sir?'

'Yes,' Eadweard stoops down to the small child sitting quietly beside him. 'Florado, you will go now with Emily, and she will settle you in. I will come and visit you.'

He looks down at the little boy, and quite against his own desire feels his eyes fill with tears and a strange pain searing through his body. *It could have been different* a voice screams in his head, *you don't have to send him away.*

But he will not listen to that voice. That voice led him astray, seduced him, betrayed him, deserted him.

He touches his son on the shoulder.

'Goodbye, Florado.'

And the child, obedient as usual, looks up at the tall man with the beard. 'Goodbye Sir.'

* * * * *

Here is something that I cannot imagine, Beth, and I am absolutely certain that you cannot imagine it either. I cannot fathom how Eadweard managed to bring himself to abandon Florado at the orphanage, and then to abandon him again at the ranch in Texas. He must have been so convinced that Florado wasn't his, and I suppose of course that Florado was a constant reminder of Flora, the woman who broke his heart. But for me the idea that someone could abandon family, which, after all is what Florado believed himself to be, is hard to bear. But this could be my own guilt talking, because I once walked away from what turned out to be my only chance to bear a child in this world.

We could imagine, though, couldn't we, the sadness of that small boy, only two, without either possible father, without his mother, in a tall brownstone building in New York. Was he well treated? We know that he was first placed in the care of a Catholic orphanage, and that Eadweard moved him to a Protestant one, and deep down, somewhere, he must have felt something, mustn't he, because he paid for his care. If he truly felt nothing, why would he have done that?

And then one day, when Florado Helios Muybridge is 10 years old, the only man he knew as father, arrives to pick him up, to take him out of the city to a ranch in Texas. New York to Texas. Not the most obvious leap Beth. In fact, the mind boggles. How did it come about? It bothers me, it truly does. Did Eadweard have friends in Texas? Highly likely from all his photographic wanderings. Was he staying with them? Is it a coincidence that Texas was where Eadweard had his accident?

I'm sure I've told you that as an older man Florado was almost the spitting image of Eadweard. There could be virtually no doubt that Eadweard was Florado's father – from his looks alone. If Eadweard was my grandfather, then that also means that Flora was sleeping with her husband and her lover.

And then there is a horrible curly thing in there as well, the question mark of my life, the idea that a man in his 50s slept with my young sister/mother. Is that idea as repugnant to you as it was to me Beth? It was to me, I can tell you, for so many, many years. But finally, I came to terms with it. I decided, rightly or wrongly, that it was sheer loneliness that drew them both together. It was not an old man and a young woman, it was two people thrown together in an isolated place, neither of them adept at making friends, and somehow, they found each other, for long enough to make me. I hope this is a correct interpetation, I really, really do.

It's a curious thing trying to write about your own beginning. Something I shall come back to, I think. All the time what I'm brought up against is that there is so much information about Eadweard's achievements, Eadweard's glorious career, Eadweard's obsession with bodies and movement, his lectures, and awards, his status as a man of science, of the arts, of the world, and all the time such a *blank* around his emotional life, and the emotional life of those around him, those connected to him, those separated from him.

But a life is not just facts is it, Beth? In the end, perhaps, a life is anything but facts, in the end a life is only the emotions we've felt, the love, or lack of it, we've experienced. At least, that is how it feels for me, as I come towards the end. The 'things' I've done don't seem to count for much, but the flash of red on a robin's breast causes me to gasp with joy. It enters my soul.

And perhaps, on that note, let us return now to Eadweard, let us join him at that point where he is about to finish with the experiment begun five years before. Money talks. Always. He had a job to finish for Leland Stanford and finish it he did.

* * * * *

Leland Stanford is waiting, and he is anxious: 'Are you ready?'

'Almost.'

Leland Stanford lets out a sigh. 'They're getting impatient.'

Muybridge snorts. 'Let them wait. They are here to serve our cause, not us theirs.'

Fiddling with his fob watch, Stanford looks down on the man who is fiddling with his meticulous preparations, adjusting a knob there, checking a wire here, and wonders, not for the first time, why he felt drawn towards this particular photographer. There must, he thinks, have been easier people to work with. Easier, yes, he tells himself now, better, no. Over the past five years there have been occasions where even the stress of completing the railroad has paled into comparison against this project. The possibility that he might have to pay for a murder defence, for instance, certainly hadn't occurred to him when he and Muybridge had first agreed on the desired outcome of their collaboration. It was a funny thing, he thought to himself, watching Eadweard continuing his adjustments, how life works out sometimes. After all, he and Jane had almost not commissioned Muybridge to photograph their house; they'd had two other photographers in mind, but there was something about Muybridge's technical prowess that had won the day. It wasn't, and he smiles to himself, his friend's charm – or lack of it – that was for sure, And then, while Muybridge was so carefully photographing their house, he, Leland, was actually in the process of buying Mayfield Grange, being so excited by the very idea of what he was going to do there, that it had seemed obvious, coming home one afternoon, to confide in the photographer, only to find that here was someone as obsessed with movement as he was. More so, perhaps. Certainly here was the fine detail person, the person who could turn his ideas into reality. Well, it had been a long time coming. He sighs. It had cost him a small fortune, but they were close now, so close.

Muybridge stretches his long frame. 'Sir,' he announces, turning to his mentor, backer and friend with a dramatic sweep of his arms. 'We are ready to make history!'

The two men walk out together, one tall and angular, the other short and stocky. As they approach the huddled group of newspapermen and racing aficionados, they seem almost to the observers to visibly swell. One young reporter on his first assignment will write later: *'The charisma of these two men should not be under-estimated. The sheer force of their personalities should have been a warning to those who felt that perhaps this project would fail, that failure was simply not an option.'*

And now the moment is here. The scene is set on this beautiful June morning in early summer on the racetrack at Stanford's Palo Alto stock farm. On one side of the track stands a whitewashed shed, with an opening a metre high from which the viewer can see a dozen cameras, all standing to attention in a row. On the other side of the track a sloping white backdrop is hanging to enhance the contrast. 12 are spread down the racetrack, each connected to a different camera.

'Gentlemen,' says Stanford. 'Let us take our places! We are ready to begin. Mr. Muybridge if you please, Sir.'

At these words, the Press pick up their weapons – the pens and cameras that will take the news to the world, thinks Muybridge: *Leland Stanford and Eadweard Muybridge have proved the impossible, or worse, Leland Stanford and Eadweard Muybridge's failure to prove...*

Muybridge takes up his position by the cameras, waves a flag and the horse is off, racing down the track and tripping – without even realising it – the wires, one by one as if they are the speediest of dominoes. And even though Muybridge knows he is right, even though he and Stanford have travelled this journey enough times to know that there is no doubt, his blood races, his palms sweat. In the few seconds it takes for the horse and rider to travel the distance, he wonders: *Did I get it wrong? Are we wrong? Is it possible? It has taken six years to get to this point. What if they are wrong?* His mind wanders for a moment. He can still remember his response to that book – what was it called? *Animal Mechanism: A Treatise on Terrestrial and Aerial Locomotion* by Etienne Jules-Marey; the excitement he felt that someone out there was thinking about movement, and, of course, if you thought about movement, you thought inevitably, about a horse. In fact, in a way, it was that book that was responsible for everything up to and including this moment, because it whetted his appetite. He *knew* after he'd read it, that he could do it, he could turn racehorse training on its head. It could become a science, not just genetics and guesswork.

The shout goes up. The horse, the wonderful Occident, has done exactly as asked.

'Gentlemen, gentlemen,' says Stanford. 'You will have to wait a little longer while these plates are processed. This is not an immediate result you know.' But he is grinning from ear to ear.

Eadweard calls his assistant. Together they begin the journey towards the fulfillment of Leland Stanford's dream, which has become Eadweard's – to prove that at one point in the gallop, the horse is suspended, for the tiniest moment in mid-air – all four hooves off the ground, rider or no rider. A gravity-defying moment, a moment where science and the art of photography, and a horse, all come together into nothing less than perfection.

Chapter 22

Home

Pain is speeding me up, Beth. I no longer have the luxury of time. My mind is so full of the things I want to tell you about: the trial, Tony's help to me, (you would, I'm sure, guess that he would help me) the inevitable divorce, which gave me my freedom, even before Liam was out of jail. And then there was the other thing, the thing Liam thought the police found, but in fact which I found.

When Liam was charged, bail was set at $100,000. It was so much money, and to be honest I was relieved. It was far too much for me to raise, and I did not want him out, which Tony, Jim and Mary knew full well.

I did not want to see him. I knew that if I saw him, I might lose my self-control, that I would look into those blue eyes, and forgive him, and I did not *want* to forgive him. Jim went to see him for me, to assure him that we would do our best to raise the money. Liam, crying, Jim told me, had mentioned every last dollar he had in the bank, and people who owed him for jobs not paid, and then he had said to Jim, gazing at him very directly: 'Tell her to be careful of the horse shelter in the first paddock, the edge is raising up. I'd hate a horse to cut itself on it.'

When he got to me later that afternoon, Jim told me. 'I don't know Rosa,' he said. 'I had a feeling he was telling me something that might help him, but I've no idea.'

I was still wounded and co-dependent enough to feel a small percentage of concern for Liam, so I said to Jim, 'Well, let's go and look, shall we?'

And so we did. We walked around that blessed shelter about 10 times, inside and out, and we could see nothing. So often, since then, I've wondered about this. It was spring, we'd had a good season, there was grass around the edge of it, nothing was lifted up, it didn't look dangerous – it looked like a shed.

'You'll have to tell him the shed is fine,' I said to Jim, and he nodded.

'I'll tell him,' he said, 'I'll go right now.'

When Jim told Liam that as far as could see there was nothing wrong with the shed, Liam went very pale and very quiet apparently. 'So,' he said, 'there was nothing wrong? Nothing at all?'

Jim had shrugged. 'Nothing that we could see.'

'Those fucking bastards.' Liam thumped his fist on to the table in the holding room where Jim was talking to him. 'Those fucking bastards.'

We couldn't raise his bail. Can you imagine for me what that meant? He was taken to the Wagga Wagga prison, the door slammed behind him, to wait it out until he came to trial. And I was *safe*. For the first time since he'd hit me, I felt safe. I had already begun the complex process of recovery, but what kept me away from him was simple; it was hard work.

I was working full-time with Jim and Mary, just to keep things going, and in between I was trying to work out what to do with the horses, with the land, with the dogs, with the house.

And in the middle of all of this, I received a miracle.

Can a miracle also be a crime? I've certainly had to reconcile those two opposites. I will tell you now the thing no-one, except you Beth, has ever known about, about how I found the small tin box buried beneath the corner of the shed in the front horse paddock, near their shelter. We'd had a week of flooding rains and one morning when I was out giving hay, I noticed that the rain had unearthed very slightly a tiny, raised edge of something. I wondered what it was, and if it was something that could be dangerous for the horses, and so I went to look more closely.

$100,000 in cash Beth.

$100,000 of ill-gotten gains that I should have turned in, but I did *not*.

The $100,000 Liam knew about, that could have paid his bail, that could have brought him home that afternoon.

The knowledge immediately flooded me that *this* is what he'd meant. That this money was his money (albeit illegally obtained). It's what he wanted us to find, what Jim had told him we couldn't see; and therefore Liam had made the assumption that the police had found it in their search of the property.

Do you hate me?

I justified taking it, and I still do. It was my payback for the year of abuse, for the anxiety left with me forever. I had been the most honest person I knew, balancing people's books within a cent, and here I was, almost unsurprised by the magnificence of this gift from God, as I saw it.

I hid it in the house. I pretended that I did not have it. I continued with the messy business of sorting out my life, of separating myself from Liam.

I will fast-forward here, because time is truly of the essence, and although I will join the dots if I have time, this is what I wanted to tell you, Beth, that this money, and my small savings brought me here, and bought me here.

I knew, you see, that I wanted to go back to the mountains, but not right into the mountains this time, no, I knew I wanted to live somewhere near a town, somewhere near water, somewhere where mountains surrounded me. And that is how I came to find Mount Beauty, and the country surrounding it. It's how I came to come home. And there is something else, before you think too badly of me. But I don't want to tell you quite yet, I think I want to save the better ending to that story, just for a little while.

* * * * *

There is a little bridge-building that needs to be done, isn't there?

I can't quite take you from there, to here, without a small join in the middle, but I will try and keep it brief, and to the point.

I carefully put back the edge of the shed. I flattened the earth, I left no trace, and I took the money.

I presumed that when Liam had said 'Bastards', he meant that he thought the police had taken it, and I'm sure he did think that. At first I worry that perhaps the money belongs to someone else, or that Liam owes it to someone, but as the days went by, and with it now hidden, like the child's game of Pass the Parcel, in layers of secrecy, in several different places, in case one lot was found, it became obvious that nobody nobody was going to ask, or enquire, or search or bully.

But of course, there's the little question of Liam, of the property, the animals, and most importantly of my future.

As a Catholic, the idea of a punishing or loving God runs deep; heaven and hell are in our DNA, but so too is the idea of divine protection, and Archangels and Angels, are, to most Catholics, real people, people to whom one turns in a crisis.

And so, I will never know if it was because I had enough faith left in me, despite the batterings I'd received, to still carry the idea of divine help deep in my heart, or some unknown and invisible source of support that protected me during this strange time, but protected I was, Beth. I've often wondered if perhaps some heavenly forces of my ancestors, of Flora, of my sister/mother, my mother/grandmother, my father/grandfather, of Florado, most surely my father, of Harry and Eadweard too, who came together and said *enough is enough*.

Had I learned the lessons I was supposed to learn? Had I simply survived these strange twists of fate in order to become a woman, living in the country, with a small trucking business, taking horses here and there for people? And why did I become such a woman? What was the purpose of my life? To meet you, to become your family? To discover the true nature of love? To - and here's a hint as to how I managed to straighten myself out – create my range of exotic Mt Beauty Olive Oils. They were a bit of a shock to the locals to be honest, in the beginning, but in the end they were my brainwave Beth. Who would have thought that bottles of extra-virgin oil with sprigs of rosemary, or a chili, or bulbs of garlic, would save my bacon? Or even put the bacon on the table, at least before I became a vegetarian.

But I get a little ahead of myself, because first what happened, was that Tony found out about my plight. Still connected with the Riverina, he was sent a clipping from a cousin about the 'drug lord' languishing in jail. Which was, let's say, a bit excessive, but if Liam saw it, it might well have pleased him.

Tony comes to find me. He gets in his car and drives down to see me. It's a gesture of friendship that I've never, ever forgotten. I really had no idea about how friendships worked, to be truly honest. At that time, I really didn't have any. I had Mary who was kind, but acquiring 'friends' – that was not a skill I brought into the world with me this time around, or so I had always thought.

It was a few months after Liam's arrest, and I was on a trajectory towards recovery. I remember I was in the kitchen, and I was preparing myself a dish from my childhood, a Spanish omelette. I was never much of a cook, not until I truly began to look after myself here, but I'd begun to have the glimmerings of interest again in some level of self-care, and Mary had given me a dozen eggs from her chooks. I had potatoes and onion, and as I drove home from work, I thought about the cooking of it, how, after I'd fed the animals, I would sit at the kitchen table with a glass of wine and savour every mouthful. How, after dinner, I would lock every window and every door, so I could feel safe, even how I would pile the furniture in front of my bedroom door, and I relished this idea, I have to tell you, because then, I could sleep. I'd moved the dog kennels closer to the house. I knew they would alert me if someone, anyone came near. There were three dogs at the time, and Liam, well, he'd just always bred more kelpies to sell, or drown if he couldn't be bothered selling them.

I wasn't having any of that, even in my bruised state. I'd had the dog, Butch, desexed, and his girls, Ruby and Fly as well. Fly, always the timid one, picked on by her bigger, older sister, had managed to wheedle her way out of the kennel and dog runs and into the house. Or had I suggested it to her? I don't really remember, but she was a bit of a lost soul, my darling Fly, and we found each other through our mutual neediness. She made me feel less alone.

This night, the omelette night, the night that Tony arrived, I'm in the house cooking, a glass of wine nearby, Fly curled up near the fire, when I hear the car.

I remember holding the spatula in my hand, suspending it over the pan, while a million tiny needles dart in my brain. Is it the police? Is it Liam, suddenly released? Is it someone looking for the money?

Butch and Ruby start to bark, and Fly, as she hears the sound of a footsteps, turns from my little friend into a ravening beast, as she snarls furiously, scrabbling at the front door in her eagerness to throw herself at whatever intruder this is.

Then I hear his voice.

'Rosa? Rosa? Are you there? God damn it, dogs, shut up!!'

Tony.

I just have the foresight to turn the pan off.

'Yes,' I shout back. 'I'm here. Hang on.'

At the front door, I grab hold of Fly's collar. 'It's okay girl,' I tell her. 'It's a friend.'

Not convinced, she stays in guard dog mode, so that when I open the door Tony is greeted by both of us, me welcoming him, and Fly most definitely not.

He grins. 'Well,' he says. 'Someone's watching out for you. Shhhhh girl, I'm a friend, not a foe.'

'Fly,' I say, in part for want of something better to say. 'That's her name.'

'Fly. Come on Fly, take it easy.'

Hearing her name, Fly's hackles drop and she begins to relax, and the other dogs, the momentary diversion over, settle as well.

Tony steps towards me and as he did Fly growls, a deep, guttural growl that tells both of us she meant business. I'm surprised and it actually makes me wonder if the dogs had known what went on in the house, but I also feel a ping of relief. I have a protector I think, even if I dont't need her right now.

'It's okay,' I tell her, and pat her. 'Come on in,' I say to Tony. 'She'll be fine. Just let her come to you when she's ready.'

Tony walks into my kitchen, and suddenly it seems as if I saw him only yestrerday, and as soon as he's in, Fly relaxes. Pretty soon he's sitting at the table with a glass of wine in his hand, and I'm back at the stove, cooking an omelette for two.

The one thing I notice: we hadn't touched. If Fly had not been there, I think I would have walked straight into his arms. Would they have opened for me? But I knew, back at the stove, curling up the edges of the omelette, that this wasn't a social visit. He'd heard about Liam.

So in due course, we eat our meal, talking about this and that, skirting around the real reason he's here, chatting about his married life – which had most definitely worked out better than mine – his work, my work, Jim and Mary, until finally, after I make us a cup of coffee, he gets to the real reason.

'I wanted to make sure you were alright,' he told me. 'I heard about Liam, about your husband. I'm worried about you. Do you need a lawyer?'

Would you like, Beth, to know the long or the short of it? I would tell you the long, but it would take too long. So it must be short. Cutting to the chase is a daily activity of mine these days, and even though these occasional digressions into an emotional past are interesting enough for me to want you to know about them, what I'm finding is exactly that – it's the emotional past that interests me, not the factual, this-because-of-that past.

We didn't sleep together. I think I would have, just for the sheer comfort of it, if he'd suggested it with more than his eyes. But I had enough pride not to ask if the way he looked at me meant that he would like to, and enough sense (you might say at last) to know it would mean trouble. We ate, and talked and drank into the night, and when he left to go back to his motel, we hugged like the old friends we were, and I felt a whole heap lighter, knowing there was someone I could turn to for advice.

'I'll be there for you the whole way if you need someone,' he tells me as he's leaving. 'If you need a lawyer, or if you need advice I can't give, I'll find someone. Out of this, good will come, mark my words, Rosa.'

I didn't tell him about the money.

I have never, ever told anyone about the money, until you Beth. If you want to tell Will about it, that's your business, if you want anybody more than yourself to read my story, then that is your business, but I am going to the grave with that secret intact, because you will not read this until I am no longer here. But I got that money back to Liam - in a roundabout way, but I managed it. I was a thief who stole a thief's money, but I balanced the scales, and along with it, my pride.

But that night I did tell Tony about my worries. What did it mean that Liam was in prison without bail? Was he likely to be found guilty? Would the police keep on coming after me? How could I protect myself from Liam, or from anyone else he was involved with? Should I move, stay, divorce him?

'Divorce him. Of course.' Post-omelette, glass of wine in hand, on that point Tony is adamant.

Once I start talking, I remember it's hard to stop, but Tony is clear. He points me on the path towards a strategy. At one point he gives me the clue to my future life.

'Can you start again, Rosa? If you can start again without taking anything from here, except what belongs to you, then your divorce will be much cleaner, and I don't suppose Liam will come looking for you,' Tony tells me. 'If men like him feel as if they've been taken advantage of, it burns a fire of revenge in them, and you don't want that.'

I *don't* want that. I didn't want *that*. I turned the words over in my mind. I could start over, thanks to the money I could start over. I'd been thinking I needed to sell the house, to take my share, to do something with the house, but I didn't have to. I was under no obligation, only to the animals. That was easy, I'd find homes for Butch and Ruby, and Fly, well, Fly would come with me. The horses? A bit more complex, but I'd sort it out.

'No,' I said to him. 'I don't want that. I can start again. I have some shares I bought when I sold my parents house. I can start again.'

And that is how Tony came back into my life for a while, as an advisor, as a friend, as a lawyer, helping me through the minefield of the next few years as I extricated myself from the mess I'd created because of a pair of blue eyes.

But in due course, as I did 'start again', and I took charge of my life, we fell out of touch with each other.

He visited me once here, about 15 years ago, and I think it came as a surprise to both of us to see our age reflected back to us in the other. He told me of his children, and of their plans to travel once he'd retired, and how much he was looking forward to retiring. Before he left, he said what seemed like the oddest thing to me.

'I've always envied you Rosa,' he says, as he gets into his car. 'I've envied you knowing you wanted to live in the country. I got caught by the city, and now that I'm heading towards retirement I'm finding all I want to do is to create a garden, and I wish that I'd done it before I got so old and arthritic.'

It seemed so odd to me that someone as successful, as well-rounded, as sane as Tony could envy me, that I didn't even know what to say.

'We've lived our lives, that's all,' I tell him. 'It's all any of us can do. Live our lives.'

We hug, and it's a big hug.

To be honest, I think deep down we knew we would never see each other again.

I was in a relationship with my dear Peter when I heard that Tony had died. With Peter I had finally reached a sense of balance and peace, and perhaps it was because we chose never to live together. He had his place in Mount Beauty, I had mine here, and as you know Beth, we had a good connection, the pair of us.

But I was glad he wasn't with me the morning I got an email from Tony's wife.

I start up my computer that morning, and the first thing I see is Tony's surname blinking out at me. I remember that I yawned and stretched, still sleepy, a cup of tea on the desk, just a routine check of email before I got to my morning chores.

Dear Rosa (I read and for some reason my heart skips a beat),

It's with a great deal of sorrow that I write this email to tell you

that my beloved Tony passed away two days ago of a heart attack. I know that you and he were close, and he often spoke of you with great fondness. I wasn't sure how to let you know but your email was in his work computer, and the firm has kindly allowed me to access it, in order to send emails to those people we feel would want to know. I will be sending out details of the funeral soon, and if you would care to attend you would be more than welcome.

All the very best,

Sophia

Dead. Tony. Wihout me knowing.

Grief again. Howling grief and loss, on the floor with it. Sounds that cause the dogs to howl outside, the very walls to shake with it. Grief for time passed, for a good friend lost, for a lover gone, for one of the few links to my early days no longer there – for, and I understood this completely – someone I could rely on under any circumstances to be there for me. But now, he isn't there, he's died with his wife by his side; he was beloved of her, as he should have been. I had been loved by him, and he by me, but we had not been each other's beloveds, but in that moment my griefstricken heart feels no difference.

And then there is *the* thought, the sudden piercing painful thought, *but I will die next*. Which isn't true as it turns out, I had to lose another precious love from my life before I would begin to feel the tide of time turn so fully against me that now I can feel the water up around my knees rising up, inexorably, inevitably.

Now though, I am not scared, but then, oh then, I was grasped with a bitter fear by the utter pointlessness of life.

I spend the morning in a state of shock, experiencing that strange duality where one minute everything seems futile, and the next, even the act of making a cup of coffee, life seems so precious and fragile.

Peter rings me in due course, and love him as I do, I still bring my layers of obfuscation into play, I buy myself some time, tell him I have a bit of a sore throat and that I'm going to tuck up for the day to take care of myself. He asks me if I want him to bring anything out to me.

'No,' I say. 'That's fine. It's not bad. I think I need a little rest. We can catch up tomorrow.'

'Of course, gorgeous,' he says. (He always called me that: gorgeous, as if I was in any way gorgeous by that time.) 'Tomorrow. I'll call you then.'

And he leaves me to my undisclosed grief, and to my memories.

I did not go to Tony's funeral. I couldn't have told you exactly why not. I had legitimate excuses I know. It was a long way, it would have taken a lot of organizing to get away quickly, there were the animals to take care of – I could extend the list as far as I wanted, really, but the fact is I did not *want* to go. I think I couldn't bear the thought that I would see what a complete life he had without me, how much, despite our care for each other over the years, I was not in his life.

There was another funeral I didn't go to. But this death I did not know about, not until Jim and Mary came to visit, and told me about it, and about something else too.

They had finally decided to retire and pass the orchard to their children, and they'd decided to do some traveling. They'd always had a caravan, but now they'd upgraded to something more upmarket, with all the bells and whistles an elderly couple needed to enjoy life on the road.

When they arrive, all cheer and hugs, Mary insists on making coffee and tea in the caravan.

'Oh, let me Rosa,' she says, when I protest that they're at my place. 'It's all so new and *shiny*.' And indeed, it's almost luminescent in its modernity. Mary is glowing almost as much as her new toy while she shows me all the gadgets it comes with, and Jim sits at the small dining table beaming with pride. I couldn't bring myself to tell them I prefer their old one, that this new one seems claustrophobic to me, so I ooh and aah along with them both, admiring every clever latch and hidden storage place.

When we're all all three of us sitting down, Jim looks straight at me.

'Have you heard?' he says, abruptly.

'No? Heard what? I haven't heard from anybody.'

Mary holds out a hand to *shhhh* him, always the nurturer.

'It's Liam, Rosa,' she says, gently. 'He's dead.'

Oh God, how I wish I was not in that tiny, confined space. My body wants to slip to the floor – with what? With grief and relief in equal measure. I can feel myself sobbing, with no control over the tears falling down my face.

'How?' I ask. 'When?'

Mary puts her hand on top of mine. 'A few weeks ago. He'd been sick for a long time. Lung cancer.'

'Thank you,' I say. 'Thank you for telling me.'

I can feel a crack in my armour opening up to these two. 'I always thought after he got out, he would come and find me,' I say. 'I thought he would come and punish me somehow.'

Mary looks at me curiously. 'He was never going to come after you,' she says. 'Didn't you know?'

'Know what?'

'Your friend Tony, the man who came down to help you when Liam was first in prison, he paid him a visit,' she tells me.

'I don't understand.' I'm truly confused. Why would Tony have paid Liam a visit once he was out of prison? Why would Jim and Mary know about it? Why would they even remember his name?

Well, Beth, it transpired they knew his name because Tony had given it to them. He'd gone to see them after he'd visited me that first time, when Liam was still in jail waiting for his trial. He'd left them his card, he'd said to them *if you ever need me, ring me.*

'After Liam got out, he was saying terrible things about you Rosie,' Jim says. (He never did take to the name Rosa.) 'He kept saying you'd stolen things from him, that he was going to come and get you, and we were worried for you, we truly were.'

And even though the danger is well and truly over, my blood runs cold at these words. My anxiety, my pounding fear at night, my guilt that the money I'd taken was blood-money, that Liam would find me and kill me, trembles again through my veins while at the same time warm liquid safety, as sweet as honey, coarsed through me. I was out of danger, my heart told me, and Tony had *again* taken care of me. But I hadn't been safe, my brain tells me, firing darts at me, I'd been stupid, so stupid. How had I lulled myself into a false feeling of security? Thought, after a few years had passed, that Liam had given up on the idea of finding me? How could I possibly have imagined that Liam would decide not to come after me? Of course he would have. He was always going to find me, somehow, some way. If you can feel retrospective fear, I felt it then.

'Do you know what Tony told him?' I ask them.

Mary shakes her head. 'No idea. We called Tony and asked him to come down we were so worried about the crap Liam was spouting. He came almost straight away, went to see Liam, and after that there was no more bad-mouthing you, love, nothing. Liam virtually went to ground. Harry gave him a job working in his shed, and that's where Liam was until almost the day he died. He worked, drank and smoked, and died. He lost his place of course, it got sold out from under him, but you would have known that.'

'No,' I say, 'I didn't. One of the things Tony worked out with me was not to go after any of the house when we got divorced. I didn't want anything to do with him that might mean he could trace me.'

'Oh,' Mary's brow creases slightly, 'but then how…' and her voice trails away. She looks at Jim, and they both look at me.

'I was lucky,' I say, standing up. 'I got this place for a song. I had my savings from Mexico, and from my years of working.'

And inside, I'm thanking Tony from the bottom of my heart for his protection of me. I might never know what it was he said, or threatened, but I had been safe since that moment, and now I was safe forever more.

Oh Beth, I can remember as if it was yesterday the circumstances that led me here. When I finally pulled up with Fly at Tawonga, we were (literally) dog-tired, and there was an old motel – you know the one on the corner of the lane – that allowed pets. On an impulse I booked us in. No camping that night, the thought of falling into a bed was too sweet, and that night, after I'd fed us both, and walked Fly out under the clear night sky, we fell into bed and drifted off into sleep almost immediately. When I woke up it was to the sound of birdsong and sunshine, and some tightly wound spring in me relaxed, just a little, enough for me to breathe deeply, to stand still, to think to myself that perhaps, before we moved on again, we might take a few days rest.

During that 'rest' while we were exploring the area, I took to looking in the local real estate agents' windows for something to rent, somewhere, where I could just land for a few months, or a little longer. And that's when I saw this place, *mi casa*, although I did not know that at the time. It was described as being: 'A small stone house in an idyllic rural setting for rent. The house is also for sale.' Well, the 'For Sale' part didn't interest me at the time but hiding in the bush in a rented small stone cottage, that certainly did. I think the real–estate agent, Janet, was surprised that anyone should want to look at it. It was, she explained to me, as we drove out there, a deceased estate. It was on the market, but nobody was making any offers, and so the children of the couple who had both died, had decied to rent it out, but to also keep it on the market. As a rental agent she wasn't entirely happy about this situation, she led me to understand in a roundabout way, because it meant that no-one who wanted more than a three-month (although renewable) lease was going to stay.

Also, she told me, as we arrived at the bottom of the driveway: 'It has its quirks.'

And it did, Beth. Hot water was only available through the wood stove, the house itself was run down, none of the doors fitted properly, there were some rotten planks in the verandah, the bathroom was probably built at the turn of the century, and the toilet was outside.

Shall we go there for a minute? Shall we leave Jim and Mary suspended in limbo? They can wait. I'm sure they would be happy to wait.

Janet is describing things to me.

'You don't have to do look after the land, obviously,' she says. 'It's 150 acres. A local farmer agists his cattle, but he doesn't use the 10 acres at the front.'

We're walking around the perimeter of the house as we talk.

'There's an outside toilet,' she says, and looks at me, probably, I imagine waiting for that to be the clincher for me, that I'll say, well, thanks but no thanks. But I simply nod. Because I'm lost Beth, lost in a world where I am already repairing, building, planting.

She shows me the fruit trees, in this springtime heavy with scent, and the old barn, jam-packed to the rafters with old 'stuff'.

'I'm organizing someone to come and empty this,' she tells me. 'We haven't had many people look at it, but the feedback is that people would rather the barn was empty.'

Then I think perhaps she thinks she's being a bit negative, because she flashes me a bright, toothy smile. 'But it is beautiful, isn't it?' she says, ʹand very lucky for around here because it has a natural spring on it, so there's always water.ʹ

And I nod again, because, to be honest, I don't really care whether the barn is empty, or the toilet outside, or the whole house falling into a state of disrepair, or whether there's a spring, or not, I want to *live* there, and I want to live there *now*.

ʹHow much did you say it was for rent?ʹ I ask casually, lightly.

ʹIt's $200 per week, but to be honest I think we could be a little negotiable if you'd like it. You're the first person to look at it that I think the owners would be happy with,ʹ she tells me.

As I follow her back into town, Fly sitting up on the back seat, her nose pressed to the window, her tail making happy thumping noises, I know that I am about to be the luckiest woman in the world. I am about to land in my own personal paradise.

And that was it Beth. By the next morning I had a signed lease, for $150 per week, with Janet's warning: ʹYou know it's for sale, so you'll need to keep it tidy if there's anyone that wants to see it,ʹ ringing in my ears, because I had no idea how I would manage to buy it, but that was my plan, right from the word go.

This is what I did. I got a job as a book-keeper two days a week in town, I got Fly a companion, her dear friend Lottie – both of them gone to dog heaven a long time ago now – and I built a dog-run for the days I wasn't there. I got my Medium Rigid license, and I bought a small four-horse truck, I advertised my transport services, and when, after three months, my lease was renewed, and again three months later, I was ready: I had a job, I had a business, I had much more than the deposit. I made an offer, and thanks to the fact that no-one had shown the slightest bit of interest in the property, because for most purchasers, there was no value at all in the house, I got it, as they say, for a song.

Of course, you know the story of Exotic Oils. Well, you know the real story. I was never going to put my name out there for Liam to find. Instead, I invented an Italian version of me. It even says it on the bottle, doesn't it?

'It all started with a dream. Missing the taste of chili infused oil from her native Italy, one night Sofia Romano had a dream of creating a range of exotic olive oils. Choose from Sofia's range of rosemary, garlic, lemon or chili-infused oil to add an exotic element to your cooking.'

I liked the idea of an Italian Rosa, it was a kind of homage to Gio and Maria.

What I remember most about those first few years here, working so hard, balancing my job with moving horses, creating the oils, selling the oils at the markets at the weekends, finding stockists, building the business, that I was so tired, I could fall asleep anywhere, at any time. But I was determined I was going to save up that $100,000 and give it back to Liam. It had been a gift, but it was a gift that needed returning, otherwise, I knew I could not live with myself.

In the end, the solution came to me so simply, so beautifully, that it was as if the universe was just waiting for me to understand it. The money needed to be returned, but not necessarily to *him*. It needed to go out into the world and do good again. These illegally gotten gains, needed to stand up and be counted, and create their own good karma.

But you know what I found during those years before the solution presented itself? Before I met you both and rediscovered family, I discovered resilience, and I discovered, which I suppose should not surprise you, my maverick nature. I discovered that although I like – even love – individuals, I am not a team player. As people began to know me in the nearby towns, they would ask me to things, or to join the local Country Women's Association, or to join a choir, or well, almost anything really. And I couldn't. Sometimes I would try, but even the attempt to turn up at something where people were gathered, where questions might be asked, even in the friendliest of fashions, was too much for me. I would succumb to anxiety, and retreat to my place, to my world, this world – the land, my work, the horses, the oils. It was *enough* already. Enough contact with outsiders, enough conversations, enough to deal with, enough with the constant river of shame running through me that I had allowed my life to be derailed at so many points. I was never going to let that happen again. And I never have.

Then on top of all the work was the house, because it demanded my time and energy, and when I had put aside the money towards Liam, almost anything spare went on repairing the stone walls, then later putting in a decent kitchen and bathroom, so that when I met you Beth, it was the place – I hope – of comfort and warmth that we all feel it to be.

But to go back now to Jim and Mary; I understand immediately what they're both thinking. I wonder if Tony had guessed after he'd spoken to Liam and said whatever he'd said to shut him up. What had he said? I think about Tony's Italian family. The whole district, as he'd once described it to me, could be like 'The Godfather', and there were those on the good side, and quite frankly those not. Tony could have used fair means or foul to scare Liam off.

Jim and Mary are relieved to end the conversation.

'Come and meet the horses,' I say, 'and take a look at my citrus trees, Jim.'

Jim nods, back on safe turf, and off we go, and that was that.

Except of course that when Peter comes out for lunch on the verandah and we have a more cheerful, quiet time, Mary hugs me as they leave, and tells me; 'You've done well there Rosa, he's lovely, and so's your place,' I am left to my thoughts, and strange indeed they are.

That night, lying in Peter's arms, I give a silent prayer of gratitude to Tony for his help, and to Jim and Mary too, for their protection. And I say a prayer, too for Liam's soul. I forgive him for his abuse of me, I ask forgiveness for taking the money and I hope that by finding a use for the money I am absolved. *Two wrongs*, I feel I can hear God's voice whisper to me, *don't make a right, Rosa*. And perhaps that is true, but perhaps sometimes that is *not* true. In this case my 'wrong' allows me to get away, to find this place, to make a business, to build a life, to meet you all, to meet Peter, and to then repay the wrong.

How do you repay $100,000 when you don't want to go near the person you've 'borrowed' it from? How do you repay $100,000 in cash without putting it into a bank account? How do you repay it, and let the person know, without being in touch with him? This was not an easy problem to grapple with Beth, it gave me months of headaches, going this way and that.

How do you repay it, when you don't, in fact, want to?

You know, don't you Beth, if you think about it, if you join the dots, what I did in the end. You walk past it every time you go to town, if you park near the bottom of the carpark, and past the backend entrance to the supermarket, you will have seen – even if you have not noticed specifically – the small plaque that says: *'The accommodation wing for this refuge was made possible by a donation from R. McDermott.'* The last time I would ever use that surname. I donated $100,000 to the building of the accommodation for the Safe House for Women and Children in Albury/Wodonga. Of course, I didn't tell Liam.

It was quite accidental, or not, depending on your point of view. I wouldn't say that the problem kept me awake at night, or only occasionally, anyway, or that it stopped me from continuing to lead my life, but it was there, gnawing away at me – how should I return the money?

One morning, I happen to be shopping, and as I walk down the main street, two young women sitting behind a table outside one of the town's dress shops, shake a tin at me as I pass.

'We're collecting money for the women's shelter,' one of them says to me, seeing me glance in their direction.

I stop, and fidlle around in my bag for some change.

'There you are,' I say, pushing a $5 note in.

'Thank you.' The young woman beams up at me. 'That's very generous.'

I smile back at her. 'It's an important cause,' I say.

And I walk away, clutching the leaflet in my hand. No more thought of it then, but the next day, clearing out my bag, the leaflet is there still, and as I look at it, and think about all the women, of all ages being sheltered there, their lives, I hope, being saved, it comes to me – this was where Liam's money has to go. This is the absolution, the repayment. He would never know, but I was safer that way, because if he never knew I'd taken it, he would never coming looking for me, he would never know where I was, and he would never, ever know that his stolen money was providing safety for abused women.

It was neat. It was fitting, and it was what I organised, with very little trouble, very few questions asked, and far less bureaucracy than I'd imagined. When people are being offered money, I discovered, they're pretty keen to get it done and dusted as quickly as possible. Within a few days, it was *done*. And then I walked away from that money, that giving. They insisted they wanted a plaque. I gave them the name: R McDermott. I didn't go for the unveiling. I told them I wanted it to be anonymous, but I was happy enough for them to use R McDermott if they really needed to thank me. It was enough. That was the end.

You, of course, knew Peter. No need to tell you the story of his place in my life in those last years of his life, and of the dear companion he was to me, before I, before we, lost him on that terrible night.

But you don't know how we met. And it's light and funny, which I think would be a relief right now, for us both I should imagine.

So this is how it came about: I'm shopping at the supermarket, I can remember it very clearly because I was standing near the end of one of the aisles, at the corner, looking at the tins of tomatoes on special, and wondering if I wanted whole tinned tomatoes, chopped tomatoes, or tomatoes with herbs.

I'm in a world of tomatoes, when a man walks backwards around the corner, dragging rather than pulling his trolley, and bumps into my trolley so hard, my trolley bumps into me and knocks me over!

'Hey!' I say indignantly. 'Watch where you're going!'

'I'm so sorry,' the man, Peter, says. 'I've got one of those stupid trolleys with a bung wheel.'

He bends down and offers me his hand. 'Let me help you up.'

'I don't need any help,' I say brusquely, rearranging myself.

He looks at me, with a certain, I don't know, laughter in his eyes. 'No,' he says. 'I can tell you wouldn't.'

'I don't even know what that means,' I say, stomping off, away from this nuisance of a man. Who follows me.

'Can't I buy you a cup of coffee then? As an apology?' he asks, walking behind me, dragging his wretched trolley and talking to me over his shoulder.

Another woman, I remember, is coming down the same aisle, on the opposite side.

'If you don't watch out you're about to take out someone else,' I say.

He turns his head. 'Oops.' He stops until the woman passes him, and I take my chance to get out of the aisle and into the checkout line, but, as luck would have it, he manages to get in behind me.

'Look at that,' he says cheerfully. 'No-one behind me, so we can keep talking.´

I sigh inwardly, possibly outwardly as well. *Why,* I wonder, *is this man pestering me?*

´I'm concentrating,´ I say, carefully putting my items on the conveyor.

´I'll help you,´ he says, plunging into my trolley and picking up random items.

´There is an order to this.´ I say, my heart thumping. I just wanted this annoying man to GO AWAY. I ostentatiously take out the items he'd taken out of my trolley and put them back in, taking out the ones I wanted. Cold foods together, tinned foods together, bottles together, soft packages last and together.

´I bet your cupboards are tidier than mine,´ he says, watching me.

´I'm sure they are.´ I pay for my shopping, and give him a glance, my eyes suddenly registering him. He's nicely dressed, he looks like a country man through and through with his jeans, boots, checked shirt and an oilskin jacket. He's grey-haired of course, and with the brownest eyes I've ever seen.

´Right,´ I say, suddenly eager to get away. ´Well, goodbye…´

He nods. ´Bye…?´

´Rosa.´

´Bye Rosa. I'm Peter.´

I just smile and push my trolley out into the sunshine towards my car, and quickly forget him while I unload my shopping into the back of the cruiser. It's chilly, the beginning of autumn, the first sudden real sense of cold in the air, and after I've finished unpacking I close the door, and think I should zip up my jacket, before I head for the café, my usual stop after my shopping. But my zipper gets stuck, and the more I try to pull it up, the more uneven it gets. I was just beginning to think I'd actually have to take the jacket off and step out of it, which would have been a) inconvenient and b) cold, when Peter, whose car is (of course) parked right next to mine, simply comes up to me.

'Here,' he says. 'Let me help you with that.'

And he does. He stands there, while I try to look away, fiddling with the teeth in the zip to get them even, and every now and then, our eyes meet, and I don't know what he sees in mine, but in his deep brown pools I see all my Mexican ancestry, every pair of laughing brown eyes I've ever known, and try as I might to keep a distant look to me, I can feel myself soften. Much *more* than soften, I can feel a river of heat run through me. I haven't stood this close to a man since Liam. I'd sworn off them forever, and now every nerve is tingling, despite me willing my body to behave itself, to make itself like the ice it was accustomed to being.

'There!' he says. 'Done. You need a new jacket.'

'I do not,' I say indignantly. 'This one's perfectly fine.'

'Yes,' he says, 'and about 20 years old if I'm not mistaken.'

And me? I immediately arc up and feel cross again. I just want him to go away.

'Well,' I say. 'Thank you.'

'Think of it as a repayment for barging into you. Now,' he says, 'let me buy you a coffee. I know you have one after your shopping. I've seen you here before.'

And, so I reluctantly agree, and that, dear Beth, is how it started.

I don't have to tell you much about the Peter years, do I Beth? Because it was during this time that I was suddenly from being a single, lonely icicle to a woman with a lover, and a surrogate family, and a home, and my horses, the ones I kept after I stopped the small trucking business and the oils had taken over. The three most precious – Princess, my original Golden Girl, passed now of course, the mother of Freya and Thor. Soon I will see her again, very soon.

I had a dream the other night, Beth. I dreamt that Freya was three years old again, and she and I were at the beginning of our training journey together. I was riding her with just a rope-halter and reins, and we were at the edge of a camping ground. She was still young and a little hesitant, but I encouraged her on, and soon we were going in and out of the trees behind the grounds, until suddenly we were on a path going up a mountain. I urged her into a trot, and soon she was into her beautiful, even Quarter Horse canter.

In the dream we ride and ride, Beth, we ride over a mountain, and down the other side, to a farmhouse where people welcome us, giving us both food and drink; and then we ride along a busy road back towards a town where – in the dream – we live. We are free, and we are together. I'll miss her when I go, but I'll stay and watch over them, Princess and I together I'm sure, and Peter of course, Peter will be there, watching as well.

But although you may feel you know the life Peter and I shared, you didn't see the secret life, the life I have to tell you about my darling friend, the bedroom life, if you will. Older sex is *good* sex Beth, to my own surprise, I might add. And as I think about it now, perhaps the kernel, in many ways, of this story of Eadweard and Flora and Harry and Florado, and of me, and my life is sex, when it comes down to it, it is as simple and complicated as that, really.

Hang on to that my friend, through these days of children, of wilful teenagers of Will so tired he falls asleep at 8.00pm, of you frustrated, exhausted and depleted. Hang on and be kind to each other because out the other side lies a different landscape, a deep and sensuous river of physical affection without the constant rollercoaster of fluctuating hormones – and in your case interrupting children – without the battleground noise of the war of the sexes. It ends, Beth. At least it did for me, and I hope it does for you.

I miss Peter every day. I thank my lucky stars for the time we had together, and for the fact that the cancer was quick. So quick. Six months only from diagnosis to his departure from this earth. I have long conversations with him still Beth, about what I should do about replacing a broken tap or mending a bit of fence. He was never backwards in coming forward with his opinion of how I should manage my place, was he?

I miss his laughing brown eyes, his sudden sweet kisses when I was being cross or stern about God knows what, his savouring of every moment of life, always in the moment. Old as I am, as close to the end as I am, I miss the sex, Beth. That's the truth.

Of course, Peter's life was complex. You knew that, although there was much I didn't tell you; his anguish over his ex-wife's decision to move to Perth when his two children were small, overnight and with no warning. Her sudden re-marrying, the blocking of him out of their lives as much as she could. He even went to Perth to live, to try and be close to his daughters, but Yvonne wasn't having any of that. She put up so many blockages to his access, in so many subtle and difficult ways, that in the end he came back here, to the area where he was born, where his parents and grandparents lived, where he had family.

He knew as well as me, the loss of famiy: he knew what I did not know – the pain of your children growing up without you. When the girls were finally old enough to make decisions for themselves, he offered them fares to come and visit him, and they did come, which was solace of a sort for him, but there was so much water, so much wounding, so much they did not understand, that it was awkward.

When he first got sick, I told him: ´Write to them Peter, tell them your truth.´ To his credit, he did. And they came again, as adults, as parents themselves, to spend time with him. I got out of their way as much as possible, so they could get to know their father, before he left this earthly plane, and they were grateful; although to be honest, Beth,

I think they were even more grateful when they heard that everything he owned was being left to them, and not to me. (Although not quite everything, there was provision made for me before and after he died, and I'm grateful for that. It was never anticipated.)

What would you tell me you remember, Beth? Coming here for dinner with Will and the kids, I hope. Our stews, and roasts and baked dinners, the desserts one of us would make, the firepit outside, the red wine, and conversations, and above us, the stars of the mountain sky, so bright, so clear, so close to the infinite secret of the universe.

The secret I am getting closer and closer to knowing, Beth. The secret of going home.

Chapter 23

Returning Home

Eadweard walks slowly down the gangplank, and as he places his foot once more on English soil, he knows with certainty what he had suspected when he began to set his affairs in order – that he has turned his back on America. He has come 'home', and everything has been prepared. He knows he should feel content at this turn of events, that he has a home, and family, to come home to, but what stabs through him is not the warm feeling of homecoming, but the sharp needle of failure. Failure that he spent *so* much money on the Chicago World Fair for the promotion of his Zoopraxograph, and that audiences still preferred to see – and in his mind he sneers over the words, *the dancing girls of Cairo* – to his invention. He has often found himself disappointed with the human race, he thinks, but rarely as much as with this last effort. And it has cost him – not just money, but pride. He is not as young as he was, even the physical effort of the preparation of the hall, the creation of the book and the plates for sale, all this effort took its toll. He wonders if perhaps he would have felt this exhausted disappointment so keenly when he was younger, he suspects not. *My own life has taken its toll on me,* he thinks, *but it was not always so.*

He nears the bottom of the gangplank, and turns, seeing once more the young man he was so many years ago, so different he can scarcely comprehend he is the same person. Even his own name has been carefully chosen over time, adjusted until its calibration, as he likes to think of it, has become exactly what his personality required.

Yet for all the years he has lived away, he has still always felt the immigrant's malaise, the strange uncertainty of constant, inevitable yearning that has drawn him back here for his final days.

'Mr. Muybridge? Sir?'

The young man has been given a photograph and there is no mistaking the tall, slightly stooped figure, with the long white beard and snowy-white hair.

Eadweard walks slowly towards the waiting carriage.

'Thank you,' he says. 'You will find my bags back there, with the luggage. The rest will follow.'

As they pass through the lush English countryside, Eadweard is surprised, as always, at how quiet, how serene, how almost like models of themselves the villages and towns are, picturesque and somehow miniature, as if reflecting the size of the island they are built upon.

So different to America, he thinks, as the memories flicker through his brain: Yosemite, of course, the desert, the goldfields, New York, San Francisco – the brash young cities and towns springing up, and yet still so much wilderness. Then there is the other place. The place he would rather not think about. The place, the incident – the life – he will not think about.

At Rosewater they stop to rest the horse. Eadweard strides ahead into the inn.

'I shall order us lunch while you see to the horse,' he says.

'Sir...' Matthew calls after his rapidly retreating back.

'Yes?'

'I have my lunch.' He points to the box on the top of the carriage. Not his place, he knows, to eat with his employer.

'Nonsense.' Eadweard taps his cane on the ground. 'You will eat with me. Anyway,' he says, taking pity on the young man's doubtful face. 'I need the company.'

And indeed, by the time the horse has food and drink, and Matthew arrives, lunch is served at a table window.

'So, Matthew Stanton…' the old man's English accent has softened with all the years away, there is a slight lazy drawl to his voice. An American accent, Mathhew supposes, although he's never heard one. 'How old are you?'

'Eighteen, Sir.'

'Eighteen. Three years younger than I was when I left. You want to know why I left, Matthew?'

'Why, Sir?'

'I left because of death.'

'Sir?'

'My father, John, was a corn and coal merchant here in Kingston. He was a good man, Matthew. He died when I was 13, then when I was 17 my older brother died, and later, when I owned a bookshop in America, my younger brother George came to work for me, and died. Perhaps if I had realised that there is no point in trying to outrun death I might never have left, Matthew."

'I'm sorry, Sir.'

'Don't be sorry,' Eadweard takes a sip of the glass of red wine in front of him. 'Things have come full circle now because I have come home to die, Matthew. That is the truth of it. I've stopped trying to outrun death. I realised the faster I was running, the closer 'He' was getting. He has more breath than me, you see, so I have changed tactics and come to meet him. I am going to slow down and sit still, and perhaps that will out fox the cunning old devil for a while.'

'But Sir…' Thomas is at a loss to know what to say.

'It's all right, Matthew.' Eadweard looks at his young employee sympathetically. 'I don't need comforting. All I require is that you keep me company, and perhaps I shall tell you stories of my glory days from time to time if the mood strikes me. I still have some books to put together, and some lectures to give, and when I'm not working, you can tell me about what is happening around me. We shall take visits out here and there, who knows, maybe you and I will even venture forth to a racetrack or two. I enjoy being in the presence of horses.'

Thomas nods.

'My parents mentioned you were in the newspapers, Sir, something to do with movement, wasn't it?'

Eadweard smiles. 'It was Matthew. It was exactly to do with movement, as you say.' He stretches his arms back and yawns. 'And now I think we should recommence our journey. I may even find it incumbent upon me, if the road is smooth enough to close my eyes for a few moments, before I face the overwhelming excitement of being back in the bosom of my family.'

Matthew laughs. 'Fair enough, Sir. I shall be as quiet as a mouse.'

In his room Eadweard begins to settle himself. He carefully opens an old, battered suitcase and takes out his books, his old travelling clock, his binoculars and his notepads. Settling himself in the armchair in the corner of the room, he covers himself with a blanket and breathes a sigh of relief. *Whatever home is,* he thinks, *this will do.*

His head is throbbing tonight. The old injury is making its presence felt. He feels his head gingerly, running his fingers over the uneven ridge on the top of his skull. He has often wondered what course his life might have taken if he had not had his brain opened to the world. *Perhaps that was what created his destiny*, he thinks, the opening to his brain drawing in so many – too many – sensations, as if he was taking in the whole world at once. He knows how solid he was before, and he knows how fluid he became after, prone, as all those who have ever had a care for him since have told him, to being irrational and unpredictable. What sort of life might he have had? His mind drifts off into pleasant avenues of improbability, a seller of fine antiquarian books until the day he died, perhaps, or a grand invention making him so rich he could live with the toffs on Nobb's Hill and never work again. Maybe, he thinks, as he drifts off into sleep, I might have married a different woman, we might still be married now, and it would be my wife taking care of me, instead of me ending my days in my cousin's house.

* * * * *

History tells us, Beth, that Eadweard spent the last 10 years of his life consolidating his reputation as a time-lapse photographer. He was, quite simply, everywhere. He believes the ancient Egyptians understood exactly how animals moved, and that knowledge was lost until his photographic investigation. He's in *The Times*, he's sending books to universities and libraries around the world; his occupation on the 1901 English census is given as *Zoopraxographer*, not *photographer*, reflecting his invention of 'moving' pictures; books are published, he lectures, and all the time he photographs: naked men, naked women, animals, all caught in the most minute detail of movement possible, forever and forever and forever.

On March 14, 1904, in failing health from his prostate cancer, he writes his will, dying one month after his 74th birthday.

In his will he leaves his watch to Florado. Why? In an attempt to reconcile that just the grown man, still living in Texas, was his son after all? To give a message – most literally – that if he could, he would turn back time? A watch then was important, Beth, a gentleman's fob watch, not just a 'thing' but a sign of standing in the community. What it tells me though, is that Eadweard *thought* of Florado, of his possible son; he hadn't forgotten him, despite the years since, his public life, his apparent lack of care. He thought of him, and if he thought of him, he thought of Flora, and of Harry. Of that, I'm sure.

In a last irony, for someone who so carefully chose his name, adjusting until it suited his complicated needs, the stone marking his ashes has his name spelled *Eadweard Maybridge,* and the crematorium register calls him, *Eudweard Muybridge.*

Chapter 24

Horses

Have I been saving the best until last? Or, more likely, am I nervous to write this bit Beth? The final bit, the piece of the jigsaw puzzle that explains 'me'.

These days I sometimes feel that I'm at least 50 percent horse, and I have become convinced that part of me has been a horse all along. I have become so acutely aware of the slightest nuance of communication with my two beloved companions, and not just with them. It seems if I take myself to town, and there are too many people around, my 'horse within' flares up, feels contained and scared. She wants to break free, get away. I have the devil's own job persuading her not to run.

But I suppose I should start from the beginning. Because, in a way, horses have had their own parallel life within my life, and if it had not been for Liam, I would not have found the animal that was destined to become my healer, my teacher and my mentor.

I expect you are used now to me jumping here and there, Beth, so let us go back, back again to the time, when I have made the decision to get out of Liam's place, to file for divorce, to move on. I had no plans at that time to have horses in my life, other than a vague longing to see the brumbies in the high country again, and the sense of peace I got when I went to feed the horses in Liam's paddocks. I did not know that horses were sitting in the bedrock of 'me', waiting to make their presence felt.

I was lucky in one way, because at the time of Liam's arrest there were only six horses on the property. Three of them were due to be delivered by him to their new homes, and somehow, in the muddle of the room he called his office, I found those order forms. Somehow, I mustered enough courage to call the prospective owners and tell them that Liam's truck had broken down, and that I would be organizing another trucking company to pick up the horses. I told them that the horse would arrive a few days later than they were expecting, but that they would be with them soon. They were understanding, and one of them, a mother, said to me: 'Julie can't wait to get her new pony, she's so excited.'

I thought of the pretty grey pony, so calm and steady and quiet from the moment it had arrived, and I was glad that Julie was getting a good one. There had been a few that had arrived to stay before the next part of their journey, and let's just say they weren't horses I would have wanted arriving on my doorstep, but Liam had a way with horses, as he had with women at times, I suppose. The horses never saw him drunk, and it seemed as if he saved his best self for them. I think perhaps part of what kept me there with him was how he handled horses – his firm kindness, his ability to settle them down, and not over-react when they were in high adrenalin mode. I had no idea that just by watching him, I was learning skills that were going to become a huge part of my future life.

It was logical work Beth: do this, do that, ring this person, ask Jim and Mary if they knew someone who did horse trucking – they put me on to the President of the local Pony Club – so I could find a trucking company, and get those three horses to their destinations. I paid for it myself. I wanted it done and dusted so that all would be left would be Liam's three, his 25-year-old Quarter Horse, bought 12 years before for camp-drafting. He'd been competitive in his day, old Buster, Liam had told me when he'd introduced me to him.

'He's given me some glory days, Rosa,' he'd said, and the old chestnut had nuzzled his master. 'He's safe with me,' he'd said. 'He'll live his days out here.'

Safe with him. How could he keep a horse safe, and not his wife? What strange broken piece in him allowed him to be kind to his horses, and not his wife? You can see, can't you Beth, even now, even after he's been gone for so long, and I am content, how that question will remain unanswered for me forever. I can hear your calm voice saying, *but he was an abuser Rosa, an alcoholic abuser,* and that is true, and yet, and yet, and yet...

When Buster had retired, Liam had bought himself, as horse people do, another younger Quarter Horse to continue competing on, but poor old Peppy came into his life just as Liam's trucking business was taking off, soon to be followed, I suppose, by his forays into drug trafficking, his bouts of drinking, and me. So Peppy, a solid 14.3hh bay with two white socks and a blaze, was, as they say, 'wasting away' being a paddock ornament. And with Buster and Peppy was the last of the trio, the plainly named Fred, a two-year-old, not yet broken in, a project for Liam, he'd said, in his spare time, but there he was too, nothing being done, and no future of anything really, now bail had not been met.

I was lucky Beth, this little herd being such three quiet geldings, even young Fred – Steady Freddy, I nicknamed him pretty soon. I had no idea, to be honest, how many difficult horses were out there, and if Liam was my abuser, at the very least the gift he gave me was that I had to step up to look after these three, and in looking after them I had to get out of bed every morning, feed them, be responsible for something other than me and learn how to handle them. In those first few muddled months, before Tony came down on his mercy mission, Jim taught me so much about horse care, and again, although I took it on board because I *had* to for their sake, I still never thought in my wildest dreams that it was leading me to a career as a horsewoman.

So as my heart and soul mended, just a little, and I gradually made plans with my meagre savings (not counting the shed money), to move on, to get out of there, to get back to the mountains and somewhere where I hoped against hope Liam would never find me, these three became a conundrum for me. I couldn't take them with me, I couldn't sell them, but how could they stay there? Who woud pay for their feed? The dogs were easy, Fly was coming with me no matter what, and to be honest, as kind as Liam was to his horses, his dogs as far he was concerned, were just something you had because country people have dogs. The two boys, both Kelpies desexed now, and with good working-dog lines would go to Jim and Mary's cousins who had a large property out of town. Mary told me they'd be happy to keep the dogs for however long Liam was in prison, and that they'd let him know the dogs were safe.

One day when we are busy sorting out the dog problem, I ask Mary: ʹWhat about Fly? What do we say?ʹ

ʹLeave it to me,ʹ she tells me. ʹMaybe Fly meets with an accident.ʹ

ʹAnyway,ʹ I say, ʹhe probably won't even ask about her.ʹ And to my knowledge, he never did.

I talk to the horses, to Fred, Peppy and Buster, every morning when I give them their hay and check their water. I like standing by the fence watching them. I quickly learn the hierarchy: feed Peppy first, Buster second and Fred third. A couple of times Fred challenges Buster, and Buster holds his own, but I wonder for how long. I tell them about my dilemma, and I tell them everything Liam had been doing. They would stand and munch their breakfast, while I would ramble on and on. Sometimes the catharsis is too much for me, and I end up in tears, and I say to them: ʹSo you see, that's why I can't take you with me.ʹ

I try to find homes for them, separately or together, and the closer I get to leaving, the more I worry about what to do.

One morning, a chilly winter's morning when my breath is making warms puffs of steam into the air, I ask them all: ʹCan't you sort it out?

Can't you pull something out of the air? I want the best for you, I really do, but I don't know *what* the best is.'

For a brief moment Buster looks up at me from his hay. His gaze locks into mine, just for a few seconds, but I have the weirdest impression he's saying, *well why didn't you ask before?* And that is my first experience of horse magic, because that evening, not long after I'm back from work, Mary rings me. I'm surprised to hear from her so soon and I wonder if I've left something undone at work.

'What's up?' I ask.

'Well,' she says, 'I might have an answer to your problem. Claire's just rung me to ask me if I know anyone who might have somewhere for a young woman to stay for a while. Her name's Lilly, and she's been at the caravan park for a few months. She really loves it here, and she's found work in town. She wants to stay, but she's had enough of a tent in the cold, she's looking for somewhere not too expensive. It might cover the costs of the house. She's had horses of her own, so she could look after the horses, too...'

I'm amazed, stunned, really. How had Buster managed to solve a problem I'd been working on for so long?

'Wonderful,' I say. 'Perhaps she can come over and meet me here tomorrow?'

And just like that it's all organised; Lilly will come over in the afternoon after work, and we'll see how it pans out. When I go out to give the horses their evening feed, I pat Buster while he eats.

'Well,' I say to him. 'You worked quickly. How on earth did you manage it?' Because somehow, blame it on my Mexican blood, I have absolutely no trouble in believing that Buster had understood me, and had somehow pulled off this small miracle. I can even swear I feel a gentle kind of knowing, spreading up into my hands as I stroke him. And there was this feeling that somehow everything will be alright.

Gradually, we put the pieces of the jigsaw puzzle together. Lilly will come and stay straight away. There's enough money in Liam's account – I know, because I do his books – to cover, with the help from Lilly's rent – horse-feed, electricity, gas, his mortgage and rates for a year, all going well. One morning, not long before I leave, I wake up at the crack of dawn, and a thought occurrs to me that if the police freeze his bank accounts because the money in there is illegal, what will I do?

What will Lilly and the horses do?

Well, that is a conundrum. I have access to his accounts, I could transfer money to Jim and Mary, but then I might be implicating me, and them. I just want to know that the horses will be okay, and as I lie there, worrying this way and that, Buster's voice comes to me clear as bell. *Don't worry,* he says. *You've looked after us. We'll be fine. And thank you.*

And just like that, the worry lifts. I know I've done everything I can. Nothing else is my business. It's time, I think, to start getting ready. All being well and the money lasting a year, something will work itself out. I thank Buster, and after breakfast I ring Jim who says he will go out and talk to Liam.

I almost, so *almost,* leave Lilly with some of the shed money, but the night before I was due to go, the Cruiser packed with all my worldly belongings, I lie in bed, and find a quiet space inside me, and into that space comes the words: *Daughter, don't leave her the money.* To this day Beth, I don't know if it was my sister/mother, or my mother/grandmother, or a Higher Power, even perhaps an echo of my Catholic background, a saint coming forward out of the shadows; but whoever she was, I thank that voice, and tell it I will not. What I do instead is to tell Mary and Jim that if Liam is not forthcoming with horse-feed money to tell me and I will send money once I've settled.

What I know the next day as I drive away, the farewells done and dusted, is that another chapter of my life is closing. I had no idea what was going to happen to Liam, but I knew one thing; there would be me, there would be Fly, and there would be – some day –some horses. That is as far as my imagination can go that last night, whilst I add up what seems to me to be the train wreck of my life.

I didn't know then, what I've said to you before, that what I was, what I am still, is a survivor. I think Beth, and I know it's a long way off for you, but it was in my sixties that I began to realise, that I'm still standing, as the song say, when so many others are not. But this fine morning, with the sky the bright cerulean blue, and just the slightest breeze blowing, I drive off in the morning after breakfast with Fly in the passenger seat beside me, both of us survivors, both of us battered and bruised but moving on Beth, moving on towards my final landscape, towards all of you.

* * * * *

I take off my wedding ring. As we drive towards towards the mountains, I wind down the window and throw it out, just like that. And even though the divorce was yet to come, I swear I suddenly feel as free as a bird. By the time Fly and I reach Jindabyne I've built a dozen castles in the air, spent a million dream dollars, and thought long and hard about my future. What is it I really want to do? I wanted to be around horses I knew, but it was hardly a career for a middle-aged woman who knew next to nothing, I was sensible enough to understand that, but still, a tiny, pulsing beat of my heart keeps the word going, *horses, horses, horses.*

At Jindy I buy food for lunch, and eat with Fly down by the lake, and begin topractically think things through. I'm going to need an address for mail, I realise, but I don't want anyone knowing a street address, no matter where I end up. Then and there, I make the decision that even if it is a few hours away from where I find myself living, a PO Box is a good idea. I can give it to Tony, to Jim and Mary, to anyone who has business with me in the future, and if I have to drive a while to get my mail, well,

I'm used to that, and it will help me stay hidden – out of sight of Liam, because, until I know what kind of sentence he's going to get, I'm still terrified that he will somehow get off and come looking for me.

Two things happen next.

I put Fly back in the car, and we drive to the shops. I leave the windows down and told Fly I won't be long. I walk into the Post Office to organise my PO Box, and when the woman in there asks my name, out come the words: 'Rosa. Rosa Maria de Martinez.'

And then, suddenly, as if I've been hit by a jolt of lightning, I know Jindabyne is the wrong place for me. I know I want to change states, to be as far away as possible from Liam, and yet still close to my mountains, and the brumbies. I want to be hidden Beth, hidden in the hills.

'Sorry,' I say to the woman behind the counter. 'I just forgot my ID.'

She sighs, as if to say, of course you have, and I almost run out of there, as fast as my legs can carry me. I leap into the car, and Fly smothers me with delighted kisses.

'We're off again, girl,' I tell her. 'But where? That's the million-dollar question.'

And of course, the million-dollar answer to that, is here. Out of New South Wales, and into the Victorian side of the mountains, not far from Mount Beauty, in the back blocks, but with the mountains accessible from everywhere.

And now you know the story of this place, how I found it, and how all things came from here: my small trucking company, my exotic oils, which has allowed me to stop using the truck for horses and start using it for produce, something I never saw coming either. And Pete, of course, the last man, and without a doubt, the best man in my life. And then, all the time, the research driving me further and further into my alternate reality in my search for my grandfather, so that I spend hours talking to Eadweard (although he never did reveal much), Flora and Harry, and my own mother, my beautiful sister/mother, and my grandparents, my parent/grandparents.

To be honest, I communicate more with dead people than real people, Beth. Another reason to be so thankful for you, my real live family, in the midst of my imaginary meanderings, and my hours and hours spent in books, at the library or on the computer. Trying, for some reason, in an obsession certainly worthy of Eadweard, to make sense of my ancestry, while the world around me gently showed me that in the end the important things were this: I exist; I was loved; I am loved; I love.

A last story, Beth, of how Princess and I came to be together. Can you bear one last story?

So here I am, imagine it Beth. I am my own woman again. I've traveled a long, hard road to my home, and I don't yet own it, because first there's Liam's blood money to pay back, and I haven't quite got there again with my savings, but I'm getting blood out of a stone, Beth. I am resourceful to the extreme. I double-use my truck for ferrying horses from time to time, and other times carry oils and fruit from my small orchard, and vegetables from my vegetable garden to the local markets. I find stockists for the oils. I am in fact, I will realise many years later, and discuss with you over a cup of tea, ahead of my time, and all my book-keeping and innate marketing, and design and love of writing and photography all come to the fore, and I find, to my immense surprise that I am a Woman of Many Parts.

But I don't have a horse of my own. Fly is still with me, although she will leave me soon, as our animals usually leave this world before us, she is slowing down now, but always my faithful companion. I still dream of a horse of my own. I go, as you know, as I did until only a few years ago, up into the mountains to watch the brumbies. I drive, then walk and hike and sometimes camp, and watch the herds up near Kiandra, and further in, and over on Mt Buller. I know some secret spots, far in from Long

Plains. I know the deep and hidden places, and I love to watch them. In a way, before I met you and Will, and later your children, I think what I saw in the brumbies was what was missing from my life – family.

I do miss being strong enough to walk those hills, to watch the interplay. The lead mares guiding, chivvying the herd; the stallion, sometimes stallions, guarding the territory. Can I say here that a major misconception of stallions is that they always fight – they do not, they often have long-lasting friendships, and I have often witnessed stallions grazing together. Even though in any wild herd it will come down, as it does with any wild animnal, to survival of the fittest. Then there's the babies learning their place, thrown out of the herd for any misdemeanour by a mare, often not even her own dam. Then when the foal – colt or filly – shows remorse, licking and chewing, head down, asking: 'Please can I come in?', the mare lets them back into safety, to kindness, even to a mutual grooming session. The child learns the lesson. Herd harmony is paramount because it leads to safety, and parental and teacher supervision is always there. I think that is why I never, ever tire of them, Beth, and why I dream of them so often.

Eadweard, I imagine, dreamt of horses too, maybe even of the mustangs he must have seen, but he dreamt of the human form too, men and women, and other animals, seeing always the energy and movement contained within the form. But for me, since I first saw them all those decades before, there has always been something about the brumby that has drawn me back to them every time.

So how it happens Beth, is like this:

The phone rings, and I answer it.

'Are you the woman that trucks horses locally?'

The voice is abrupt, raspy, a smoker's voice, I immediately imagine.

'Yes,' I say.

'I've got this mare. I want to sell her. She's no bloody use to me. Can you take her to the saleyards at Echuca for me?'

Now, I have always hated it when people are angry at horses, and to me, it seems as if it usually hides a deeper anger at themselves, but I took a breath.

'I can,' I say to her, 'but you know the knackeries buy from there as well?'

'They can chop her head off, for all I care,' the voice rasps at me. 'The bitch threw me three times. Teach me to take a fucking brumby.'

Well, Beth, the hairs on my neck stood on end. Then and there I want to offer her money, but I'm already clever by now. I know people like her, if I offer to buy this horse, there's no way she'll let me. She's got it in for the mare, and she'll have it in for me if it looks as if I'm going to intervene, or as if I know better than her, so I play it very cool.

'I'll probably have a run going there in the next week,' I say politely. 'I can book you in if you like?'

I don't tell her I won't take horses to Euchaca, not since I found out what happened to the first and only delivery of horses I took there. I keep my business small, private and simple. But I'll *pretend* to get this mare. I have a knowing, Beth, just like that.

On the appointed day, five days later, I travel to this woman's place, near the border, and I've already told her the mare will be the first horse I'm picking up, so she won't be suspicious about my empty truck.

When I drive into her driveway, it's what I expected. Ramshackle, slovenly. An old tractor minus its wheels beside a barn filled to the brim with junk, a small yard filled with mud, and in the middle, a palomino mare, once gold, now mud-coloured. Her thick neck, long, tangled mane, her strong shoulders, flat back and heavy rump all screaming 'brumby' at me. She looks defeated. Everything about her says she's given up, and my heart opens in a flood of feeling and memory. This mare, she's lost her family, Beth; this mare, she's been abused, this mare, she's lost hope.

The woman comes out to me where I've parked the truck near the yard.

'I don't know how you'll get her on,' she says, 'but then again, that's your problem. Here's your money.' She almost throws $250 at me. 'I'll come back and collect it if you can't do the job,' and she walks away with never a backward glance, and I'm pleased Beth, I really am. I don't want her here with me. I know she would stop any chance of the connection I had to make, and I need to use everything I've ever seen in the wild with this horse, and *now*.

I have feed and hay with me, so the very first thing I do is to throw some lucerne into the yard, as near as I can get it to her. For the first time, she looks up, and I swear if she was a person, you would have seen someone with tears pouring down her face.

'There you are darling,' I tell her. 'You're safe now. You're going to be safe.'

She looks down at the hay, and I can tell she hasn't eaten in a while, she chows down like there's no tomorrow, but she's watching me, and her ears are alert, I know she could go into defence mode in any moment, but I also know, that if the woman has ridden her, she's had a saddle and bridle on her, she's had a headcollar and leadrope, she's been led. I just have to get her to trust me. That's everything and that's all.

As slow as I can go, I enter the yard, and I take no notice of her, I just keep up some gentle conversation.

'How about you come home with me, Princess?' I say to her, and the name slips out just like that. 'Beautiful girl,' I tell her. 'I'm sorry for all your losses.' I swear she pauses in her chewing, and looks at me. But still, I take my time. I notice she has virtually no water in her bucket and what's in there is filthy. I'm lucky that it's in front of her and not behind. I wouldn't trust her back end at the moment, I think to myself. I take the bucket, empty it, clean it, refill it and carry it back in, still talking all the time, keeping my eyes down and away from her, turning my body slightly away, staying at this moment, submissive. I have a bag of carrots with me, and I think well, if she's been handled, perhaps she's used to carrots, and indeed, when she's finished her hay, with me standing well away I stretch out my hand, and yes, she takes the carrot, but from as extreme a distance as she can manage.

Something attracts my attention, a noise, a bird – I don't know what – but I look up and I see the woman standing by her front door, arms folded, looking at me, and I know suddenly that she's looking for an excuse for this not to work, for her to get her money back, shoot the horse and pretend it was the only thing she could do to assuage her guilty conscience.

I look at the mare full on for the first time, and she looks at me with surprise, and a bit of fear.

'It's okay,' I tell her. 'It's going to be fine. But we have to work now, and we have to work fast.'

I have a rope with me and standing away from her I flick it at her, holding my right arm out and flicking it with the left, she steps back, and a huge relief goes through me, she knows something, for sure, she's not going to turn and kill me or charge me.

'Come on Princess,' I tell her. 'We can do this. You just have to move away from me.'

I flick again, and she moves back, closer to the yard edge, and again I encourage her to break away from me, so that suddenly, she does, with a flick of her legs in my direction and a toss of her head, and she's off at a trot away from me.

'Good girl,' I tell her. 'Come on, keep moving.'

And she does, she's sweet and steady, not coming on too strong, not avoiding me. If I had to choose a horse to 'rescue', I think, this one is the goods.

We work together for a little while. I put a little pressure on her, and she gets a little anxious, head up, neck rigid, so I release, and she goes slower, now flicking her ears towards me, and gradually she lowers her head, she starts to lick and chew, she starts to engage.

I think that if I had the time, I would stop her and go the other way, but already this has taken me close to an hour, and I know we don't have much longer. I have to take a great big step into trust, and hope that it's enough. That without the pressure of a saddle and bridle, she will recognise kindness, or at least she will understand what I want. I stop 'herding' her, I turn away, I lower the rope, and I wait. I count to 10, very, very slowly, and just as I'm getting to nine, and I think I don't have her, we're going to have to start again, I feel her warm breath on my shoulder. I hold a carrot out sideways, no looking at her, and she takes it gently. We stand there for a moment until she's finished and then I walk away a few steps.

Oh Beth, was she with me? Yes! I can see her at my shoulder, then a little behind me, then at my shoulder, as I walk, and turn and she follows, and soon, oh my God, how I hope not too soon, I stop and she stops beside me, and I reach up to give her a scratch. She holds herself stiffly for a moment, then as I simply scratch and scratch and scratch, she relaxes, and gently now, gently as you can Rosa, I slip the rope over her neck.

'There you are my beautiful one,' I tell her. 'Great job.'

I reach into my jacket and take out the headcollar, and attach it to the end of the rope, and offer her another carrot piece, and now I slowly, slowly lift the headcollar over the nose, behind the ears, and she stiffens again, so scratch, scratch, scratch until she softens, and I have her!

Suddenly I notice the woman begin to walk down towards me, and I know if she gets to Princess (already named in my mind) before I get her on the truck, all hell will break loose, and so I tell the mare with as much honesty and strength as I can: 'This is for your life, darling, you have to come with me now. I know it's soon, but it's for you,' and I move away. And that good horse, she walks with me to the gate of the yard. I open it, and we walk out together, up the ramp of the truck, where I have a haynet hanging for her. I tie her up, and give her more carrot, then quickly now, push the barrier into place, click the latch, out of the truck, raise the back.

The woman is almost on me, I run around the front, jump in start the truck, just as she gets to me.

'Hey!' she says, and I know she's going to say: 'I've changed my mind.' She wants this horse dead for one reason or another, one way or another, maybe even because Princess has done exactly as I've asked, and the woman is furious about that too, but she's not killing this one, not on my watch.

'Sorry,' I shout at her over the engine. 'I'm running late for the next one. I'll let you know how she goes.'

And just like that, foot down, slam the truck into gear, and off we go up that driveway and out, and I'm trembling and sweaty and nervous. Because the next bit, I haven't even thought out. How do I *not* take her to Euchaca, since that's what the woman's expecting? And she'll be expecting her money as well.

But just at that moment, I know that now the mare has left the property, the woman's lost all interest. She's back inside, she's poured a drink, she's lit a cigarette, she's watching television. She doesn't care. I could say anything now and she'd accept it.

What I do, is I drive Princess home, because the woman won't be expecting to hear from me until that evening, or even the next morning anyway. When we get home, I unload her into the garden paddock next to the house, and although she's tense, she doesn't explode, not until the leadrope is off her anyway, and then she bucks, and farts and snorts, and takes off like a chunky golden dragon, breathing fire around the trees, until she gradually slows to a trot, then a walk, then lifts her head to look at me, and then drops it to graze on the fresh green grass.

The next morning, I ring the woman, and I will not give her a name, because she does not deserve one. I tell her that my truck broke down.

'I'm really sorry,' I say. 'I had a problem with the brakes, I had to come back to my place.'

Well, she just swears at me. 'That doesn't help my fucking bank balance, does it?'

I don't tell her that if this brumby mare went to the sales, she'd be lucky to fetch $200 as dog meat, she already knows that. I just apologise.

'Look,' I say, 'I may not be able to get back to Echuca until the next sale. How about I buy her from you, and then you don't have to worry about the money, or registering her for sale.'

I can almost hear the woman shrug, and then her brain ticking over.

'Alright,' she says. 'You can have the bitch. $1,000.'

Well, we both know that's laughable, but I've already had $250 from her, so just to give her the satisfaction of a haggle and so I don't appear to be a complete pushover, I say: 'What about $800?'

There's a pause. '$850,' she says.

'Done,' I say. 'Give me your bank details and I'll put the cash in there in the next hour.' Then just for good measure I say: 'I don't suppose I'll get that at the sale, but I've put you out, so I'm happy to do the right thing.'

'Yeah.' The woman has zero interest. She gives me her bank details, I tell her the money will be in her account by lunchtime and she hangs up, and that's it, Beth.

Princess is mine.

So that is what I do. I go into town, and I deposit $850, and I get a receipt, and I ring the woman one last time. There's an answering machine on, so I don't have to speak to her. I just tell her the money's gone in. Then I go and stand on my verandah and look at my muddy golden girl grazing quietly in the garden. I have no idea how long, or what the journey we are going on together will be, but I know that I love her unconditionally already, and that she will spend the rest of her life with me.

Which, as you know, Beth, is what happened. I promised Princess a family, and after six months of us working together, and my eternal promise to her that she need never be ridden, I found a beautiful Paint stallion nearby and Princess had her Thor and Freya, who grew up knowing only kindness and love, and they of course, became my riding horses, while Princess held her position as the matriarch, right up until the very end when we had her put to sleep so quietly, didn't we Beth, at the ripe old age of 32, when I knew without a doubt that she wouldn't last another winter, and she was so ready to leave this world – as ready, I think, as I am now.

In fact, soon I will be too tired to write anymore today. The pain in my arm is not good tonight. So bad in fact that I wonder… but then I have thought that before, and here I've been, up making a cup of tea in the early morning light, working on these pages.

Will I be here tomorrow? I have no way of telling. I just pray that whenever it comes, it's quick. But whenever it is, I leave you this manuscript as my way of telling you I love you, dear one, you are *mi familia.* À demain, as they say in French, see you tomorrow…

Chapter 25

Beth

'Beth.'

Beth stirs in her sleep, and the voice comes again. 'Beth.'

Beth opens her eyes and sees Rosa standing in their bedroom door.

'Rosa!'

Rosa puts a finger to her lips. 'Shhh.'

Beth smiles and pats the bed beside her, as if it's the most natural thing in the world that Rosa should be in their bedroom in the middle of the night.

'What time is it?' Beth asks sleepily.

'It's early – or late – depending on your perception. Around four I think, although suddenly time doesn't seem very important.'

Beth nods. 'No, of course not.'

Rosa sits on the bed, and it seems to Beth as if she is shimmering somehow. She almost feels that if she tried, she might be able to put a hand straight through her old friend.

'Are you alright?'

'Never better.'

Beth realises, and somehow it doesn't surprise her, that Rosa is looking much younger than usual – about the age she'd been when Will and Beth first met her. Rosa reaches for her hand.

'You are my family, you know,' she says. "Mi familia." She glances at Will sleeping beside Beth. 'All of you.'

Beth nods. 'Of course. I know that.'

'You'll look after Thor and Freya for me, won't you? And Bella?'

'Why? Are you going away? You didn't tell me...' Beth looks at her friend closely. 'Where are you going?'

Then, with a touch as light as gossamer, Rosa's finger touches Beth's forehead.

'I've already gone, my love,' she says. 'But you know that. There's a will, that's why I'm here. To say goodbye and tell you there's a will. You'll find a letter on my desk, along with something else...'

Beth begins to cry. 'But I don't want you to go. Rosa...'

Rosa smiles, and stands up. 'It'll be alright, Beth. You'll see.'

Beth starts to sob. 'No,' she says, over and over. 'No... no.'

It was the dream that did it.

'I've got to go and check on her, Will.'

Beth is standing by the stove, waiting for her morning coffee to rise through the tiny Italian coffee machine she uses for herself. The bitter-sweet aroma fills her nostrils, and she stretches for a second, already anticipating the sweet, strong taste in her mouth; the wonderful perfect moment of the first coffee, before the children are awake, before the day starts. Will, a tea man himself, is sitting at the table, stirring in his two sugars. *His hair looks rumpled,* Beth thinks to herself, automatically putting a hair trim for Will on her never-ending list of tasks. Sometimes, she thinks, the list is the devil's way of taunting her. Take something off the list, and two more things are added – a list to take her to infinity.

But now, this new thing on the list, that she needs to visit Rosa, there's no waiting on this one. This is pure compulsion.

'I had a dream, Will. Rosa came and said goodbye. I have to check.'

Will strokes his morning stubble. 'You've been wrong before, you know,' he says, but he is not unsympathetic. 'I mean, the doctor could be right, there could be a case to be made for her going into a home if you're going to worry about her all the time.'

'Will.' Beth brings her coffee to the table and stretches out a hand towards her husband. 'You don't even mean that. You're worried too.'

'You could ring first.'

'Will! I'm going. You can get the kids ready for school this morning.'

Will nods in resignation. 'Okay, but I'm sure she's fine.'

But Beth knows there is something wrong as soon as she turns off the main road onto the lane that leads to Rosa's place. Thor and Freya are agitated, cantering up and down the fence line, and when they see her car, they whinny.

'Shit.' Beth speeds up, taking the corner into the driveway far faster than usual, faster than she should. As she heads towards the homestead she can hear Bella barking, on her chain still, and a cold chill runs through her. She knows. She is already imagining: *In the bed? In the bathroom? Did she fall?*

Beth brings the car to a sliding halt underneath the big old gumtree near the front door. She is calling Rosa's name even before she gets out.

'Rosa… Rosa… Rosa!'

The dog barks, Thor and Freya whinny, but there is no answer, and Beth skids through the house, her hand to her heart – through the living room where she notices the upturned chair near the desk, but there is no body, nobody there, the bedroom, but no, nothing there, the kitchen – nothing. She pauses for a moment, confused. Maybe, she thinks, maybe it's nothing, maybe Rosa went for a walk, or had a moment of forgetfulness. She breathes, a deep breath, so deep a small amount of steam escapes. *Winter is coming,* she thinks. When she finds Rosa, she has to talk to her, tell her she can't stay out here alone.

'I'll take the rugs off the horses and let Bella off,' she says out loud, and nods to herself. *Yes.*

She walks towards the back door, imagines for a moment, Rosa coming back from an early morning walk, sees her walking in, the kettle going on, stoking the wood fire. Gingerbread, a chat.

The door is slightly open.

As Beth pushes it, she sees her old friend, sprawled at the bottom of the three steps.

'Rosa!' The word explodes out of her. 'Rosa!' But she knows, immediately. Her friend has fallen, her friend is dead. She hurries to the body, and touches Rosa, giving an involuntary flinch at the coldness of her, and as she begins to cry, she realises as she has never realised before that Rosa was the closest thing Beth has had to a mother, she realises how central she was to the success of her marriage, how she was even a grandmother to her children. As she sits there, the tears of grief falling so fast they make make small circles in the sandy ground, images of Rosa float in and out – Rosa massaging her feet when she was pregnant, Rosa opening her arms to her when Beth arrived after a row with Will, Rosa's cups of tea and coffee, Rosa minding the children, or leading them around the paddocks on Freya and Thor.

Freya and Thor... Beth looks up, startled out of her reverie, to see the two horses, quiet now, looking at her, and Bella, quiet too, her head cocked on one side. *They know,* thinks Beth. *How do they know?*

She can almost hear Rosa's voice: 'Come on, my preciosa. It's time. Help my loved ones. There is nothing more you can do for me.' Beth reaches down and gently strokes Rosa's bruised cheek. She wonders whether she needs to call people before she takes care of the animals, but she can hear Rosa's voice again, clear as day. 'Look after my animals Beth, then call.'

Beth lets Bella off her chain, and the dog runs immediately to Rosa, stopping a few feet away from her, confused, her tail suddenly between her legs, her hackles up. 'It's alright old girl,' says Beth, tearing up again. 'You'll be fine, you'll come with us.' A tiny, fearful thought dashes across her brain, a flicker of gunpowder: what can she and Will do with the horses? They don't have room, or the feed, or the money to look after them – and what will happen to the house? She thinks of Rosa's fight with James Jarvis. Will the house be sold now for development? In death will Rosa have lost the fight she'd won in life? Did Rosa have relatives she and Will don't know about? She collects hay from the shed for the horses, feeds them and unrugs them, the pair of them, together since the day Thor was born, graze side by side, and when she's done, Beth stands for a while between them, a hand on each of their backs.

'It's going to be fine,' she says to them, reassuringly. 'We'll look after you somehow, I promise.'

She pats them both, and calls to Bella, heading for the house to start the next bit, the bit that she really doesn't want to do because it's going to make it real. She passes Rosa where she's fallen, and walks back around to the front door, and Bella follows her inside, standing near her food bowl, her tail wagging.

'It's alright for you.' Beth, not for the first time, wishes life was as simple for humans as it is for animals.

Automatically she puts on the kettle to make a cup of tea and calls Will.

* * * * *

Waiting for the doctor, waiting for Will, waiting for... the next step, Will had said: 'They'll probably have to do an autopsy.' And the blood in Beth's veins seemed to turn to ice. Cut her friend's body? Cut into her beloved Rosa? When anyone can see – she was old, she fell over.

Beth wraps her hands tightly around her cup of tea, pushes the image out of her mind, wanders through the house, touching the everyday objects she never took much notice of before. She glances into the bedroom, to the rumpled, just-got-out-of bed. *Too hard for today* she thinks, and closes the door. She pauses at Rosa's desk – there's a large pile of manuscript on it, printed out next to the computer. It had always surprised Beth that Rosa could use a computer, when Beth herself was so not interested in technology. Rosa had always had some unusual interests, Beth thought: cars, for instance, astrology, technology, photography, a passion for horses; how did all of those fit together in one elderly woman?

Beth sits down, and pulls the pile towards her. As she does, she notices a small envelope at the back of the desk, under an old paperweight with a frozen forever teal green wave inside.

Will & Beth, it says on the envelope.

Beth stares it, half-wishing it would go away. *Did Rosa know then, she was going to die? And what would she be writing to them about, and what is this, this – book – in front of her about?* She opens the envelope slowly, trying to put off the moment when she will hear her friend's voice from beyond. Hard enough now for her, she thinks, suddenly remembering how a friend's father had died when she was a teenager, and how her friend had been distraught when she'd got a postcard from her father, posted on a holiday several months before he'd died.

But there is nothing to do but be brave and open it. And so, she does.

Dearest Will & Beth,

If you are reading this, then you and I know what has happened. I am not here anymore, or at least, not in any earthly form. I can't know exactly how this has happened, or when, but I hope and pray that it has passed relatively peacefully for all our sakes. This letter is written for several reasons, the first I shall get out of the way quickly, for this is the business part.

This is to let you both know that there is a will with my solicitors, Earle & Thomas, in town, and there is also a copy of the will in the third drawer down on the left-hand side of this desk. In it, I leave everything to you both. Lock, stock and barrel. There is only one condition, and although it is not one I can enforce from where I am, I am sure that you will see this in the same light as me, and that is that you will never sell the property for development, and if possible you work towards creating a nature reserve to protect it in perpetuity, so that perhaps when it is your turn to leave the planet, this land may stay as undisturbed and pristine as possible.

My dears, you are the closest thing I have to family, and I have left you EVERYTHING. It's yours to do with as you wish. There is money in the bank, there are my animals, there is the house and all its contents. I hope perhaps you will think of living here, perhaps rent out your home so you can create extra income, but whatever you do, as long as you hold onto this land, I will be happy.

I know that Thor and Freya and Bella will be happy with you. I think we all know neither of the horses have many years left on Earth, and I certainly hope that when they pass, I'll be there to greet them.

Look for me in your everyday lives, in the breeze that passes through the bottlebrush, in the rippling of the creek, in the birdsong of the morning chorus, for I will certainly be here, watching over you. You, and your children have given me kindness, love and generosity. You've both taught me that it truly doesn't matter if we don't know where we come from, or even who we are: if we are loved, and love in return, then we have family. Here, in this valley, I found my tribe, and I found peace.

Lastly, and for no other reason than for my own amusement, I have spent the last few years writing a book – or writing something, I'm not sure what you would call it, but stories about me, my history, and my grandparents. Just a memoir, but I hope, perhaps a memoir you will both enjoy. It's also yours to do with as you will. Burn it after you've read it, if that's your inclination. Perhaps the saying that all of us have one book in us is true, and this was mine.

If it's possible to miss people on the next plane of existence, I shall miss you all, and, at the same time, as you know, these last two winters have been long and hard for me, so I hope that I have been set free from this earthly body to roam in the realm beyond, where only love matters, for now, and forever, pure, simple and true.

I love you both, and I know that you love me, and I thank you.

God and Goddess bless you.

All my love, for now until eternity,

Rosa.

Beth's heart is thumping, possessed it seems of an entirely different rhythm to its normal steady beat. She instinctively holds her hand against it, as it leaps, like a caged bird against her chest cavity. She thinks she will pass out. *Rosa has left them everything!* She glances around her – *everything?* She stands up. Rosa has left them this house, with its beautiful thick stone walls, its slate floors, the large pot-belly stove and the old verandah? *This house* so entirely different to their weatherboard shack, freezing in winter, boiling in summer. A kind of crazy, whirling energy seems to fill her body, she feels an outpouring of love and gratitude towards her friend that transcends, for the moment, all her grief. *That she would do this for us,* Beth thinks.

Beth feels the need to move, to do something, anything to steady herself, to wait for the moment – soon now surely, when Will will arrive, when she will tell him this extraordinary news. She steadies herself, holds the paperweight in her hand, feeling its cool weight. She notices again Rosa's manuscript. She'll take it home with her tonight, she thinks, and then at the same moment as that thought, she has another – that she will come here to read the book, while everything is sorted, while she and Will come to terms with this gift, with this new life. She will come here, and sit at this desk, and think of her friend, and read her book.

Beth pulls the manuscript towards her:

Light and Shadow, she reads,

The story of Eadweard Muybridge, Flora Shallcross Stone and Harry Larkyns - as told by their granddaughter, Rosa Maria de Martinez.

Prologue

Dearest Beth

The truth is, there is no truth.

For example:

My grandfather was a murderer. He shot my grandmother's lover dead. The name he became known by was not the name with which he was born. He was not a purveyor of truth...

Epilogue

Beth raises her head from the desk, where she's been writing for the past few minutes. She can hear the boys larking around outside. It'll be dark soon, time to light the fire, supervise homework, feed the horses, feed the dogs, feed the family, and have a cup of tea with Will to discuss the next day's orders for the oils. She pauses for a moment in her thoughts, the image of their latest oil, Exotic Rose Oil, and the words on the back of the bottle.

This beautiful Rose oil, infused with the luscious scent of Bulgarian Rose, has been created as a lasting tribute to Sofia Romano, the founder of Exotic Oils, a much-loved member of our family and of this community.

Would Rosa have loved it? Beth believes so. She'd wondered whether to 'out' Rosa as the creator of the range, but finally she'd decided that if Sofia Romano was the name Rosa wanted, then that was the name it was going to stay. It's going well, this latest addition, particularly in Melbourne where customers can't seem to get enough of the Exotic Oil range. Really, there is nothing wrong with any of part of their lives at the moment, Beth reflects, apart from the tiredness she and Will feel at the end of the day, but it's tiredness she's grateful for, with every inch of her body.

What a gift their friend has given them. No more poverty for her family, for their lineage, she hopes.

She breathes a big sigh out and observes her handiwork on the desk.

Dear Katharine Winton, she reads,

It was lovely to chat with you the other day, and I'm so happy that you are keen to read the manuscript my friend Rosa Martinez left for me, with a view to becoming an agent for the manuscript.

I look forward to hearing from you in due course.

All the very best,

Beth McDonald.

Acknowledgements

I first started the novel *Light and Shadow* in 2010, driven by my continuing passion for both horses and photography. Those passions let me inevitably to the photographer Eadweard Muybridge. However, when I first discovered Muybridge's equine movement studies, I was unaware of the numerous tragedies surrounding his life, and it was those which sparked my ongoing interest in another arena entirely, namely how often women in history are lost, or forgotten, or somehow fall by the wayside.

Muybridge was still a young man when he almost died in a stagecoach accident which undoubtedly caused an ABI (acquired brain injury); later there was his marriage to Flora Shallcross Stone, a young woman half his age, and only a few years after that his shooting dead of her feckless lover Harry Larkyns. Muybridge's subsequent trial, and the fact that he was found Not Guilty, quite probably hastened the end of Flora's life. After Flora died – at only 24 of typhoid – Muybridge refused to bring up Florado, the son that was almost certainly his (if photographs are anything to go by), leaving the little boy in two different New York orphanages until Florado was 10, when Muybridge arrived to take Florado to a Texan ranch, where Florado lived for the rest of his life.

My starting point was simply that I had chanced upon and loved (in fact was somewhat obsessed by) Muybridge's famous photograph of a horse captured in mid-gallop, with all four hooves off the ground at the same time. In the beginning, it was that image alone that set me off on the trail of discovering more about Muybridge, an eccentric and brilliant man – in many ways an upstanding example of a Victorian patriarchal male, in other ways a man way ahead of his time. It was Muybridge who pioneered the use of multiple cameras to capture motion in sequences of photographs, including horses, nude men (often himself), women and various animals over and over again to determine exactly how they moved; he also invented the Zoopraxiscope, the first known device for projecting moving images, and was also the inventor, believe it or not, of the first washing machine.

The deeper I delved, the more complicated the story. How could a self-admitted murderer be acquitted? How could a jury refuse to follow the judge's orders that if they were to find him Not Guilty, they must find him Insane? How could he, no matter that his young wife had had an affair, leave her destitute after the divorce, refuse to pay alimony, and in a very real sense, condemn her to death? Why, since he refused to acknowledge Florado as his son, did he pay for his years at the orphanage, and leave him his fob watch?

My meanderings, and conversations with friends, took me to many books. A close friend, Zoe Humphreys, was instrumental in gifting me two invaluable books – the absolutely essential *Motion Studies, Time, Space and Eadweard Muybridge*, by the esteemed Rebecca Solnit and the massive Taschen tome, *Eadweard Muybridge, the Human and Animal Locomotion Photographs*. Further research took me to Rebecca Gowers wonderful book, *The Scoundrel Harry Larkyns and his Pitiless Killing by the Photographer Eadweard Muybridge*; I also discovered *Eadweard Muybridge* by Marta Braun; Rob Winger's *Muybridge a poem in three phases* and Dover Publications *Eadweard Muybridge, Horses and Other Animals in Motion - 45 Classic Photographic Sequences*.

In my two previous novels, *Women and Horses* and *The Hidden* I had already explored a dual timeline, and I knew I wanted to do the same with this novel, which for some years was merely jottings and the glimmer of an idea. I also knew that horses, beyond Muybridge and Larkyn's interest in them, would inevitably enter stage left, because horses inhabit not just my real life, but my creative life and my dream life. To be honest, I didn't really have much choice, I knew that even if I tried to keep them out, they would no doubt gallop in and make their presence felt. But for the time being, with no idea what this contemporary timeline would be, I got further into my research, and the shadowy figures of both Flora and Harry began to make themselves known to me. I began to ponder on the shame, humiliation and despair that Flora must surely have felt after Harry's murder, which also led me to her past, and what might have caused her to marry a man twice her age.

As I began to think, and dream, about Flora more and more, I also began to think about Florado – let's say for the sake of the most plausible argument, Flora and Eadweard's son, who was run over by a taxi in Texas in 1944. What kind of life had he led? There seems to be virtually no record of him. He never married; he didn't have children. I had a feeling that loneliness, or a sense of somehow being an outsider, seemed to be a common denominator for these historical figures. And then one day, it occurred to me: What if Florado had fathered a child? And if he had, who would that child be? From those meanderings, Rosa was born – fictionally, if not in reality – and the novel began to take shape.

Light and Shadow is a novel written through the eyes of an 80-year-old woman, and I've aged 15 years since I first had the idea. My guesses about what old age is like, weren't initially written from my own personal knowledge. 15 years later, and having recently turned 70, I have much more of an idea about old age, and it's not all beer and skittles by a long shot. Nevertheless, Rosa remains resolutely young at heart, as, I hope, does her creator. I've given Rosa my passion for horses, for Australia, for wild landscapes and for brumbies, but right from the start she was her own person, and as a writer I've appreciated her insistence on my keeping her character consistent.

Writing historical fiction is to walk a fine line between fact and fiction. Most of Eadward Muybridge's story in the novel is based in fact, and a lot taken specifically from reports of the trial, newspapers of the day, or from reference books. Harry Larkyn's childhood and careers are also well documented. Less well documented is Flora's life, and some of it I have shape shifted to suit my feeling of the woman she was – a feeling which was seriously challenged several times. I suppose in the same way that the script of a book has to be trimmed to fit the length of a film, so too in one book it's difficult to sum up three real lives, and one imaginary life. Like many women, in the past I have experienced unpleasant circumstances around sexual relationships, and as a child I was occasionally subjected to both emotional and physical abuse. I wanted to give both Flora and Rosa a voice that reflects what can happen to women when shame, insecurity and vulnerability lie at their core. Domestic violence and violence against women are persistent problems worldwide, and I wanted to draw attention to the fact that gender and power inequality has affected, and continues to affect, women through the ages.

Curious coincidences abounded as often happens during a writing project. Perhaps the oddest was when I'd finished the manuscript and was at a bit of a low ebb about the next move. When Rosa moves to Sydney, I'd settled her in a tiny corner of Rose Bay, near the shops beside the golf course, where I'd stayed in the 70s with a friend for a few weeks. When my daughter moved out from home, she found a flat just around the corner from the Rose Bay shops, and suddenly, when I visited her, I was catapulted back into Rosa's world. Visiting Anna, in what, in my imagination, is Rosa's place, helped me to continue to believe in the book.

As well as Zoe's divine intervention with books, I have a list of people to thank, first and foremost being my wonderful agent Jeanne Ryckmans from Key People Management, who, after the novel had been almost snapped up by two publishers, only to fall at the acquisitions meetings because the female character was too 'old', persisted with the project, putting me in touch with Bonita Mersiades, the powerhouse behind Fair Play Publishing and Popcorn Press. The publishing process with Bonita was easy right from the start, particularly because she gave me free rein – to use a horse analogy – to create a cover concept. I owe her a debt of gratitude for that, and to my designer Mathilde Noblet, who worked assiduously on my concept, and the many diverse items I sent her to include in her design, to gradually create a cover which I think captures much of the emotional and physical landscape of the book.

I guarded this particular novel close to my chest, and very few people read it, or even knew about it, during the many years it came together, but when it was ready to be shown, I was blown away by the testimonials given to me for the book by Rachel Ward, Sally Colin-James and Sue Woolfe. Between the three of them they created an overall testament to the book which encompasses everything I feel the novel is about, and I would like to thank them for the care and attention they gave to *Light and Shadow.*

There are several people who have encouraged me on this long road, particularly my fellow horse-loving friend Jane Camens, and my horse-loving poet friend, Robbie Coburn. As with Rosa, my horses have been my teachers and mentors, and without their continuing life lessons, I would not have been able to write this book. They may not be able to read their thank-you, but perhaps an extra serving of hay on the day of publication will let them know how grateful I am to them.

Last, but of course, by no means least, are my family – my husband Greg, my sister Charlie and my children, Sam and Anna, who have been there right from the beginning, through the middle and to the end, and I thank all four of them for their continuing support of my creative endeavours.

Candida Baker
August, 2025

Previous Books by Candida Baker

Fiction

Women & Horses
The Hidden
The Powerful Owl

Memoir

The Heart of a Horse

Non-fiction

Yacker - Australian Writers Talk About Their Work
Volumes 1, 2 & 3

Anthologies

The Penguin Book of the Horse
The Infinite Magic of Horses
The Wonderful World of Dogs
The Amazing Life of Cats
The Wisdom of Women

Children's Books

The Baby Angels Counting Book
I Know That!
Belinda the Ninja Ballerina

Poetry

Wanderings: A Journey of Minds (with photographer Ken Ball)
Memories Imagined (with photographer Ken Ball)

OTHER BOOKS BY POPCORN PRESS

High Heels and Low Blows

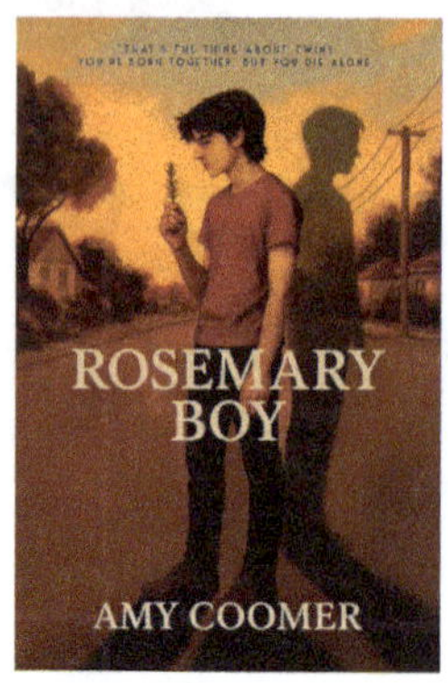

Rosemary Boy

RIPPA!

The End of the Game

Abebi

Game

POPCORN
PRESS